THE EXILE OF ELINDEL

CAROL BROWNE

"It's all about the story!"

Burning Willow Press LLC

Spartanburg, SC

Burning Willow Press, LLC (USA):
3724 Cowpens Pacolet Rd., Spartanburg, SC 29307

This edition published in 2017 by Burning Willow Press, LLC (USA)

All rights reserved.

Without limiting the rights under copyright reserved above, no part of this publication may be reproduced, stored in or introduced into a retrieval system, or transmitted, in any form or by any means (electronic, mechanical, photocopying, recording, or otherwise) without the prior written permission of both the copyright owner and the above publisher of this book.

The scanning, uploading, and distribution of this book via the Internet or via any other means without the permission of the publisher is illegal and punishable by law. Please purchase only authorized electronic editions and do not participate in or encourage piracy of copyrighted materials. Your support of the author's rights is appreciated.

The persons, places, and events of this novel are works of fiction. Any coincidence with individuals past or present, is merely that, coincidence.

© Carol Browne, 2017
© Donna Marie West, editor, 2017
© Loraine Van Tonder, Ryn Katryn Designs, cover design, 2017
© Lori Michelle, The Author's Alley, interior formatting, 2017

For Harry

Chapter One

Britain—500 CE

IT WAS HARD to talk to trees. They were deep and dark within themselves and spent most of their time asleep. Elgiva touched the rough bark with her fingers, lightly at first. Her desire to act reverently was great, but her need for comfort was stronger. Pressing her body against the tree, she wrapped her arms around it.

"Forest-Lord, I need your help!" she begged in a quavering voice. "My name's Elgiva. My people are . . . my people were the Eldrakin. I need your guidance . . . please . . . if you could . . . if you would . . . "

She couldn't continue, and for a time, her slender frame was racked with sobbing, while the oak leaves danced above her head, their shadows capering on the grass, carefree as summer butterflies.

"Your arms are warm, little elf, but they need to be much longer if you wish to embrace me."

Elgiva sniffed back her tears and listened, but the tree's voice could be felt, rather than heard. It flowed like dark waters under the earth.

"You've seen many things in your life," she said, dabbing at her eyes with her ragged sleeve. "Would you be willing to give advice to an elf who has lost all hope of home?"

"I would," he replied, "for the elves are my friends. I am Derryth, and I do not forget those who pay me respect. I recall those others . . . it seems but yesterday. Druids, they called themselves. Now they are gone. All gone forever. All of them slain."

Elgiva tried to be patient. Time had no meaning for Derryth, and he would never understand the need for haste that governed the lives of shorter-lived creatures.

"Yes, all slain," he went on sadly. "Then came others from across the grey sea. Bricks and stones and wars. They were always building, but I cared nothing for their works. And now, these Saxons . . . tree-slayers. I feel the anguish of the forests."

"Yes, the wilthkin. They're cruel and selfish."

"But elves . . . I like. Speak, child."

"I need your guidance, Derryth. I was a servant in Elindel, but I've been sent into exile . . . for treason. I'm banished from all Elvendom and must fend for myself, but I don't know how. Where will I live? How will I survive the winter? The food I brought with me from home is gone. All I have is this amulet." She held it up for him to see, and for a moment felt extremely foolish, but then she remembered that Derryth had senses beyond mere vision. "It was given to me by a wardain . . . Lord Bellic. He was my friend, my teacher."

"I know of him," said Derryth.

"You do?" Elgiva was astonished.

"Do not be surprised. He travels far and he speaks with the trees. His heart is good. Speak further, child."

"The amulet has the power to protect, and it gives off warmth if the giver is within three leagues of it," said Elgiva, "so I think, I hope, he intends us to meet again."

"How is the amulet used?"

Elgiva thought back to the day she left Elindel. Briar, the wild cat, had carried the gift to her in his mouth and given her Lord Bellic's message.

"I must speak its name, and it will work whatever spell I wish," she said. "But if I use it for sport or gain or any evil purpose, it will rebound on me. Apart from this gift and my servant's rags, I have nothing else in all the world."

"You have the world," said Derryth softly.

Elgiva didn't understand. She peered up into his branches and tried to conceal her disappointment. Derryth seemed to be falling asleep; she could sense him drifting away. Her impatience made her protest far more shrill than she intended, and it startled birds in the neighbouring trees.

"Derryth, I've been wrongly accused. I only ever did my duty, and they sent me away from home . . . forever. Derryth! Are you listening?"

She felt a tremor run up the trunk, as though the great tree were chuckling.

The Exile of Elindel

"The Eldrakin . . . how they sparkle," he said. "Be calm. I feel your innocence . . . but little elf, there is blood on your head."

Elgiva pressed her forehead against his trunk and fought to hold in her tears.

"But still," he went on, "I am happy to help you. I do this in honour of Faine, your First-Father, the founder of Elvendom. It was his love for the trees and beasts that gave us this boon of speech. Let us not squander it."

"Then tell me, Derryth, what must I do?"

Derryth drifted again. Elgiva sighed with impatience and ran her fingers through her hair. Finally, he spoke.

"You must change," he stated simply.

"Change?"

"The amulet. Tell it to change you. You may not walk abroad as an elf," he said. "The wilthkin will not shelter you . . . kill you, most surely, I think. Your own kind have renounced you. You have no skills to survive alone, and winter will be hard this year."

The breeze rustled harshly through Derryth's leaves, as if to add weight to his words, and a shiver skittered down Elgiva's spine.

"If you appeared to be . . . what you are not . . . help would be given willingly," Derryth went on. "Then safety. Until Lord Bellic comes to your aid."

"You think he will?" she asked.

"He is a wardain, child. He will not abandon his friends."

Elgiva wasn't so sure, but she didn't wish to call Derryth's regard for the wardain—the royal elves—into question, so she made no comment. "So what must I change myself into?"

"You must become a Saxon."

Elgiva's mouth fell open at this suggestion, and she pulled away from the trunk. Perhaps she had chosen the wrong tree. His great age had clearly addled his sense of reason.

Another tremor ran through his trunk and his leaves seemed to crackle with laughter. "These hewers of trees are hateful, yes, but they overrun the land, little elf. Everywhere. Like ants. You have travelled east into their domain. The Saxons are masters here. Will you elude them forever? Who will help you, if they do not? Do elves not need companionship, too? I have no love for the race of men . . . wilthkin, as you name them . . . and the Saxons I like least of all, but they are most hospitable and always look after their own. Shelter will not be refused you if you are one of them."

"Perhaps you're right," she said. She had to admit his suggestion wasn't as foolish as she first thought.

"The Saxons . . . you will learn from them, for everything is a lesson, child. They will teach you how to survive. Then, after winter, travel on. Spring will be early. Warm."

"You think so, Derryth?"

"I know it. I know many things . . . unknown to you . . . Ah . . . "

Elgiva frowned, waiting for him to continue. She feared he might be drifting off again.

"Derryth! Did you have more to say?"

"Ah . . . little elf, yes," he murmured, at length. "This amulet. Tell me . . . how long will the spell endure?"

She shrugged. "Until I undo it, I dare say."

"Let us hope so, my child. Good. So, you have had my advice. Rest here awhile, for you need time . . . to decide if you will take it . . . or not."

She sensed the ancient oak tree had said his piece and he would say no more. His consciousness was sliding into sleep, so she sat down in the hollow between two of his thick, knurled roots and leaned her back against the stout trunk. It was true. Surely it had to be true. Bellic would one day seek her out. Throughout her sixteen years of life, he had always been her teacher and friend, and he was a good elf with a generous heart; he wouldn't abandon her to her fate. But if for some reason he didn't come, she would have to find some cave or wood, far away from elves or men. The thought of such solitude appalled her. She pushed it aside. All she needed to focus on now was surviving the coming winter.

It was decided, then.

The amulet of lapis lazuli hung on a leather thong around her neck. She clasped it firmly in her hand. She didn't know how to use magic but supposed a formal tone was best. Self-consciously, she cleared her throat.

"Siriol, hear me and work my will. In the name of the one who gifted you to me, do as I bid you. Help me walk unremarked upon into the world of the wilthkin. Change me into a Saxon maid with yellow hair and eyes of blue. Do as I command you, until I bid you otherwise, and . . . Siriol, I, er . . . so be it."

Elgiva waited for several moments, holding her breath, but nothing unusual happened.

Stillness stole over the grass and she relaxed, her body sinking as though it wanted to merge with the tree bole behind her. Her morning's walk had exhausted her, and she was tired. Birds now sounded as though they were singing a long way off.

She yawned, but she didn't want to fall asleep. She needed to know the spell would work.

But still her hair lay, black and gleaming, over her shoulders. She reached up slowly and touched a pointed ear. Nothing had happened.

Behind her, the tree was now deeply asleep, and perhaps his advice had been as unreal as the magic he had told her to call upon.

Magic.

It was hard to believe in such a thing.

Chapter Two

SHOUTS ERUPTED FROM a nearby wood and sent the birds screeching and chiding into the summer sky.

Elgiva was startled. The cries were those of wilthkin. There was a harshness in the pitch of their voices, and the underwood cracked loudly beneath their heavy tread. No elf would cause such a disturbance.

She thrust herself upright, clawed strands of hair from her eyes, and her fear-sharpened hearing caught the swish of arrows among the trees. So the wilthkin were hunting.

These men were on foot; she couldn't hear any horses. If need be, she could easily outrun them.

She brushed the dirt and leaves from her clothes and prepared to continue her journey, but almost at once, she faltered as the cries abruptly changed, becoming peals of laughter, and Elgiva glanced back at the wood. The sounds were inviting, and curiosity moved her to seek out their source. She had never before seen a wilthkin. No harm, surely, in taking a quick peek at them? She touched the oak tree, seeking advice, but Derryth slumbered still, so Elgiva set off to investigate. Perhaps she ought to be afraid, but she was strangely calm. She crossed the meadow and stopped at the marge of the wood.

After a moment, she stepped between the trees. Her sandals sank into the leaf-littered ground as she crouched among the shadows and peered through the foliage, compelled to seek out these wilthkin. A tall elm creaked above her and for a moment, she steadied herself against its sturdy trunk.

In the still, green silence ahead of her, an arrow whispered through the air, and Elgiva stiffened and held her breath. The wilthkin were nearer than she had thought. She strained her ears to catch their words.

The Exile of Elindel

"Missed again, Elric! Perhaps we should ask them to stand still for you." The voice trailed off into guffaws of laughter.

"Ha," cried a second voice. "Taunt me, would you, Deor, when you've hit nothing all day yourself?"

"You're forgetting something, Master Elric," said a third man. "Your cousin has pierced the heart of a hawthorn and caught an old robin's nest."

"By Grim, you saucy rogue!" the first voice retorted. "I'll have your eyes for gaming pieces!"

"In that case, my lord, they'd see you lose."

A gasp of pretended fury was followed by the sounds of a scuffle, while the owner of the second voice—whom Elgiva presumed to be Elric—complained at the lack of discipline.

"Come on. Let's find a wild boar," urged Elric. "We can take its head back as a trophy."

His companions agreed and followed him deeper into the wood, while Elgiva shook her head. What coarse and clumsy creatures. Were they as ugly as their voices? She wanted to find out, so she followed quietly in their wake, letting their noise be her guide.

At one point, her path was blocked by a fallen tree. As she clambered over the toppled giant, a mantle of silence fell over the wood; the hunters were lying in wait.

A sudden whooping noise to her left made her heart jump into her throat. The men were nearby, far too near. She crouched in the shadows and waited.

"By Frigg! You got him. Our luck has changed!"

She recognised Elric's voice.

The owner of the third voice sounded weary and bored. "It's just a young hare, Master Elric. He strayed from the meadow, little knowing he'd end up as sport for a slave."

Elgiva's lips curled into a smile. This man's appearance was a mystery to her, but she could almost picture the long-suffering look he would give his master.

"Even so, Godwin, that was well done," said Elric.

"Well," said Godwin, "I thought I'd show my betters how it's done. After all, you can't eat an old robin's nest, no matter how it's cooked."

"Does this bastard never cease?" Deor demanded. "Who said you could hunt, anyway? A serf bearing arms indeed. Let me remind you, Godwin, you're supposed to carry our gear, be our beater, and shut your noise."

"If I did that, my lord, I'd make a very poor beater."

"By the blood of the gods!"

In her hiding place, Elgiva grinned. As far as quick wits were concerned, the serf had the upper hand. As a servant herself, she took pleasure in it. Tucking her long hair behind her ears, she crept a little closer.

"Deor, listen!" Elric hissed. "I think I heard a large animal over there in those bushes, if your noise hasn't driven all the game away."

Silence settled once more on the wood, and Elgiva edged closer, until she finally spotted the hunters, crouched and unmoving among the shadows.

Her elven senses, so in tune with the natural world and all of its creatures, told her the beast they sought was some yards behind them, grouting among the ferns. This was something these wilthkin with their limited sensibilities couldn't know. She could almost picture the boar and share in its consciousness as it began to scent the air. Its rough flanks shuddered with loathing. A muscular male with gleaming tusks, its mind held a bitter memory: a memory of men and arrows and pain.

Suddenly, it burst from the underwood, aiming itself at the men.

Before she realised what she was doing, Elgiva cried out. "Lord Elric, behind you!"

At this, the hunters sprang to their feet. The man she assumed to be Elric spun round to avoid the boar that hurtled madly towards him. His companions fumbled to nock their arrows, but the beast had gone, smashing its way back through the bushes, as startled by the warning shout as those it had sought to surprise.

"By Frigg," cried Godwin, "that was close!"

"You all right, cousin Elric?" asked Deor.

Elric glared at his companions. "Who called my name?" he demanded.

The other men shrugged.

"Who called?" he shouted, scanning the trees and bushes ahead of him.

From her place crouched among the woodland plants, she

The Exile of Elindel

watched him draw an arrow from the quiver at his back and raise his tall, curved bow. Nocking the arrow, he drew the bow string taut.

"Who are you, girl? Where do you hide? Come out and show yourself."

Panic raced through Elgiva's veins. What mad impulse had caused her to shout a warning? Why had she cheated the boar of his quarry?

Looking down the shaft of the arrow, she saw the sharp tip, the sleek, black feathers, and felt the tension of the bow and the hunter's sinews. Elric was young and determined. He looked like a man who would stand there all day, if need be, and he had heard a female voice. Perhaps he had more sport in mind, of one sort or another, but he might be in for a shock. Perhaps she could sneak quietly away...

"Show yourself and be rewarded, or hide and be hunted!" declared Elric grandly. "You have nothing to fear, if you mean no ill!"

Elgiva's heart thumped in her breast, but there was nothing for it; shakily, she got to her feet. Momentarily startled, Elric lowered his bow.

"Approach," he commanded.

Reluctantly, Elgiva edged forwards, stopping within a few yards of the men.

Oh, Faine, they'll kill me.

Elric looked her up and down, his eyes an icy blue. He was a Saxon, and she guessed about the same age as herself, but he was tall and well-muscled for his age. He had the manner of a lord sure of his authority.

Her silence seemed to unnerve him. He turned to his cousin, the blond hair brushing his shoulders as he did so. "What are we to make of this, Deor?"

Deor's lip curled as he considered her. He, too, was tall and young, but the paunch that overhung his belt suggested a softer life than that of his companions. Twin garnet brooches flashed on his breast, and his scabbard gleamed with amber studs. He was altogether too well-dressed for hunting.

"Don't ask me," he replied with a shrug. "Godwin has put me in a bad humour. Whatever I say will bode ill for your rescuer—if it isn't mocked first." He thrust out his chin and glared at Godwin. "But she's not one of my father's serfs, and if she isn't one of yours, she has no right to be on Lord Othere's land."

Folding his arms, Elric turned to the third man. "And what do you say, Godwin?" he asked, as though granting him an undeserved honour.

Elgiva looked at Godwin. He must be at least ten years older than his companions, though she couldn't be sure. Wilthkin had much shorter lives than elves, and guessing their ages was difficult once they had reached a certain maturity.

His plain apparel marked him out as a man of low rank, and whereas his masters sported immature beards, he was clean-shaven. Bellic had told her a few things about wilthkin so she supposed this man was a Briton; his shoulder-length hair had a coppery sheen, and he had a dark, gentle beauty that was strangely appealing.

He folded his arms across his chest, smiling impishly at Elric, but Elgiva sensed tension behind the smile. He gazed at her for a moment with what she could only describe as regret, then he spoke.

"If I wasn't a man of honour, I'd say I was glad my wife isn't here." It seemed he had said what was expected of him. Elric smirked appreciatively. "But Master Elric, this girl has perhaps saved your life. True, she's a trespasser, but a most welcome one in that case." His tone became more flippant. "Besides, she's young and looks half-witted, so I think we should be merciful."

"How dare you! I have all the usual number of wits and more besides. Don't taunt me . . . or I'll call back that boar and watch him make a meal of you all." Forgetting her fear, Elgiva tossed back her head defiantly.

Godwin and Elric stared at each other, and Godwin spoke with a wry grimace, "Well, apart from the language of my betters, I speak a few words of the Celtic tongue. I know some Roman phrases, too, I learnt from Aethelwulf the Sage. But now I find myself surpassed. I couldn't claim to be fluent in Boar."

"And why not, when you are one?" Deor put in with a satisfied pout. "So, what do you say to that, then? I've learnt to beat you at your own game."

Godwin regarded Deor as though he were an imbecile, and then he said, "And why not, my lord? I beat you at yours."

The Exile of Elindel

Deor spluttered indignantly, but before he could respond, Elgiva spoke up.

"Enough!" she cried. "I saved your life, Lord Elric, and you've no right to toy with me."

Godwin lowered his gaze, while Elric's eyes glittered dangerously. Elgiva's anger became fear, and the impulse to flee made her turn on her heel.

"Stay, friend," commanded Elric. "We did not mean offence."

He placed a hand on her arm and she turned to look at him. She tried to appear affronted, despite the fear that clogged her throat.

"You know what I am, Lord Elric, so why don't you put an end to me now and spare me this cruel sport?"

The three men looked at each other blankly.

"What are you, then?" asked Godwin, who by some unvoiced agreement seemed to have been delegated to speak. "Apart from another damned Saxon, a trespasser on Lord Othere's land, and a saver of great men?"

Elgiva's mouth fell open. A what?

In the silence that followed, her mind laboured to make some sense of it all. A veil shifted from her perception. She glanced at her hands and noticed that they looked different, somehow, the skin pink and a little coarser. She had changed. But when?

Help me walk unremarked upon into the world of the wilthkin. Change me into a Saxon . . . The spell had taken effect in the order in which she had spoken it. The magic was real.

"What is wrong with this girl?" asked Deor. "Surely she is elf-shot."

Elgiva glared at him before she could stop herself, but he seemed hardly to notice her reaction.

"Master Elric," said Godwin quickly, "this creature has a fine spirit, which I think we have offended. Your father would—"

"Speak not of him," snapped Elric. "I know how to behave."

He frowned petulantly, then turned in Elgiva's direction, as if to speak, but she ignored him. Instead, she was drawn to the serf. She saw his concern and kindness clearly, but also the pain and complexity he kept hidden behind a veil of humour. She needed to acknowledge his support.

"Thank you," she said simply.

Godwin appeared mildly surprised. He looked Elgiva up and down in her shabby servant's clothes. And what eyes he had. They were blue, like those of the Saxons, but a deeper blue that gave him an open, honest appearance. She fancied she saw a light in them that had been dimmed by harsh experience. She stepped carefully towards him.

"I see sorrow and loss in your eyes. It makes me a little sad." No sooner had she said it, she cursed herself and, overcome with embarrassment, lowered her gaze.

There was an awkward silence in which the songs of the woodland birds were unnaturally loud. Elric and Deor shuffled their feet.

"You're wise beyond your years," said Godwin, his gaze both wary and quizzical. "Do you have the second sight?"

"Er . . . no," said Elgiva, baffled. "I recognise sorrow, that's all. It's my companion, too."

By now, Elric was clearly growing impatient. "What's your name, girl? Where is your home?"

"My name is Elgiva," she answered, "and home is wherever I find myself. My people have banished me."

She saw their shocked expressions, and her throat constricted.

"Banishment from home," said Elric, shaking his head. "That's the worst thing in the world."

"Now I feel sad for you," said Godwin, his brow creased with sympathy. "So young and so alone, with no lord to protect you. What on Earth did you do to deserve it? Was your crime so great?"

She looked at each of them in turn. She hadn't intended any of this. All she needed was food and shelter. No further involvement was required. Not with these barbarians. Why had she trusted them with the truth, when lies were all they deserved? She had committed herself too hastily. And Derryth was a fool.

"I've been wronged. But I'll tell you my tale, and perhaps you can judge for yourselves."

"Tale-telling comes later," said Godwin with a smile. "First, you must sample our hospitality." He turned to address Elric. "This creature looks half-starved. Your father would be angry if we didn't offer food and shelter to an ill-used Saxon maid."

They were going to take her back with them, which, of course, was what she wanted, but her elven instincts were appalled. She had forgotten who she was. These people were her people's enemies.

But . . . she had no people anymore.

Siriol, this was all a mistake!

Elric's forehead furrowed at Godwin's suggestion, but Elgiva recoiled from the prospect of help as though she had been offered a quick death.

"No, I can't," she protested.

Her intractability appeared to both annoy and bore Elric. He sighed and rested his arm across Godwin's shoulder. This gesture conveyed an unexpected depth of affection, throwing Elgiva further off balance. She had assumed the serf was her ally because of his lowly status, but despite the arrogance of the younger man, she saw now there were genuine feelings of friendship between the lordling and the slave.

"I'm sorry, I must go," she said shakily.

"Come, girl, let us help you. We shall be honoured to share our food and hear your sorry tale." Elric's tone took on a sharper edge. "How can an exile refuse?"

How indeed? Elgiva was bereft of words. All she could think of was her home, the only world she knew and understood. It was lost to her forever. And now, thanks to Siriol, she had even lost herself. It was all too much to bear.

"Other tribes wouldn't be so hasty in their trust," Elric said. "Now, we must get going. We're two leagues from the settlement and I, for one, don't intend to go home empty-handed."

He turned abruptly and marched away, his bow slung over his shoulder. Deor, with a grin of relief, gathered up his bow and arrows and trotted after his cousin. Godwin stooped to pick up the remainder of their gear, and then he held out his hand towards Elgiva.

For a moment, she chewed her lower lip, still weighing the need for shelter against the instinct to flee. His reassuring smile seemed to be inviting her to trust him.

It galled her to admit it, but already she liked this man.

She took his hand, allowing him to lead her away, and with that small act, she felt she had committed herself to something momentous, yet she had no idea what it was.

As they walked through the wood, Elgiva toyed with a strand of her hair. Lost in thought, it was some time before she noticed her hair was now a golden yellow. Of course, Siriol had brought about some change, but she had hoped for an illusion, not a physical fact, and the knowledge of her complete transformation made her gasp with shock. Every muscle in her body tensed.

Godwin turned to look at her, clearly concerned by the tightening of her grip. Forcing a smile for his benefit, she told him she had stumbled on a tree root. But she was frightened to be so changed, more frightened still to know the cause. Magic was something the wardain used. It was fearsome and capricious. Underlings like her could only wonder at it and seek to avoid its wrath.

As she left the wood and felt the clean sunshine on her skin, she chided herself for her cowardice. Though Siriol's magic frightened her, it was good magic and as natural as the air she breathed. It was Lord Bellic's magic.

And if they couldn't be together, at least this was something they could share.

Chapter Three

THE HOME OF LORD OTHERE'S people was a well-established and prosperous place, and Elgiva had never seen anything like it. Her people lived unobtrusively in their tidy forest dwellings, while these wilthkin needed an abundance of space in which to live out their brief and brutal lives.

As she was taken through the gates, the stronghold opened out before her, around twenty acres' worth of bustling activity, and within it were three dozen or more rectangular dwellings of varying sizes, all with pitched, thatched roofs. There were also work sheds, pens, and stables. Smoke hovered in the late summer air, and the stench of burning rubbish made her wrinkle her nose in disgust.

But the noise surprised her more than anything else: the chatter of people doing their chores; the barking of dogs and the bleating of goats; the raucous laughter of warriors, lounging near the stronghold's gates; the screams of children playing tag; and, somewhere, the laboured clanking of a loom.

She tried to take in all of the details as Godwin led her past the great hall.

"I suppose your lord will put me to work, sweeping floors and scrubbing tables," said Elgiva.

"Well, we won't have you sweeping and scrubbing just yet. We generally feed our guests before we stick a broom in their hand." Godwin's artless eyes flashed her a look full of gentle humour, and she couldn't help but smile back at him. "You're not a servant tonight. Your place will be at the high table, next to Othere himself."

Her smile disappeared. "It will?"

"A stranger with a tale to tell? You're worth your weight in gold, Elgiva."

Elgiva swallowed hard. "I see."

"But no need to worry about that now. We've some time yet before we eat, so I'd better find you a place to stay. We're a little cramped here at the moment, but we're building some new dwellings in the spring. Of course, you must have a servant's quarters." He grimaced in apology. "For the time being, you're welcome to share my home, though I'm afraid you will have to share it with my family."

She inclined her head. "You're very kind."

They strolled across the settlement to the servants' quarters. Godwin walked up to one of the dwellings, pushed open the rickety wooden door, and invited Elgiva to step inside with a sweep of his arm and a grin on his face.

"There's a spare place over there," he said, pointing through the gloom.

Elgiva peered across the hut and saw a low wooden frame. On either side were partitions of osiers.

"I'm afraid that's the best we can do for now. I'll get you a pallet from somewhere."

"I'm accustomed to nothing better," she said, hoping he wouldn't take offence.

"Neither am I." He grinned.

"Where's your family, Godwin?"

"My wife, Rowena, will be preparing food. My two young daughters are playing somewhere. They're usually with their friends. And I must be getting back to the hall, but I'll light you a fire before I go."

The fireplace was a pad of clay in the centre of the room with several three-legged stools beside it. Elgiva chose one and sat down. As the fire caught hold and she had more light, her eyes were drawn to a glinting object hanging high on a wall. It was a fine sword, and it seemed out of place in this meagre dwelling.

Elgiva pointed towards it. "How does a serf come to own such a weapon?"

Godwin moved to take the sword down and show it to her. "My only link with what has been . . . or might have been." He sat down on a stool beside Elgiva and ran his fingers over the hilt. "Back then, I was the son of people I can't remember, bearing a name time has erased. I was perhaps five years old, and our village was attacked by

The Exile of Elindel

Saxons. They took me, but they killed my sister. I've never understood why she had to die." For a few moments, he fell silent, composing himself, and then he quirked an eyebrow at her. "I had the sword with me that day. I don't know why. Nor do I know why I'm telling you all this."

"You were young to have such a weapon."

"Yes, it's odd, but the sword has always been with me, I think. I keep it un-honed. I'm not permitted to bear arms here, of course, but I was allowed to keep this. When I was older, Othere told me I tried to defend myself with it, to the great amusement of the raiders. When one of them tried to take it from me, he was badly cut. In fact, he lost three fingers. Othere said they all roared with laughter. Such things amuse them no end. He decided that because I'd defeated one of his best warriors, I could keep the sword. It's still the subject of a joke among the older men in the mead hall, when they're all drunk and feeling nostalgic."

"And the man you wounded?"

"We've been friends ever since. So, there you have it; how I came to be at Othere's, bearing the name he gave me."

"Godwin, they killed your sister and made you a slave."

He glared at her. "These things happen. You must know that. Has your tribe never gone to war against the Britons, against each other?"

"But didn't you ever think of running away?"

"Where should I have run to? I had no idea where my people were. I still don't. Don't tell me what I should have done. I was a child when it happened. I had to accept it. The Saxons have treated me well. Othere was more like a father to me when I was a boy. Then I grew up and it no longer mattered. Do you understand? The Saxons are my people now."

"Godwin, I'm so sorry."

He touched her arm reassuringly. "Don't be, please. Perhaps you're right, but I can't change what happened. If I could, I would have had them kill me instead of my sister."

"Doesn't it bother you, not knowing who you are, or might have been? Don't you hate the Saxons for taking that away from you?"

"What good would that do? It wouldn't change anything. We have to accept things as they are and just get on with life."

"But I can't! I won't. What happened to me, it's wrong. It's not fair. It's just not fair!" Elgiva hid her face in her hands and burst into tears.

Godwin put his arm around her and pulled her gently towards him. "But you'll be all right now. Lord Othere will look after you."

"What makes you think I want your master looking after me? I want . . . I need my own people."

The Saxons *are* your people, Elgiva."

This only made Elgiva sob afresh. "Godwin, I don't know what to do."

"If you're afraid of the future, would it help if you knew you had at least one true friend? Well then, upon my oath, I'll be that friend, and I vow to be your protector if it's within my power. I pledge this with all my heart." He placed his hand upon his breast, and then his gaze shifted to the fire and he frowned. "I don't know why I'm saying such things."

Elgiva had no idea what to say next, but her awareness shifted to the sword that now lay across his knees. There was something odd about it, a curious feeling she couldn't explain.

"You say the sword is un-honed, but it looks incredibly sharp," she ventured.

"A trick of the light. It's quite dull. I couldn't cut butter with this." He ran his thumb hard along the edge of the blade to show her how blunt it was, and then he stood up and replaced the sword on the wall. "I'd better go and tell Lord Othere about you. Stay here and rest. I'll call for you later."

With that, he was gone.

Elgiva drew a deep breath, trying to accept the strangeness of the day. Clutching the amulet to her breast, she begged it to maintain the spell, but she also prayed she would not forget who she really was.

The feasting was drawing to a close, and the air in the great hall was thick with smoke and sweat and the tang of roasted flesh. Inside this impressive building were splendours Elgiva hadn't expected. The massive high table bore gleaming goblets and golden platters, all reflecting the light. Benches stood ranked among the thick stanchions that supported the roof with its rafters of ash. On the

The Exile of Elindel

walls hung silver-tipped drinking horns, colourful tapestries, and polished war-gear, and by the great hearth, a brace of huge deerhounds watched the newcomer warily.

It was clear that what she believed about the wilthkin wasn't quite true. She had thought their homes would be dirty and dismal, but the great hall was spacious and orderly; the wooden floor had been recently swept, the torches were lit, and a fire blazed on the great clay hearth. Polished and arranged with care, helmets, swords, and axes gleamed bravely on the walls.

Of course, they're still barbarians, surrounded by the spoils of battle, she thought.

The chatter and laughter of many voices resounded within the hall. Elgiva longed for the cool, open air. She swallowed the last of her bread and cheese, gulped down some wine to calm herself, and watched the great dogs that were grouped by the hearth. They were fighting over a thigh bone that had once belonged to some hapless beast. The manner in which they addressed each other made Elgiva sigh. They were clearly as arrogant as their masters.

Someone was trying to attract her attention. It was Othere, seated on her right. Godwin had brought her to him at the beginning of the meal. Elgiva's mouth had been dry, and she had feared the Saxon lord could see her trembling. Tall and draped with fur, Othere looked like an angry bear, with strong hands, a battle-scarred face, and a voice accustomed to being heard.

He thanked Elgiva for her part in saving his son from the boar's attack, but when told of her exile, his face darkened. He shook his head, and his grey beard whispered against the silver chain that hung about his neck. His eyes had the sharpness of steel. Deceiving him wouldn't be easy.

But Othere said no guest in his hall was called to account on an empty stomach, and with that, he had left her alone to gnaw on the bones of her apprehension.

Now, however, it seemed he was ready and eager to hear her tale.

"You have feasted well, child? Perhaps you will honour me with the tale of your unhappy exile? I cannot believe you an evildoer, unless your innocent looks are deceptive."

Feasted well? Though the Eldrakin used the horns, hides, and bones of beasts that died in the forests, since the time of Faine's pact with the animals, they had never eaten flesh. Bread, cheese, and russet-coloured apples had sufficed at Othere's table this evening.

Elgiva drew in a deep breath and expelled it quickly to steady herself. "I may have done evil, my lord, but it wasn't my intention," she said, and she cleared her throat. "I tried to protect my master. I knew he was in danger. He had placed his trust in men who were really his enemies. I chanced by their hiding place one day and overheard their talk. They were plotting against him, my lord."

Lord Othere drew closer, clearly intrigued to hear more.

"I was angry. For all his faults, he was still our master, and we had sworn oaths to serve him. I had to keep it to myself, and you might wonder at that, but to be honest, I was afraid." She paused, as though it saddened her to recollect the past, but it was the effort of choosing her words that made her hesitate. One slip, and she risked revealing her true identity. "Who would believe someone like me, if I accused my betters?"

Bellic would, of course, but he had been absent, as he frequently seemed to be when he was most needed.

"I decided, if I was to save my master, I must take action myself." She paused again and gulped some wine. "Well, my people are skilled at archery, as are yours, I dare say. So, as I knew where my master's enemies planned to meet him . . . kill him, I went there with a bow and some arrows. I climbed a tree and waited."

Elgiva was growing in confidence now, and this time, she paused for dramatic effect. She took another sip of wine, while Othere sat stiffly attentive.

"My lord arrived for the secret meeting his enemies had requested and soon his arch-enemy, who was also the Chief Counsellor turned up with his fellow conspirator."

The conspirator was called Tarkinell. She shuddered as she remembered his gaunt, mean face and greedy eyes. She had never liked him, but still it had surprised her to find him in league with the Chief Counsellor.

"This man diverted my lord's attention and engaged him in conversation while the Chief Counsellor stepped behind him and drew a dagger from his robe. But I was ready. Did I intend to kill the Chief Counsellor? I don't know, but I pierced him to the heart."

The Exile of Elindel

Elgiva glanced at Othere. His mouth was set in a thin, hard line, but otherwise, he showed no reaction.

"My master looked up and saw me, and while he called for the guards, the other man picked up the dagger and hid it in his tunic. Then there was general confusion, as guards and servants appeared from all sides. I was shaken from the tree, and the other conspirator feigned outrage and told everyone my master had been my intended target. Nobody listened to me. The Chief Counsellor a traitor? What a ridiculous notion! And there I was, a low-born slave, with a bow and arrows, guilty of murder. I was beaten unmercifully. The conspirator egged them on to prevent me from speaking up for myself. I think they would have killed me, had a high-ranking friend not intervened."

She smiled as she remembered Captain Merrill and hoped he hadn't been punished for standing up for her.

She sighed deeply and took more wine. By now, her head was beginning to swim and the heat in the hall made it hard to breathe freely. She leaned against the tall chair back and tried to relax, but it wasn't easy. She could see in her mind those awful moments following her arrest. She had thought King Thallinore would strike her dead with his magic, but oddly, he withheld his power, in spite of his fury. Outrage had no doubt robbed him of the capacity to act.

She swallowed to ease her tightening throat. It was easy now to look sincere. Too well, she recalled the curses and blows and the feeling of helpless despair.

"At length, I was dragged away. I was put in a cruel confinement, underground in a dark, dank cell. If some sort of trial was conducted, I was never told. Eventually, they hauled me out and banished me forever. I thought they were going to execute me, but perhaps they thought exile was worse. I dare say they were right." She shrugged and took a sip of wine. "So I can't return to my people's land. Ever. On pain of death. My home is lost to me."

And Bellic had said nothing. He sent Briar with the amulet. He asked Alsiann, leader of the royal herd, to be her escort. But he said nothing, not even goodbye.

Elgiva started as Othere banged his large fist on the table. "If what you say is true—"

"I swear it, my lord."

"Then your lord was unjust and foolish. He lacks the knowledge required for a lord to rule wisely and well. A lord must be a father to everyone, high or low. He must know their needs and value their worth. He must give justice to everyone. Your master did not permit you to speak in your own defence. A lord such as yours can never have the respect his title merits."

Elgiva imagined that Othere truly believed what he was saying, but removed from them by his rank and wealth, did he really know the worth of his people down to the lowliest serf? And yet, were royal elves really any better?

"It is foolish to trust without question the men who crowd around one, eager to give advice," he went on. "Such men are often dissemblers whose hearts nourish secret ambitions. They are often not as true as the lowly servant who tends the hearth."

"Like Godwin?" she asked. He was across the hall, clearing away the remains of the meal in the company of some other serfs, while his betters continued to laugh and swill beer.

"Ah, my favourite servant! An honest wight, indeed. More so than these noble sirs you see about me, mouthing wise words. Position and wealth do not nurture humility."

She wanted to cock an eyebrow at this but managed to look sincere.

"Yet even so," she added, "he belongs to the race of our enemies."

He raised his eyebrows. "That is so. There were many battles with different tribes at the time when Godwin was taken." He paused for a moment, and the gleam in his eyes looked more like relish than recollection. "Our children were also abducted in raids. But now we live in a time of peace. Our enemies have retreated west, and those that were taken, on both sides, are no doubt content to be where they are. Godwin is one of our race now."

"I dare say you are right, my lord."

She lifted her beaker to her lips but found it was empty. Othere reached for a jug of wine.

"Permit me to offer you more," he said.

He filled her beaker to the brim, and Elgiva smiled. Seldom did a lord wait on a servant.

"You treat your guests very well. I am, after all, a mere serf." Perhaps her remark had been ill considered, because he narrowed his eyes fractionally. Hastily, she added, "And a serf without a master. As an exile, I can expect nothing from anyone, but I dare to ask something of you, my lord Othere."

"Ask."

"I need food and a place to live. You are convinced of my innocence, I hope. Would you let me stay here and serve you? If you deem me worthy, of course." If it weren't for the loosening effects of the wine, these words might have choked her.

Othere weighed her request, while Elgiva's guts churned with impatience. Eventually, he said, "I consider you most worthy."

"Thank you, noble lord."

He chuckled. "An interesting creature you are, to be sure. You are a serf, yet your manner speaks of higher things."

"I was well taught, my lord."

"So it would appear. I was told you may have tales for us. In sooth, I confess my hospitality was not entirely unselfish." He studied the rings that adorned his fingers while Elgiva gulped down more wine. "Hearing you were a traveller, I had hoped that you would repay me by giving us news of foreign parts, as well as some new stories. We have few visitors these days, now that things have quietened down. Some diversion is always welcome. So, child, from whence do you come?"

"From beyond the hills to the west," she replied.

"The stronghold of the Britons?"

"Oh, er . . . yes, my lord. But our settlement is very large, and we have many warriors. As for the Britons . . . " She shrugged. "A disorganised rabble, bemoaning their lot and fighting amongst themselves. They know what's best for them and leave us well alone."

"Perhaps . . . yes," agreed Othere. "It must be as you say. But enough of such matters for now. It is time we had some tales and verses. Perhaps you have some stories for us?"

Elgiva gave him a weary look. "Forgive me. I don't wish to offend, but I am very tired. My mind is confused by the day's events. If you have no objection, my lord, I should like to retire."

Othere looked disappointed, but he clearly wanted to uphold his image as the affable host. "Of course, my child. I can see your fatigue. I will not keep you from your rest."

She bid him good night, left the table, and slipped out through a side door into the evening's chill embrace. Its freshness hit her like a wall of stone, making the wine surge in her veins, and she staggered for a moment before the giddiness passed. Her gown felt damp and cold on her skin.

The full moon had risen, and an afternoon storm had rolled away to a distant sky. Leaves and blades of grass were silvered under the spell of the moon, robbed of their reality, but Elgiva's senses felt their being.

It was then she experienced a pang of compassion for these wilthkin with their narrow views. They would never see life with her elven perception, never know the feeling of oneness with even the smallest living thing.

A burst of fresh carousing from the hall, and her communion was profaned. She sighed and walked towards Godwin's hut. Now she wasn't just a servant; she was a servant of the wilthkin. It was truly unthinkable.

She hoped it would be a short winter.

And what had happened to Bellic? Was he sitting in King Thallinore's hall, listening to Caspell's harp, or reading some dull, old manuscript in his cosy, fire-lit room? Did he wonder what had become of her, or had the giving of Siriol absolved him from all responsibility for his former pupil, from the guilt of letting them drive her out?

But he wasn't responsible for her at all. He had only been her friend. Friends weren't responsible for each other, were they?

Even so, he was still a wardain, and he had power. He could go wherever he pleased, do whatever he liked. Surely one day, he would seek her out?

Yet, could it be even he believed she was a traitor? He knew her better than that, didn't he?

That night, Elgiva went to her bed feeling lost and alone, but the days that lay ahead of her weren't as bad as she had feared.

Many months passed and a hard winter came. The rivers were choked with ice, the mean huts scoured by blizzards, but in the great hall there was food, warmth, and company, of sorts, and Elgiva did her duties without complaint.

Elgiva's skill in handling livestock was generally admired, and no one ever suspected that being able to talk to the animals was the reason for her success. She seized this as her chance to gain a little privacy and asked if she could have a pallet in the stable. Her devotion to her master's beasts was praised, but what would the Saxons have thought had they known she preferred the company of animals to the company of men?

Guilt, however, gave her no peace; guilt for living a lie. She wasn't used to the feeling and hadn't expected it. After all, they were only barbarians. What had she to feel guilty about? Didn't she work hard for her keep?

And with the guilt came anger at the situation she found herself in. Her life should never have been like this. It wasn't right. It wasn't fair.

But the amulet's spell endured, and soon the winter was growing old. Still, there was no word from Bellic. Elgiva longed for the first signs of spring, when she could leave this place, undo the spell, and be herself again, running free in the leafy woods.

Chapter Four

IT WAS A grey dawn near the end of winter when tragedy fell upon the settlement. An army of warriors appeared in the east, marching over the frosty fields. Cold sunlight flashed on their shields and swords.

Panic scattered Lord Othere's sentries, for peace had made them complacent and they were late in sounding the alarm. The people were jolted out of their sleep, not knowing quite what the danger was, and they were unprepared for the threat of bloodshed.

Elgiva, however, was aware long before the sentries knew what was happening. In the deep straw of the stable, she was dragged from her sleep by a premonition. She sat up and listened intently. Her companions were restless, and a small, nervous pony nudged her with its muzzle.

After dressing, she set off for Godwin's hut, where she found all of the occupants sleeping. She shook Godwin by the shoulder and tried to convince him they were in danger, insisting they hurry to find Lord Othere. Confused and frowning, he pulled on his boots and yawned his apologies to his wife Rowena, and then he stumbled after Elgiva as she ran to the hall.

By the time they reached their destination, the alarm had been given and warriors were starting to take up arms. A half-dressed servant came tearing towards them, still wrestling with the buckle of his leather belt. He thrust Elgiva and Godwin aside and barged into the hall.

"Have you heard? We're attacked," he yelled.

Godwin looked horrified, and then he called after the man. "Kern, wait!"

But Kern, his bare feet slapping on the wooden floor, was already on his way to rouse Lord Othere.

The Exile of Elindel

Elgiva and Godwin followed him. They reached the high table just as Othere appeared at the curtained entrance of his chamber, a mighty scowl upon his craggy face. Kern came scuttling in his wake, and Othere rounded on him.

"By all the gods, what's toward, you rogue? Why am I tumbled from my bed at this hour?" he demanded. "Is the settlement ablaze?"

"It's Beortnoth," Kern almost shrieked. "With a great army, a very great army, my lord, and almost upon us."

"By Grim," roared Othere. "That murdering bastard is after my lands again." He gave the servant a mighty shove. Do not stand there gibbering, Kern. Get my sword and helm and see that everyone is awake."

Kern darted off in terror, and Othere strode towards the dais, a dangerous frown upon his face. "A dawn attack. There is no honour in that."

"My lord," Godwin said, "they'll be here before we're ready. Can we hold the gates against them? Perhaps we should talk—"

"Talk? How much talk has there been with that bastard and his mercenary scum? How many truces has he broken? Did he not agree to keep to his side of the river? He covets my land, Godwin. He will not give up until he has everything I own. But I will see him dead first."

Godwin lowered his gaze. "Yes, lord."

"He has been biding his time, gathering strength. It is a blood feud and must end in blood. We must commit ourselves to battle and pray that the gods are with us. We must hold the gates, and if we cannot, we will fight to the very last man." His keen eyes narrowed with resolution. "Whoever is sound in limb must take up arms—even you, Godwin."

A spasm of anxiety passed over Godwin's face, but he merely nodded.

"Hurry, man!"

Godwin straightened himself, gave Elgiva a brief, tight smile, and hastened from the hall. She stared after him blankly, wanting to express her concern, but finding no words for the purpose.

At that moment, another side door flew open. In its throat stood a trembling Kern, behind him a background of chaos as people ran in all directions, shouting in fear and panic.

"My war gear!" cried Othere, as though he were greeting a long-lost friend.

Elgiva watched him from the corner of her eye. *You're actually enjoying all this.*

As if for the first time, the Saxon lord seemed to notice Elgiva. "Find yourself a place of safety, child," he said. And with that, he hefted his longsword in both hands and strode out through the hall's main doors, Kern trotting in his wake.

Elgiva sighed and leaned heavily against the high table. Now what? This seemed like a good time to leave. The world of men was one of violence and mayhem, and she had seen the awakened savagery in Othere's ice-blue eyes. He thrived on warfare; they all did. Without it, what were they but farmers and storytellers, growing fat and bored?

She didn't intend to shed her blood in the name of some petty, territorial dispute. If she sneaked through the rear of the hall and out across the compound . . .

Her plan got no further. The image of Bellic's stern face rose in her mind and in his wise, old eyes, she could see more than a hint of reproach. He would, no doubt, have reminded her she owed a great deal to Godwin and his family, and even to Lord Othere. To run away now would be an act of betrayal.

She wrestled with her feelings, but there was only one honourable course to take, and at length, she made for the main doors. People were running everywhere, and it was impossible for her to make sense of the chaos. The clash of swords rang in the distance. That could mean only one thing: the raiders had already forced their way in and were fighting with Lord Othere's men.

But what could she do to help?

She drew the air deep into her lungs in an effort to steady herself. She needed to consider her part in defending the people who had given her shelter, but any help she gave would have to be limited to those she considered her friends.

What had become of Godwin, who had gone unskilled to join the defenders of the settlement? Perhaps already slain, his corpse lay, spilling blood before the gates of the stronghold. She wasn't prepared for the indignation such a thought provoked, but she had to acknowledge that, wilthkin or not, he didn't deserve to die like that. She was powerless to help him, but perhaps she could ensure his family was safe.

Elgiva stepped over the threshold and hurried to Godwin's hut; in her haste to get there, her own safety was forgotten.

She found herself hoisted into the air. Twisting round, she came face to face with a tall, blond warrior. His fierce eyes glittered with triumph.

"You'll make a fine gift for my father-in-law, Othere's dog!" he snarled.

Elgiva kicked out angrily and caught him on the shin. He howled with rage and loosened his grip, but recovered before she could struggle free.

"Siriol, curse him with the pox, the blister, and the scab!" she screamed.

The raider laughed and slung her over his brawny shoulder. She beat her fists in vain against his muscle-hard torso. Restraining her legs with one hand and clutching his longsword with the other, he strolled away with his prize.

"How dare you!" she cried. "How dare you!"

In the distance, she saw the servants' dwellings, and she was being carried in the opposite direction. Tears of frustration welled in her eyes. Godwin had been her friend, and she had to help his family.

When she thought of Rowena and the two little girls, desperation stirred up all manner of wild imaginings: scenes of destruction, slaughter, and rape.

"Siriol! Siriol! Why don't you help me?"

But the amulet didn't respond.

Try harder. Try harder.

Perhaps the amulet wouldn't help, if in doing so it caused harm to another? But her heart was so full of *hate*. She must get free. She must help Rowena. She raged at herself and her fists were clenched so tightly they ached.

Concentrate. Try harder. Do you want to end up as a spoil of battle?

Siriol, why don't you do something? You're supposed to obey me!

Could she penetrate the amulet's passivity with her mind, forge some kind of link between her need and Siriol's power?

She needed words to awaken its might, but her mind was completely blank. She needed the words she had never been taught...

What were the words? What were the words?

"Stop struggling now, Othere's dog, or my sword will spill your guts," snarled the raider.

His threat provided the spark. Her anger flared with a heat she feared would consume her if it found no release. She poured it into Siriol in a moment of exquisite focus.

"In the name of Faine, protect me, Siriol!"

A glow of power responded to her need. At first, it centred on the amulet, but it grew more vague, more diffuse. A strange warmth spread throughout her body. It set her nerve ends tingling, and her skin shivered with gooseflesh. She hadn't expected this. For one awful moment, she feared Siriol couldn't separate its mistress from her enemy. The use of the amulet had never been explained to her. And now it was too late.

The power grew. There was an excruciating moment of calm, as if Elgiva were poised on the lip of some bottomless chasm. Did Siriol feel her hesitate?

She surrendered herself to the power.

"Siriol, strike him now!" she cried.

Something contracted inside her. Then she felt an explosion, which seemed to be in her mind. An intense stab of hot pain passed from her body into that of her captor, and she was flung aside. He yelled in agony and fell to his knees.

For a moment, everything went black in her mind. Why was she sprawled in the dirt? She forced herself to her feet. Her legs felt weak and boneless. Her head reeled and nausea griped her guts. She held the amulet in a trembling hand and glared at it.

"Whose side are you on?"

Her gaze flew to the stricken raider, who was rolling on the ground in pain. A strange desire to gloat on his agony rooted her to the spot, as though she were witnessing some personal achievement. At the same time, it was sickening and she longed to be as far away from the horror of it as possible. Of course he deserved his pain, but surely, Siriol, this was too much?

When she had control of herself she tore her gaze away, left the man moaning on the icy ground, and ran to the servants' quarters.

The Exile of Elindel

Once inside the hut, Elgiva could hear the children whimpering with fear. She quickly moved towards them to offer reassurance, and they clutched at her robe. She hugged them both.

"Don't be afraid. We'll be all right," she said. She glanced at their mother. "Rowena, they might ransack the huts. You must find somewhere safe to hide, where they won't find anything worth the bother of searching. The defences are breached. We must move quickly!"

Clasping Rowena's hand, Elgiva dragged her out of the hut, the children's fingers still clamped to her robe. Fires blazed everywhere as they burst into the stark, cold light. A premonition of danger made Elgiva brusque, as she urged her charges behind an overturned cart.

Three raiders tore past, one brandishing a torch. They were searching all of the huts for treasure, though the servants' dwellings had little to offer. But Godwin's proved more lucrative. To the cheers of his companions, a raider emerged with Godwin's sword and flourished it triumphantly.

Elgiva frowned and clenched her fists at the sight of his greedy smirk. Godwin's only link with his past was now in the hands of scavengers. And she could do nothing about it.

The man with the torch set flame to the thatch. As the fire took hold, his lips drew back in a fierce grin of pleasure. He joined his companions, and they dashed off again on the trail of plunder.

Elgiva watched through narrowed eyes as the figures were lost in the billowing smoke. Rowena gaped at the loss of her home, and the children whimpered and clung to their mother. For a time, they watched the little hut burn, as though they were paying their last respects.

"Huts can be rebuilt," said Elgiva, "and you're all safe and not in there."

Rowena's lip trembled as she tried to smile. "Elgiva, yes. We must thank the gods. For that, for you. You saved us."

Elgiva lowered her gaze. Rowena's gratitude stung her conscience. After all, she was merely discharging a debt. That and nothing more. "Come," she said. "Follow me."

They trotted behind her as she led them towards the stables. The fences were smashed, the animals taken, and for the moment, all was quiet. She ushered them inside.

"I can't think of anywhere better, Rowena. If you hide in the straw, perhaps you'll be safe. They can see the place is empty, nothing here for them to steal. But keep a look out for men with torches." She turned to the children. "You must be very, very quiet. Still as two hares in a meadow." She placed a finger on her lips, and the children nodded, eager to please.

She hugged them again and turned away. She had been of some use to her friends and now could leave with a clean conscience.

Rowena peered out of the shelter. "I wish I knew if Godwin . . . if . . . " She swallowed and turned away.

"He can take care of himself." *Another lie, but what else can I say?*

Rowena turned to face her. "He's no warrior," she said, and her face was streaked with tears.

Elgiva sighed and got to her feet. "I'll find him and bring you news."

Rowena tried to grab her arm, but Elgiva was far too nimble. Ignoring Rowena's pleas, she left the stable at a run, breaching the wall of greasy, grey smoke rising in front of her.

She hadn't intended any of this, and she certainly didn't want it. Godwin and his family had reached her in ways she hadn't expected. Yet still, she needed to prove her integrity, to herself, if no one else.

Then she would be free.

As she pelted towards the mead hall, she made herself a promise. If she escaped from this place with her life, she would march straight back to Derryth and give him a very large piece of her mind.

Chapter Five

Deor, fatally wounded, lay stretched at the feet of his comrades. The warriors couldn't move him to a place of safety, for the battle was raging all around them, but they tried to shield him as best they could. Their battle cries still rang bravely in the air, and their swords were slick with the enemy's gore.

Beyond the wall of the stronghold, just out of the archers' range, Beortnoth sat on a great black horse that raked the earth with its hooves. He watched the embroilment like a god of war and laughed at the missiles that fell short of their target. The sight struck terror into Othere's men.

Godwin glanced down at Deor. "My lord, how do you fare?"

"I'm dying, you stupid bastard. Forget me, man . . . the foe!" He choked on the blood that rose in his throat, his face as white as the frost.

A fresh wave of raiders surged to attack. Godwin parried blow after blow until his head swam. That he still lived amazed him, but years of hard work had given him the muscle to wield the mighty longsword Elric had found for him. At least now he had a shield, too, for Deor could hold his no longer, and he had Elric beside him. Many times, he thanked the gods for the younger man's quick reactions. Now they were part of a sturdy line of battle-seasoned warriors, and while these veterans stood at his side, Godwin could count on their protection.

He swung at his assailants, trying to disable them before they came too close, but he was growing more fatigued. Only the need to survive kept him going, gave him the strength to continue hacking and slashing with the ponderous blade. He was glad to have left his own sword behind. Too short, too blunt for this bloody work.

Weariness warped the world around him, but he battled on,

compelled to keep the flashing blade in motion. It seemed he had always been here, whirling this blade, and always would be. The foe kept coming, the foe would keep coming, and at his feet, Deor's lifeless body mocked him with its sightless gaze.

Deor was dead. This realisation shattered Godwin's concentration.

"Godwin, look out!" cried Elric.

Godwin looked up and saw a long blade poised in the air above him. Numb to the core and unable to move, he watched his death descend.

He was knocked aside and thrown among the corpses on the ground. A battle-hardened warrior now stood in his place, and with practised ease he dispatched the marauder, as if such things were the reason for his existence.

The grey-bearded veteran flashed him a grin of fellowship. It was Cerdic, Elric's tutor in swordplay, a good-natured man who had always treated Godwin like an equal.

Cerdic tucked his sword under his arm and, with his right hand, helped Godwin to his feet. His left hand was unfit for the task, as three of its fingers were missing. Briefly, they grinned at each other like the old comrades they were, before Godwin retrieved his own sword and staggered back to the line of warriors.

He gritted his teeth and held in his mind's eye the images he fought for: his wife, his children, his lord. His home. He clung to these symbols of permanence. It was the only reasonable thing to do.

Oh, Grim, don't let me die like this!

Elgiva soon found the hub of the conflict. A seething mass of warriors were battling for control of the area before the stronghold's gates. The latter hung from their hinges, like the broken wings of some great, trampled bird.

Drawing closer, she spotted Elric. His face was grey with effort, and his sword dripped with blood. She felt a pang of compassion. Though he looked like a man, he was the same age as her. He shouldn't be forced to risk his life in so desperate a manner. His courage made her stand back and look at her own.

She searched the turmoil feverishly. The air blew about her in acrid gusts, sharp with smoke and the reek of gore. Her eyes stung and watered so much, all she could see was a meaningless blur.

Scrubbing away the tears, she edged carefully forwards. The ground was churned and trampled by combat, strewn with weapons and injured men. And then she saw Deor, twisted and still. Blood trailed from his mouth. His eyes were wide and staring, but he saw no more of this world. His pale, clenched fist still gripped his shattered sword.

She found Godwin—alive or dead, she couldn't tell—lying beside the wall of the stronghold. The intensity of her reaction surprised her, but of all the wilthkin, Godwin was the one she most wanted to survive.

Avoiding the blades that sliced about her head, she ran to his side and knelt. His hand still gripped the hilt of his sword, and it filled Elgiva with dread, as a picture of Deor flashed into her mind.

"Godwin!" She shook his arm, and the weapon slid from his grasp. "By Faine, you're alive. Listen. Godwin, listen. I've hidden your family. They're safe, do you hear me? Godwin!" She found herself shouting, angry at him, at herself, at everything. "Wake up, Godwin. Wake up, damn you!"

His eyelids flickered open, and he gave her a vacant look.

"You can't stay here. You'll be hacked to pieces." She shook his arm again.

"Am I not . . . already . . . then?" His voice was hoarse and weak.

Sighing with impatience, she struggled to heave him upright. Slowly, they crawled and stumbled away from the thick of battle, and then she let him rest.

"Your head is bleeding, Godwin. Is that your only wound? You're covered in blood. Not all yours, I hope." Her nose wrinkled at the stink of gore.

"Something hit me," was all he said.

She tore a strip from the hem of her robe and began to bandage his head.

"You said they were safe," he ventured.

"Your family? Yes. I hid them in the stables. I saw Othere while I was looking for you, and he promised he would send men to rescue them. They'll be all right. Don't worry."

She smiled at him, and he relaxed. His honest gaze beamed gratitude at her, and she wished she'd been less abrupt with him.

"Othere's hurt, but he'll be fine, too," she told him.

"I'm glad, Elgiva. While he's alive, there's hope for the rest of us."

She arched her eyebrows. "Hope, Godwin? He's an old, wounded man. Your warriors, they're dead, they're injured, they're outnumbered. Can't you see, it's only a matter of time?"

"We'll be taken, then, Elgiva. We'll be slaves of Beortnoth." A sudden look of horror widened his eyes. "Elgiva, they'll take my daughters!"

She saw his fear, and she also saw herself, making pies in the kitchen of the great hall with Godwin's wife, while his two little children played with the leftover dough. She remembered laughing with them, and for a while, she had known what it felt like to have a family. Her pulse was pounding in her throat as she fought to control conflicting emotions. She ran her fingers through her hair, trying to compose herself, but his pain and her own anger demanded her attention. And not merely her attention.

She jumped to her feet. "This has gone on long enough."

"Elgiva, where are you going?"

Elgiva didn't respond. She crept towards the stronghold's gates, her back pressed to the wall, and all the while, she searched the ground for the weapon she needed.

With a major effort, Godwin stood and tottered in her wake. His vision swam from the exertion, but when it cleared, he saw his friend lift a tall, curved bow from the body of a fallen archer. Then she selected a single arrow and ran towards the gates.

The warriors at the entrance were too engrossed in battle to notice the girl who darted among them. One swung his axe half-heartedly, but she ducked beneath his arm; clearly no one was going to stand in her way. Godwin pursued her as best he could, too numb to care for his own well-being. The conviction that he should follow her was too compelling to ignore.

Elgiva ran through the shattered gates and came to a halt about thirty yards from the line of warriors that were ranked around Beortnoth. They bristled with contempt at the sight of her, her slight form dwarfed by the bow. Their master's eyes narrowed above his

The Exile of Elindel

hooked nose and for a moment, he seemed to consider the threat, but then he let out a roar of mirth.

"My lords, we are undone!" he cried in a booming voice edged with malice. "A fierce war-maiden is upon us!"

His men greeted his words with hoarse laughter.

With a grimace of effort, Elgiva struggled to nock the single arrow.

"By the time you have that weapon under control, if you can, little serf, my warriors here will have cut you down," Beortnoth promised sternly. "Othere must be desperate, indeed, to send his half-grown serving women to fight his battles for him!"

His men raised their bows and nocked their arrows, while others unsheathed their swords, unhurried in their complacency.

"Siriol, hear me," whispered Elgiva. "Raise a wall of power before me so that their arrows will not strike me."

Planting her feet firmly on the earth, she drew a steadying breath and held it. Her elven instincts, her whole being, were focused upon the mastery of the bow.

The warriors mocked her with their insouciance, clearly not the least bit alarmed, but before they could prevent it, their haughty master was pierced to the heart.

Godwin staggered from the stronghold just in time to see Beortnoth drop slowly from his horse's back. The animal reared and galloped away, while the warriors stood open-mouthed and gawped at their fallen leader. But several had the presence of mind to let their arrows fly.

As the missiles swished about Elgiva, Godwin stumbled forwards. Each step he took jarred his throbbing head. Vaguely, he realised he had left his sword behind. He was weaponless, defenceless, but it didn't matter now. His friend was his only concern. And he was too late to save her. He hadn't kept faith with his vow.

Horns blared the news of Beortnoth's death, and the ranks of the enemy scattered in confusion. The higher-ranking men retreated on horseback; the rest were left to flee as best as they could. Godwin shifted his line of vision and gasped when he saw Elgiva. She lay stretched on the ground like a sacrifice, a bristling of arrows piercing the earth around her, like carelessly planted saplings. In his haste to reach her, he tripped and stumbled to his knees.

When he regained his feet, he found himself facing the stronghold. His breath caught in his throat. Like a broken dam, the gates spewed forth a flood of retreating men. Some were injured, some carried plunder, and many were fighting still as they tried to get away. A few had taken captives, children who squirmed in their captors' arms and screamed to be released.

The retreat emboldened Othere's men and cries of triumph rang in the air.

Godwin stood transfixed by it all. A tidal wave of men bore down on him. He had to reach Elgiva, but before he could summon the strength to move, the surge of marauders had swamped him and he was carried along.

Someone grabbed hold of him and encircled him with rope. He struggled but was overwhelmed by the crowd of fleeing men. As if from a long way off, he heard the horns of the settlement bellowing victoriously. He fought for a last look at his home, but all he could see was a pall of grey smoke that rose from the stronghold, like a gasp of exhaustion.

Bewildered and bereft of hope, he allowed himself to be dragged along by the yelling mass of raiders. A blur of armour and swords blocked everything else from view. They hauled him down a grassy slope and over a narrow brook. A raider, his thick arms cradling booty, crashed heavily into him, and they fell into the water. Goblets and plates clattered and splashed. His captors jerked him upright and urged him on with curses.

Ahead of them, ponies and wagons waited beneath the trees. The animals neighed in terror at the sight of the angry horde, and their eyes glittered white.

Godwin was bound securely and then hurled into one of the wagons to lie among the sacks of booty. For the second time in his life, he was just another spoil of battle. With a sickening lurch, the wagon began to move.

Chapter Six

Night had already fallen by the time Godwin came to his senses. He lifted his head and gasped at the pain that pierced his skull, but gradually his vision cleared and he was able to focus on his surroundings.

He was slumped on the cold earth at the edge of a clearing, leaning against a tree, and bound to it with rope. His chilled body was stiff and bruised, and a crust of dried blood tightened the skin of his face. He ached to stretch the cramps from his limbs.

The night's icy breath crept into his bones. He shivered and scanned the trees around him, but he had no idea where he was, nor how he came to be there. He remembered being in a wagon, and he ought to be at the settlement of Beortnoth's people by now, but clearly he was in the middle of nowhere.

About four yards from where he sat, a small fire blazed invitingly. A cooking pot hung over it on a makeshift spit. A delicious aroma wafted towards him, and his stomach clenched. He had eaten nothing all day—assuming it was the same day—and a void inside him yearned to be filled.

A man he assumed to be his captor, or one of them at least, squatted beside the fire. He was rubbing his hands to warm them, his scowling face lit by the flames. He glanced impatiently over his shoulder and searched the surrounding trees, and then with a curse, he turned to the pot and stirred its contents with a stick.

Godwin tested his bonds, but they were secure. Wearily, he resigned himself to whatever his captors had planned. A noise in the undergrowth snatched his attention. A man in a cloak emerged from the shadows and made for the fire. His companion looked up with a grunt of annoyance.

"Have they fixed that wheel yet, Ealdred?" the man by the fire asked morosely. "At this rate, we'll never get home."

The newcomer warmed his hands over the flames. "Stop moaning, Harold. That's all you ever do. I told you, it's a tricky job. Edgar thinks it's past repair."

"Shit. That's all we need. This jaunt's been a nightmare from start to finish. We've had more bad luck in one day—"

"Shut your noise," said Ealdred, "and give me one of those oatcakes. I'm starving."

Harold ignored him. "We should have left the ruddy wagon. Gone back with the rest of them."

Ealdred seated himself by the fire "And leave all that stuff? I'm not going home empty-handed. Anyway, there wasn't room in the other carts for us and all the spoils. How many times must I tell you?"

"No room, aye, and why is that? All those kids they took, that's why. What use are they? Take adult prisoners, that's what I've always said. The higher ranking the better. You get more ransom then."

"We won't get much ransom for these two. A couple of serfs."

Hearing this, Godwin looked around to see if there was another captive in the clearing. Now that his eyes were used to the dark, he could make out more of his surroundings. He noticed something to his left and thought he detected movement. Was it a small figure, tied to a tree as he was?

In the distance, a howl shattered the calm of the glade. The marauders stiffened and drew close to the fire.

Godwin dragged his tormented gaze away from the cooking pot. His mind was clearer now, and some of his strength was returning. He tried his bonds again, but still it was no use.

The howl sounded once more in the darkness. A solitary wolf.

Godwin's fellow captive let out a howl so similar to the wolf's, the men by the fire sprang up with cries of alarm and fumbled for their swords. Godwin would have leapt up too, had the ropes not prevented it.

"By the gods!" yelled Harold.

"A wolf!"

"Too bloody close for my liking!"

The Exile of Elindel

The men peered round in all directions, and another howl reached their ears, this one from the distance. They sagged with relief and reseated themselves, evidently persuaded that both sounds had the same origin.

"Night air playing tricks on us!" said Ealdred.

"Aye, a wolf won't come this close to a fire."

But from Godwin's perspective, the last howl had seemed much nearer than the first. The wolf was drawing closer, and Godwin had the strangest feeling it came in answer to the other captive's call. An insane idea, perhaps, but one he couldn't shake.

"It's ready now," said Harold as he prodded the stew with a stick. But a moment later, he jumped to his feet in horror and stared across the clearing.

Ealdred's mouth fell open in shock when he followed Harold's gaze.

A wolf with silver-grey fur emerged from the shadows.

Two men appeared from the opposite side of the clearing. If they had been entertaining thoughts of supper, these were soon abandoned, and they threw down their torches and bolted. The two marauders by the fire were quick to follow their example.

"They always travel in packs," screamed Harold as he fled. "Let them eat the captives!"

They crashed through the bushes in a frenzy of fear, desperate to make their escape. From beyond the trees came scuffling and cracking sounds, the nickering of horses and the bellowing of oaths. Godwin listened as they galloped away, leaving their prisoners to the mercy of wolves. He held his breath and prepared for the worst.

For a long moment, nothing happened, and the night seemed to thicken around him. Then the great wolf turned slowly towards him, and a visceral panic lurched through his body, as though all of his organs were rushing to his feet.

But the wolf wasn't joined by others of its kind, nor did it seem in a hurry to eat him. It paused and sniffed the air with its long grey muzzle. The full moon, rolling free from clouds, turned the wolf's fur an eerie silver. Paralysed and helpless, Godwin watched the beast consider him, its amber eyes gleaming.

The great wolf turned, its large paws soundless on the frosty grass, but Godwin found no relief from his fear. The animal strode across the glade towards the other captive. Once there, it stopped and lowered its head, and its jaws opened and fastened on something.

Godwin felt his heart would stop; the other captive was being devoured!

He struggled wildly against the ropes. Then, breathing hard, he stopped and listened. There were no screams, nothing to indicate that carnivorous fangs were at work. All he could hear was his own ragged breathing—and the wolf was wagging its tail.

"Thank you, Greyflanks." Shaking off the chewed ropes, the captive got to her feet. She stretched herself exquisitely and then stroked the animal's head.

By Frigg . . . It's Elgiva! Godwin gaped at her as she strolled across the glade.

Kneeling beside him, she untied his ropes.

"Elgiva?"

"Yes, that's right." Her lips curled into a mischievous smile. "You look as though you've seen a ghost."

"But . . . I was sure you were dead!" Liberated from his bonds, he rubbed his wrists and flexed his arms. His mind was so crowded with questions, he couldn't give voice to them all.

"I pretended to be, and if I'd done so for a few minutes longer, I wouldn't have been taken. Curiosity overcame me." She tucked her hair behind her ears and smiled. "Are you all right? Can you stand?"

"Yes," he said vaguely. "I'm fine." With her assistance, he climbed to his feet.

"Godwin, this is Greyflanks." She pointed towards the wolf. "And we were very fortunate he was in the area. I recognised his voice at once and . . . er . . . sent him a cry for help." Her eyebrows drew together, and a tentative smile touched her lips. "I spoke wolf, of course, so I didn't alert the raiders."

"Of course." Godwin frowned in bewilderment.

The animal leaned against Elgiva, and she stroked its large, soft ears. "You see we . . . we're old friends."

"Old friends." Godwin feared his grip on reality was not as firm as he had believed.

"Godwin, I . . . " Then she stopped, her features fraught with misgiving. She cupped his elbow with her small hand. "You should sit down. You don't look well. Our captors left their supper. A shame to waste it, don't you think? And I'm sure you must be hungry." She led him unresisting to the campfire, and they seated themselves in silence.

Gradually, the warmth restored the feeling to his limbs, and Godwin's stupor began to recede. He ladled some stew into a wooden bowl and as he did so, he tried to grasp the strangeness of his plight. He offered the food to Elgiva, but she pointed to the wolf.

"Serve the guest first," she said with a grin. "Then yourself. I'll eat these oatcakes." To the question in his eyes, she said, "Haven't you ever noticed? I don't eat animal flesh."

"Why not?"

"Well . . ." She stopped, chewing her lower lip before continuing. "It's not the custom of my people."

"Oh."

He stared at her for a moment before gingerly placing the bowl of stew before the wolf. Then he reached for a second bowl and filled it for himself. The wolf regarded him briefly, as though in silent thanks, then set about devouring the stew with obvious enjoyment.

Elgiva sat chewing an oatcake and staring into the fire, her large eyes reflecting the flickering flames. Godwin watched her while he ate and his mind worked.

A young girl having a wolf for a friend? A wolf as docile as Othere's hounds? And why was she being so quiet? They had been involved in a battle, abducted from the settlement, and miraculously saved by a wolf, but it didn't seem worthy of comment, as though such things were commonplace. There was an awkwardness between them that had never been there before, and he couldn't cope with this silence. What was she hiding? Had he offended her?

"Did you rear him from a whelp?"

She was startled out of her thoughts. "What?"

"Your friend. You tamed him, did you not? Does he do tricks as well?" Perhaps it was all quite plausible, really. What were Othere's dogs, after all, but domesticated wolves? As for her claim to have spoken wolf, that was clearly a joke.

"Tricks?" She sounded annoyed.

"Redwald had a dancing bear once."

The flash of anger in her eyes brought an end to his questions. He sighed and stared at the fire.

When Elgiva finally spoke, the unexpected harshness of her tone unnerved him. "He's completely wild—as he should be. I met him a few years ago. He was half-grown then, and his leg was caught in one of your people's traps. They had no business laying their vile snares so close to my people's lands." Her voice was rising in scale with her anger. He saw her check herself, and then she drew a deep breath. "Well, anyway, I freed him, and Bellic tended the wound. It was lucky I found him when I did, or he might have lost half his leg." She glared at Godwin, who suddenly felt the need to apologise, as though he had set the trap himself. "We haven't seen each other since, but he hasn't forgotten me, and I haven't forgotten the sound of his voice."

Now Godwin was even more baffled. How had she found the courage to approach an injured wild animal? And how could she tell one wolf's howl from another?

Elgiva lifted her gaze. For a moment, she looked at Godwin with something approaching hatred, but he returned her gaze and her features softened.

"I'm sorry," she said with a sigh.

He managed to smile at her. "What for?"

"I expected some quip. Some dismissive remark. I thought you were like the rest of them, but of course you're not, are you?"

His eyebrows drew together. He had no idea what she meant.

"I'm going to tell you something, something you ought to know. You've been a good friend to me, Godwin, and perhaps you will still be my friend after I've told you the truth." She shrugged her slender shoulders. "Or perhaps you'll hate me. I don't know. I just know I must tell you my secret. This lie, this disguise, I hate it. And when I've told you, I'll leave you in peace. I'll go to the forests, to where I belong, or to wherever . . ." She swallowed hard and turned her face away. "I'll never bother you again."

"Elgiva?" He reached out to touch her, but she recoiled from him, so he sat back and waited, concerned by her sadness and desperate to know its cause.

She shifted her position. Drawing up her knees, she hugged them to her chest. It was then that Godwin noticed the tear in her sleeve just above the elbow, the smear of dried blood caked around it. One of the arrows fired by the raiders must have snicked her flesh. Frowning, he got to his knees.

"You're injured. Let me tend the wound."

"Please," she said steadily, "sit down and listen."

Godwin acquiesced with a shrug. "Very well. You can have your say, but that wound should be tended. After you've told me—"

"After I've told you, you won't care, believe me. You'll run for your life, or you might want to kill me."

"What in Frigg's name are you talking about?"

"Just sit down and listen."

She glared at him and refused to go on until he complied with her wishes. The wolf watched him, too, and Godwin felt any offence he gave Elgiva wouldn't escape the notice of her lupine companion.

"I didn't want to deceive you," she said, with a pleading look in her eyes. "Believe me, I meant no harm. It was something I had to do to survive. I needed food and shelter, and there was nowhere else to go. What you see, my present form, it's one I took upon myself by the agency of . . . of magic." She paused and ran her fingers through her hair, and Godwin's heartbeat quickened in response. "I'm not what I appear to be. I'm one of those beings feared by your kind. I'm . . . I'm . . . Godwin, I'm an elf."

That knock on the head had clearly done him more harm than he realised. None of this made any sense. If Elgiva hadn't looked so sincere, he might have laughed out loud. He didn't know how to answer her, but he had to say something.

"Elgiva, is this a jest?" Her scowl told him plainly that it wasn't. "Forgive me, I don't know, I've no idea what you expect me to say. I'm not even sure this is really happening."

Godwin wanted to lighten the mood, to make her the friend he knew, but everything seemed to have changed between them. He didn't know how he should react, and she appeared unwilling to help him. He hadn't yet recovered from the trauma of abduction, and his mind was still at the settlement, where elves lived only in tall tales and sagas.

"I thought you were different once," he admitted. "Well, a bit mystical, something like that. But this . . . If you really are an elf, I guess you could put a hex on me, but it wouldn't be a bad one, would it? You'd never do that to a friend."

He raised his eyebrows expectantly, but perhaps he was being presumptuous. Elgiva was frowning at him.

"I can't anyway," she said. "Only the wardain—the elves of royal blood—have the gift of magical power. I'm just an underling. Ordinary. In Elvish, we say 'nar-wardain'."

"But you talk to wolves," he protested.

"That isn't magic."

"It isn't?"

"Yes, well, it is and it isn't. Basically, elves and animals are able to speak to each other. It all goes back to our founder, Lord Faine. His love for animals, and theirs for him, created a magical bond. That's why we don't eat their flesh. It happened a very long time ago. It comes from the spirit, a feeling of oneness." She looked at him then, and he tried not to show how completely lost he was, but clearly he failed. "Let's just say there are many different kinds of magic. There's high magic and low magic, and low magic can be quite commonplace."

"What else can you do?" he asked. He might as well be discussing the weather. Where his emotions should have been, there was nothing but a great black void. He suspected that fatigue was partly to blame. Perhaps he had actually fallen asleep and this was all a dream.

"My senses are very acute. I can talk to trees, if they're willing, but sometimes, I think it's better not to." She paused for a moment and smiled to herself. "Some elves can see into the future. I can't. I don't think I'd want to, either. I dare say mine isn't worth the looking. Apart from all that, I can't do much, but I'm good at household chores." She gave him a sideways look.

"You forgot to mention one thing," he said. "Your skill at archery. You saved the settlement, you know."

Godwin's attention shifted, as images of the day's ordeal danced through his mind. Had he actually fought in a battle? There had been pools of gore on the grass, a man falling from a horse, warriors fleeing in panic, huts belching smoke. Had he been a part of all that?

"You're taking this very lightly," she said. "Have you listened to me at all? I've just confessed to being an elf. An elf, Godwin. Don't you believe me?"

"What?" Despite her insistence, it still seemed quite unreal. "I've known you many months, and now you confront me with this. What in Frigg's name do you want me to say? I'm sure I've no idea." He looked to her for guidance, but she turned her face away. "Well then, why don't you tell me how you managed to change your appearance? You said it was with magic, yet you say you don't have any."

Leaning closer, she pulled the amulet from her robe and showed it to him. "Bellic is a wardain. The great-uncle of my lord, I mean king. King Thallinore, who is ruler of Elindel, where we live. Where I used to live. Bellic gave up his rights to kingship in Peranduil—that was his home—so he can follow his chosen pursuits. He's a seeker of knowledge, so he's often absent from Elindel. He likes to wander and talk to sorcerers and animals and even wilthkin—that's our name for men—and he often wears a disguise so he can go where elves aren't welcome. Bellic is wise and compassionate, and he taught and befriended me when I was a child. He didn't have to do it. A nar-wardain doesn't need much education, you know. Perhaps he took pity on me for some reason. Perhaps I even amused him."

"And perhaps, like you, he needed a friend," said Godwin.

She reflected on this in silence. At length, she said, "He gave me this amulet. Its name is Siriol. I used it to change my appearance, but something went wrong at the settlement. I believed it was protecting me when I went to kill Beortnoth, but as you can see, it wasn't. If it had been, I'd be completely unharmed. I dare say my survival is all down to luck and nothing else."

She looked down at the gash on her arm and probed it with her fingers. A grimace of pain winced across her face. "It's the loss of trust that hurts most of all."

"Perhaps it doesn't know you now, if you've changed your appearance," said Godwin.

"While it's in my possession, it must work my will. That's the way with amulets, Godwin. They can't be fooled by outward appearance."

"I wish I could say the same."

He hoped his humour would lighten her mood, but her pained look told him otherwise. A period of thoughtful silence loomed. He decided to forestall it.

"We've talked enough for now," he said. "I want you to know I'm still your friend, but I need more time to take in what you've told me."

She accepted this with a weary nod, sighed, and climbed to her feet. "Stay here and rest. You look exhausted. And I need some time alone." Turning away, she headed for the encircling trees.

Chapter Seven

THE SOUND OF laughter drifted towards Godwin, like music beyond the trees, and he turned in time to see Elgiva step from the bushes and walk in his direction. The wolf pranced beside her like a fawning puppy.

"I wish you could speak to wolves, Godwin. They know so many pleasing tales. How do you feel today?" She sat by his side, her golden hair like sunshine, and her smile more carefree than any smile he'd seen on her face before. "I'm sorry I let the fire go out, but never mind. It's such a lovely morning. And you've missed the best part of it already."

The lightness of her manner showed no trace of the previous day's ordeal. It was almost as though she wanted to forget the secret she had shared with him. He had no wish to darken her mood, but now that he had recovered from his traumatic abduction, there was only one thing on his mind: the fate of his family.

"Later, we'll look in the wagon," Elgiva went on. "There may be food in it."

"Elgiva, where in the name of the gods are we?"

"I don't know. And neither does our friend here. He and the pack got separated several days ago. They were out hunting, and being the fastest runner, he lost them all. Got carried away in the thrill of the chase, I dare say."

"Elgiva, please, I need to know where we are, how to get back home. Rowena and the children . . . " Anxiety stopped his throat. There were no words for the panic that raced through him.

"I'll see what I can do." She got to her feet and squinted at the sky.

He watched her with a puzzled frown. What on Earth was she doing?

"I think we're in luck." She pointed at the clouds.

"What?" He stood and followed the direction of her arm with his gaze, but saw nothing of any interest. And yet . . . what was that dot he could just make out, circling lazily above them?

"Hey!" Elgiva waved her arms, and the black dot spiralled down.

The dot drew closer, and Godwin could see it was a hawk. It hovered awhile and then swooped down to them and landed in a tree. Elgiva approached it, while Godwin stood with folded arms, not knowing what else to do. Elgiva talked to the bird, but he couldn't imagine why.

At length, Elgiva returned to his side. "She flew over a settlement yesterday. Many hours before dusk, she says. She stopped to rest in a tree and watched. There were fires being put out and people dead or injured. She remembers seeing a large building and a Saxon woman in an amber-coloured robe. The woman had two little girls at her side, and they had dark red hair and were dressed in blue. And a tall older man was with them. The granary had been pulled down, and there were loads of mice—"

"Forgive me, but I have no interest in the fate of Othere's mice."

"As you wish." Elgiva looked away.

He sighed. "Sorry. Thank you for this news. So my family is alive, at least. And Othere, too. How far away is the settlement?"

"All I know is it's due west. Birds don't measure distance the way we do. My guess would be several leagues."

"When do we leave?"

"We?"

"We can't stay here. Be reasonable, girl. Beortnoth's men are bound to return. They've left a wagonload of booty. Where else can we go but home?"

"Home?" Her tone was edged with acid. "Your home, perhaps, not mine." She cocked her small fists on her hips, clearly intending to make her position clear. "I told you, Godwin, I'm an elf. My home is in the woods. That's where I belong and should have stayed, but for some very bad advice. I can't return to Othere's. I must help Greyflanks find his family. Then I'll fend for myself."

"But you saved the settlement. They'll hail you as a heroine."

"You'd have me pile deceit upon deceit," she went on. "Not only would you have me lie about my appearance, you'd have me pretend to be brave, too. I told you, Godwin, I believed the amulet would protect me. Do you think I'd have been such a fool otherwise?"

"Perhaps I do. You're fool enough."

From her expression, he could tell his remark had stunned her, but he allowed no hint of apology to soften his gaze.

Abashed, she looked away and ran her fingers through her hair. Then, in a calmer voice, she said, "There's nothing for me among your kind. I don't need their adulation. I don't belong there. I never did. It was all a great mistake."

"By Frigg, we fed and sheltered you," he said. "How can you be so arrogant?"

"How dare you judge me, wilthkin? By Faine, why can't you just go home and let me live my life?"

He shrugged and sighed. "Very well," he said. "You must do as you please. You saved my family, so I've no right to stand in your way. I'm in your debt."

Elgiva hesitated for a moment. "You're not in my debt. I was only repaying your kindness towards me. Now we're even and ... and I'm glad your family is safe."

He smiled at her and nodded. "I made a vow to protect you, but I can't abandon my children. Still, I need to know you'll be safe. Where will you go?"

"That's not your concern. Go back to Rowena. It's your duty, Godwin. But you'll have to go alone. I won't go back to Othere's. I can't. Have a safe journey home." She turned her back on him.

Godwin grabbed her arm and made her look at him. "Is that any way to say farewell to a friend?"

Despite his frown, he hoped his tone was gentle. He was desperately trying to understand, to make some sense of it all before she made her escape.

"Friends should be curt in their goodbyes and spare each other pain," she replied.

"You do care about me, then?"

Her cheeks reddened, and she snatched her arm from his grasp. "That's neither here nor there. By Faine, what do you want from me? Your family needs you. I need no one. All I want is my freedom. If you need me to admit that I've felt friendship for a wilthkin, then I admit it. Satisfied? Now, let us part."

"We shall, but not like this. I feel I only half know you. Before I go, would you grant me one favour, in the name of friendship?"

Elgiva narrowed her eyes. "What might that be?"

"I want to see you as you really are. You owe me that. I've never seen an elf. I need convincing that such things exist."

"Still you don't believe me." Her face flushed with rage.

"Indeed I do," he protested.

"What good would it do?"

"If I don't know the truth, it'll haunt me forever. I don't deserve that, do I?"

Her smooth brow wrinkled with doubt and frustration. "That might not be a good idea."

"Why not? Are you horrible to look at?" He smiled good-naturedly, but she scowled all the more.

"It could be risky. Bellic told me that some elves have the power to enchant wilthkin simply by their appearance," she said.

"What do you mean?"

"How can I explain something when I don't understand it myself?"

The wolf began to fidget uneasily, and Elgiva glanced in his direction.

"We need to be going," she said. "This delay distresses Greyflanks."

"Then change now. Please. Then you can go with him and I can go back to my family."

Elgiva thought for a moment, clearly torn between conflicting emotions. "But what if I can't? What if Siriol won't obey me?"

He held her gaze as steadily as he could. "There's only one way you can answer those questions."

She shrugged resignedly and drew a deep breath. "Very well. There's nothing else for it. I'll do as you have asked. But I will not accept responsibility for the consequences."

She turned and put several yards between them. She folded her hands around the amulet.

"Siriol," she said in a quavering voice, "hear me and work my will. I beg you, reverse your enchantment. Restore me to my true appearance." She cleared her throat and then tightly closed her eyes in concentration.

The Exile of Elindel

Despite his wish to see her as an elf, Godwin's entrails knotted with trepidation, but he clenched his jaw and ignored the inner voice that urged him to run for his life.

"Siriol," continued Elgiva, more strongly, "tear away this deception. Take the dawn's blush from my skin, the summer sky from my eyes, the autumn gold from my hair. I no longer need the protection of this disguise. I wish the spell undone. So be it."

Elgiva waited, her breathing quick and shallow, the anxious beat of her own pulse resounding in her skull. Would the amulet's magic affect her as violently as it had when she used it at Othere's settlement to free herself from the marauder? So far, there was no giddiness, nausea, or weakness. The merest sensation of passing wafted through her soul, but it had no more power to alarm her than the draught from a butterfly's wing.

Beside the dead campfire, the wolf whimpered softly.

Elgiva filled her lungs with air to stop her shaking. Her throat felt as dry as the ashes of their fire, and it forced her to swallow before she could speak. "Well? Has anything happened?" she asked, but Godwin didn't respond. She opened her eyes. Her friend looked like a man bereft of all his wits. She watched him warily. "I take it something has."

Godwin stood motionless and seemed struck dumb, but there was a look of wonder on his face. Elgiva had to admit she was relieved it wasn't revulsion. The depth of her own vanity made her angry.

"By Faine, don't stare at me like that." And to her surprise, she stamped her foot.

"You're beautiful," he said. "Your face...it's perfect. You could be a goddess."

Her lips parted, but astonishment left her mute. For a while, they stared at each other, neither knowing what to say. Then Godwin gathered himself together.

"If it wasn't for those strange, pointy ears, I'd mistake you for a Briton."

"Strange ears?" Her hands came up to cover the offending articles, and as far as it was possible for an elf to blush, she did. "Are you satisfied now?" She strode towards him and searched his face. "You can understand what I'm saying, I suppose?"

"Of course I can," he replied. "And your skin is amazing, you know. So pale and smooth..." He reached out to touch her face.

She tilted back her head in a gesture of dismissal. "Now, in the name of Faine, be gone."

She stood still and waited, but Godwin didn't move. Unable to endure the intensity of his gaze, she turned her back on him and folded her arms.

"Elgiva . . ." He hesitated a moment and then seemed to reach a decision. "Let me come with you. Just a little way."

With an angry glance behind her, she shook her head at him.

"I thought the matter was settled. What about your family?"

"I know they're safe, and Othere will protect them. They're his property, after all, and he's a fair master. And they'll believe I'm held captive at Beortnoth's. They won't expect to see me until Othere bargains for the return of prisoners."

"And will he?"

"Of course he will. He's our master. He wouldn't abandon any one of us."

Clearly some fascination for the creature that had magically appeared before him had driven all other considerations out of Godwin's mind. Elgiva shook her head with exasperation. She had feared this might happen.

"This is awful. You're enchanted, aren't you?" She sighed. "What have I done?"

"I have to see you settled somewhere. How can I leave you now? Especially when the sunshine gleams on your hair like that. I'd never know where you were or if you were all right."

"Would it matter?" she asked him.

"You protected my family. You saved the settlement. You probably saved my life. Don't I have a right to care in return?"

"Of course you do, when the caring is real. But this is just an enchantment, Godwin."

"I don't know what you mean, but I never noticed before how beautiful your eyes are. A man could drown in those big dark eyes of yours."

She knotted her fingers in her hair and fought with her growing impatience. "If it's adventure you're after, you'll get no adventures travelling with me."

The Exile of Elindel

"To me, freedom itself is an adventure, and anyway, I made . . ." He flinched from her dark gaze. "I made a vow to protect you. I can't go back on it now. Not until you're safe somewhere."

"So, my friend, you made a vow, but now you're enchanted and you don't know what you're saying. Can you even hear yourself? I had no idea an enchantment could be so powerful. To make a man abandon his family like this."

"You can't really stop me anyway," he said. "I can't leave you."

He smiled ingenuously, and Elgiva shook her head. "Very well, Godwin, I see I have no choice. I can't stand here forever arguing about it. I've tried to dissuade you, but I don't think it would matter what I said to you now. You're under an enchantment. Well, so be it. It might be quite pleasant to have some company—at least for a while. I can only hope you'll see sense and go home soon." She looked him up and down and then shrugged. "Right, then. There's a stream beyond those trees where you can bathe and wash the blood from your clothes. But don't be too long. We must be on our way."

She turned on her heel and left him.

Chapter Eight

GODWIN HAD BATHED his wound in the chill water and scrubbed the gore from his grey woollen tunic. Although he was far from clean, it was the best he could do. He joined Elgiva as she searched through the spoils the raiders had abandoned. They found two water-skins, some dried fruit and bread, and a large, round cheese wrapped in a cloth. Godwin put them all in a sack which he volunteered to carry, and all the while, the wolf padded round them, trying to contain its impatience.

With a grimace of satisfaction, Godwin uncovered a small knife, and he thrust it into his belt. Then, for a moment, he drifted. When he returned to his senses, he was staring at Elgiva, as though she were something precious and awe-inspiring. Her long-suffering expression told him better than words that he looked as foolish as he felt.

"Are we ready to leave?" he asked.

"We've been ready for ages," she told him, "but you were somewhere else."

"I'm sorry." He slung the sack over his shoulder and turned to walk away.

"A moment, if you please."

He turned. She hadn't moved. She was leaning against the wagon with an arch look on her face. "Something wrong?" he asked.

"Well, two things. Firstly, where are you going?" she asked. "We haven't decided which way to go yet, and I think our friend is the one to choose. His instinct is better than ours."

Godwin nodded. "Of course."

"Secondly, are you blind?" Her eyes sparkled at him mischievously.

Godwin gave her a questioning look. In answer, she reached into the wagon and snatched aside a piece of cloth. When she lifted her arm again, it was with a gesture of triumph.

"My sword! Elgiva, they took my sword!" He dropped the sack, ran to her side, and grabbed the weapon. He gazed at it in disbelief, as though it were an old friend he hadn't seen in years. "This is good fortune indeed!" he cried. The weight of the blade reassured him and somehow, he felt whole again.

"Now we really are ready for the road that lies ahead," she declared with a smile. "Greyflanks, lead the way."

Dusk was falling as the three companions stopped for the night in a sheltered clearing. Following Greyflanks's instincts, they had walked many leagues in a northeasterly direction, though they had no way of knowing where they were or exactly how far they had travelled.

The land was thickly wooded, and the absence of tracks made the going hard, but at least there was plenty of wood for their fire, and Godwin found a stream of clear water with which he replenished their water-skins.

Elgiva and Greyflanks flopped down on the grass, while Godwin set about making a fire, striking sparks from a stone with his knife and using dry moss for tinder; it was a laborious business, and soon, his forehead was slick with the effort.

Elgiva tried to comfort the wolf. "When morning comes, I'll stop a bird and we'll ask if it's seen any wolves. Do you feel we're going in the right direction? Well, tomorrow will be better. We'll be rested then." She caressed his large head, and the wolf leaned against her and licked her face. "We'll soon get used to travelling, and then we'll pick up more speed. But perhaps you'd rather go on alone?"

"Wolves don't care to travel alone," said Greyflanks. "It's not in our nature. Alone is bad."

Elgiva didn't care to confront the truth of this. Godwin sat rubbing his hands by the fire, but he was looking at her, his eyes glazed with adoration. Elgiva drew a long breath and leaned closer to the wolf.

"There," she said, "is one who, as yet, knows nothing of his aloneness, for he's seen an elf and dwells with enchantment. This is all a dream to him. I feared it would happen, and I did try to warn him, didn't I? He should have remembered me as I was, but wilthkin won't be told. And when the enchantment finally fades, reality will come as a shock. I wish I knew what to do for him, Greyflanks. I wish Lord Bellic were here."

She slumped back down on the grass with a sigh. In the sky above her, the shadow of night pursued the sun towards the western horizon.

"Elgiva, I'm starving," Godwin complained.

"You'll have to get used to it," she said. "We have to be sparing with our food. We're not in the mead hall now."

"Perhaps we could hunt?" he suggested.

"Hunt with what? Your sword?"

He shrugged and lowered his eyes.

"Have a piece of bread, if you must," she said. "Greyflanks might hunt tomorrow. Perhaps he'll share the kill with you. At least the enchantment hasn't robbed you of hunger, unlike your common sense."

"What enchantment?"

"I tried to tell you before. Some elves have the power to enchant, merely by their appearance, and I seem to be such an elf. Don't ask me to explain. I can't. I believe it wears off, given time." Godwin smiled, as though she were talking nonsense, and this provoked her anger. "No one explained such things to me. I don't know how to end the enchantment, but I do know that you've left your family because of it . . . because of me. You've abandoned your home and your kin, and you just sit there, Godwin, as if it didn't matter at all."

But Godwin continued to smile at her, and she felt her hands clench into fists. She wanted to shake him, though she doubted it would do any good. She crawled towards him and grabbed his sleeve.

"I wish you'd see sense and go home. I don't want this on my conscience. I won't . . ."

Something large was heading towards them, slashing through the bushes. The wolf sprang up, his hackles raised and a snarl about his lips. Elgiva and Godwin jumped to their feet to confront the unknown threat.

A huge figure burst from the trees and blundered into their midst. He wielded an axe that would have tested the strength of three average men. His massive shoulders were draped with furs, which added to his bulk, and from his chin hung a great blond beard. He was a Saxon and a giant, seven feet tall, at least.

He planted himself before them, and the firelight glowed on his cheeks.

"Intruders!" he roared, lifting the axe, and his brows drew together into a scowl.

He took a few steps forwards . . . and Godwin, Elgiva, and Greyflanks took several steps back.

While he looked them up and down, Elgiva and Godwin held hands, like two small children caught robbing an orchard, each comforting the other.

Greyflanks moved slowly, as though he intended to circle the threat to his friends, but the giant flourished the mighty axe and made a bold sweep before him. Clamping his tail between his legs, the wolf slunk off behind his companions.

For a long, tense moment, they all stood in silence.

There must be some place in this world that didn't belong to someone. Once again, Elgiva was trespassing, but this time, she didn't have a disguise. Well, somebody had to do something, and it might as well be her. She peeled her hand from Godwin's grip and stepped towards the giant. Then she halted and swallowed hard.

He planted the axe before him, its edge a flash of gold in the firelight. From beneath his craggy brows, he watched Elgiva guardedly. She made a small bow and looked up, trying to smile and hoping it wasn't just an awkward grimace. His stern expression didn't waver.

"My lord," she ventured, her heart thumping in her breast. "I'm Elgiva. I'm an elf, as you can see. These are my friends. Godwin—a Briton—and Greyflanks, son of the wolf-queen Whitefoot. We're sorry to trespass, and we meant no harm. We can move on, if you wish."

The giant studied each of them in turn but made no move to answer.

"Perhaps we can make amends for our intrusion," said Elgiva, "and invite you to join us in a humble meal?"

Elgiva moved back to Godwin's side, and they glanced worriedly at each other. Godwin looked alarmed. He was probably worried the giant would eat all of their food. Despite their situation, her lips curled into a smile. She cursed her perverse elven sense of humour, which found reason for mirth in so ridiculous an observation, but the giant responded to her grin.

"Joskin, I'm called," said the giant. "You one of Tandrin's elves?"

"Er . . . who is Tandrin, my lord?"

"Ha," said the giant. "I'm no lord!" The companions flinched, but the giant beamed as though Elgiva had done him an honour. "Tandrin, king of the elves. Round here, that is. Nice bunch they are. Not very chatty, though." Despite his deep and resonant voice, he spoke in an awkward, jerky manner, as though he had little practice with speech.

"I'm from Elindel," Elgiva said.

"What you doing here?"

"I . . . er . . . lost my way."

The giant nodded knowingly. "Happens to the best of us. What you got to eat, then?"

He tucked the axe under one arm and sat down cross-legged by the fire. Elgiva and Godwin looked at each other, and then they followed his example.

"Is . . . is there a settlement near?" Godwin asked.

"East. Many leagues," said the giant. "Wondering where I come from, are you? I live alone. Have to. Understandable, really. No fun being different. Even as a lad. Always so tall. Don't know why. Parents a bit on the small side, see? Always seemed to frighten people. And there's another thing. About being big. People think you're special. They want to have a go at you, too. You get no peace. Lord had me marked down for his champion. Might have had to kill someone. So I ran away."

Godwin grimaced and held out their sack of provisions. The giant helped himself to some bread with a courteous nod of thanks.

"Not a bad bit of bread," he opined, laying down his axe. He must have noticed Godwin's look of relief because he laughed. "Don't worry, man. Use the axe to chop down trees. Or scare people off. Never to hurt. Can't stand the sight of blood, you see. But who's to know that, eh? Gave you lot a fright, at least! But if you'd all ganged up on me, don't know what I'd have done." He laughed again, an honest laugh that held no trace of malice. "How come you're travelling with a wolf?"

The Exile of Elindel

"He lost his family," Elgiva explained. "We're trying to help him find them."

"Very obliging, I'm sure. Poor thing must be fretting. Tell you what. Come back to my cave. Better shelter than here. A good night's sleep set you up for travelling. I've got elf-wine, too." He winked at Elgiva. "How'd that suit you?"

Elgiva looked at Godwin, and he nodded his agreement. "You're too kind, Joskin."

"Bless me," exclaimed the giant. "You can never be that!"

"We'd be honoured to stay at your home."

"Good. Don't get many visitors. None, really. Food, back home. Meat and stuff. Elves leave me some things now and then. Very grateful I am, to be sure. Only wish they'd stop for a chat. But elves are wary. Never mind. I've got friends, why yes, bless me! There's Shredwing and one or two of my furred and feathered friends who pop in now and then. Many a creature old Joskin has raised that fell from the nest or lost its kin. Animals never forget you know. Don't care what you look like, either."

Raising a piece of bread to his lips, he took a nibble. Elgiva fought the urge to stare, but she couldn't help herself. She had fully expected the food to vanish in one almighty gulp; instead, she found herself put in mind of a great bearded hare chewing grass.

"Perhaps I am a lord, as you said," chuckled Joskin. "Lord of the Beasts. Yes, I like that. Course, you can't talk to them. Unless you're an elf, that is. 'Cause they don't follow, you see."

He brushed the crumbs from his golden beard and drew a small handkerchief from his tunic. He wiped his mouth with it, as though he had eaten a feast.

"Think we'll be off now, if that's agreeable. Don't like to leave the old place too long. Especially at night. Understandable, really. Never know who's abroad, do you?" He rose to his feet and towered above them. "Nice evening for the time of year. Still a bit chilly, though. Take a brand from the fire, if you would, little elf. To light us on our way."

Elgiva did as she was instructed. Godwin kicked dirt onto the fire and picked up their sack of provisions. Greyflanks padded softly behind them as they followed the giant's lead.

The cave where the giant lived had been carved from a stony ridge of land and was hidden from view by the ancient trees and undergrowth around it. Before the entrance stood six tall rowans he had planted in an orderly line; they were trees that had power against hexes, he said. The cave was also Joskin's doing. He had hewn it out of the shallow escarpment with his powerful hands.

"Ruined all the tools I had. Just the axe left now," he said, smiling at his own accomplishment.

He guided his visitors inside and set about making a fire a few feet from the entrance. While he worked, he told them how the elves had spied on him, admired his perseverance, and left him gifts outside the cave while he slept. Sometimes they left food or wine, sometimes knives or pots or beakers. On several occasions, he had found injured birds, which he cared for until they recovered.

Each time he released a bird back to the wild, the elves would leave him a special gift. It was usually something good to eat—fruit cake was a particular favourite.

The cave was a cheery, comfortable home, despite the cold, unyielding rock. Two deep stone ledges ran parallel to each other down both sides of the cave, and at intervals, they were draped with furs. Rough niches in the walls accommodated flagons and bowls, and there were brackets for holding torches.

Elgiva noticed a number of tapestries pegged to the walls of the cave and enthused about their detail and colour, unprepared for the giant's response.

"One of them was an elvish gift, but I did the others myself. Elves left me some stuff, you see, so thought I'd have a go. Suppose they're okay. Makes it look cosy. Only one problem: the spiders. Spiders get behind 'em. Can't stand spiders. Can you?" His massive frame shuddered, but then he laughed. "They probably can't stand us! And spiders need a home, too, eh? Anyway, cobwebs, good dressings for wounds." He raised his eyebrows.

Elgiva was charmed by his eccentricity. "You have a lovely home. In fact, I've never seen better."

A glow of modest pride mantled the giant's cheeks. "Though I say so as shouldn't, it's true. Make all my own clothes, too. Don't like

The Exile of Elindel

to kill for the skins, of course. Elves don't like it, either, so I take things already dead, if I can. But now and then—" he shook his head sadly, "—have to set some traps. Understandable, really. Got to eat, you know."

By now the fire had taken hold. Joskin lit four torches and positioned them on the walls. A cheery glow spread into the cave, and near the back, the travellers saw more of Joskin's handiwork: a smooth perch fastened to a stave of wood. And on this perch and blinking in the light was a bird—or something resembling a bird. Its wings hung down like tattered rags.

"Aye, that's Shredwing," the giant said, following their gaze. "He was a fledgling. Wildcat got him. Saved his life, but couldn't fix him. Did what I could, but as you see . . . Wings beyond repair."

"He's some kind of hawk," said Godwin. "My lord had one just like it."

Shredwing inspected the visitors, his black eyes gleaming like small polished pebbles.

A sweet scent suddenly filled the cave, mingling with the wood smoke. Joskin grinned when his guests sniffed the air.

"Burn herbs with the wood. Nice, eh? Please sit down. I'll do you a meal. Just have to warm up that comfrey soup. I've a stew of winter vegetables. Bread, too, and some honey somewhere. And by the looks of you two, I need to find fresh bandages. You've been in the wars, I'd say. Well, a noggin or two of Tandrin's wine soon put you to rights!"

Chapter Nine

THE NIGHT WAS waning when Elgiva woke, wondering where she was. The dark ceiling of Joskin's cave hung above her, and everything had a reddish glow, cast by the embers of the fire. She slid from under the fur coverlet, her skin tightening at the loss of its warmth, and searched for her leather sandals. Something had woken her, something that waited outside the cave. A runnel of dread ran down her spine.

She had an inexplicable sense of impending danger, but it was too insistent to ignore. An unnamed instinct stopped her from alerting her companions. She must face this menace alone.

She left the cave as quietly as she could. Her heart pounded in her throat as she peered between the rowan trees and searched the night. Whatever had awakened her, it beckoned. She held her breath and listened, but her ears detected nothing, save for a silence as dark and empty as an abandoned crypt.

It would soon be daybreak, but the sun had yet to rise, and the dark beyond the cave swarmed with potential horrors. She stepped out from among the rowans, relying on her acute senses to make out her surroundings. An unnatural calm gripped the night and as her sandals whispered against the cold grass, they sounded abnormally loud. She feared they would betray her presence.

After a while, she came to a stop and searched the trees. Thin strands of mist curled along the ground, cold and clammy, like an exhalation of sickness.

She hugged her shoulders, knotted her fingers in the cascade of her hair, and shivered in her ragged robe. All around her, the silence seemed to be drawing into focus.

"Who is it?" Her throat was too dry for her purpose. She

swallowed and licked her lips. "Who's there? I know you're there. I can . . . I can feel you!"

Feel you.

A flash of silver sliced through the dark, and Elgiva gasped in fear. Her arms came up to shield her face as the beam struck a rock several yards ahead. It exploded with a whoosh and sent up thousands of splinters of light, which fell to the ground and sizzled in the mist.

A shape now stood upon the rock, its form concealed in a black, hooded cloak.

Elgiva clutched the amulet to her breast. Her hands were white with terror. "In the name of Faine, who are you? What sort of trick is this?"

A soft, sly voice spoke back to her. "Why should you fear magic?"

"What do you want?" she pleaded, her voice a croak of fear.

"To see for myself."

"To see what?"

The dark shape sniggered but made no answer. Instead, it swept its cloak aside, and a cloud of sparks flew out and covered the ground with beads of light.

Elgiva stepped back unsteadily, resolved to flee.

"Stay!" commanded the creature.

It raised a skeletal hand, and the forefinger swung towards Elgiva and pinned her against the darkness, holding her like a rivet of bone. No elf, no wilthkin, ever owned such a hand. Her legs threatened to buckle beneath her. This had to be a nightmare; she was still asleep in the cave. But no, it was all too real.

"Who are you? What do you want?" she cried. "I have . . . I have an amulet!"

The creature laughed derisively. "I am Death, and I have come for you."

It began to radiate a sickly green light, enveloping itself in a caul of brilliance that pulsated with force. The light grew in size until the trees behind it were bathed in its angry glare. It reached for Elgiva, like a foul stench creeping along a breeze, and she was helpless. The creature's power throbbed in the darkness.

Within the taut coils of her fear, her instincts screamed at her to run, but her limbs had turned to stone.

Siriol, Siriol, help me . . . help . . .

With a shriek of glee, the creature increased the throb of its power. Elgiva's mind was suddenly invaded by an inexplicable force. She became divorced from herself and watched from a great distance, waiting for the horror to unfold.

Something broke inside her. A dam burst open, and a flood of defiance surged to her assistance. "You're not Death. No one dies like this! In the name of Lord Faine, whoever you are, you have no right. I'm defenceless. Stop this!"

Her hooded opponent merely intensified the probing of its power, renewing its attack on the barriers of her mind, and behind its virulence, there was a thrill of laughter.

How dare you!

She had to master her fear, find the strength to resist. Her enemy's power was narcotic, lulling her into a trance, but part of her mind was feverishly active, gathering might of its own. An inner resource she couldn't name was pleading for recognition.

She forced herself to concentrate. She must expel this being from her mind.

It seemed they were revolving round each other, like autumn leaves caught in a gale, though they both stood motionless, rooted to the earth. Within Elgiva's breast was an unfamiliar feeling, a burgeoning heat. It expanded in desperation and then flared with boundless joy, as if it were nearing some long-wished-for focus. It filled her with strength . . . but how it seared! Like scratching an open wound.

Stop it, please . . . stop it.

The creature probed her with its power all the more, but as it breached the privacy of her mind, it revealed something of its own.

Elgiva recoiled, alarmed at the discovery that this being was a wardain. But who?

She strengthened her will and kept the creature at bay, but its power still battered at the threshold of her mind. Self-defence required so much effort she felt as if the blood was boiling in her veins. Her mental anguish scaled upwards, becoming physical pain.

Why are you doing this to me?

She couldn't stand this any longer. She prepared herself to die.

Suddenly, there were shouts in the distance, from what seemed like a hundred leagues away. Someone called her name. Someone she knew: the voice of a friend. With a mighty effort, she strove to gain her freedom, and a great light flashed in her brain.

Then she was herself again, on her hands and knees, with the shock of the cold grass on her skin and the world canting madly around her. She was free, but engulfed by fire and soaked with sweat. Her robe clung to her skin like a membrane, and her scorched lungs heaved for air.

She managed to lift her head. Through a throbbing red mist she saw her attacker, standing calmly on the rock, his concentration either broken or willingly curtailed. His cloak was wrapped around him, and a sheen of spent magic shivered along his form.

"Excellent," he whispered. His voice had changed completely, its edge of malice gone. "I'm sorry about the theatrics, but that was an entertaining battle. I think we shall meet again."

As she watched through the tears that stung her eyes, his flesh seemed to grow transparent. Gradually, he faded like mist and then, in a moment, was gone.

Her limbs folded beneath her, and she fell face down in the dew. Between her ragged gasps, she vaguely heard someone running in her direction. She was gently rolled onto her back, and relief flooded her mind, for in the first light of dawn, she recognised Godwin.

"Elgiva, by Frigg! Who was that? What happened?"

Elgiva couldn't respond.

"Are you all right? Elgiva?"

"I'm sick," she croaked. "I feel . . . so sick."

He cradled her in his arms; it was a good feeling.

"Who was that?" persisted Godwin. "What did he do to you?"

"Hold me . . . hold . . . "

She floated on a sea of nausea and clung to Godwin as her only anchor until the heat within her gradually dwindled and the world decelerated around her. As the dizziness passed, it left her with a feeling of violation. Moreover, some change had occurred at the very core of her being. Some inexpressible wrath or madness hungered for release. She didn't understand it, but whatever it was, it scared her. She pressed herself closer to Godwin, desperate for warmth and strength.

"Greyflanks woke me," he explained. "He seemed concerned.

Stood there staring at the cave mouth, but wouldn't go out. I knew you were in danger anyway, even before I realised you weren't there."

"The wretched enchantment," she gasped. "It links us."

He ignored this. "Elgiva, are you hurt?"

"Oh, no, not hurt," she said shakily. "It wasn't that kind of fight. It was . . . it was all in the mind." She took a deep breath to compose herself. "He was looking for something. Something in me. He was thinking 'easy prey,' but I wasn't." She paused and slowly shook her head. "I defended myself, but I don't understand. Perhaps it was Siriol. I just don't know."

"Who was he, Elgiva?"

"He was a wardain, Godwin. Very powerful, too. I thought . . . I thought he would turn me to ashes. I felt him holding back. It was almost as though he was testing me."

"Why?" asked Godwin, frowning. "Forgive me. I don't even understand how you can fight someone in your mind. Why was he testing you?"

"I've no idea," she said.

"How did you defend yourself?"

"I don't know that, either. Somehow, I just did. All of my strength fought half of his, but somehow, I defied him. Was it the amulet?" She pulled away from him. She sat up and combed the hair from her face with a hand that trembled badly, aware of the need to regain some composure. "He was holding back. Was he waiting for me to weaken or just prolonging the sport? I was done for, I know that, but then you shouted and broke his concentration. Godwin, if you hadn't . . ."

Overcome by exhaustion and fear, she needed his support again. He held her in a tight embrace, and they sat in silence for a time. All around them, the darkness was lifting and birdsong announced the dawn.

"Come back to the cave," he advised her at length.

She nodded weakly and allowed him to help her to her feet.

"We must continue our search for the wolves tomorrow, and you'll need some rest before we go."

She gazed into his honest blue eyes. "Godwin, no, you must go home. That wardain said we'd meet again. If he returns . . ."

The Exile of Elindel

"How can I leave you when your life is in danger? If you still insist on finding Greyflanks's family, I'm going to make sure you do. Then you're coming straight back to Othere's with me if I have to carry you, kicking and screaming, every inch of the way."

"Look at me, Godwin. I can't go back to Othere's. I'm an elf!"

"But Siriol . . ."

"I don't know . . . if Siriol still works or not." She covered her face, unable to hold back the fresh tears.

He faltered for a moment, and then he hugged her again. There was a hitch in his voice when he spoke. "I'll find a way."

Chapter Ten

Having said farewell to Joskin, Godwin, Elgiva, and Greyflanks continued on their way. They had travelled two leagues before noon but saw no sign of wolves, and the birds Elgiva questioned offered little in the way of help.

"Your family must have moved," surmised Godwin while Elgiva translated his words. "They could be looking for better hunting. Perhaps they're looking for you."

He felt like an idiot, talking to a wolf, but knew better than to say so.

Late afternoon saw them dragging their feet along a narrow valley, where a thin stream bubbled over stones and rocks. They were brought to a halt by the faint cry of a wolf in the distance. Greyflanks stiffened and lifted a front paw tentatively, as though preparing to follow the sound. He threw back his head and howled his response. They waited for an answer but were to be disappointed.

"He says it's Blacktail, his uncle," explained Elgiva. "He's a long way off, and it doesn't seem likely he heard Greyflanks call back."

The wolf pawed at the sparse grass, and then his wet nose scented the air. With a wag of his tail, he spun to face his companions, a growl rumbling deep in his throat.

"He's going to try a bit of hunting," said Elgiva.

Greyflanks streaked off down the valley, while Godwin sighed at his retreating form. "Might as well make camp."

"Why not," said Elgiva. "We've walked enough for today."

Together, they clambered out of the valley and searched for a sheltered spot. They were in an area where scything winds had levelled the shrubs and twisted the trees. A group of large boulders stood in a heap, like a family of stones in the wilderness, and they set up camp beside them.

The Exile of Elindel

It was nearly dark by the time they had gathered enough wood to make a fire. Greyflanks returned soon after. He had caught and eaten an elderly goat, but he spared Elgiva the details, and while his friends ate their own meagre supper, he told them all about Blacktail.

Blacktail was an elder of the pack, and a veteran of many battles. He had only one eye, and his snout was badly scarred. His restless spirit made him often absent, wandering and exploring. Greyflanks guessed the old wolf had been off on one of his expeditions when they heard his call, and he might be as lost as they were.

Night darkened the sky by degrees as the travellers sat huddled before their fire, each of them thinking of the home they had left or lost.

Elgiva stared into the fire. Clearly, the elation Greyflanks had felt at hearing Blacktail was fading and even a stomach full of goat was no compensation for the loss of his pack. There was nothing she could do for him but hope they would find his family very soon.

The meeting with the wolf's family wouldn't solve any of her problems, however. What was she to do with her life, once their quest was over? Could she live with the wolves? Living life as a nomad was unthinkable. It might be fine for Bellic and Blacktail, but it held no appeal for her. Yet, what else lay in store for a nar-wardain like herself, banished forever from her people's lands?

Had Thallinore discovered the plot against him? Did he regret the expulsion of the person who had managed to thwart it? No, that was unlikely. And even if he had, recalling her from exile would make him look foolish in the eyes of his subjects. Thallinore was too proud to admit he had made a mistake. And after all, why should he bother? She was no one of any importance, when all was said and done. He had always despised her anyway, and was probably glad to have her off his hands.

She thought then of Eldreda, the old crone who had been Elgiva's guardian. She was overseer of the king's household and had taught Elgiva her domestic duties. Drunk more often than not, she answered every question and rewarded every mistake with a swipe of the cane she always carried. She had repeatedly told Elgiva to be grateful, for the king had given her a status far in excess of her merits.

When Eldreda had disappeared, no one ventured an explanation for it, and Elgiva wouldn't have dared ask for one, even if she had cared. No doubt the cruel hag had fallen down a well one night after a bout with the wine.

As for herself, Elgiva had accepted that her origins were somehow shameful. Even Bellic had evaded her questions on the subject. Either he didn't know, or he couldn't bear the truth. Perhaps her parents were criminals and she was the last in a long line of traitors. The irony was her treason had been warranted.

Now, added to all of her unresolved questions about the past and her fears for the future was a new and undeserved terror: a powerful wardain had chosen her for his sport. But why?

Tears were very close. She lay on her side and curled herself into a tight ball of anguish.

Godwin glanced down at his friend. Firelight gleamed on the silken hair that fell across her cheek, obscuring her delicate features. Her slender form looked frail and childlike in her tattered gown. She looked like a beggar's daughter, or some lorn and hapless infant abandoned to the mercy of the world. He wished he had a blanket to protect her from the night.

Her vulnerability hurt him, so he looked away and studied the campfire. Despite his fatigue, he was wide awake. He was restless and edgy, poised between his past and his future, like a man who has abandoned one and can't find the other. The mental fug that had cocooned him for some time shifted and relaxed its hold. Unwelcome thoughts now drifted to the surface of his awareness. He hugged his knees and shivered, but it wasn't the chill of darkness that filled his veins with ice. Rather, it was the burden of the guilt he carried.

Why hadn't he returned to his wife? The question stung him like a dart of self-loathing. She must surely believe him dead or enslaved. And his dear little daughters, what were they thinking? He wondered if he would ever find his way back home.

Home...

A picture of Elric flashed before his mind. What had become of the lad? Othere had survived, but the fate of his master's son was a mystery. And what of Redwald, Kern, and Cerdic? What of the countless others, childhood friends and fellow serfs? How he longed for news of them, for some assurance the security of home was the same as it had always been.

He gritted his teeth to stifle his frustration. His sword lay beside him, glinting in the grass, and he touched it with his fingertips, as though it were his only anchor in an ocean of anxiety.

Home...

Where he was merely a serf, a man of little consequence, the lowest of the low. Where he wasn't even allowed to wield the sword that was his birthright. Hadn't he earned one brief taste of freedom after all those years of service?

He looked down at Elgiva, now safe in the arms of sleep. That strange night outside Joskin's cave, when he found her lying on the ground, he'd seen a glow in the depths of her dark eyes, like the luminous gaze of some fierce, wild creature. Had he merely imagined it? Had it been a trick of the light? It was yet one more weird happening to exacerbate his confusion. And why was he still following her? He shouldn't be here. He was only getting himself more lost and more involved in things he didn't understand. He had no idea how to be with his family and protect Elgiva at the same time. His heart ached with the misery of his impossible dilemma.

I'll find a way. His words returned to him now, and they mocked him.

The enchantment tightened its grip so suddenly that all Godwin could do was relax into contentment with a soft sigh, his tormented thoughts sinking back down into darkness.

The following day, they travelled on, but they never heard Blacktail again. Despite the advent of spring, winter refused to leave without a fight and scattered frost and rain in equal measure.

Godwin became resigned to the fact that hunger and cold were his constant companions, but he had chosen them of his own volition, so he forced his sore feet onwards and kept his complaints to himself.

That night, they made camp under an ancient elm. Lord of a desolate kingdom, it stood alone on a wind-scoured plain of thin and scrubby grass. In the distance lay a nebulous shape, a large, dark blur of forest.

They had eaten the last of their rations but drew comfort from the blazing fire. They had gathered wood throughout the day, determined not to suffer a cold and cheerless night.

Even so, Godwin's mind was elsewhere. It had wandered over the mirthless miles to the mead hall of Lord Othere. There, men would be drinking and laughing, and joints of meat would be dripping juice onto the silver platters, ignored by a rabble already too full to move. His mouth watered at the image.

For a while, Elgiva and Godwin talked, until weariness and the warmth of the fire compelled them both to sleep.

Elgiva woke up suddenly, instinct warning her danger was near. She listened for a moment and then struggled to her knees. Her movement disturbed her companion.

"What's the matter?" Godwin muttered drowsily.

He levered himself up onto his elbows, clearly surprised to see Elgiva on her hands and knees, listening to the night, like a terrified animal.

"Quiet!" she hissed.

She picked up some of their surplus wood and threw it onto the fire.

For a moment, the crunch of grass that sounded in the dark could have been nothing more than the sighing of the wind, but it soon became apparent that something slow and ponderous was drawing towards their camp, was about to breach the firelight that strained against the night.

"What's that noise?" gasped Godwin. "And where's . . . By Frigg!" He sprang to his feet in alarm.

Elgiva joined him as the shape of the intruder shambled into their midst. It lumbered out of the shadows, a materialised horror, bear-like and monstrous. Halting, it scented the air then raised its bulk on stout, hind legs. Cords of drool hung, sparkling, from its jaws.

"What on Earth?" cried Godwin.

Elgiva swallowed hard. "A shendkin . . . Faine, no!" The words tore her throat, and her blood turned to ice.

Since childhood, she'd been warned of these eldritch beings. The obscene experiments of a long-dead wardain gave them life, Bellic had told her, but she'd always suspected that such tales were inventions, designed to make naughty elf-children behave. Now the truth stood before her, clothed in flesh and all too real to dismiss.

The shendkin swivelled his large brown eyes in her direction and fastened his gaze upon her with carnivorous glee.

Godwin was on his hands and knees, scrabbling for his sword.

Despite her fear and revulsion, Elgiva stood firm, refusing to flee. One thing at least she remembered from Bellic's interminable lessons: an elven incantation against evil magic, which he had made her learn by rote. There was power in the words, he had said. Now, silently, she thanked him.

Her blood roared in her ears, her pulse throbbing in her throat. Even though she doubted the amulet, she clenched her fist around Siriol and forced out the words as steadily as she could.

"Though you have hair or feathers, claws or beak,

"Though you be tall or tiny, one or ten,

"Though you be dead or living, you are weak,

"And so will fade like moonlight on the fen.

"No matter what you be or what you seek,

"Depart from here and never come again."

As she spoke, the words provided a base on which to plant her courage, and her voice became stronger, drawing authority from the verse. Her whole awareness centred upon it and upon the enemy before her. Nothing else mattered. The campfire became an insubstantial flicker in her eyes, the encircling night a swart blur of irrelevance.

Godwin managed to scramble to his feet. He took his place at Elgiva's side, but fear overcame him and his sword dangled in his grasp.

The shendkin appeared to be visibly affected by the incantation, and it listened raptly while its claws raked the air. Frustration shuddered in its shaggy hide. The skin on its snout wrinkled, and its lips curled back from its yellow teeth in a snarl of impotent rage.

Godwin fought for self-control and turned to Elgiva in supplication. The sight of her hit him like a bludgeon. His friend was no longer a small, frail figure, but appeared to have blossomed in stature and presence. She glowed with smouldering power, and her eyes shone with vehemence. He couldn't name the force around her, but he felt it all the same. The very air was taut with it; it throbbed all around him like a tortured nerve. The night pressed down upon him like a weight he couldn't carry, but he fought to stay on his feet.

The incantation spoken, Elgiva drew a brand from the fire and flourished it at the beast. The tips of the flames flared momentarily blue and echoed the glint in her eyes.

"Be gone!" she commanded.

The creature reared for a moment in a last gesture of defiance, then it was on all fours again, watching her with eyes that were surprisingly soft and sad. Their innocence seemed incongruous in such a feral face. Elgiva tensed, the breath catching in her throat. Whatever power she exuded seemed at that moment to gutter and fade.

The shendkin turned away and loped off into the darkness.

Terror drained Godwin's strength, and his legs folded beneath him. He was suffocating with awe. He had seen something impossible, unreal, and its horror still hummed in his ears.

The violated night was filled with the sounds of howling and yapping. Dark shapes materialised out of nowhere and whirled past the campfire. They were wolves, and they pelted after the shendkin. Hugging his chest, Godwin listened to their snarls and the screams of the creature as the pack leapt upon it and tore it apart. The noise of rending made the gorge rise in his throat. Was this really happening, or had he gone insane? He shot his companion a terrified look, desperate for reassurance.

"The gods protect us!" he cried. "Elgiva?"

She placed her small hand on his shoulder but didn't meet his gaze. "It's all right," she said in a trembling voice. Her fingers pressed his flesh. "It's all over now, Godwin."

Weakness overcame her. She covered her face with her hands and swayed where she stood. Before she lost her balance completely, he roused himself and got to his feet, grabbing her by the shoulders. Shortly, she raised her head and her hands fell to her sides. She took a shuddering breath.

She looked at Godwin, tried to say something, but could only gape at him. Her eyes were mirrors of exhaustion.

Presently, Greyflanks came trotting towards them and announced his news with joyful barks.

The Exile of Elindel

"He went off earlier, following a familiar scent," stated Elgiva. Her voice sounded flat and abraded. "He's found his family. You were right when you thought they'd moved. To the forest over there, in fact. He brought them back to meet us—fortunately."

Godwin sighed with relief. He never thought he would be so glad to see a pack of wolves. "They've killed that thing, then? They'll dine well tonight."

Elgiva let out a cry of protest. "No natural creature eats the flesh of a shendkin!"

Godwin's brow knotted with incomprehension. "Why not? What is it? I've never seen its like."

"Never mind that now," she said sharply. "I haven't . . . I can't explain." She rubbed her forehead and screwed up her eyes, as though her head were splitting. "We're being escorted to the wolf camp. There's food and shelter there. Put out the fire."

Godwin obeyed and kicked out the camp-fire while Elgiva stumbled after Greyflanks. She had the air of someone fleeing unbearable truths, and until the enchantment pulled him after her, Godwin fought to summon the strength required for forward motion. His head was spinning with hunger and fear, and his recent experience had appalled him. He ached for knowledge or guidance, for anything that would help him come to terms with what had happened.

But no one was there to help him. A monster that couldn't exist had attacked them and been chased off by a magical spell. A pack of wolves had swarmed to their rescue. Not even Othere's minstrel could invent a tale like this.

The enchantment had him once more between its teeth, and he forced himself into motion, following Elgiva into the brooding darkness.

CHAPTER ELEVEN

GODWIN HELD FAST to Elgiva's hand and trusted her to lead him to the wolf camp. Her superior night vision was equal to the task, though they stumbled over tree roots and their progress was slow. At last, they reached a clearing where a den beneath a mound of earth lay half concealed by ferns.

"We're here," she said.

He set to work and gathered wood for a fire. Hunger, cold, and darkness made Godwin's movements clumsy, and the noisy greetings of the wolves only worsened his unease. Explaining to their hosts her companion's need for heat and light, Elgiva went to help him, and they had soon collected sufficient wood to build a substantial fire.

Once the fire had taken hold, Godwin could see the wolves more clearly. To his surprise, Queen Whitefoot personally thanked him for playing his part in the return of her son. Elgiva conveyed the wolf's gratitude to him, and he bowed politely—and self-consciously—in the animal's direction.

By now, his need to talk with Elgiva was the only thought in his head, but she seemed too busy with the wolves, and he didn't want to intrude. Completely out of place in this world, all he could do was content himself with warming his bones by the fire. At length, despite his anxiety, he resumed his sleep where he had left it.

After breakfast the following morning, Elgiva expressed the desire to be alone and disappeared into the surrounding forest. The wolves also wandered away, and while Godwin was becoming less anxious in their company, pretending to be at ease in the presence of so many sets of sharp teeth had been something of a strain. Now he could relax and take advantage of the opportunity to rest.

The Exile of Elindel

As evening fell, it carried with it a cloying dampness, and mist coiled among the tree trunks. Godwin concentrated his efforts on building up the fire, the only thing that would preserve him from the cold night ahead. He was so engrossed, it startled him when Elgiva appeared from the trees. He struggled to his feet, determined to have his questions answered, but when he saw her hag-ridden features, there was only one he could ask.

"Elgiva, are you all right?"

With a weary nod, she sat down beside him and held out her hands to the fire. He seated himself next to her and waited for her to speak.

"I'm sorry I was away so long. I lost all track of time. Did you mind? The wolves don't bother you, do they?"

He shook his head. "Don't fret about me. Where have you been, Elgiva?"

"Oh." She shrugged. "Just out there. Thinking."

"A lot to think about, I expect." He rested his forearms across his knees. "Do I have your attention now?"

She turned her head, one eyebrow arched. "Yes, of course."

"Would you care to tell me what a shendkin is? I've never seen anything so hideous."

"Of course you haven't. They keep their distance from your kind. Their only aim in life—if life it can be called—is to slaughter elves and eat them."

Godwin was horrified. "What are they?"

"Shendkin aren't animals. And yet, they are."

"Riddles are all very well in the mead hall—"

"If you think I'd waste my time on riddles, you're very much mistaken," she snapped.

He sighed. "I'm sorry. Please carry on."

Elgiva drew closer and folded her hands in her lap. "They're not true animals. Bellic told me they were some kind of hybrid, corrupted by dark magic. An evil wardain called Smirill created them many generations ago. Royal elves do sometimes go bad, and Smirill dabbled in things Faine warned us against. Smirill lived in Misterell, a strange kingdom shunned by other elves to this day, and he spawned these creatures by interbreeding natural beasts in the presence of black magic. The animals he chose were aberrations and all deeply flawed. In due course, his vile experiments left us with the shendkin. Smirill was mad but believed himself a creator, a genius. He thought he had the right, as a wardain, to pervert the natural order of things, but no one has that right. In the end, he became so corrupted by the forces he wanted to control that, one day, according to legend, he exploded."

Godwin couldn't help himself and burst out laughing. Elgiva frowned at him, clearly a little hurt and angry.

"I'm finding this impossible to believe," he said. "Well, the bits I understand."

"Don't blame me," retorted Elgiva, thrusting her pert nose in the air. "It was you who wanted to hear it." She turned her back on him indignantly. "As I was saying, Smirill exploded because the pressure of the evil within him was too great for his flesh to contain. The forces he thought to master merely rebounded upon him. So, he was no more, but the evil lived on in the things he created. They are few in number, I'm glad to say, and they don't seem able to produce young. They're slow and elusive, but they don't die like natural beasts. A strange power sustains them. Some part of the dark might Smirill invoked is still at work, defying mortality."

Godwin shivered. "At least they can be killed, like other animals."

"By a pack of wolves, certainly," she agreed, "but many an elf, caught alone by a shendkin, hasn't had the good fortune to have a pack of wolves to hand. We, indeed, were very lucky." She paused and shook her head. "You know, for a moment I doubted my eyes, Godwin. I was as shocked as you were. I've never seen a shendkin before, though I've heard all the tales. I suppose I didn't really believe them. It's hard to believe in something you've never seen, and the shendkin rarely come close to our forests. They prefer to pick off lone travellers, and an ordinary elf, lacking magic, is helpless."

"But," he said, "you weren't helpless."

"Bellic taught me the incantation. He made me learn it by rote from something he called *The Book of Weirds*, and he made certain I had it by heart. He said there was power in the rhyme, enough to hold a shendkin at bay, so an elf can escape. Shendkin are slow, clumsy things, easy to outrun."

Godwin wasn't convinced. "So, why didn't you run?"

She lowered her eyes evasively. "Well . . . I wanted to."

The Exile of Elindel

"You didn't stay on my account?"

"No, Godwin, you were always safe. You're not a shendkin's idea of good eating."

"Is that a compliment or not?" he asked, trying to lighten her mood.

"It's a very good thing for you and your kind."

She fell silent, clearly reluctant to continue, but Godwin's curiosity had yet to be satisfied.

"Tell me, then, Elgiva, if these things were created by some mad old elf, why do they want to eat elves?"

She thought for a moment and toyed with her hair. "Revenge, perhaps? Who knows? I feel sad when I think of them, Godwin. Even more so since we were attacked by one."

"Why so?"

"Did you see its eyes? A hideous face, yet it had disturbingly beautiful eyes. It all felt so wrong, somehow. There was a pleading look in those eyes, and I wanted to do something about it. You don't understand, do you?"

"You may be right about its eyes," said Godwin, "but I was terrified, Elgiva. I just wanted it dead."

"It's not their fault, though. The shendkin are abominations of nature, the work of madness. Surely they can have no peace."

"No, perhaps not."

"This is what happens when we get above ourselves and think we can defy the laws of nature, Godwin. Bellic told me the wardain are well-schooled in such matters and know there's a natural limit they mustn't go beyond." She hesitated, and a frown creased her brow. "Schooled or not, I wouldn't want the responsibility of such power. I mean, it must be a temptation to see how far you can go . . . I dare say."

She changed her position again, to sit hugging her knees with her back turned towards him, as though she were closing the door on his questions.

"You still haven't answered my question," he said.

She looked round at him sternly, unsure of his meaning.

"Why didn't you run?"

"There was no need," she replied with a shrug. "The incantation sufficed."

"From whence came your courage?"

She frowned at him, puzzled. "The words gave me courage, and I—I had Siriol."

"I thought you said Siriol doesn't work."

"I—I don't know. Look, you didn't run, either. So what? Let's be honest, shall we? We were both too scared to move."

He watched her steadily. "Yes, let's be honest, Elgiva. It was you, wasn't it?"

She glared at him as though he had hit her, and then she scowled at the fire. Her rigid posture told Godwin not to question her further. He knew nothing about elves or incantations and even less about shendkin, but one thing he did know: when Elgiva spoke the potent rhyme, the force he had sensed came from her, not the words. How he knew this was yet another mystery. He had hoped his friend would explain it all to him, but now was not the time. Her confusion seemed to equal his own.

"Talk to me, Elgiva, please," he said.

"Something is happening, and it makes no sense," she said. "My life in Elindel left me ill-equipped to deal with all the things I've been through since I left, so how shall I talk about it?"

"Tell me how you felt."

"What do you mean?"

"When you used the incantation."

She shrugged. "Strange. Hot. Dizzy. Sick. And it's happened before. When I used Siriol to defend myself at the settlement, and again when I defended myself outside Joskin's cave. But Godwin, when I used Siriol to change my appearance, I felt nothing. And it didn't protect me from that arrow, did it? I wish Bellic had told me about magic, about this wretched amulet. It frightens me."

She took Siriol from around her neck and clenched it in her fist. There were tears in her eyes.

"One thing I do know for certain. Siriol can't be trusted." A frown of determination seamed her brow. "I can't use it again. I won't."

She drew back her arm, but before she could hurl Siriol at the fire, Godwin seized her wrist.

"No!" he exclaimed forcefully. "By Frigg, there may be purpose in it yet. Wasn't it the gift of a friend?"

"I used to think so, yes," she sobbed.

The Exile of Elindel

"So is there any wrong in it?"

For several long moments, her dark eyes opposed him, then she relaxed and he loosened his grip on her arm.

At length, she said tentatively, "I just don't know what's happening. Godwin, I feel different."

With that, she stumbled to her feet and dashed towards the forest. He didn't know the right words to use to call her back, nor even if he should. He was left, once more, with only his thoughts for company, and the doubts and fears he harboured began drifting to the surface of his mind.

Now that Greyflanks was back with his family, was this the end of the adventure? Moreover, this shendkin business was frightening. It was all outside his ken, weird and unfamiliar. And now his friend had grown distant and strange, and he didn't like it at all.

This isn't my world. None of this has anything to do with me.

But he couldn't be parted from Elgiva. Some prohibition he couldn't name made it impossible. And what of the threat from that unknown wardain?

Wardain. Even in his thoughts, the word sounded strange.

He drew out his sword and studied it. There was something reassuring about a sword, even if one lacked the skill to use it. It was real and irrefutable, something to cling to when everything else was fear and illusion. He pressed the flat of the blade against his overheated forehead. The touch of the cold metal was soothing.

An instant later, a cleansing wind blew through his mind, scattering his muddled thoughts like chaff and leaving reality behind it, all fresh and painfully exposed. He sat up straight, as though he had sprung out of a trance. What in Frigg's name was he doing here?

He must go home, but he had no idea where it was, or where *he* was. This realisation panicked him, and tears sprang unexpectedly into his eyes at the thought of Rowena and his daughters.

He had to go home, and yet he wanted to honour his vow to his friend, but he couldn't be in two places at once.

What was he going to say to Elgiva?

Godwin was still agonising over the future and his role in it when Elgiva returned in the early hours of the following day with roots and herbs for them to eat. He was more than glad to see her, having resolved to confront her with the fact that he was determined to go back home.

But once again, when he looked at her face, he found himself lost for words. She had a peculiar glint in her eyes, a glint he had seen there before. It was disconcerting and elvish—and strangely appealing—so he dumbly accepted the food she offered and waited for her to speak.

But the chance for discussion never arose. There was a sudden commotion beyond the trees. Howling and yapping rang through the forest as the pack swarmed into the glade. Their tails were thrashing with excitement, and they chased each other about.

Elgiva smiled at the celebration. "Blacktail has returned."

At that moment, an elderly wolf trotted proudly into their midst, followed by a rabble of youngsters. He pranced towards Elgiva, nuzzling his kin aside, and sat before her. His snout was raked by old scars, and his left eyelid sank into an empty socket.

Seeing the animal's battle scars, Godwin found himself reminded of Cerdic.

Elgiva inclined her head towards Blacktail, and he greeted her with throaty growling.

"What's he saying?" Godwin asked.

Elgiva listened to the animal for a while. At length, she turned back to Godwin. "He said if I am Elgiva of Elindel, he has a message for me, from a woman he calls a friend to all the woodland folk. A stag brought her news from an elf, a great elf who is in peril. This elf's plans have been ruined, whatever that means, but he spoke of me and told the woman to find and help me. She must tell me things he would have told me in person, but he can't search for me himself, although sometimes he can venture out in spirit."

"What?"

"That's what Blacktail said. He also told me I can trust this woman because her house is under elf-ward. I suppose that means it is protected by magic, so she is an elf-friend. We have to prepare to leave and follow Blacktail. He's just gone to tell Queen Whitefoot where he's going. If this woman can be trusted, as Blacktail maintains, then perhaps I've found shelter at last. I dare say the great elf he spoke of is Bellic. There's no one else who would bother to help me. I'd hoped I wasn't forgotten."

The Exile of Elindel

"But Blacktail said your friend was in trouble. How can he help you?" protested Godwin. "Perhaps he needs you to help him."

Elgiva's smile vanished and she narrowed her eyes, anxiety etched on her face. To Godwin, she looked like a child chased by ghouls with nowhere left to run. His protective instincts rose to the fore, and his cowardice cringed in their shadow. She was his vulnerable friend again and she needed his support.

"Perhaps Bellic intends this woman to shelter you, but there's definitely something wrong," he said. "If he's as powerful as you say, then why is he in trouble? Instead of finding a place of safety, you could be walking into danger. Might the elf you met outside Joskin's cave—"

"No!" she cried. "Don't speak of it. I've no idea what's going on, but if it's Bellic who summons me, then I have no choice. And if I can help him, I will. At least I must find out what's wrong."

"We must both find out. I really need to get back to my family, but if this woman will shelter you, then you'll be safe. I can leave you there, knowing you'll be cared for, and she might be able to tell me how to get home."

She stared at him with fear-widened eyes, and he thought she was going to object, but she said nothing. He suspected facing danger all alone was something she couldn't bear, that secretly she desired his company but was far too proud to admit it. Her fear reassured him. It made him feel wanted and useful. When she was distant and strange, he was lost, but now she was in need, and this need made him strong. It was something he understood and could fight. Weakness and fear were well within the scope of his mundane powers.

When she finally spoke, they were words he had not expected.

"You seem different, somehow," she said. "More like your old self. I believe the enchantment has lifted completely."

He took her hand and squeezed it. "I don't know about that, but I do know we should leave now and find out what's going on," he told her. "If Bellic's in trouble, then perhaps his purpose in sending this message is to make sure you, at least, are safe. Maybe he can get himself out of the mess he's in, and when he does, he'll know where to find you. No point in looking on the black side just yet." He began to collect their few belongings together.

"Godwin, there's something else, and it may be of interest to you. Blacktail has been exploring for several days, and when he saw you, it reminded him that he'd come upon a tribe of people who look like you."

Godwin spun to face her. "Britons?"

"I think so, and they're in the general direction we'll be travelling, though Blacktail can't be more specific than that."

Godwin digested this information, and then he frowned. "But they're so near. Othere told me the Britons had all been chased far to the west and north."

Elgiva touched his arm gently. "If we do meet this tribe, they might have news of your other family."

Godwin had no idea how to respond. For some reason, his heart beat faster and he needed to move. He shouldered the sack of provisions and offered her his hand. "Blacktail is here, Elgiva. Let's get going."

During the morning of their second day of travel it began to snow, leaving the air fresh and clean, but so sharp that it burned their lungs and drew water from their eyes. As Elgiva and Godwin plodded on wearily through a snow-draped wood, a cheery voice greeted them, jolting them out of their gloomy thoughts.

On a branch a few yards above them sat a young male blackbird, his dark eyes twinkling.

"Hail, travellers, and well met," he cried. "Hail from the leader of the dawn chorus! I am Aderyn. If you are Elgiva of Elindel, I come to bid you welcome in the name of my mistress!"

"Hail, Aderyn," called Elgiva. "I am who you say and I'm honoured to be so greeted by the fairest songster of the woods."

The clear, pure notes of the blackbird's voice trilled like laughter from his throat, and he swooped low over their heads, alighting on a tree stump beside them. "Across these fields before you and over that rise yonder, you will come to a plain that slopes down to a wood. There dwells my mistress in her little house. Before dusk, you will reach it. Tarry not. Supper awaits. I must go and tell her you are come."

With that, the blackbird twitched his tail and soared into the air.

"Aderyn, wait!" Elgiva cried.

The Exile of Elindel

"I go," whooped the bird. "I fly. Follow me!"

And he was gone, winging his way over the fields before them, his dark body swooping and climbing with ease.

Elgiva turned to Godwin and told him what the bird had said. She hesitated, chewing her lip.

Blacktail stepped forward, studying her for a moment with his one good eye, and then nuzzled her hand with his dry, scarred nose. "The bird speaks truly. Follow his directions, and you will not go astray. As for me, I must go home. You have no further need of my guidance. Farewell, my friends. I hope we shall meet again."

Chapter Twelve

THE SMALL HOUSE stood with its back to the frozen woods. Its coarse brown thatch was hoary with snow, and grey smoke drifted above it. The door of the house opened, and an elderly woman appeared on the threshold, waving her hand. Elgiva stopped walking and looked at Godwin.

"That must be her," she said.

The woman called to them and waved again, and they pushed on through the snow. As they approached, the old woman hurried out and threw her arms around Elgiva.

"My dear, how good it is to see you after all these years," she exclaimed in the Celtic tongue. "And how you've grown, and so pretty, too!"

Startled, Elgiva pulled away. "We'd rather you spoke Saxon," she said, "if you can."

The woman raised her eyebrows at this, but she shrugged and nodded. She asked for no explanation, but Elgiva seemed to regret her earlier curtness of manner and offered one.

"My friend was brought up by Saxons."

"My dear, I will speak any language you wish," said the woman, "for you are as dear to me as if you were my very own child."

"I've never met you before in my life," retorted Elgiva.

The old woman laughed. "Well, how could you remember, indeed?" She looked them up and down. "By the stars, a fine pair of scarecrows you look, poor chits! Yet never fear, there's room inside my little house for all of us and a nice, warm fire and a good, spiced caudle to warm the blood. There's water to wash and clean clothes, too. Come inside, my dears, please, and let us thaw you out!"

She gestured towards the door, but the travellers waited and looked at each other.

"Come," she beckoned with a good-natured smile, while tugging at their sleeves.

They both regarded her with blank stares.

"Who are you?" asked Elgiva.

"Why, I'm Kendra. Has Bellic never mentioned me? By the stars, he's not ashamed of me, I hope." Kendra laughed, but the jest meant nothing to Elgiva.

"You clearly know who I am. This is my friend, Godwin."

"A fine-looking lad. A Briton, in sooth! They have such wonderful eyes." Godwin looked embarrassed, and Kendra chuckled. "Forgive me, my dears. No doubt you're wondering what kind of creature I am? My parentage perhaps makes me somewhat strange in manner. My mother was a Briton, but my father, on the other hand . . . my father was an elf."

Kendra put her hand on Godwin's arm. "Young man, I think you to be an honest wight, but be aware if you have evil in your heart, for my home is under elf-ward and none who seeks to do me harm may cross this threshold scatheless."

Godwin gaped at this and looked to Elgiva, clearly needing her guidance, but she wasn't able to give any and all she could do was shrug.

Godwin drew a deep breath, closed his eyes, and stepped inside the house.

Nothing happened except for a strange sensation, as though he had walked through a membrane of gossamer, but almost immediately, he became aware of the cosy warmth, the flickering of candlelight, and the smell of the gruel wafting from a pot over the fire. His stomach also noticed and began to growl. Smaze from the cooking curled up towards the rafters, where dried herbs hung in bunches.

When her guests were both inside the house, Kendra closed the door and moved towards the hearth. She indicated three stools beside the fire. Elgiva and Godwin glanced at each other before they took their seats.

"Did you feel nothing?" asked Kendra, reaching over to stir the gruel.

Unsure of her meaning, Godwin shook his head.

"Ah, that is odd. You can't feel the Earth-magic? You sensed it, Elgiva, when you stepped through the door? A shivering sensation, at least? I'm surprised that your friend is so unattuned. The Britons well know the feeling of magic. They have an affinity with the Earth, you see."

"As I said," Elgiva reminded her, "Godwin was brought up by Saxons."

"I confess I know nothing of Saxons," said Kendra, "but perhaps they think more of war and the getting of gold than they do of mystical matters."

"That's not true," put in Godwin, and then he faltered, not knowing how to continue or why he felt so defensive.

Kendra smiled. "No matter." She ladled the gruel into two wooden bowls and handed them to her guests. "I like to think of my den as a sanctuary. I never turn away any creature that needs a bit of help. That's why we're here, to help each other, and by the looks of you two poor waifs, you arrived just in time."

Once Kendra had cut some slices from a round loaf of bread and offered them to Elgiva and Godwin, she took her place by the fire.

Godwin sniffed at the contents of the bowl, hoping she wouldn't notice, but her eyes missed nothing and her peals of laughter filled the room. It was so infectious that Elgiva joined in.

"Trust me, lad," chuckled Kendra. "I'll not poison thee, for you're Elgiva's friend and there's too little good in this world. I'd poison bad folk, I suppose, and think no more about it, but they poison themselves as it is, I think, and don't need my assistance."

Godwin flushed with embarrassment and started to eat the gruel.

It was while he was mopping up the last of it with a chunk of bread that Kendra tapped him on the arm.

"That's a fine sword you have there, Godwin," she said. "Do you think I could take a look?"

"What? Oh, yes. I suppose you can."

He drew the weapon from his belt and handed it over without a second thought. Any ideas of mistrust had been overcome by the fire and the meal. She studied the blade with interest.

"From whence does it come?" she asked. "Who made it?"

Busy with chewing, he merely shrugged.

"'Tis a fine thing indeed," she said, nodding. "But indeed, by the stars, this is odd. Know you the meaning of these patterns here?"

Godwin swallowed. "Er . . . no."

She nodded to herself. "Most odd."

By now, Elgiva had also stopped eating, and she and Godwin stared at the old woman.

"A rare gift," murmured Kendra. "Has it always been yours?"

"Why, yes," said Godwin. "I've had it since I was a child."

"I see."

"Is there something wrong?" he asked.

"Wrong? Ah, no. No wrong in this," said Kendra. She looked at her guests for a moment and then smiled. "No matter, my dears. I should say no more."

She returned the sword to him, and Godwin was puzzled by how reverently she handled it.

After a pause, Kendra went on. "I must ask you one thing, my dears. Are you travelling on together?"

Elgiva ventured a reply. "Godwin was planning to see me settled somewhere before returning to his home. From the message you sent with Blacktail, I'd hoped that you—"

"I would gladly welcome you if I could, but you are not meant to stay here," said Kendra, interrupting her. "And if you were to part from your friend, I think that would be unwise. I feel, somehow, that your destinies are linked."

Godwin looked at Elgiva, but it seemed neither of them knew how to respond to Kendra's statement.

On the hearth lay a long iron poker, its tip blackened by years of use. Kendra leaned forwards, picked it up, and began to poke at the fire. Her eyes had a dreamy look, and she seemed quite content with the silence, but Elgiva had questions she needed to ask.

"Kendra," she ventured, "are you going to tell me why I'm here? Blacktail said you had things to tell me."

Kendra replaced the fire-iron and then reached across to her left. Lifting a leather-bound book from the floor, she placed it on her lap.

"Yes, my dear, you have been very patient, but now it is time, I think. Do you know what this is?"

Mystified, Elgiva shrugged her shoulders. "A book, I suppose."

Kendra laughed. "A book, indeed! But a most important book. Elgiva, 'tis the *Ninth Book of The Chronicles of the Eldrakin*."

Elgiva frowned dismissively. "There are only eight," she said.

Kendra gave her an arch look.

"Aren't there?"

"So it was believed for many generations, my dear. Ah, me, I have so many matters to relate. Where to begin? Forgive me if my talk grows wearisome and confusing. 'Tis a complicated story."

Kendra looked at them both in turn and then cleared her throat and opened the book on her knee.

"You know, Elgiva, that the chronicler, Silvanuil, left eight manuscripts in which he had written the history and lore of Faine and the Eldrakin. Bellic taught you all this, I think, when you were just a child. But some time ago, another manuscript came to light, and this is it, the *Ninth Book,* the *Book of Prediction.* Can you guess who found it?"

Elgiva looked at her askance. "Lord Bellic, I suppose?"

"The very same! His wanderings have resulted in this gift, though he was not the very first to find it. Well, before I tell you my story, let me show you this." She turned several pages and indicated that Elgiva should look. "This is a copy, one of only two that exist. The original is in Misterell."

"Lord Bellic went to Misterell?"

"Yes, and he has the other copy. The original has decayed, and parts are missing, but see you this?" She pointed at a passage in the book. "Read."

Elgiva leaned forwards and began to recite:

"The Stone's Discoverer,

"Orphan and slave,

"Shall unlock the door . . . "

She stopped and frowned at Kendra. "What does it mean? What stone?"

"One thing at a time, my dear," said Kendra. "As I said, the original was decayed and the rest of the verse has been lost, but it says in the passage before this that the stone will be found in the thirty-ninth generation of Elindel—you see, it mentions Elindel specifically—and you, my dear, are the beginning of that generation. The contents of this book of prediction were given to Silvanuil by Zallic, prophet of Faine, First-Father. The stone is the Lorestone, left by Lord Faine to redeem his people at a time of future peril. It was his parting gift to Elvendom. And perhaps the time of peril is upon us, but more of that anon.

"Many years ago, Bellic chanced to find the legendary land of Misterell, and he met and befriended the king, Eldruin. They shared a common interest in histories and lore, and some years later, on a subsequent visit, Eldruin told Bellic of a remarkable discovery.

"Misterell was the home of Lord Faine, the very first kingdom of the Eldrakin and the seat of the Founder's power. It was during repairs to the royal hall there that an ironbound box was unearthed. Within it were the remnants of the *Book of Prediction*. Eldruin gave a copy to Bellic in the name of friendship. Though like all Misterellians, he preferred isolation from the rest of the Eldrakin—they bethink themselves rather special, I ween—he was a good elf and not averse to sharing knowledge for the good of all. I do not think it meant a great deal to him, but Bellic read the manuscript, and in it, he saw many things of importance.

"Well, there are gaps in the text, and we must interpret what's left as well as we're able. In the deciphering of this book, I trust Bellic, as I trust him in all things, and this Lorestone is, he believes, to be found by you, Elgiva. This legacy is to be used now, by you, to save Elvendom from the evil that threatens it."

Elgiva made to protest, but Kendra reached out and patted her arm. "It will all become clear, Elgiva. You see, the Lorestone is a thing of awesome and unknown power, and Bellic is convinced it is hidden in Misterell. Where it is and how it may be found is uncertain. In the *Ninth Book*, in the passage just before the one you read, there is mention of the forest's heart and then this." She turned back a page and tapped with her finger at the relevant part.

"A door that is not a door,
"A key that is not a key,
"United, a hidden power will free."

"You said it would all become clear," said Elgiva, "but all you can offer me are riddles."

Kendra studied her guests for a moment. "Ah, my dears, forgive me. You are somewhat surpassed by it all. Let us drink a little ale together, and I shall tell you of Elgiva's past. It may prove of greater interest." She set the book upon the floor and shuffled into a corner of the room, where she seemed to merge with the shadows.

"My past?" exclaimed Elgiva. "Do you know who my parents were?"

"I do, in sooth," said Kendra, returning to the fire. In one hand, she held a tall clay jug that she set upon her stool and, in the other, three silver goblets. Elgiva toyed with a strand of her hair, trying to control her impatience, as Kendra gave them a goblet apiece and filled them both with ale from the jug. She smiled at their reaction to the richness of the drinking vessels.

"A gift from Lord Bellic, in fact." She sat down upon the stool, took a long draught of the dark ale, and then smacked her lips with pleasure. "Ah, this bog myrtle was gathered at just the right time." She looked at them both and chuckled. "You look so glum, my dears. Drink up! This is the finest gale beer you ever will have tasted. It will do you good."

Elgiva sighed with frustration. "How do you come to know all this? What is your connection with Lord Bellic?"

"First, my dear, I must tell you my tale. I fear I have postponed the telling. Perhaps I know it will shock you, and it will sadden you, too. You want to hear it . . . and you don't."

Elgiva turned her face away, determined that the old woman should not see how scared of the truth she was.

"Your forebears, Elgiva, are the wardain of Elindel, and I suspect you will prove to be the finest fruit produced by that particular family tree."

Despite her decision to remain aloof, Elgiva jumped to her feet in disbelief. The goblet fell from her fingers and clattered across the floor. "What are you saying?"

The old woman held up her hand in a gesture that asked for patience. "I tell you that you are a wardain, child, and the king who sits on Elindel's throne is a fool, a knave, a usurper, and he is also your cousin."

"Thallinore, my cousin? He can't be. I don't believe any of this."

"I do," broke in Godwin.

They both looked at him.

"Well, I do." He lowered his eyes. "I know Elgiva's a wardain. I know she has power. I've felt it."

Kendra smiled with satisfaction. "Then you're not totally blind to the Earth's magic, Godwin? I am glad. So, Elgiva, you have used your birthright already?"

The Exile of Elindel

"No, I haven't. It was Siriol." She drew out the amulet and showed it to Kendra. "Bellic gave me this, to protect me."

Kendra touched the amulet and then shook her head. "I think not, my dear. You're mistaken. There is no power in this."

Elgiva scowled at her, refusing to believe it, but Kendra's gaze was adamant. Glaring at Siriol as though it had betrayed her, Elgiva thrust it back inside her robe.

"The amulet has a link with Bellic, if that is some consolation," said Kendra.

Elgiva turned away and frowned at the fire, her mind in turmoil. How could any of this be true? Or even real? She was a wardain and Siriol was a lie, a piece of rock and nothing more. Her closest friend had betrayed her. In spite of that, she was expected to rise to some horrendous challenge and go to Misterell. The very name of the place had filled her with dread since she was a child.

Kendra sighed. "I'm sorry, Elgiva, but I have a duty to perform, and I must proceed with it. This is my tale. Try not to interrupt. I've digressed more than enough already. Pour some more ale and listen well." She set her own goblet on the floor and glanced at them both in turn.

"Now," she began, "I left Peranduil with your great-uncle Bellic twenty years ago—yes, your great-uncle, Elgiva. We journeyed to Elindel, he as escort for his niece, Erlina. Elindel's king, Modron, had a younger brother, Ner, who was next in line to the throne and was to marry Erlina. I went along with Bellic, being always uneasy without his protection—and I wanted to see the wedding.

"Now, Modron had a bastard son—that's Thallinore, of course. Yes, Elgiva, a bastard, begat of a wench called Eldreda, herself a mere nar-wardain. Modron had never married and had no legitimate heir, but the lack did not concern him, for like Zallic, he had the gift of foreknowledge. After the wedding, he took your great-uncle aside and told him what he had seen in his many prophetic dreams. Ner and Erlina would have but one child, a daughter. She would have power to surpass all other elves, and this power would come to her in the form of a gift. What kind of gift, he knew not. He felt this future child was ordained to be a great ruler of Elvendom—its redeemer, in fact.

"Bellic respected Modron and always kept in mind what he had said. After the wedding, Bellic decided to stay in Elindel until his niece was settled in her new role.

"In the fullness of time, Erlina conceived. Then poor Modron caught an ague and died, and Ner was suddenly king. Thallinore had, by this time, fallen in with Tarkinell—a rogue and arch-manipulator. Tarkinell knew Thallinore was weak and greedy, and they became close friends. What passed between them, who can say, nor who did the deed that followed. I suspect Tarkinell convinced his friend of his right to rule as Modron's only child.

"So we may never know who poisoned Ner, but he was, and so left this world before his time. We were numb with grief, and none more so than Erlina. The shock induced delivery. I was with her when she birthed you, child, and I was the first to hold you in my arms. Yes, Ner and Erlina were your parents. Sadly, your mother died soon after you were born. I think her heart was broken."

At this point, Kendra was obliged to break off from her narrative to wipe the corners of her eyes with her sleeve. Tortured by this unexpected disclosure about her parents' deaths, Elgiva could do nothing but sit open-mouthed and wait for the old woman to continue.

"Before Erlina died, she asked to see Bellic," Kendra went on. "She begged him to protect you. She told him she suspected her husband had been murdered and she feared for the safety of her babe. You may not know this, Elgiva, but the wardain do not attain magic till puberty—and a good thing, too, I'm sure. Imagine power in the hands of naughty elflings! Erlina wanted Bellic to ward you until you could fend for yourself, so he put you in my care, and for many months, I tended to your needs.

"So your parents were gone, and Bellic took it upon himself to speak to Thallinore concerning the fate of the kingdom. At that time, he had no reason to suspect your cousin of any duplicity or malice, and when Thallinore offered to be the regent until you were of age, your great-uncle accepted. There was no one else with a claim to the throne, and Bellic was an outsider, related to the royal house by marriage only, so his right to interfere was limited.

"It was then that Bellic heard from Eldruin and was invited to Misterell on a matter of some importance. And so, my dear, he left you in my charge and was away some time. Alas, in his absence,

THE EXILE OF ELINDEL

Thallinore proclaimed himself king. No doubt Tarkinell egged him on. No one in Elindel was able to oppose him—he does have powers, you see, be they somewhat weakened by his mother's blood. So we had to accept it. Of course, we had no reason then to believe he did it for any other end than the good of the kingdom.

"As for myself, with your parents dead and Bellic away, I realised I had no friends in Elindel and would not be used with kindness. Sadly, I have not found favour with any race. My strangeness has always set me apart. You see, it's hard to conceal one's ancestry, my dears."

She hooked her long grey locks behind her ears, which were pointed, like Elgiva's. Grinning, she continued, "Of course, you know why Bellic went to Misterell. The *Ninth Book*. When he returned, he found your cousin secure in kingship, so he confronted him about Elindel's future.

"He learned that Thallinore objected to my presence, so he agreed to send me away. Indeed he was glad to do so, knowing I would be safer elsewhere, especially as he himself would often be away. This is the home he found for me. Anyway, Thallinore told Bellic he had plans to found a dynasty of his own, and you would be excluded from the succession. In his heart, perhaps, Thallinore feared what you might become. Did he know about the prophecy? Who can say? But Bellic did, and he alone had read the *Ninth Book*.

"Your cousin told Bellic he was welcome to stay in Elindel, if he so desired. And Bellic made him promise no harm would ever befall you. He expected your cousin to be honourable, no doubt, and in turn, Bellic promised you would not know your true identity. You will remember taking the oath of fealty to the king when you were old enough to do so, Elgiva, but only the nar-wardain are required to take it. Bellic, as a full wardain, could act against Thallinore anytime he wished, if Thallinore gave him cause to, and the king knew his power was unequal to your great-uncle's. He would have been afraid of the consequences if he harmed you.

"Thallinore had you put in the care of Eldreda until it could be decided what should be done with you. Fear for your safety no doubt prompted the idea that sprang into Bellic's mind." Kendra paused for a moment and shook her head. "I'm not sure my next disclosure will be very well received. However, it must be made. Bellic suggested an announcement be made to the effect that you had died of a childhood illness. In reality, you would be brought up in the royal household as one of the servants and would grow up believing yourself lowborn, knowing nothing of your origins. What's one more parentless babe in the servants' quarters? No, Elgiva, do not speak. You misjudge Bellic. Do you not see, my dear, that this kept you safe and allowed your great-uncle to stay in Elindel and keep an eye on you? It also fulfilled the prophesy—'Orphan and Slave.' As you grew up, Bellic taught you as much as time allowed without arousing suspicion. He taught you things unknown to other menials. And to him, it all seemed to fit. He was preparing you for your destiny, and he, in turn, was able to travel when he wished, having no need to fear for your welfare. My dear, do not scowl. Do you not think he had another aim in mind?"

By now, Elgiva was too confused and angry to even care.

"Do you not think a wielder of great power must be a creature of humility, a being mindful of the needs of others and aware of the importance of justice and mercy?" asked Kendra. "Would not a slave know more of such things than someone accustomed to wealth and flattery and selfish indulgence?"

Elgiva gazed into the fire, her mood suddenly altered. Images stirred in the sea of her memories. Thallinore, Lord Bellic, the royal horses, and the servants' quarters, the daily round of chores, her homespun gown with its ragged hem. These were the day-to-day realities of her childhood in Elindel. But her childhood was just another lie. She swallowed the knot in her throat.

"But I have no power," she said.

"You are merely unpractised," said Kendra. "Perhaps Bellic presumed too much, but there was no one else to protect you. He could have gone away and taken you with him, but Thallinore would have tracked you down; you were a threat to his sovereignty. And it was better you should stay where you were and come to know the workings of Elvendom and of the kingdom you would one day rule. Bellic is a wardain and wise, my dear, but by the stars, he's not infallible. Do not hate him, for he loves you dearly. In you, his dead niece lives again."

Unable to comment, Elgiva acknowledged Kendra's words with a slight nod of her head.

The Exile of Elindel

"Your childhood passed and no one knew your true identity, except for Bellic, your cousin, and Eldreda . . . and Tarkinell, of course—"

"And Alsiann," Elgiva broke in. "I think Alsiann always knew." Kendra and Godwin both frowned, and she smiled. "The leader of the royal herd."

Kendra nodded. "Well, you showed no signs of magic, Elgiva, but no more should you have, for you believed yourself a nar-wardain. Without a tutor in magic, your powers did not develop. But you were being watched. Tarkinell was always alert to the stirrings of your power, ready to advise his master that the time had come to dispose of you—as Eldreda was no doubt disposed of, when her love of wine and mischief-making threatened to loosen her tongue. Bellic made more frequent journeys, searching for somewhere to hide you away, where he could teach you the application of magic. He felt the first part of your training was over, and he also suspected Tarkinell was planning a little accident, something that would rid the king of your presence without giving rise to suspicion.

"But no sooner had Bellic found the ideal place, when you got yourself banished. In many ways, it was well-timed. There was no need for Bellic to spirit you away, inviting suspicion and trouble. Tarkinell, of course, had a hand in the plot you foiled. He was second only to the Chief Counsellor and probably thought it was time to move nearer the throne. It would have availed him nothing, of course. As a nar-wardain, he would have been deposed sooner or later, but Tarkinell is mad, I think.

"As you know, Bellic did not follow you. He wished to appear indifferent, perhaps even ashamed. It suited his purpose. He had no wish to leave Elindel at that time, for he was fearful for its future and he believed it would be easy for him to find you when he wished. And he gave you the amulet, of course, but I must leave the explanation of that to him, when you both meet, as I hope, by all the stars, you will."

"Shouldn't we?" asked Elgiva.

Kendra shrugged. "Who can say what meetings the future holds? Things in Elindel are not what they were."

"And Bellic is in trouble," said Elgiva.

"From what I hear, they're all in trouble. Let me tell you what I know, when I have found a good place to start." Kendra stooped awkwardly to pick up her goblet, and after a long drink and a moment to arrange her thoughts, she continued. "You realise that when you slew the Chief Counsellor, the position went to Tarkinell?"

"I helped him," cried Elgiva. The shock of this information made her fists clench together in her lap.

"Yes, but be that as it may, he has told his master that documents exist dating back to Faine knows when, according to which the kingdom's nearest neighbour, Urith-Endil, was once a province of Elindel. He has persuaded Thallinore that it's time to claim it back. 'Tis absolute nonsense, of course, but for now, a state of war prevails between the two kingdoms."

Elgiva gasped in disbelief. "War? That's madness, Kendra!"

"Madness, indeed, and meanwhile, your cousin grows more grasping and more cruel. Severe penalties are meted out to anyone who opposes him. He means to destroy those he cannot bend to his will. But there is something else I must disclose, and it's the main reason why your uncle cannot leave."

"Several days after you left, my dear, a traveller came to Elindel with a retinue of elves. He claimed to be Vieldrin, Misterell's new king. Since Eldruin's death, he had been putting his realm in order, he said, and had now decided to visit other kingdoms and lay to rest the reputation of his own. He maintained that his mission was one of friendship and peace. Your great-uncle knew him from his visits to Misterell and may already have had some inkling of his true nature—I did hear that Eldruin's death was suspicious. Well, Vieldrin fell in with Tarkinell and Thallinore, and I'm sure he soon knew everything they did, but being Eldruin's son, he alone had access to the *Ninth Book*. I believe Bellic spoke out against Vieldrin or his cronies, and certainly the war, but whatever transpired, he made himself an enemy. His last message gave me little cause for hope, Elgiva. He asked that I help you and tell you all I know, for he's unable to act."

"But why?" demanded Elgiva.

"I know not. I know only that he cannot leave Elindel."

"Kendra, Bellic is a wardain. He has great power."

"To you, little elf, mayhap. But your great-uncle is ninety-five—three times Vieldrin's age, I'm sure. He's weary and has spent his life in study, not in the practice of magic. While you have seen him as some kind of god, his powers as a wardain are no more extraordinary than those of any other."

"Why are you telling me this? I can't bear it!"

"Be calm, my dear," counselled Kendra. "You have work to do in this world. Things to learn and a destiny to fulfill. Perhaps the future of all Elvendom is in your hands alone." She reached out to touch Elgiva's arm.

"No," snapped Elgiva, pulling away. "I have no power. Modron was wrong, and Bellic, too! And the wretched *Ninth Book*!"

"I did not expect you to react so selfishly," chided Kendra. "Bellic is relying on you."

"How else can I react?" Elgiva stood up and paced back and forth, her eyes flashing angrily. "One minute, I'm a servant, a nothing, and the next, I'm a wardain with magical powers, ordained to rescue Elvendom. How can I save Elvendom? It's ludicrous. What am I supposed to save it from? And if this Vieldrin surpasses Bellic, then he'll surpass me, too. Kendra, I have no magic!"

She came to a halt behind Godwin and, after a moment of hesitation, placed a hand on his shoulder, seeking reassurance from his sturdy friendship.

Kendra frowned at her. "No courage, either."

Enraged, Elgiva sprang forwards, uncertain of what she meant to do. Godwin quickly caught her arm and held her back, and she twisted round to confront him. His eyes narrowed, and she knew he was urging her to show forbearance.

She sagged against him, her arm around his shoulders.

For a while, they were silent, and then Elgiva spoke. To her own ears, her voice sounded small and defeated.

"What must I do?" she asked.

Kendra held out her hand. Elgiva clasped it and then knelt at the old woman's side. With her free hand, Kendra stroked away the angry tears running down Elgiva's cheeks.

"My dear," she said, "it seems there is but one thing you must do. Find the Lorestone and use it."

"Yes . . . but how?"

"Let us hope that Faine will show you the way." Kendra smiled, but then her expression hardened. "You ask what the danger is. I do not know, but it is certain. It is great. The *Ninth Book* would have it so. And it is Bellic who told me. I may not doubt him."

"The King of Misterell, is he the danger?" wondered Elgiva.

"He may be. Or part of it," said Kendra.

Elgiva tightened her grip on Kendra's hand, and her heart brimmed with fear and revulsion. "I think we've already met."

Kendra nodded. "He's bound to know all about you."

"He's evil, Kendra," Elgiva said. "Am I to oppose him? I can't!"

"What happened, when you met?"

Elgiva shook her head and pulled back her hand.

Godwin's forehead creased with concern, and he looked across at Kendra.

"If you won't tell her, I will," he said.

Elgiva made no protest.

"Elgiva said he was testing her," said Godwin. "He could have destroyed her, but he refrained. Why would he? Is she more powerful than he expected?"

"Sadly, no. Elgiva is only a wardain, Godwin, and one wardain cannot know the strength of another until it is tested. If Vieldrin, being stronger, then chose to withdraw, he must have had a very good reason to want her alive." Kendra sighed. "There are so many things Bellic would have taught you about magic, Elgiva."

"Can't you teach me?" asked Elgiva.

"Think you that I have magic, child? It's not for me to teach the uses of power. I have the gift of healing. I read the stars and the runes. I'm a keeper of arcane knowledge. I talk to trees and animals. There are many kinds of magic, my dears. That a tiny acorn can become a great oak, what is that but magic? But I know nothing of real power, the sort royal elves use. One thing, however, I do know is that you must not play with it. Magic is a gift, not a sport, not a toy. It must be used wisely and for all the right reasons. There's always the danger, without proper schooling, of magic being misused."

"You say you know nothing of power," Elgiva said, "but be honest, Kendra, you know a great deal about everything."

Kendra chuckled. "By the stars! Much knowledge may be gained by study, they say. There's no mystery in that. But 'tis wrong to credit my poor pate withal. My sources are not extraordinary. Perhaps my

The Exile of Elindel

knowledge, too, was ordained and we have all been chosen for a purpose."

"Who chose us?" asked Elgiva. "Faine?"

"Who can say, my dear?" replied Kendra. "But suffice it to say, if we are chosen, we must accept our destiny and strive to fulfil it."

Elgiva drew a long breath. "Misterell."

"Yes, my dear, the Lorestone," said Kendra.

"But where is Misterell?"

"Many leagues to the northwest . . . I think."

Elgiva frowned at the uncertainty in Kendra's tone. "You think? Don't you know exactly?"

Kendra shook her head. "Why can things never be simple? Give me some more of that ale, my dear. I'm hoarse from all this talking. A moment or two to gather my wits, and then we shall speak of Misterell."

Chapter Thirteen

Kendra held out her goblet, and Elgiva filled it with ale. The old woman quaffed the gale beer, wiped her mouth on her sleeve, and placed the empty goblet on the floor.

"Misterell," she began. "'Tis the most magical of all the elven kingdoms. Everything about it is strange, and 'tis a place that breeds legends and myths. Faine First-Father loved it—"

"This, I know," Elgiva said.

"Yes. Be patient, child," said Kendra. "Other kingdoms have always feared it. Thus did its rulers seek to protect it and ward it against the outside world. The land is enchanted, and 'tis a hard place to find, for it has turned in upon itself and withdrawn. Bellic is the only elf I know ever to have been there. Whatever lies within Misterell, you must find out for yourselves."

"Is it really an evil place?"

"I do not know," answered Kendra. "Some legends would have it so, for it turned against the Founder, despite his love for it. All I know is the spell that surrounds it makes travellers stray from their path. Bellic tried to find it many times before he succeeded. The forest wove a spell of confusion to protect itself from outsiders. Eventually, Bellic focused his mind on the enchantment itself and followed it to its source."

"But if he entered Misterell and left unharmed, it can't be an evil place," said Elgiva. "And wasn't Eldruin a good king and his friend?"

"So I was told," replied Kendra, "but we can all appear to be what we are not. And Misterell can do likewise. If Bellic returned unscathed, perhaps it was only because Misterell wished him to."

"Or because Eldruin wanted to trick him," said Godwin, "and the *Ninth Book* is a lie."

Elgiva and Kendra looked at him, and he shifted in his seat.

Uncertainty hung in the air above them, and doubt coiled in the shadows, as dark as despair.

"Of course, my dears," Kendra said. "There's only one way to find out the truth about Misterell. You'll have to go there and see for yourselves."

"If Bellic wouldn't tell you what the truth was, it must be something bad," Elgiva said. "I don't think I want to go there. In fact, I don't think I want any part of this." Her inner tension was becoming too much to bear. It propelled her to her feet. She glowered down her nose at the old woman with all the petulance she could muster. "Why can't someone else find the stone? Someone with real power? Why me? Why pick on me?"

Kendra smiled. "Elgiva, don't be childish. Someone has to find the Lorestone. Why shouldn't it be you? Think you other wardain can leave their lands without protection to go gadding about after legends? Has Bellic had the time or the opportunity to tell them all he knows? Would it be wise for him to do so? And would they find the Lorestone if they tried?"

"Why shouldn't they?"

"Because it's not their destiny, child."

"Destiny! I'm sick of that word. I don't believe in destiny!"

"Nevertheless, it's a fact," said Kendra. "I'm older than you, Elgiva, and I have seen and heard and felt many things. I have discovered that too often, we disbelieve when there's no solid proof, and all we achieve is to close our minds to the unknown wonders of this world. We narrow our vision and are left with nothing but the bare bones of existence. I have learned 'tis better to keep the mind open."

Kendra looked at her with a gentle smile, but Elgiva was unable to return it. The weight of all her responsibility seemed to crush her, yet it appeared there was no one else to carry it. "I have no choice, do I?"

"We all have that," said Kendra. "We all have the freedom to act in whatever way we think is best."

"The very name of Misterell fills me with dread, and I won't pretend I can see any sense in going on this fool's errand."

Kendra clearly saw fit to ignore this remark. "Apart from the trouble in Elindel, other elven kingdoms may soon fall prey to

Thallinore's greed and the schemes of Vieldrin and Tarkinell. Wilthkin lands as well, perchance. For those who desire to take and possess, boundaries have no meaning. The Lorestone may be the only hope for us all. Be it a legend or a lie, it must not go unexplored.

"Now, Misterell," said Kendra. "You must go northwest till you reach a great forest. Not only is this forest large, but long and narrow too, and you will have to decide if you're going to walk through it or go round it. The latter course will cost you a day of travel, at least, but to cross the forest will take a few hours. That seems straightforward, but it may be unwise to brave that place without the protection of magic. Bellic calls it the Forest of Shades. It lies under some kind of spell—perhaps the influence of Misterell. Well, you will have to decide for yourselves. But if you cross it, be aware, and do not stop until you are safely on the other side. I think even the trees are dangerous."

"How can trees be dangerous?" asked Elgiva.

"I dare not imagine, for I have never been there. Well, once you're through the forest, keep going northwest and hope you find what you seek. I cannot give directions. Landmarks may be inconstant. Be ever on your guard against danger and deceit." Kendra glanced at her guests and then nodded, as though her task were done. Then she got to her feet. "All this talk has made me hungry. I made a fruit cake yesterday. I think it's time we ate it." She turned to walk away and then stopped. "You asked me a question, Elgiva, which I have yet to answer. Forgive me for forgetting. You wanted to know the connection between your great-uncle and myself."

"Kendra, I'm sorry. I didn't mean—"

"Bellic is my father."

A sly grin of amusement stole across Kendra's face. She turned quickly and shuffled towards her shelves, while Elgiva and Godwin stared at her back in silence.

The night matured, and Elgiva and Kendra continued their discussion of elven affairs. Lulled by the warmth of the fire and the potency of the ale, Godwin's attention drifted away from his surroundings.

He was a little envious of Elgiva. She was learning the truth about her past, something that would never happen to him.

The past was one thing, but what about the future? Great danger loomed ahead, and if he went with Elgiva, he might get killed and never return to his family. How many days had he been absent already? He had no idea.

He glanced at Elgiva. She seemed so small and frail, despite the powers she supposedly possessed. She looked like a vulnerable child. How could he envy such a tormented, self-doubting creature? She still needed him. He had made an oath. And Kendra had advised them to stay together.

Elgiva might not believe in destiny, but he did. Deep inside, in a secret place where dreams and hopes were hoarded against a time of emotional famine, he felt it to be true.

He had been born a free man, but the Saxons had taken by force whatever birthright had been his.

They killed your sister and made you a slave. Did you never think of running away?

Othere had been a fair master and yet, by Frigg, what right had he to make slaves of others? Godwin realised how deep his anger ran, how much he resented Othere and all he stood for, but he also had to confront his jealousy towards Elric, who had landed like a cuckoo and ousted Godwin from his master's paternal affection. The shock of these conflicting emotions staggered him.

There were things in his life that had to change, but how he did not yet know. Perhaps all he could do was go with Elgiva and risk whatever stood in their way, be it shendkin, forests, evil elves, or anything else. It might test his mettle, might show him what kind of a man he really was. Perhaps that was *his* destiny.

He stared at his empty goblet. He was clenching it so hard, his knuckles were white.

As he sat there, immersed in his inner turmoil, a small voice called to him from the distance. Then a hand touched him gently on the arm and jolted him back to reality.

"Godwin, are you all right?" asked Elgiva. "You're trembling. Are you ill?"

"I'm all right." He returned to staring at the fire.

"We've been cruel, Elgiva, excluding this poor young man from our talk," said Kendra. "No doubt he's bored, and when folk get bored, their minds start to wander, and who knows what they might dwell on. He has things that trouble him, just as we do. Forgive us, Godwin. I think we've talked enough. 'Tis late, and you two look fit to drop. I've some soft straw pallets in there." She pointed towards a curtained chamber. "A good night's rest is what you need."

Suppressing a yawn, Elgiva stood up and bid good night to her friends, and then she made her way towards the curtained chamber. Godwin pushed himself to his feet and prepared to follow her lead, but Kendra had more to say.

"Before you retire, Godwin, there is something I wish to tell you. I do indeed see more than most people, and I see in your heart the great burden you carry. You are being torn in two. Please believe me when I tell you that your family is quite safe. Your home will be there for you when you return, but until that time, you must stay with Elgiva. I feel you may be the only person who can help her fulfil her destiny, and perhaps you need her to fulfil yours."

Godwin grinned. "I have no idea what you're talking about, but I *do* believe you and I thank you. I care so much for Elgiva, and I want to help her, but she would never understand how much it hurts me to be away from my daughters especially, and I don't want her to know, either."

"She will not hear it from me, but do not be so quick to assume she's ignorant of your pain. You know her better than that, surely? Now, away with you and sleep well."

The next day, during their preparations to leave, Kendra gave Godwin a stout sacking bag filled with whatever food she could spare. It had leather straps that looped over his shoulders. A seemingly bottomless chest in the curtained chamber also provided him with a new linen shirt, woollen tunic, and cloak.

Having bathed and shaved and eaten a good breakfast, Godwin had sharpened his sword on a whetstone, and although the sky was dark with the threat of snow, he felt equal to whatever lay ahead.

Elgiva was now attired in a grey woollen robe. Over this, she wore a brown hooded mantle held below the throat by a silver clasp.

There was one more treasure in the cavernous chest.

"A fine sheath for a fine blade. 'Twas made in Peranduil," said Kendra, handing Godwin a leather scabbard.

The Exile of Elindel

He accepted her gift. The old Godwin had now been discarded along with his servant's rags, and he fancied he had the aspect of an errant warrior intent on bold deeds.

Everything had changed since their meeting with Kendra, taken on a different perspective. They were starting out on a new adventure, but one with a worthy and serious purpose.

Chapter Fourteen

GODWIN'S ELATION WAS starting to waver. The weight of the pack he carried was impinging upon his sense of adventure, and he knew he was still playing the servant's role, for he had volunteered to carry all of their gear. Too late to start complaining now, and there was no point in feeling resentful. It was entirely his own fault for wanting to appear so strong and dependable.

Elgiva was walking some way ahead of him, cocooned in thought. He noticed a tension in the way she carried herself, a stiffness in her shoulders that was so unlike her usual graceful posture. Perhaps he should leave her in peace, but he couldn't cope with this protracted silence. To lift her spirits, but mostly to vanquish his boredom, he caught up and tried to set a conversation going.

"By Frigg, it's cold. I thought we might be in for warmer weather by now."

She smiled at him. "We are. Be patient. You wilthkin are obsessed with the weather. Believe me, this is the last snow we'll see before next winter."

"Are you sure?" he asked.

"Kendra said so. She knows much about weather-lore."

"I see."

This conversation was leading nowhere. He needed to be more direct; his friend was troubled, and there was no sense in skirting round the problem.

"Do you think Kendra spoke the truth?"

"About the weather?" Elgiva asked.

"No. About . . . you know."

Elgiva frowned and gazed towards the horizon. "I'm confused. I can't believe it, yet I have to. I'm wondering if I dreamed it all, or if it was the gale beer. If it's all true, then it's too much for me to take in. How can I say if she spoke the truth? I don't know her."

She turned towards him with a look of helpless anger. "How could they do this to me, Godwin? They keep things a secret for all these years and then tell me who I am and what I'm expected to do, like it or not. I've got these powers, so I'm supposed to act accordingly with no time to adjust. Here we are, searching for a place that may be impossible to find and a stone whose location is unknown, and we're doing it because two long-dead elves had visions. Doesn't it all seem a bit vague and pointless? I mean . . ."

She stopped and spread out her arms. "We've nothing definite to guide us. It's not fair, Godwin, and they could . . . they could at least have given me time to get used to the idea of being a wardain. They expect me to act differently, but I'm still just me. Imagine, Godwin, if someone came up to you and said, 'Oh, by the way, you can fly, but we didn't want you to know until now, because now we need you to fly to the moon for us.'"

Godwin nodded and searched for a better topic to lighten the mood.

"Why don't you tell me about Lord Faine?"

Elgiva looked taken aback, and then she smiled. "Ah, Faine, the First-Father, the Founder of all Elvendom. He was a wardain long ago, in the days before elves had either magic or the gift of universal speech. I don't know where my people, the Eldrakin, came from, but we were in this land centuries before the wilthkin. Faine united the Eldrakin into one kingdom with himself as the first king. It fell to him to discover magic, or rather, it was granted to him by the Earth Spirit."

"How?"

"Bellic told me Faine understood all things are one. He was one with the Earth and its power. They communed with each other."

"I still don't understand."

"Sometimes Bellic's lessons were a bit beyond me, too," she said. "Let's just say that by being what he was, with his kind heart and integrity, Faine earned the respect of the Earth Spirit and so was granted a share of the Earth's magic. And he became a great leader and king, yet he always maintained he was merely a servant of a much higher power. Whatever you wish to call that power—love or good—it is the life force that sustains the universe."

Godwin frowned and tried to stretch his mind around the concept of something larger than a settlement. "Kendra implied his spirit may still be working for the benefit of your race," he said, knowing himself to be surpassed by the topic, but eager to show his interest.

"Let us hope so, Godwin. We need all the help we can get."

They travelled for two more days, while the snow melted around them and the grey clouds fled before the strengthening sun. The leagues drifted by unrecorded in Elgiva's mind. Even the spring unfolding around her couldn't distract her from her gloomy thoughts, from the dread that dogged her footsteps.

Soon, she spied a dark mass on the horizon. It could be none other than the Forest of Shades. It sprawled across the land like a monstrous animal, sleeping or lying in wait.

As Elgiva and Godwin approached the outer marge of the forest, it almost reared up at them, as though frozen in the act of pouncing. In the late afternoon silence, Elgiva fancied she could hear the old trees chuckling softly to themselves, though it was only the breeze rustling in the dry branches. Still, she was uneasy. She hadn't expected them to find the forest so soon, or to find it so grim and forbidding. Now it stood before them, not like an ordinary forest, teeming with natural life, but like a huge, quiet beast with a simmering mind, brooding in the shadows. She was overwhelmed by its size, by the density of the trees, the thickness of the canopy of leaves. Young saplings marched out from among their elders in straggling twos and threes. They looked like sentries, alert for any intruders, and an atmosphere of coiled hostility hung above them like a pall of smoke.

She turned to Godwin, and it was obvious from his expression that he felt the same way.

"Not the most welcoming of places," he said.

"I think we've heard too much about it, or perhaps too little. We're afraid of the unknown, that's all." She tried to ignore the icy shiver that skittered up her spine.

"I'm not so sure. I may be a thick-skinned wilthkin, but it doesn't feel right to me, yet what I can see looks normal enough." He turned to Elgiva and smiled. "Of course, I've been fooled by appearances before."

Elgiva ignored this remark. "It's a natural fear of dark forests and wild beasts and nothing more."

"Maybe so," he said, "but the beasts in this particular dark forest are a bit too quiet for comfort."

They stood and listened, both holding their breath. The forest was still and deathly calm, as though it, too, listened. Elgiva chewed her lower lip. She wasn't familiar with forests like this, with such a sinister silence. "What shall we do, then? It blocks our path to Misterell. You can see how big it is. Can we spare the time to walk around it?"

"Why should we?" Godwin folded his arms and glared at the trees. "I think we'd be mad to be scared of a forest. The trees can't hurt us, can they?"

Elgiva shrugged. "I don't see how. But I don't like it, Godwin. It doesn't feel right to me. Perhaps we should make camp here and cross it in the morning."

"No, let's carry on," he said. "If we let this get the better of us, when worse things lie ahead, how shall we cope with those? Come on, Elgiva. I thought elves lived in forests?"

"Not forests like this!" she declared.

Godwin extended his hand, palm upward. "It's starting to rain, and I'm not getting soaked out here. We'll have more shelter among the trees. Kendra said it would only take a couple of hours to cross the forest, so we can walk through it now and make camp on the far side. We'll sleep much better, knowing it's behind us."

"But remember what Kendra told us? We mustn't stop for any reason. Do you think we can make it before nightfall?"

"We can try," he replied. "There's a few hours of daylight left yet."

"Are you being sensible, or just very brave?"

"I'm trying to be both."

Elgiva considered the dark forest and then said, "Very well. Lead on."

Inside the forest, it was much darker than they had expected. The branches were coiled like snakes above them, blotting out the light.

A strange gloom filled the air, a chill as dank as a dungeon seeped into Godwin's bones, and the soil gave off a rancid odour beneath his wary feet. He looked at Elgiva, and her expression indicated she was equally uneasy, but they had committed themselves to crossing the forest and they had to keep going. However, the underwood grew thicker as they pressed on, and they gradually lost their sense of direction. Soon, they began to appreciate the folly of their decision.

They knew they shouldn't stop, but it was useless to continue. When they reached a glade that offered relief from the tangle of thorny shrubs, Godwin suggested they make camp. Slipping his arms out of the straps, he lowered his pack to the ground with a sigh of relief. Elgiva didn't argue with his decision and helped him gather wood for a fire.

Godwin spread his cloak out beneath a towering elm. "The soil's damp," he said, frowning. "I hope it doesn't seep through my cloak."

Elgiva sank down upon it. "I'll soon complain if it does."

Godwin stacked the wood a few yards away and got the fire going. Such menial tasks held no mystery for him. He could have done it in his sleep. Soon, the wood was crackling with bright flames that nudged the darkness back against the trees.

"What have we left to eat?" asked Elgiva.

Godwin inspected their pack of provisions.

As he spoke, he shared out the food between them. "Some cheese . . . oatcakes . . . dried fruit . . . bread. And there's something I've been saving for a time of extremity." With a grin and a flourish, he drew out a jug with a stopper in the neck. Removing the stopper, he sniffed expectantly at the contents. "Gale beer . . . and by Frigg, it might have gone off! It smells like horse liniment."

Elgiva let loose a peal of laughter. It echoed through the brooding forest and then faded into silence.

Godwin drew his breath in as a chill ran up his spine. "The fire won't last long. We're going to need more wood." He shuddered at the thought of being plunged into darkness in this cold and gloomy place. "Perhaps the ale will warm us before it rots our guts." He tasted it and screwed up his face. "It's not so bad."

They sat in silence and shared the food and ale. Godwin emptied the last of the ale into his mouth and cursed at the bitterness of the dregs. In a sudden flare of temper, he swung back his arm and hurled the jug across the glade with all the strength he could muster. It struck against one of the nearest trees and broke into jagged pieces.

Elgiva sighed at his outburst, but she said nothing.

The forest's oppressive aura asserted itself more strongly, and Godwin became aware of the rain as it sifted through the leaf canopy above him. It resembled the angry hissing of serpents. He began to feel queasy. He blamed his nausea on the ale, but suspected fear was the real culprit. If only he could hear the hoot of an owl, the scream of a fox—natural things, things he understood. But this creeping darkness wasn't right. This dread of something intangible had no remedy known to him.

He wrapped his arms about his chest, trying to maintain control. Curse Kendra for putting ideas into his head.

"I don't feel very well."

Elgiva's announcement startled him, but he pulled himself together. Sliding his arm round her back, he drew her to his side. As though she were an ailing child, to distract her from discomfort, he began to tell her a tale he had once heard in the mead hall, a hundred years ago, it seemed. But he couldn't look at her. The effort of focusing made him giddy.

He chattered on while she listened raptly. As he continued with the tale, a story about a dragon and the man who went to slay it, a change occurred in his mood.

He ceased and looked around like a man who had lost his way. He scowled at the encircling trees, and Elgiva tugged at his sleeve.

"What happened next?" she asked him.

"What?"

"The story, Godwin. You were telling me a story."

"Frigg take the stupid story. What about this forest?"

"I don't know what you mean."

"If there are any monsters here, I'll wager they're too scared to come out."

He struggled to his feet, while she watched him through half-closed eyes. "What monsters are these?" she asked.

He cocked his fists on his hips. "That old crone Kendra has frightened us stupid. Come on now, admit it."

"I don't know." She sighed and supported her head with both hands.

"What if she made it all up?" he persisted. "There's nothing wrong with this forest at all. It's lies, by Frigg. Just lies."

"If she lied about the forest, then she lied about—"

"Dangerous trees? Shit. We've been here for ages, and they're not attacking us, are they?"

Elgiva gasped as he drew his sword and waved it at the shadows.

"If you're so bloody dangerous, come on, then. Do your damnedest! You know who this is?" He flung out his arm, swaying drunkenly, and pointed at Elgiva. "This, my friends, is an elf-queen. No, *the* elf-queen, the ordained one!"

"Godwin, please . . ."

"This is a wardain, you stupid bastards, and if you give us any trouble, she'll sort you all out, don't you worry."

"You're drunk."

Godwin spun round to face her. She had covered her mouth with one hand, trying to stifle giggles, but he had no time for her perverse, elvish humour; he wanted to see her eyes alight with the stirring of magic. He couldn't resist the urge to goad her.

"You're the greatest of elves. Why don't you prove it? Kendra would want you to practise."

"But you said she made everything up."

"What are you waiting for? Are you afraid?"

"Kendra said not to—"

"What right has she to tell you what to do?"

"What right have you?"

He shrugged with mock indifference and sheathed his sword. "I'm disappointed. I thought to find some courage in that icy heart of yours."

She pushed herself upright. Beside the elm, discarded branches lay among the shadows, and she stooped and grasped one. Then she turned to her friend.

"Courage enough to knock your brains out!"

She circled him, waving the branch, but he merely laughed. "I don't expect you to change night into day, or anything like that. Can't you do something about the fire? It'll soon be out, and we'll be cold. That's using magic wisely, I'd say. Of course, if you can't, if it's too much for you . . ." He shrugged, but inside, he was churning with fear and excitement. "Perhaps you're not up to much after all."

The Exile of Elindel

Violence bloomed in Elgiva's eyes. She gripped the branch with both hands and exerted enough force to snap it in two.

"We can all snap rotten twigs, you know. Is that the extent of your powers?"

There was a wicked grin on Elgiva's face, and he grinned too. The air reeked of conspiracy. Godwin had the conviction that they were the victims of this conspiracy, but also players in it. There was a chaotic mix of love and hatred in his heart that went beyond all the bounds of reason. There was no going back for either of them. The game must be played out for good or ill.

Chapter Fifteen

ELGIVA HURLED THE riven branch into the shadows, and then she swept back the gleaming darkness of her hair. "You want fire, Godwin?" she asked with a chilling softness. "Then you shall have it!"

Her gaze was feverish with the possibilities of power, and it made excitement seethe in Godwin's breast. His legs felt boneless, incapable of support, and anticipation left him breathless. Entranced, he watched her turn towards a tree behind him. She raised her arms, as though in greeting.

No, no, no! Imprisoned in a dark chamber, deep within his mind, a tiny voice pleaded, but he pushed it even deeper and crushed it into silence.

The tree was gnarled and brittle-barked. Its denuded branches strained upwards to the canopy above, where they burst into leaf, as though the air below the forest's roof were poisonous to life.

"I know no suitable incantations, so this will have to do," said Elgiva. "I command you, denizen of the dark forest, I compel, I order you to take fire and perish. I, Elgiva, Queen of Elindel would have it so. It is my will."

Her voice began strong but soon trailed away to embarrassed giggling. After a while, it became apparent that nothing was going to happen, and silence fraught with apprehension swooped into the glade. Elgiva glanced at Godwin, who frowned with frustration, his expectations thwarted.

"You've not done it right," he said.

"I've not been taught. I don't know what to do. I feel . . . I feel silly."

"And so you are, by Frigg."

"Damn you, then I'll try again."

She inhaled and flexed her fingers. Her eyes closed and a furrow of effort appeared on her brow. Her hands clenched into fists.

Her eyes sprang open, shining with confidence, and tossing back her long hair, she once more confronted the tree.

"You hideous, evil tree," she cried, "I command the Earth-magic, and you will obey me. I order you to take fire and perish. As I say, so mote it be!"

Still nothing happened, but time passed and the sky grew heavy with darkness.

Elgiva stood glaring at the tree. Her pulse was a painful thump in her temple. She had found the magic. It welled up in her, a tight shiver of passion that crawled along her nerves, seeking an outlet. A strange, alarming sensation and yet, it pleased her even so. But nothing had happened. The power needed direction. Her impatience flared upwards, boiled like magma. She stamped her foot in frustration, and almost at once, she felt the heat leave her in a dizzy rush of force that sucked the strength from her limbs.

"This is ridiculous," Godwin fumed, spinning round to face her. "How can a tree just burst into flames?"

A roar of hot air sent him staggering. In amazement, he turned and gaped at the tree, which was now engulfed in fire. Grinning with delight, he rushed up to Elgiva and grasped her by the shoulders. "You did it, by Grim! You did it!"

Elgiva pushed him away. "Faine, oh, Faine! Look what I've done! Godwin, this is murder!"

"What do you mean? Elgiva, look. It's wonderful!"

She glared at him and for a moment held the conviction that he was the most loathsome creature on Earth. "But the tree is alive. Alive!"

"So? It's only a bloody tree. Trees don't feel, you stupid girl."

She stepped forward, knotted her small fists in the fabric of his tunic, and tried to shake him, though she hadn't the strength. "Of course they do! I know, curse you! Because your senses don't stretch that far, you dismiss the suffering of other creatures. How do you know what a tree feels? You're not a tree!"

He grabbed her by the wrists and easily unhooked her hands from his tunic.

She raged at him. "This is all your fault. You provoked me!"

"You were easily provoked."

"You wanted me to do that," she said, gesturing towards the tree, "to satisfy your need for excitement. You're just like all the rest of them. A bloody barbarian. You're cruel. I hate you!"

"Don't think the feeling isn't mutual. You think you have all the answers, don't you? You and your Faine and your bloody magic. You're an arrogant little sprite from the woods, and you've no right to preach to me."

She flew at him in a desperate rage, kicking and flailing her fists, while he tried to fend her off. The shadows billowed up around them, gyrating about the burning tree. Flakes of its blistering flesh wafted skywards, while the rain steamed in its branches.

As the rain grew heavier, it began to sift through the lattice-work of branches and its whisperings cooled the frenzy in the glade.

A mist lifted from Elgiva's mind, and she reeled with the pain of awareness. Panting, she pulled away from Godwin, her muscles slack with exertion.

"Stop! Godwin, let me stop it. Let me save the tree!"

He was deaf to her plea and didn't reply. Without warning, he struck her hard across the face and sprawled her in the grass. Stunned by the blow, she was helpless to resist as he pinned her to the ground. Her vision occluded by whirls of darkness, she watched him unsheathe his sword. Firelight danced along its edge like glee.

No, you can't! But she couldn't say the words.

Elgiva fought the blackness in her mind and struggled in Godwin's grip. The forest shivered in its cloak of darkness, and a pulse of desire left its murky heart to thump beneath her in the cold marl. Or perhaps it was her own heart pounding with fear at what her friend planned to do. "The forest is angry," she managed to wail. "Listen! Can't you hear it? I've done murder. It will kill us both!"

"I'll save it the trouble of killing you," he said with cold, mocking laughter.

Leaning forwards, he pressed the edge of the blade against her neck, with the pressure of a kiss and the spite of an old adversary. His arms trembled, as though they feared to obey him, but his mouth was set in a grim line of cruelty.

He dragged the blade across her throat.

The Exile of Elindel

Elgiva winced. It was only a shallow slice, but the blade left a line of fire on her flesh, and a sticky wetness trickled down her neck. The smart brought tears to her eyes. "Fool. We'll die. We trespass!" She grabbed his wrists to hold him away.

"It's all your fault," he growled at her. "Everything is your doing. You seduced me from my family."

"You seduced yourself."

"You've an answer for everything, haven't you? You're evil clothed in flesh. As all elves are. You're demons. You're filth. Every last one of you!" His eyes burned with an intensity that was nothing short of madness, and it left Elgiva so empty of will, she could hardly recall who she was. "It's my duty to free the world from the tyranny of evil elves."

He raised his sword arm. For a moment, he held it high, trembling and poised to strike. Yet the blade did not fall. Instead, his eyes widened in horror.

"Oh, Grim, Elgiva! The gods know, the gods know. I can't! I could never." He hesitated, shivering, in the grip of conflicting desires, as if torn by some inner struggle. Finally, lowering the sword, he looked at it with a grimace of disgust, seeming to see it for the first time. "What?"

He hurled the blade aside. It spun through the air with a flash of silver and landed in the bushes. Godwin looked down at her, his expression full of remorse, and snatched her to his breast.

"Elgiva, forgive me! Am I mad? What in Frigg's name was I thinking?"

"It wasn't you. The forest," she said, "it's using you. You must fight it, Godwin."

He pulled away from her, studied her face, and then frowned at some inner turmoil.

"Godwin, listen to me. There are voices whispering in your mind, I know. I can hear them, too. Sly, seductive voices. Ignore them. The trees are making sport with you. Don't let them use you."

But even as she implored him to be strong, the forest's coercion seized hold of her again. Its madness flooded her mind. She was aware of it now. It was the collective intelligence of the trees. It was their only defence against intruders, but it was also their sport. Together, their warped and savage wills became an awesome weapon.

She knew herself inferior in the face of such dark power. Appalled though she was, she didn't have time to wonder what had spawned such unnatural spite. All of her mental resources were needed to try to block out the forest's will so it wouldn't discover her weaknesses and turn them all against her.

But it was a battle she couldn't win.

She became aware of Godwin's lean strength and the way his hair gleamed red and gold in the light from the burning tree. Yes, he was desirable in a way she had never noticed before, but he belonged to someone else.

What did that matter? She had power. Power to compel, to take, to possess.

"No one uses me," said Godwin. "I am free to do as I please."

He pinned her down, and while his strength filled her with longing, the part of her mind still her own resisted him.

"Don't! The trees will force me to use my power against you."

This was what the forest wanted, to drive them both mad and watch them kill each other. She must deny them their sport, but—

But she badly wanted to hurt her friend.

Godwin released Elgiva. Drawing away, he frowned. "What am I doing?"

Elgiva hooked her fingers in the fabric of his tunic, as though their separation filled her with chagrin.

For a long moment of anguish, Godwin forgot who and where he was, forgot what act he had planned to commit. He looked down at Elgiva, his heart thudding with panic, and she regarded him with mischief in her alien eyes. Reaching up with her free hand, she ran her fingers down his cheek.

"Can you hear it?" she said. "The trees are mocking us."

He snatched her hand from his face. "That's impossible! Why should they?"

She sighed. "Because they can."

He stumbled to his feet, and the forest whirled around him. "Those bushes, they've moved closer!"

"Illusion!" Elgiva laughed.

He dragged her upright and shook her by the shoulders. "By Frigg! What's going on?"

She shook her head, as though trying to clear the confusion from her mind.

"We must leave this place, Godwin," she said, frowning up at him. "We must leave at once or never leave at all. Can you get our stuff together?" She gave him a crooked smile, devoid of warmth or humour, and he let her go. He didn't want to look at her, and a shudder ran through him.

He collected their belongings, a calm as cold as the grave now settling in his bones. He had awoken from a dream, as if some part of his mind had been absent. He hoisted their gear onto his back. Elgiva was searching in the bushes. She reached down to grasp something, and when she straightened, she held his sword. She winced, and he immediately started towards her.

"Elgiva?"

She frowned at him. "This miserable hunk of metal protests at being handled."

He stopped in his tracks. "What?"

"It stung me." Her eyes narrowed in puzzlement and surprise, but then she grew angry. "Whether you want to or not, you will do as I say!"

She flinched again, and Godwin cried, "Elgiva, for Frigg's sake, we must go!"

She turned to confront him and touched the cut on her throat.

"So you would kill me, would you?"

"Elgiva, this isn't you."

She ran towards him and lifted the sword. "I have no need of this, wilthkin. I could deal with you as I dealt with that tree, but let's do it your way, shall we?"

"Elgiva . . . what . . . "

She swung the sword at Godwin while he, taken by complete surprise, made a desperate attempt to avoid the blade as it slashed towards his head, but it caught him on the shoulder. The sword fell from his attacker's hand and landed on the grass.

He staggered under the impact, but there was no pain, just disbelief. His shoulder must be cut to the bone, but it didn't concern him. Elgiva flitted away, like a shadow among the trees, and he knew only that he must follow her and he must catch her; she had to be stopped.

As he ran from the clearing, his sword lay behind him, forgotten, on the grass.

Elgiva ran, laughing, through the trees. Magic pulsed in every vein. She was invincible, capable of anything.

She stopped in a broad glade flanked by ancient trees, and the moon's mottled face looked down at her from a ragged patch of sky. The trees faced her in their silent ranks, pale and leprous in the moonlight. Her elven sensibilities reached out to them and were appalled by what they encountered. The trees were unable to have what they most desired: the ability to walk the land, doling out pain to blot out their own. Rooted in helpless, seething anger, their malice towards Elgiva was so mordant, she sobbed when she remembered oak-lord Derryth's wholesome consciousness and gentle concern. She shrank back inside herself. But soon, her madness resurfaced.

"I know what you want," she cried. "To turn my power against me, but you can't. It's mine, and now it's going to teach you all a lesson."

Turning in a circle, she called up her powers, but there was no answer to her summons. Exhausted, she sank to her knees. Clawing clods of soil from the earth, she threw them at the trees. "Curse you, you ugly, unnatural spawn of rotten fruit! You think I'm weak, but all I need is practice. Then you'll know what fear is. Stop laughing at me, you monsters!"

Godwin dashed out of the shadows into the moonlit glade. He stopped to catch his breath and listened as Elgiva shouted at the trees. He didn't know what to do.

A quickening breeze had started up and fanned the flames of the burning tree. Fire gnawed its way towards them. They had to flee the forest.

Seeing the childish behaviour of his friend, concern for her well-being chased away the last of the forest's enchantment, and he felt sane once more.

Elgiva glared at him in protest. "They dare to defy me, but I'll show them."

Godwin strode towards her and dragged her to her feet. "Be

The Exile of Elindel

reasonable, can't you? We've more important things to do than waste our time on these sad, old sticks of firewood. For Frigg's sake, come to your senses! The forest is alight." He grasped her shoulders and shook her firmly, but his words were gentle and soft. "Can you understand what I'm saying?"

She blinked at him, clearing the tears from her eyes, and then nodded, and he released her.

"Forgive me for what I did to you, for what I would have done," he said. "I'd never, never hurt you. It was the will of the forest. At least, I have to believe that."

She shied away from his gaze and clawed the strands of hair from her face. "Godwin, listen, I . . . " She looked about her, as though bewildered to see the shards of her reason scattered at her feet. "I fear the trees haven't finished with us yet. I think we'd better leave."

He grabbed her hand and they turned to run, but to their horror, a mass of brambles reared up in their path. The underwood, stealthy and silent and rife with barbs, had crawled towards them. On what had been an open stretch of ground, there now stood a tangle of thorny shrubs.

"By Frigg, it's impossible!" Godwin cried. "We're trapped. The forest has trapped us!"

Wherever he looked, their path was blocked by shrubs and briars and weeds.

"It knows it's going to die," cried Elgiva, "and it's making sure that we die with it!"

"We have no choice, Elgiva. We must get through these brambles. Look, it's thinnest here!"

He pulled her along. Behind them, he could hear the fangs of the fire devouring the old, dry wood, and it increased his sense of urgency, but at a gasp from Elgiva, he pulled up short.

"What is it?" he demanded.

"The trees, the trees! They're helpless. They're screaming! It's all my fault." She sobbed, and her legs began to fold beneath her.

He seized her and dragged her along. "There's nothing we can do about it. And why should we care? Would the forest have cared about us?"

Brambles tried to snare their legs. Elgiva stumbled and couldn't get up; the sharp thorns dragged her down. Godwin tried to wrench her free, and the cruel barbs ripped their hands and faces.

"I can't do it," she wailed.

Godwin tried to calm her, but his throat was clogged with panic. The fire was raging behind them. "Don't give up. Wrap your cloak about you tightly. Protect yourself from the thorns."

He succeeded in hauling her upright. He pressed her body close to his and guided her through the briars. Their progress was slow. Smoke stung their eyes, and rain hissed like malice in the canopy above.

It was hopeless. The forest had won.

A brave hope flickered in his brain, one that he hardly dared voice. "If only I had my sword, perhaps I could hack a way out of this mess."

Elgiva clutched at his tunic. Her large eyes gleamed in the ochre-tinted darkness.

"Perhaps, perhaps I could," she said. "Why not?"

"Could you?"

"I have to try. I know I couldn't clear these brambles, but retrieving your sword . . . there is need." She gulped down several lungfuls of air. "I must find some words to help me focus."

Elgiva stood in silence for several moments, her eyes closed and her body trembling. Then she spoke.

"Sword of steel, hear what I say,

"Hie to your master without delay.

"Leave the place where now you sit.

"I have spoken; so be it."

Elgiva opened her eyes, and in that moment, there was a thud as something heavy fell at Godwin's feet. He stooped, touched the object, and instantly recoiled.

"Ow! It's hot!" They both laughed with relief. "Thank the gods I sharpened it. When it's cool, I'll make short work of these bushes."

Elgiva looked down at the glinting weapon. "That was easier than I expected," she said, wiping the sweat from her eyes with her sleeve. "Too easy."

"Strong magic, then," suggested Godwin.

She shook her head. There was something odd about this blade.

THE EXILE OF ELINDEL

Should she share her suspicions with Godwin? In the end, she merely said, "The sword wanted the summons."

Godwin was clearly puzzled by the strangeness of her remark and unable to respond.

Elgiva turned to him. "I'm sure it's cool now. You can pick it up." When he hesitated, she touched his arm. "Trust me."

Chapter Sixteen

A GOLDEN SUN peeped over the horizon and daylight illumined the dim, grey land. Godwin was lying on open ground, where exhaustion had left him the previous night. He sat up slowly. He had no idea where he was. His face and hands were covered in scratches and his clothes were torn by brambles, but his sword was in its scabbard and his knife was in his belt. Their pack lay next to him on the sodden earth. It seemed all he had lost were his wits.

Beside him, Elgiva sat up, stretched, and yawned as Godwin got to his feet.

"I'm soaked," he complained.

"Where are we?" she asked.

She rubbed her eyes with her knuckles and scanned the landscape, as though seeking a friend in a roomful of strangers.

"I suppose I should apologise," he said. "What happened in the forest was my fault. We shouldn't have crossed it so late in the day."

"Do you think it would have been safer at any other time?" Elgiva shook her head and got to her feet. "I think we should forget it. We survived, didn't we? Let's put it behind us."

He looked back at the forest, and to his surprise, it was now transformed into naked, black, and smouldering spars, where once, whole trees had stood. Some of them had survived on the margin, but the heart of the forest was gone.

"A blaze like that would have been visible for miles. We couldn't have done a better job of announcing our arrival. I mean, we're close to Misterell, aren't we?" Godwin scanned the landscape ahead. "Northwest, Kendra said. We'd better get moving. We'll have to skirt round that hill, past those clumps of willow. But we should have some breakfast before we go."

The Exile of Elindel

Elgiva followed the line of his gaze, while he knelt on the ground and rummaged through their pack. "What clumps of willow?" she asked.

He straightened up and squinted at the hill. "I could have sworn..."

"Perhaps my great-uncle's not an old fool after all, unless you're both prone to seeing things."

He handed her a chunk of bread. "Elgiva? I know you said to forget it, but..."

She turned to face him. "What?"

"What happened in the forest. Did it really happen?"

"Haven't we the wounds to prove it?" She lifted her chin and bared her throat. Across the smooth, pale skin was a shallow cut, covered by a crust of dried blood: the work of Godwin's sword.

"Elgiva, I could have killed you!"

Realisation widened her eyes. "And I you!" She clapped her hand to her mouth in sick horror.

Godwin touched the wound on his shoulder which, until this moment, they had both forgotten. Nauseated at what he might find, he explored the site of the injury, and the colour drained from his face. Elgiva snatched his hand away, but what she saw clearly bewildered her. Although the fabric of his tunic was slashed, the skin beneath it was unmarked.

"I don't understand," she cried.

"Elgiva? How?"

"I don't know, Godwin. But I know it happened. All of it did. I hit you with all the strength I could find, though it shames me to admit it. I should have taken off your arm! And look, we're covered in scratches. It must have happened, but why I'm injured and you're not, I can't explain. If we're close to Misterell, I'm afraid weirder things might happen yet. We need to doubt everything we see."

"Including the evidence we leave behind us?" He nodded towards the forest.

"Can we believe what our eyes tell us in such a place as this?"

"It's hard not to," he replied. "How else will we know what is and what is not?"

"Our hearts must guide us, as Bellic's guided him when he sought the kingdom of Misterell." She paused and drew a deep breath. "I sometimes wonder if it isn't all an illusion. Life itself, I mean. Do you ever feel that way?"

He took her hand. "I may have lost my bearings, but I can't doubt reality or the fact of my existence. I have substance, and so do you. Last night . . . " He paused and tried to recall their ordeal. "It can't all have been illusion. Something we shared was real. I know that as surely as I know my own name." He checked himself and frowned. "But I don't really know that, do I? It's not easy for me, Elgiva. This world is so unlike the one I know."

"And mine. Magic has always frightened me, but now that I know I'm a wardain, there's something that frightens me more."

"What's that?"

"I've no real proof that I have any magic. If what happened in the Forest of Shades was all a trick, then perhaps the power I used was also an illusion. But if my magic is real, I still have no hope of learning how to use it properly."

"Whatever the truth is, it won't come to us," said Godwin, feeling decisive. "We must seek it out."

For the rest of that day, they travelled on with grey clouds and grey thoughts for company. On the second day, the sun warmed and burned off the clouds, and the landscape around them glowed with new vigour. Woodland plants stretched out their soft, new leaves and danced in the haze beneath the trees. The air was vibrant with the sounds of spring and heavy with its perfume.

As they emerged from a wooded area and crossed a sun-filled meadow, they saw two figures some way ahead. One was a dun-coloured pony, the other an old man in a dirty, grey robe who sat on the ground beside the animal. As Elgiva and Godwin approached him, he rubbed his ankle with arthritic fingers and muttered to himself. He seemed to be frail and harmless, and Godwin ventured to speak to him.

"Hello, old man. What's amiss?"

Startled, the man's eyes widened in fear. His thin white hair, standing stiffly on his skull, gave him an air of distraction.

Godwin approached him with care. "Can we help you?" he asked.

The old man grinned at him, revealing stained and broken teeth. "Oh, what a blessing to see you, lad. Yes, indeed, what a place to be lost in," he said, his voice hoarse with age and distress.

"Are you hurt?" asked Elgiva.

The Exile of Elindel

"Ye gods! An elf!" exclaimed the old man. He made to rise but fell back with a grimace of pain.

"Don't be afraid," Godwin said. "You're safe with us, I promise."

"By all the stars! A Briton and an elf! Strange company for an old Saxon to fall in with. An' I'm safe, say you?"

"I promise you," said Godwin. "Now, what's wrong with your foot?"

"Fell an' twisted it on some rocks. By the ancients, but what I'm doin' out here, the gods themselves don't know! An' this ole pony be no use nor ornament. Stubborn, that's what she is."

"Where are you bound?" Elgiva asked.

"Like I told you, I'm lost. Travellin' for days, an' here I be, lost, with a twisted ankle an' this ole bag o' bones. Was e'er a man so tried? I was off to sell this vermin at market, but the eyes, I suppose, they've led me agley, an' I can't see the right road for lookin'."

"Where are you from?" Elgiva persisted.

"Many days to the north. I've got this little homestead, see. Some acres of land. Do a bit o' farmin'. I was on my way to the neighbourin' village. Should have been there two days since. Must have took a wrong turn back at the crossroads, but I'm a born fool, I reckon. If I don't sell some stock, I'll starve. Times are bad, see. The wife, she joined her ancestors. A cold snap took her, just like that, and my only son, he died last harvest. Got the bloody flux, he did. I had two lads helpin' out, an' they ran off one day. Well, I ask you, how's a man to live? So here I be, lost and alone, wi' a twisted ankle an' a stubborn nag what's no use but for hound meat. I think the gods are punishing me for my idle and misspent youth. My old gaffer always said I'd come to grief one day."

Godwin smiled, but Elgiva looked thoughtful and her eyes were fixed on the pony.

"Let me see your ankle," said Elgiva.

"Well, I don't know—"

"I'll not put a spell on you, if that's what you're thinking," she snapped.

Godwin glared at her, surprised at her asperity, but the man gave her a peculiar grin and held out his injured leg. Godwin tried to lighten the mood.

"We don't have much food, but you're welcome to share it," he said.

"The moment I set eyes on you, I knew you was kind-hearted," said the Saxon. "There's few as would stop for a codger like me, except to rob me, of course. But don't you worry. I've plenty of food, an' I'd be honoured if you'll partake. I've bread an' meat aplenty in that pack on the pony's back, an' you'll dine well this night—an' you, Grimalkin," he shouted, half-turning towards the animal, "you can get off up that hill an' fill your belly wi' grass! I call her Grimalkin, for she's as spiteful an' wayward as an ole she-cat." He shook his fist at the pony. "Get on, willful beast, or you'll feel the end o' my boot."

"There's nothing wrong . . . that I can see," said Elgiva, in a somewhat sardonic tone.

"Eh?" The old man narrowed his eyes at her.

"Your ankle. There's nothing broken. Perhaps you should give it a rest."

The Saxon slowly nodded his thanks. For a long moment, she studied him before getting to her feet with a sigh, and giving Godwin a look that he couldn't decipher, she walked towards the pony.

"There's some nice grass up on that slope," she said.

The pony allowed Elgiva to lead her away.

The Saxon indicated Elgiva with a sideways nod of his head. "That creature has a way wi' animals, but she don't care for men."

"Well," said Godwin with a shrug, "she's an elf."

"Suspicious, eh?"

"What? Yes, perhaps, and probably with good reason. She'll come round sooner or later."

"Hope so. Can't stand bad feelin'. Puts me on edge, it does. At least you seem a friendly sort. What do they call you, son?"

"A great many things, no doubt, but mainly they call me Godwin. My friend is Elgiva."

"An' I go by the name of Oswald. Oswald Elricson."

"Elricson," mused Godwin, suddenly missing the young lad. "I knew an Elric once. I used to work for his father."

They chatted until Elgiva returned, the pony at her side. She had a troubled look on her face. Oswald smiled in welcome, but she quickly looked away.

"Well, Oswald," asked Godwin, "what are your plans?"

The Exile of Elindel

The Saxon shook his head. "Can't say for sure. To one that's lost, any path will suit. I could travel with you a ways, if you don't mind, o' course. Might find my way back home."

"We travel alone," said Elgiva.

Godwin winced at the tone of her voice. "It's better we do," he said, making amends for his friend's curt manner. "We follow a dangerous road."

"Well, by the gods!" Oswald declared. "I've been on many a dangerous road, an' most had more holes than these rags I'm wearin'."

"How odd that someone so widely travelled should get lost going to market," remarked Elgiva.

"Look here. I never said I was widely travelled," Oswald protested, looking offended. "I've been about a bit, you know, but not all over the place. An' goin' to market, well, that's different. It's on a road I don't much use. Never fell on hard times till now, an' had no reason to go to market to sell off my only chattels." He shook his head and sighed. "You was right, lad, when you said elves was suspicious."

"But . . . " Godwin's attempt at an explanation was silenced by the hurt and angry look in Elgiva's eyes. "Well, er, we'd best be on our way. I suppose you can travel with us a short while, until your ankle's better." He glanced at Elgiva, but she turned her back on him. "Can I help you onto your pony, Oswald?"

"Nay, lad, I can shift for myself, as long as she stands still. Perhaps you'd hold her head, son?"

Godwin took hold of the leather bridle, while Oswald struggled to perch himself upon the animal's back.

"Are we ready, then?" asked Godwin.

Elgiva glared at him and began to walk ahead. Grimalkin trotted after her, as though she had heard a spoken command. Feeling somewhat dejected, Godwin brought up the rear, the image of Elgiva's reproving gaze refusing to fade from his mind.

For a while, they travelled in silence, but Godwin found that he couldn't bear the burden of his guilt, and Elgiva's manner worried him. He quickened his pace and caught up with her.

"I'm sorry about that," he whispered so Oswald wouldn't hear. "Elgiva, it's not what you think."

She shrugged. "It doesn't matter."

"Well, then, what's wrong?"

She looked at him, but he was aware that he only had half of her attention. "That pony. She won't talk to me."

"What?"

Elgiva seemed too preoccupied to pay him further heed, but he had no idea what was wrong with her. Was she annoyed because the pony had snubbed her? He dropped back, shrugging his shoulders, content to let her sulk alone.

They had covered almost two leagues when Elgiva stopped. Ignoring Oswald, she said to Godwin, "We'll stay here for the night."

"But lass," protested Oswald, "there's several hours of daylight left."

"I think your pony is tired."

"And I'm hungry," Godwin declared, adding under his breath, "not that anyone cares." He surveyed their surroundings. They were standing in a shallow dell, sheltered by a few small trees. "A good enough place to set up camp." He held out his hand to help Oswald dismount.

The old man shrugged and clambered down. "By the gods, I'm stiff! Like sittin' on top of a sack full o' stones!"

Godwin turned to speak to his friend but stopped when he saw her expression. She was watching Oswald and seemed to be quite perplexed. Her gaze slid to Godwin and became immediately blank. She strode off towards the lip of the dell and sat down with her back towards them.

The pony moved and lumbered after her.

Godwin set to work collecting wood for a fire. He glanced at his friend, but the rigour of her back defied communication. Since their ordeal in the Forest of Shades, he had come to feel they were equals, had almost forgotten she was an elf, but now her aloofness called to mind her perplexing, elvish nature. She was a being from a magical world, who talked to animals and hated wilthkin. Perhaps she was only with him on sufferance.

He chided himself. Elgiva had a great deal to worry about, and he was being feeble. A proper meal and a good night's sleep would soon put things to rights.

THE EXILE OF ELINDEL

By the time dusk had fallen, a chill breeze tugged at the trees around the dell. Godwin and the old man sat before a roaring fire, grateful for its warmth, while Elgiva continued to sit apart, like a sentinel watching the gathering night.

Hating their separation, Godwin was beginning to resent the Saxon's presence. The sight of Elgiva sitting alone in the cold was more than he could bear, and he decided to try to persuade her to join them. Leaving Oswald to finish his meal, he strolled across the dell and sat beside his friend.

"Elgiva?"

"What now?"

He frowned. "Come to the fire and eat."

"Leave me alone," she said. "I don't want his food."

"Why not?" he demanded. "Why do you sit here? Have I offended you?"

She looked at him and her features softened. "No," she said, lowering her eyes. "I don't like him. I don't know why. I just don't trust him, Godwin." She sighed and ran her fingers through her hair. "He has an unpleasant aura."

"Well, a bath wouldn't go amiss," he jested.

She cut him dead with a glare. "It's not funny!"

He sighed with exasperation. "I'm sorry. Look, I don't want him here anymore than you do, but we're stuck with him for the night. Tomorrow, we'll send him on his way."

After an awkward pause, she said, "Perhaps elves are suspicious."

"I had to explain—"

"I can explain my own actions."

"Can you?" he asked. "I'm not so sure of that. Be reasonable, Elgiva. You were far too rude."

"And you were far too friendly."

"By Frigg, I had to be! Poor harmless old man. One of us had to show him some pity. Besides, Elgiva, he's one of my kind."

"He's a Saxon!" she snapped.

"He's a human being!"

She looked at him, and for a moment, her eyes reflected something torn between hurt and envy. Then she smirked. "Is he?"

"Yes, and I felt sorry for him. I suppose it's good to talk to a normal person again." Godwin regretted this statement as soon as he had uttered it.

"I see."

He gave her a hesitant smile. "I do believe you're jealous."

She scowled. "How you mistake me, wilthkin! But I warn you; be on your guard. Something is wrong here. I feel it. What will it take to teach you caution?" She turned her back on him.

"By Frigg, you're impossible!"

Chapter Seventeen

Beside the cheery campfire, Godwin lay wrapped in his cloak, his body aching for sleep, but Oswald was a lively character who seemed to need no rest. As soon as darkness had fallen and they had settled down for the night, the old Saxon began a monologue. The history of his thrilling life was a tale long in the telling, and Godwin felt a wave of relief when finally it crawled to a close. But Oswald hadn't finished.

"You know, what puzzles me, young man, is what you two are doin' out here. You're in the middle of nowhere. You could be attacked by wolves, an' there's robbers on the road. You're miles away from the nearest village." He paused and threw more wood on the fire, then looked at Godwin askance. "You runnin' away from somethin'?"

Godwin floundered at the change of subject.

"You're not lost, surely? Such capable folk as you? Folk like me get lost all the time." His manner was affable, matter-of-fact, yet Godwin felt ill at ease. "By the way, if you want some real strong ale, there's some in Grimalkin's pack. Or if you're a man as likes somethin' a bit different, well, I've got these mushrooms, you know." He grinned in the firelight.

Godwin raised his eyebrows, then shook his head.

"As you please. They're not easy to come by, so I don't mind keepin' 'em all to myself. There's few pleasures left at my age. Not like you young folk, eh? What was I sayin'? Ah, yes. Seems to me you're ill-prepared for travellin'. Hardly any food an' no pack animals."

Godwin swallowed hard and his mind laboured. "Er, we had some trouble in that quarter."

"Robbed on the road, were you? There's worse can happen, I

reckon. Lone travellers are good sport, you know. Aye, you never can tell who you'll meet far from home, on a lone track in the dark. So, where are you headin' for now, then?"

"We're looking for a village," said Godwin.

"A village? What, Saxon? What village is that?"

"Where . . . where they breed the best pack-ponies in the land. My father wants six for his farmstead." Godwin was rather impressed with this invention, but the look of doubt in Oswald's rheumy eyes gave him second thoughts.

"An' there's another thing. I don't know why you're with an elf, but if I was you, I'd drop her. You can't go into no village wi' an elf. Folk would run a mile. There'd be a bloody riot, son. Ain't you afeard of elves?"

"I was," said Godwin, "but now I know better."

Oswald gasped, like a man whose knowledge weighed heavily upon him. "Wish I could say the same, I'm sure. I've heard some tales, but, well, best not to say."

"What sort of tales?" asked Godwin, his interest reviving.

"Nay. Happen it's all tittle-tattle."

Godwin sat up. "No, go on, but—" he lowered his voice to a whisper, "—more quietly, if you can."

Oswald drew closer and glanced right and left, as though afraid the shadows had ears. "Have you ever heard of, or seen, a man what's elf-shot? I mean, really?"

"I've heard many claim it," said Godwin, "but they were fooling themselves, I think. Some people always need someone to blame for their problems, rather than blame themselves."

"Son, believe me, I've seen it, an' I don't want to see it again." Oswald shivered. "Young Eadric it was. A good-lookin' lad from t'other valley. Well, one fair mornin', Eadric went out to the wood behind the farm, collectin' berries an' such. We all knew there was elves there, but Eadric, he didn't give a crone's cuss. That night, he came staggerin' home, wild-eyed he was, an' his face as pale as a linen clout. Said the elves bewitched him for trespassin' on their land. He took to his bed that very night an' never got up again. We all knew he had been cursed with the blister. Burnin' up wi' fever, he was. Terrible to see.

"As soon as I got wind of it all, I rushed straight over to help, but

The Exile of Elindel

I saw him breathe his last, his body a bloated mass, covered in great purple blisters. It fair turned my stomach, an' I'm not the squeamish type. To think he was once a fine young lad—not unlike yourself."

Was it a trick of the firelight, or did the old man have a sly grin on his face?

"I'm tryin' to warn you of perils your young mind is ignorant of," added Oswald.

"I'm much obliged," said Godwin. "It's a strange tale, indeed, by Grim." He lay down and made himself comfortable, hoping that Oswald had finished for the night.

"An' there's somethin' else, though it isn't easy to talk of, but I see you'd best know about it—just to be on the safe side."

Oswald frowned and hesitated, as though debating whether or not it was wise for him to continue.

Godwin sat up and stared at him, his curiosity roused.

"What is it?" he asked.

"Well, you see, son, these elves, they have a way about them. They're enchanters, see, an' can poison your mind. They take on disguises to fool us. Seems to mean something to you, lad?"

"No, no. Please go on."

"Well, they're damned clever, see, an', well, sensual. To them, seducin' a mortal man is the height of entertainment. They have strong passions, you understand, an' a likin' for trickin' innocent lads into their beds—"

"Now just a minute . . ."

Godwin tried to protest, to find the words, but logic had forsaken him. He eyed the old man. He had no reason to lie, and like all old men, he loved a good tale. There was often truth in tales, and he was well aware elves were jealous, gloating beings who hated to be crossed. He travelled with one, didn't he? Elgiva had magic, too, and cursing a man with blisters might not be beyond her reach. He remembered also, with a sudden pang, her Saxon disguise and the way she had enchanted him when he first saw her true appearance.

"Mind you," said Oswald, "you can take care of yourself, I'm sure. Took you for a warrior at first. Can't understand what a farmer's lad would be doin' wi' a sword like that. A goodly, bold weapon indeed. I've been admirin' it, so I have. Would you mind if I had a look?"

Oswald's eyes grew large and round, and Godwin saw a gleam in them that smacked of greed. He clasped the sword and shook his head. "No." He drew a deep breath and forced a smile. "No, it's dangerous. Very sharp."

Oswald shrugged. "We'd best get a bit o' sleep. Nice talkin' to you, but an ole man needs his rest, you know. You young folk don't think o' that. Good night, then. Sleep well." He yawned, pulled the thin blanket over his chest, and settled down to sleep. Then he chuckled. "Happen I'll sleep wi' one eye open, lest your friend gets a funny mood on her in the middle o' the night."

Muttering oaths under his breath, Godwin lay down once more. Fatigue had made him gullible, and he had lapped up Oswald's chatter like the credulous dolt he was. Although he refused to believe it all, some doubts still lurked in his mind, doubts that sprang from his fear of things he didn't understand: elves and magic and the unknown horrors that crouched at the marge of reality.

Finally, Godwin fell asleep.

At his side, the old man sat up. Sure that his movement had gone undetected, he shrugged off his blanket and got to his feet. He strolled across the moonlit sward to the lip of the dell, where Elgiva sat, her chin cupped in her hands. She heard him approach and raised her head.

"Your ankle has made a remarkable recovery," she observed without turning round.

He halted at the sound of her voice and chuckled.

"Thought you'd fallen asleep," he said. "I was restless, see. Needed to stretch the ole legs. My ankle was only twisted. The rest must have done it good. Mind if I join you, lass?"

"As you please," she said.

"Stars are bright tonight," he remarked. He drew nearer and seated himself upon the grass. "You're keepin' a lonely vigil out here. What you watchin' for? You got enemies?"

Something sly about his tone made her look at him. She paused and then said, "We all have enemies."

"Yet you're travellin' wi' one. Elves an' men don't mix, you know. Sad, I reckon, 'cause elves ain't bad folk. No worse than us, at least. You ain't the first I've seen, you know. The woods are teemin' wi' elves back home, but they keep to themselves an' don't cause no trouble." He shook his head. "Aye, less trouble than them damned Britons. They're a funny lot. Can't be trusted at all. But elves, they mind their own business."

He paused, and Elgiva knew he wanted some kind of response. A sigh of boredom was all he deserved.

He paused and shuffled nearer. "You know, I think it fittin' I give you some advice. Be careful o' the company you keep, lass. That friend o' yours has a runaway tongue. It doesn't matter in front o' me, 'cause I'm an honest wight an' take it all wi' a pinch o' salt. But there's some folks might wonder a bit. Might think his wits had gone wool-gatherin'."

"You underestimate me," Elgiva said at length. "Especially my sense of hearing. I know what's passed between you. I might have found it entertaining, had your sport not been at my friend's expense." She turned and gave him an icy glare. "What game are you playing?"

Oswald looked surprised, feigned innocence, and then he laughed.

"I'm not a fool," Elgiva assured him. "What's the meaning of this act of yours, and furthermore, who are you?"

"I'm a poor ole man," moaned Oswald, "an' if my mind sometimes wanders, then 'tis no fault o' mine."

"You can do better than that," she said.

There was a brief, tense silence.

"I should need to do a great deal better to fool you, little elf. I have nothing but praise for your perspicacity."

Elgiva stared at Oswald, amazed at the change in his voice. He smiled at her; a cruel and cunning smile that had nothing in common with humour. Then he sighed and stretched himself, as though set free from a tiny cell.

"Who are you?" demanded Elgiva, but she half-feared she knew the answer.

He raised a sinewy hand and stroked her cheek. Though filled with revulsion, she couldn't pull away.

"I am not as I appear, of course," he said. "You knew something was amiss, but this is such an excellent disguise that you could not pierce the illusion, could you? Well, I'm not a Saxon. Neither am I old. What am I then, think you?"

"I . . . I . . ."

"Come now, little elf, you do not need to fear me. I am your friend. Your only true friend in all the world, though as yet you cannot see it. I know your heart."

His vivid blue eyes gleamed, grew larger, and emitted an inner glow that animated his features. His hand snaked out and fastened on her arm. Drawing her towards him, he rested her head upon his lap and stroked her forehead with a silken touch. Mesmerised, her limbs relaxed. A warm, narcotic glow spread throughout her being.

She struggled to focus on her captor, and within the nimbus of power he had thrown about himself, she saw a male elf, neither young nor old, but strong and lean and handsome. His features were so perfect, they could have been sculpted out of marble by a master at the art. His high, intelligent forehead was crowned by glossy black hair which fell to his shoulders in gleaming waves, while above his large black eyes, his eyebrows arched wickedly, full of dark humour.

Yet despite his beauty, his face had a contradictory appearance, for it seemed at the same time both cruel and kind. When he spoke, his voice was as sweet as honey, but as sour as vinegar, too.

"Forgive my little disguises," he said, "but sometimes I grow bored, and when I do, I must make mischief. But this is preferable, is it not? A handsome fellow, would you not say? I assure you this is my true appearance, yet gladly will I assume another, if it does not please you. Great magic knows no limits."

He continued to stroke her brow, his touch as soft as a butterfly's wing, as soothing and warm as a mere in summer, yet as numbing and cold as a winter frost. Elgiva's eyes refused to stay open.

As she lay helplessly sprawled in his lap, she felt herself floating over fields of flowers, the Earth a pageant of colour below, the mountains glimmering in the sun . . .

No, this is an illusion . . .

She opened her eyes and blinked at the night.

"Do not oppose me," he murmured. "I mean you no harm. You see how magic can be used to subdue, how easy it is to beguile? I regret your inexperience, but I, Vieldrin, can teach you."

She struggled to resist him, to find a spark of awakening power, but he tightened the clench of his magic about her.

THE EXILE OF ELINDEL

"The King of Misterell is your friend," he purred, "and you are safe with me. Quite safe."

He lowered his head and kissed her mouth, and the pleasure of his embrace melted her resistance. Her lips tingled. The coercion of magic made her his thrall. He slowly released her and studied her face.

"We are two of a kind," he breathed. "You are safe with me. We are Eldrakin. And you are safe with me."

"Yes."

"You are safe with me. I am your friend."

"Yes."

"I am your friend. You trust me."

"Yes."

"Thallinore is a fool," he said. "He talks too freely, and I know all. It did not require a great stretch of my intellect to work out what you are up to. And I know you for what you are: a precious jewel of Elvendom. Mine, dear heart. My jewel. What would I want with a dolt such as he, with magic dulled by unworthy blood? He believes I am his protector, but he is useful to me. That and nothing more. But you, I would not use. You would not be taken in, I think. Clever little elf. But here I must apologise, for one of my disguises frightened you—though even then, you knew it was a trick. It was cruel of me, but I had to test your mettle, to see what you were made of. You have potential, I admit. And you intend to find the Lorestone, do you?"

Elgiva struggled to speak. "Yes."

"Unhappily for you, so do I."

Fighting the spell that cocooned her, she gasped out, "You were afraid of me."

"Afraid, dear heart?" He laughed. "Wary, nothing more. Wary and respectful of your little powers, my sweeting. If I feared anything, it was that I might harm you. I wanted to assess your strength. Thallinore thought you had no powers since you did not use them when he banished you. You let those scum abuse you. But even then, he feared you, for he is a cringing coward. I also wanted to determine your heart's true inclinations. How distressed I was to find it set so resolutely against me. It pained me, little elf, for I wished only to be your friend."

"My heart will always . . . be set . . . against . . . evil . . . "

"Your heart has been warped by weak elves and wilthkin. But I will win your heart, as I will win the Lorestone. You do not know your true self, but I do. Power will excite you. Power is a drug you will come to crave."

"Never."

"Be that as it may, dear heart," he said with a sigh, "you will come to realise that what I am to tell you is the only way. It is inevitable. Mark me well. You and I together, with the stone, would be invincible. As allies, we could rule the Earth. What could we not achieve together? As King and Queen of Misterell, we would build a powerful dynasty, and our children would inherit our conquests. The stain of wilthkin would be removed from this land, and all elves would kneel before us. Even Faine would seem weak in comparison to our power."

Elgiva was aghast. "You can't deceive me. You can't. You know I'll find the stone. The *Ninth Book* says—"

"The *Ninth Book* comes from Misterell. How do you know it is genuine? But harken to me, Elgiva, I will give my kingdom to you as a gift to seal the alliance between us. It was a disorganised kingdom when it fell into my lap. My father was weak and foolish." Vieldrin's lip curled. "But now I have it all in order. My subjects resented the rule of law and stuck to their idle ways. They thought to oppose me, as you do but were soon to discover the extent of my wrath. They are a mere handful now, but they always do my bidding. They have learned the wisdom of obedience. A king must be strong and brook no insolence from a rabble of inferiors."

"You murdered your own people?"

"I did what was necessary," he replied. "Do not trouble yourself with such thoughts. The loss of a few silly elves is beneath consideration. I have set my sights on higher things."

"You won't succeed. I'll find it. I'll find the stone and I'll defeat you," declared Elgiva, but her voice sounded too feeble for her purpose.

"Poor, misguided creature. Would you risk your life for those who do not love you as I do? I am King of Misterell and have never found the Lorestone. Small hope have you, and even less of using it with your adolescent powers. But so be it. It shall be a game between us. A contest. I shall enjoy that. Yet if you do not finally see the sense in what I have said and if you persist in opposing me, then regrettably, I will destroy you." He laughed, and his teeth glimmered like pearls in the moonlight. "Power, they say—those who have none—is a corrupting force, but I know it will divert you to a truer path. A path that leads to my friendship. How sweet would be the union between us? We are so alike, dear heart. And there is none to equal you in all Elvendom, none as worthy to be my queen. You will realise that I am your only hope. In fact, I am your destiny." He tutted and then frowned in mock apology. "In the name of Smirill, how remiss of me. Here I am, chattering on, and quite forgetting an important disclosure I had come here to make. It is most inexcusable. Will you forgive me? I have good news for you, my dear, though it will make your obstinacy even more unthinkable." He stroked her hair for a moment and gazed up at the night sky, sighing.

"You see," he went on in silken tones, "I was charged to tell you that your banishment is revoked."

Elgiva tensed beneath his touch but was powerless to move.

"Furthermore, the King of Elindel has given you to me. You are your master's gift to me to seal the alliance between us. As the property of your betters, you must do as they decree. So you will be my bride. The oath of fealty you made to the king in the name of that old fool Faine still applies, so you are bound to honour your master's pledge."

Elgiva struggled to rail at him, but her voice was a croak of helpless ire. "You lie."

He shook his head. "Whether you like it or not, dear heart, you belong to me. Would you dishonour your vow to Faine? Anyway, I will leave that to your conscience. It is time for me to go."

He bent and kissed her on the lips, and his power drew back, the spell of coercion lifting. Shaking the mist from her mind, she pushed herself away from him.

"I don't believe you!" she cried. "You're using me to get the stone, and once I've outlived my usefulness—"

"Do not even think such thoughts. I am your friend, Elgiva."

She tossed back her hair and made anger the shield for her fear and abhorrence. "Your spell has faded. Is that the best you can do?"

He got easily to his feet. His stately frame towered over her. "A weak spell sufficed to subdue you, my dear. Now I must go. I eagerly await our next meeting. But before I leave, should I draw your attention to something that you may already have noticed?"

She frowned.

"Your friend, Elgiva."

"What of him?"

"That sword of his . . . "

"I know."

"Of course." He turned to leave but stopped. "By the way, please keep that pony. She is a true beast. I placed a spell of silence on her after I stole her from the old wilthkin who owned her, but it is lifted now. Take the food also. I do not wish to see you starve before the start of our contest. Where is the fun in that? Do not worry, dear heart, none of it is poisoned. I fully intend us to meet in Misterell."

Chapter Eighteen

Godwin's eyes focused on another day. He noticed Oswald's absence at once. Elgiva was also missing. At least the pony was keeping him company. She stood a few yards away from him, regarding him with perfect indifference. In fact, as her jaws munched a mouthful of grass, she seemed to be looking straight through him.

He sat up, stretched and yawned. The campfire was a mound of grey expenditure, as empty and forlorn as the blanket beside him. He rubbed his eyes with his knuckles.

"Can't you stare at something else?" he asked.

The animal tossed her head and snorted.

"Where has everyone gone?"

He got to his feet. Surely, the contours of the ground were now impressed forever into his flesh. "By Frigg, you're an ugly brute," he exclaimed.

The animal flashed the whites of her eyes at him.

"If I was an elf, we could have a chat to pass the time. There's no one else to talk to round here, and when there is, they either bite your head off or bore you to death with their endless chatter." He looked about him and frowned. "Perhaps I've been abandoned. Well, no reason why I should starve."

He walked towards the pony, intending to take some food from her pack, but she whinnied at him and backed away. Sighing with impatience, he approached her again. This time, she showed him her large, yellow teeth, her brown eyes round with the promise of violence.

Godwin cocked his fists on his hips. "Well, perhaps I'll starve after all."

Whinnying, the pony turned and kicked out her hind legs, just missing him with her hooves. She galloped out of the dell, leaving Godwin alone with his hunger.

Muttering oaths, he wandered out of the dell through the trees behind him. A short walk took him to a bubbling stream, where he splashed cold water on his face. The sun was newly risen, and its rays slanted like threads of steam across the land before him. It was a fresh, mild morning and the emerald vistas called for his appreciation, but hunger was gnawing in his gut. He decided to wander back to the dell with the hope of somehow procuring breakfast.

When he arrived, Elgiva was already preparing food. The pony lounged beside her, her jaws once more munching grass.

"Hello," greeted Elgiva, "I wondered where you were."

"Me?" returned Godwin. "Where were you?"

"Just a short walk. To clear the cobwebs. It's a beautiful day."

"You haven't slept, have you?"

"By Faine, does it show that much?" Elgiva laughed.

"Well, it seems to have done you good," he said. "You seem a bit more cheerful. You should go without sleep more often."

Her eyebrows drew together, and she muttered a brief apology.

Godwin shrugged. "I understand. Don't worry. I forgive you."

"I don't need forgiveness from a wilthkin," she said. "And your understanding is given without knowledge."

Godwin bowed with mock servility and then turned to face the pony. "You see, Grimalkin, when it comes to saying the wrong thing, you can always rely on me."

Sighing, Elgiva looked at Godwin, and then she handed him a bowl of oatcakes, liberally spread with honey. "Sit down and eat your breakfast."

Godwin obeyed her command. "Where's Oswald got to, then?"

Elgiva looked away and grinned. "I believe he was on his way to market when someone stole his pony."

"Well, pardon me if I don't follow any of that," he said with a frown of exasperation.

"I'd better explain." She seated herself beside him, a mischievous glint in her eyes. She hooked her hair behind her ears, folded her hands in her lap, and told him what had happened while he slept.

He completely forgot about breakfast. "Frigg, I had no idea!" he said.

The Exile of Elindel

"Neither did I for certain."

Godwin detected a hint of smugness in her tone. "Well, I was completely taken in. I should have been more guarded. I guess you'll have no choice now but to gloat and have a laugh at my expense."

She seemed taken aback. "You're a wilthkin, Godwin. How could you possibly see the truth behind a glamour of magic? How can I berate you for lacking a skill your kind don't possess?"

"This is one of the few occasions when I've been thankful for my native stupidity. It has spared me your condemnation. But Elgiva, couldn't that nag have told us what was going on?"

"Vieldrin silenced her with magic."

He nodded and chewed on an oatcake. "So, Vieldrin sees this as a game."

"A game he intends to win." She hugged her knees and stared at the ground, the splendour of her hair like a shawl about her shoulders. "He was trying to turn us against each other, but probably just for his own amusement. He tried to tempt me with power and marriage, and he threatened me with a broken vow. It would have been easy for him to kill me, but I know why he refrained. I think he really does believe the prophecies, so I dare say he'll wait until I've found the Lorestone. Whatever his motives, there's a lot more sport to be had in waiting. Watching us struggle towards our goal, knowing he's going to kill us at the end." She sighed and lay back on the grass. "The worst part for me in all of this is he's right. Under elven law, I do belong to him."

He looked at her askance. "No, surely you don't believe that. He's using your integrity against you."

"Perhaps, but I think you know something about the nature of vows, Godwin."

"Perhaps I do," he agreed.

"If I'm no longer exiled, I am bond-servant to the king. I am his to command. If he decrees I belong to Vieldrin, then I do. I vowed such obedience in the name of Faine. No honest elf would break such a vow. Vieldrin is using my love for Faine to force me to be his bride."

"He's cunning and cruel, Elgiva. But Faine wouldn't hold you to such a vow."

"No, I know. But nevertheless . . . " She lifted her torn, sad gaze to the sky and sighed. "Godwin, what Oswald told you, when you thought him just a lost old man, did you believe him?"

The truth might be hurtful, but Godwin didn't want to lie to his friend. He skirted round the question. "It's a rule of mine to take the words of Saxons with a pinch of salt."

"Perhaps you should have believed him. You should know what elves are capable of."

"I may have had second thoughts," he said, "but I knew you weren't like that."

"Indeed?"

"You wouldn't hurt a living thing without a very good reason. Of course, I know nothing of other elves. You might be the only good one among them."

Elgiva stiffened. "You have far too high an opinion of me, Godwin," she said in a small, defeated voice. "I killed the Chief Counsellor and Beortnoth. I left a Saxon raider writhing in pain from my elf-bolt. I burned a forest alive. And there was the shendkin . . ."

"Elgiva, you had good reason to do what you did."

She shook her head. "Killing is just too easy and with real power, it can only be easier. Vieldrin told me power is a drug and I will come to crave it."

"You're not like him."

"How do you know? You say I'm a good elf, perhaps the only good one, for all you know, in which case, be glad I'm the one you're travelling with. But I'm not just an elf; I'm a wardain, and I'm completely unschooled in the use of magic. With my powers, I could easily become the kind of elf Oswald described." She paused and then added, "It would make life so much simpler."

"But you won't," he said.

"You're sure?"

"I won't let you."

Elgiva toyed with a strand of her hair. "I must confess something, Godwin. When I was cold towards you . . . I knew Oswald wasn't as he appeared. I felt he would try to turn you against me, manipulate you in some way, but I had no idea why he should. Now I know who he really was, I realise he could have used an enchantment. It would have been much easier, though I dare say not half so amusing for him. It was wrong of me, but I thought it would be a test of your friendship." She paused, but clearly couldn't look at him, fearing his reaction. "After what happened in the Forest of Shades . . . Look, I'm set on a perilous course, and I have to know who I can trust." She buried her face in her hands. "A test! Faine help me, as if you needed one. All the time you've stayed with me, when you should have been with your family, and I've been cruel and made you suffer even more. Who knows if I may not do so again? Yes, I'm suspicious, Godwin. Perhaps I'm jealous, too. I'm insecure and vain and selfish and lots of other things, but how can I measure friendship when I've known so little of it?"

Tears of shame clung to her long lashes. "I've failed you, Godwin," she sobbed. "Betrayed you. When I suspected Oswald, I should have been straight with you."

Mention of his family had wrung Godwin's heart, but he swallowed his hurt. Leaning towards Elgiva, he put his arm around her. "Perhaps you did right," he said. "Perhaps I needed a test. I'm the first to admit that I'm weak."

"No," she said. "You're stronger than me."

"Whether I am or not, you gave me a warning, remember? But I was too proud to accept it. Besides, had we thwarted Vieldrin's game, who knows what he might have done for his sport?"

"Nevertheless," she said, "I fear you must find me very wearisome. Perhaps time will cure me of many things, if you have the patience to wait." She touched the hand that cupped her shoulder, and he gave her fingers a gentle squeeze. "You're the truest of friends, and I value that more than I can say." She faltered, avoided his gaze. "So I would also value your forgiveness, if I may hope to have it."

"Always," he said.

The companions travelled for the rest of the morning. Elgiva talked to Grimalkin while Godwin watched them from the corner of his eye. He could have felt superfluous, but the sight of them made him smile, and for a time, he forgot the gravity of their quest.

It was later in the afternoon when Godwin became aware of an odd sensation in his mind, as though someone were talking to him just beyond the range of his hearing. He froze. The voice was telling him to turn aside and follow a southerly trail. Straightening himself, he glanced at Elgiva, who was walking some way ahead. He wondered if she were experiencing the same thing, but decided not to mention it, for fear of appearing foolish. To keep his attention focused, he thought of verses he had heard in the mead hall, reciting them to himself to block out all distractions.

He became so set on closing his mind to all external forces that when Elgiva called his name, she had to repeat it several times before it claimed his attention. He looked around. Dusk was falling, and on the horizon, a sprawling mass lay dark against the sky.

Elgiva and Godwin looked at each other. It could have been any forest, but Godwin knew it was Misterell: the object of their quest. He was sure Elgiva must share his conviction.

The pony suddenly cantered away, and when Elgiva and Godwin caught up with her, they found her lapping at a small, shallow pool, its edges broken by rushes. The sun was falling in the west, and they both decided to make camp.

Godwin struggled out of his pack, but he couldn't find the energy required to make a fire. Instead, he strolled to a nearby alder, whose limbs reached out across the pool, and sat himself down at the water's edge. Elgiva joined him, slumped against the trunk of the alder, and let out a sigh.

At length, Godwin fought his languor and returned to a sitting position, but the will was being sucked from his mind and his muscles felt almost useless. "I think there's something wrong," he finally managed to say.

"The enchantment of Misterell saps our will," she said. "It wants us to leave. Do you remember?"

"Bellic."

She combed her hair with her fingers and gazed at the darkening sky. "I'm convinced we should turn back, but it will pass. We must ignore the enchantment."

"I think I should build a fire," he said.

Grimalkin raised her head and stamped one hoof. Elgiva leant forward and gripped Godwin's arm.

"Be on your guard," she whispered. "We have company."

"Where?" hissed Godwin, spinning around. He scanned the foliage.

"That bush over there." She nodded to the right. "Someone's hiding in it."

"I see nothing."

"Neither do I, but Grimalkin and I can sense it."

Godwin fumbled for the hilt of his sword, his fingers clumsy with haste. "Shall we see who it is?"

She shook her head. "No, let it be. I feel it's harmless," she said. "Let's wait and see if it declares itself."

"Whatever you say." Godwin relaxed, his hand spurning the sword.

"No, draw your sword, Godwin," she advised. "We're close to Misterell. It wouldn't hurt to be cautious. We'll have some supper, and then we'll pretend to be asleep."

He raised his eyebrows but voiced no objection, and Elgiva went to fetch their provisions. After making a small fire, they ate without haste and talked awhile. Soon, it was time to bed down, and they wrapped themselves up in Oswald's blanket, resigned to waiting.

Silence settled over them and soon, their pretence of sleep began to approach the reality. At length, whatever had hidden itself moved towards them.

Godwin tightened his grip on his sword, every muscle tensed. Beside him, Elgiva seemed rigid with apprehension. The pony cocked her ears, and the whites of her eyes flashed in the firelight.

A small, dark shape crawled into the open. It crept up to their pack of food and began to rummage inside. Godwin jumped up. He seized the intruder and pinned it down before raising his sword above him. The struggling captive emitted a pitiful squeal.

"He's an elf!" cried Elgiva.

The intruder began to beg for mercy.

"Stop struggling," shouted Godwin. "We won't hurt you."

The elf relaxed a little, and his thin chest heaved as he fought for air. Shortly, he said in the Saxon tongue, "All I wanted was food."

"We'll give you food," said Elgiva calmly. "Don't be afraid. We mean no harm. Godwin, you'd better put some more wood on the fire so we can see what we've caught."

In the fire's glow, they studied their captive more closely as he bolted the food they gave him. He seemed very young, was grimy and barefooted, and his skinny frame was clothed in rags, his hair tangled with burrs. An ugly scar on his left cheek ran from his eye to his chin. His features were pinched with malnutrition, which made his black eyes seem unusually large; they looked like wells of sorrow in which his hopes had drowned.

"Now," said Elgiva, "if you've finished eating, perhaps you could tell us your name."

The elf wiped his mouth on his sleeve. "T-Trystin. My name is Trystin."

"Well, Trystin, this is Godwin, and I am called Elgiva."

The elfling's eyes grew larger. "The one the wise man spoke of?"

Elgiva was surprised. "What did the wise man say?"

"That someone would come to free us." He glanced about him. "He said it was you. But I mustn't tell. And I've kept my secret, lady."

Elgiva regarded him steadily. "How old are you?"

"Twelve, I think. I'm not sure, lady."

"Why are you out here? Where are your parents?"

The elfling lowered his melancholy gaze and his bottom lip trembled. "Dead. A long time. Killed."

"The king?" asked Elgiva gently.

The elfling nodded and turned his face away. Elgiva reached out and took his hand.

"I know your king," she told him. "He's an evil elf. Are you one of his slaves?"

"We all are," said Trystin. "We're cursed and starved and beaten. There's nothing but slavery in Misterell." His red-rimmed eyes were wet with tears, and they gazed at Elgiva in supplication. "Have you come to help us, lady?"

She shouldered his question aside. "This wise man, Trystin, where does he live?"

Trystin's disappointment was naked in his expression. "In the hills beyond the river. He came to Misterell a few months ago. He wore a cloak and a hood, so I don't know what he looks like. I was out collecting mushrooms, lady, near the edge of the forest. He wouldn't tell me his name, but he talked to me and I liked him. He told me of you and said I should meet you. He said I should help you, but I couldn't stay." At this, the tears fell freely down his cheeks, leaving trails in the grime on his skin. He smudged them away with the back of his hand. "He was kind to me, and he trusted me. He promised to visit whenever he could, and I saw him twice, at night.

The Exile of Elindel

It was good to talk to him. I could tell him things. There was no one else I could talk to. But I haven't seen him for weeks, lady."

"Is he an elf?"

He shrugged his thin shoulders. "I don't know, lady, but he spoke in the elven tongue. He asked me what was happening in Misterell, and he said no one must know we'd spoken. The king has lots of spies, he said. I was told to keep watch for you, and when you arrived, I was to help you, but I couldn't stay in Misterell. So I've failed him, haven't I?"

"You've run away," she said matter-of-factly.

"I was afraid," he exclaimed, his dark eyes round with terror. "They caught me stealing bread in the kitchens. They beat me with a stick. So yesterday, I ran away, because . . . because . . ."

"You've had enough of beatings."

Trystin sobbed into his grimy hands, and Elgiva felt a surge of compassion. She reached out and touched his scarred cheek.

"Who did this to you?"

He clapped his hand to the damaged flesh and pulled away, as though ashamed. "The Captain of the Guard," he sniffed. "Two summers ago. For insolence."

Elgiva frowned at this. "Don't back away from me. Come here." She seized his thin arm and drew him towards her. "Whatever happens, trust me. I will not hurt you." She pressed her palm against the scar.

Elgiva focused, ignoring all distractions. For what she wanted to do, she needed to find belief in her powers, to cast aside all previous doubts. No thought of failure could be allowed to spoil her concentration. It was time to consciously summon the magic and bend it to her will.

She had no strong emotion, no threat of danger to trigger her might, so she focused on the ugly scar, the disfigurement of healthy flesh and the cruelty that had caused it. Soon, her anger stirred in response to this unjust act. She brought her will, her ability to heal, and her hatred of cruelty to a point of convergence.

As she focused upon the scar, Trystin trembled in fear.

Elgiva smiled to herself as the magic blossomed in her limbs, quickened, and gathered strength. Power hummed along her nerves. It wasn't magic apt for destruction, but warm and controlled and sanative. When she felt the time was right, she willed it to flow into Trystin's face.

Trystin recoiled, clearly terrified of magic. Godwin, kneeling beside Elgiva, seized the elfling's wrist to keep him still. Godwin snatched in a breath, and Elgiva smiled.

"You can feel it too, can't you?" she said. "What is it like, this healing magic?"

Godwin grinned at her. "Like stepping out of a dark hut into the summer sunshine."

Elgiva released Trystin and sat back, breathing hard. "Now, little elf," she said with a smile. "Touch your face. Tell me what you feel."

Gingerly, Trystin touched his cheek and gazed at Elgiva in wonder. She couldn't help but be pleased with herself for removing that ugly seam of skin. The elfling's cheek was now as flawless as the rest of his young face.

"It's gone, it's gone!" he shouted with joy. "Oh, Lady Elgiva, thank you!"

He threw his arms about her and hugged her for all he was worth.

"Don't take on so," she said. "It was nothing, Trystin. Godwin, give him some more to eat. He's so thin, it makes me shudder."

"You've healed me, lady, with magic. Good magic!"

Elgiva's cheeks flushed at the elfling's worshipful gaze, and her eyes met Godwin's. He smiled at her and then handed more food to the elfling. Trystin gladly accepted it and grinned at them both in turn. As he ate, he stopped repeatedly to thank Elgiva and praise her, and he hummed a little tune to himself while his mouth was crammed with food.

Godwin warmed his hands before the fire. "You'll choke, lad. Eat more slowly, for your stomach's sake."

"I'm sorry, my lord," said Trystin.

Godwin laughed. "My name is Godwin, and I'm no one's lord, merely a runaway slave. Just like you, in fact. And Elgiva. Why, even our pony, Grimalkin. We've all escaped from slavery. You have joined a band of outlaws, lad."

Elgiva rather liked this idea. She caught Godwin's eye and grinned at him to show she approved.

"You're not from the village, then, Master Godwin?"

The Exile of Elindel

Godwin looked puzzled. "What village is that?"

"A day's walk on the other side of Misterell," Trystin explained. "Southwest. In the river valley. The people who live there look like you. We trade with them. But it's not fair. This trade is the king's idea. He's taken all their gold, and now they have to give him half their crops as well, and in return, he leaves them alone and doesn't use magic against them. But even so, they're under a spell. Grandfather calls it elf-bane. It won't let them leave the valley. I think if they try, it will kill them. We were their friends once, Grandfather says. And now their chief is old and ill. Poor wilthkin, their lives are hard."

"Have you any news of Elindel? Did the wise man ever speak of it?" Elgiva asked.

Trystin screwed up his face. "I'm trying to remember, lady, but it doesn't make sense to me. The wise man said King Thallinore has a mind fever. He wanders the forest all day and makes toy warriors out of twigs. Slow poison, the wise man says. Who is this king?"

"It doesn't matter, Trystin. He's just a watered-down version of Vieldrin. Well, I'd like to meet this wise man, but the main thing now is Misterell."

Trystin gasped and stumbled to his feet, as though preparing to flee. Elgiva stood up, placed her hands on his shoulders, and looked him in the eye.

"We're looking for the Lorestone. Did the wise man speak of it?"

Trystin looked sheepish and then nodded.

"Does he know where it is?" she asked.

"He thought he knew where it might be," said Trystin. "Somewhere deep in the heart of the forest, where Faine would go for solitude, according to the legends. I told the wise man I knew where this place was. It's called Faine's Lynn."

"So you could take us to it?"

He chewed his badly bitten fingernails and avoided Elgiva's eyes. "He made me promise to show you, lady. It's well hidden, but I can't go back. I can't!"

"Be reasonable, lad," said Godwin. "It's vital you show us where it is. We will protect you."

"No, please, Master Godwin, I'm afraid. Please. You don't understand."

"I understand that you've broken your promise."

"No," said Elgiva, "let him do what he likes." She turned to her friend with an arch look, hoping that he would guess her meaning. "So, Trystin, where will you go now?"

"I was going to the wise man to beg for shelter," said Trystin, "but now I can't. I don't care, as long as I'm away from Misterell. I'll find a cave or wood to hide in and stay there forever, if I have to."

A memory flitted like a shadow across Elgiva's mind. "A sad end for one so young." She sighed and looked at Godwin, who seemed to know what was required of him.

"You'd be better off with us, fighting for freedom, than hiding in a cave for the rest of your days, afraid to stick your head out, like a snail that fears being trodden on. But I guess you know what you want." He shrugged.

"The wise man was cruel," said Elgiva, "making you promise to risk yourself."

The elfling looked at them both in turn with a lost and anguished expression. "No," he protested. "He's not cruel! The wise man was my friend."

"So it is with sages," Elgiva went on, frowning. "What do they know of the real world? They spend all their time with books. They get children to do their dirty work instead of putting their knowledge to good use."

"No, lady, no. He's not like that. The wise man is clever and good!"

"If he were good, Trystin, he'd have rescued you," said Elgiva. "Instead, he entrusted you with a mission. You're much too young for such a burden."

Trystin chewed his nails.

Elgiva turned to Godwin. "What do you think, my friend?"

"I think we're wasting our time," he replied, "and we should get some sleep."

Elgiva nodded. "A good idea. Well, Trystin, you can stay here tonight and breakfast with us before you leave tomorrow."

Trystin's mouth opened, but no sound came out. Elgiva knew his mind was in turmoil and felt responsible for it, but she turned her back on him, joined Godwin, and readied herself for sleep.

The Exile of Elindel

Trystin curled up before the fire and closed his weary eyes, but some time later, he was still awake. He was torn between his fear of going home and the promise he had made. And there was no one in the world who could help him reach a decision. He knew what he ought to do, but he didn't want to do it. Tears welled up in his eyes again as he touched the cheek that was healed and whole.

Abandoning the warmth of the fire, he went to the shadows to weep unheard. He didn't get very far. A large shape barred his way. For a moment, he was alarmed, but he quickly realised it was only Grimalkin. He reached out to stroke her neck. She swung her head round, stared at him, and snorted with disdain.

"Want to hear a riddle, child?"

He nodded, trying to smile.

"What must you keep after giving it to someone else?" she asked.

Trystin shook his head.

"Your word, stupid!"

Snickering, the pony sidled away.

Chapter Nineteen

WHEN THE TRAVELLERS awoke the next morning, the sun had just risen and the sky was flushed with pink and gold.

Elgiva leaned on Grimalkin's shoulder and followed the wispy clouds with her gaze. Godwin sensed that she wasn't yet ready to set off on their quest, so he sat by the fire and kept himself occupied by sharpening his knife.

Trystin was sitting a few feet away, looking downcast and chewing his nails. He had just returned from bathing in the pool, and his face looked even younger without its layer of dirt.

"A wonderful time of year, spring," mused Elgiva. "Don't you agree, Trystin?"

Trystin looked up and parted his lips, but he merely smiled in an awkward manner and continued to chew his nails.

"Buds on the trees and birds building nests. Wherever you look, there's life and power, and the strange thing is," Elgiva went on, "it arises out of decay."

"I wonder what tells the birds to make nests," said Godwin. "What makes the green things start to grow again?"

"The need to survive," she said. "But in the natural world, there's a balance. The needs of all creatures must be considered. In elves and wilthkin, it corrupts. It makes the strong cruel and the weak faint-hearted." She cast a quick glance at Trystin. "Some, in order to survive, run away from whatever threatens them, and they're doomed to run forever, never finding peace of mind. Good creatures must act, or the bad ones will flourish, but they don't realise that. It's much wiser to face our fears than to drag out the torment day after day and live in some self-imposed prison. Better to try and fail than to never try at all and wonder what might have been. Wouldn't you say so, Godwin?"

The Exile of Elindel

"Why, er, yes, Elgiva. Better to die once than die a little every day, I suppose."

"Well," said Elgiva, "if we're ready, we'd best be on our way. Perhaps, Trystin, you could give us some directions before you leave?"

Trystin stared at his legs and seemed unaware that she had addressed him. Then he lifted his head and looked at them both with an expression of grim resignation.

"Lady, you're right," he said. "I could never escape the king. I could run a thousand miles away, and he'd always be in my mind. I'm terrified of Misterell, but I love it, too. And my friends, I've left them behind. That was wrong of me."

Elgiva walked towards him and drew him to his feet. "I admit, I've tried to persuade you to come with us, Trystin, because the search for the Lorestone is so important, but I've been very selfish. I haven't considered your fears at all. And that was wrong of me. I have no right to make you act against your will."

"Oh, no, you haven't, lady," he assured her. "It was what you said about spring. It just made me think of home." His eyes misted a little and he smiled, a sorrowful smile, but one full of warmth. "But you shall see for yourself."

Elgiva rested her arm on his shoulder. "Very well, my friend. Let's be strong together."

The sun grew warmer as it climbed towards noon, at which point the travellers stopped to rest. They sat in the tall grass that bordered a meadow. Ahead of them was a wide expanse of closely cropped greensward. Elgiva talked of Elindel, and Trystin listened raptly, but Godwin soon found his attention drifting.

For a while, he was lost in thoughts of summer, how his children would skip through the fields that surrounded the settlement and dance among the poppies with daisy chains on their heads. Then two hares darted across his line of vision, many yards upwind, dragging him back to the present. They ran out from the long grass and proceeded to dance around each other on their hind legs, forepaws flailing. Godwin watched their antics for a while, grinning.

"Look at them," he whispered. "They're so engrossed in fighting, they don't even know we're here."

Elgiva looked up and smiled. "Fighting, are they?"

"I envy you elves, being able to understand animals. I wish I could talk to them like you do. I wonder what two hares could possibly have to say to each other?"

Elgiva's eyebrows arched mischievously, and leaning closer to Trystin, she said, "Shall we give the wilthkin his wish?"

The elfling grinned with glee. "Oh, yes, lady! Can you?"

Elgiva began muttering words under her breath. Godwin was about to ask her what she was doing when what happened next distracted him.

"I've told you, I'm not in the mood," insisted one of the hares.

For a moment, Godwin questioned his own sanity. Not only had the hare spoken, the pitch of its voice told Godwin it was female.

"Aw, come on, Fernie," pleaded her male companion. "Ow! That one got me on the nose!"

"You'll get another if you don't back off."

Godwin raised himself from his elbows. He couldn't believe what he was hearing.

"Oh no, what's he doing here?" demanded the male as another hare darted from the long grass and joined in.

The female, now even more agitated, boxed with both of them.

"Leave me be, you buggers," she cried. "I've already made my choice of a mate, and it isn't either of you!"

Godwin was now on his knees, while behind him, the elves giggled. "You won't believe this," he began, spinning round to face them. "What are you laughing at?"

"Oh, Godwin," cried Elgiva, "you ought to see your face!"

"No, spare him that," snickered Grimalkin. "It's not a sight bears close inspection."

"I see," said Godwin. "An elf's trick, by Frigg! Well, thanks for including me in the joke, though I seem to be the object of it." Godwin was annoyed to find everyone laughing at him, and he frowned at Elgiva. However, in her eyes was a sense of wonder that even surpassed his own. Clearly, she was pleased with herself, and he tried to conceal his indignation.

Elgiva's grin faltered. "Don't be such a bore, Godwin. You're not really angry, are you? I gave you your wish. It's a gift from a friend. Will you spurn it?"

"Of course not. How long will this spell of yours last?"

Elgiva shrugged her slender shoulders. "I can't be sure. As long as you live, I hope. From now on, you will understand animals, elves, and men, and they will understand you." She tossed her head back haughtily. "That's quite a gift, you know. Aren't you going to thank me, at least?"

Her stance rekindled Godwin's anger. "Thank you? For making a fool of me?"

"Cabbage hearts!" snorted Grimalkin. "Don't credit her with Nature's work!"

As the afternoon wore on, a mild southwesterly breeze blew and clouds rolled sluggishly overhead, but Elgiva and her companions paid little heed to the possibility of rain. Misterell lay ahead of them and dominated their thoughts. A cold, grey silence floated out from under the forest's skirts, spreading like sea-fog over the grass.

The ancient trees were impossibly verdant, as if they had heard the call of spring some weeks before the surrounding land.

All too soon, the travellers were standing before the edge of the forest, confronted by a wall of trees that stood together like sentinels. Their branches overlapped and meshed, and their roots were buried deep beneath a tangle of shrubs. The travellers listened for hostile sounds, and in the shadow of the mighty forest, they felt their insignificance.

For her part, Elgiva wondered still at the forest's vernal splendour. The branches above were rife with leaves, and despite the eerie calm surrounding it, inside the forest, a host of birds filled the boughs with song. It was almost as if the birds had flocked to the enchantment of Misterell.

She gazed up at the trees; they were dour and forbidding. There was a feeling of power about them. But when she probed them with her elven senses, she found no wrong in them.

Yet, beneath their quiet murmur of life was a stern command. *Turn back.*

She looked at her companions. Trystin chewed his fingernails, while Grimalkin snorted and pawed at the ground. Godwin stood hugging his chest and gazing at the forest before him, as though it were a forty-foot wall and he had been asked to climb it.

"Well, here we are, then," he stated. "How far must we go into the forest?"

"To the middle," snickered Grimalkin. "After that, we'd be going out."

"The trees aren't so crowded inside. There are many paths and glades. I know the way, Master Godwin." Trystin gave his friends a nervous grin.

Elgiva peered up at the lofty trees. She felt like an ant dwarfed by bulrushes. This was one more threshold that had to be crossed, and she hoped she had the courage to face the challenges that lay on the other side of it. She placed her hand on the elfling's shoulder.

"Very well, Trystin. Lead on."

Chapter Twenty

IN SINGLE FILE, they threaded their way between the knuckled trunks of the ancient trees. Once this initial barrier had been breached, an astounding sight met their eyes, and they stopped and gazed around, astonished.

Inside the forest, the air seemed warmer and bird-song filled the treetops. Wherever Godwin looked, the shrubs and plants were prematurely in bloom and a rich and peppery perfume rode the silken breeze. There were tangles of elder and hawthorn and clumps of hazel, heavy with catkins. Rowans stood proudly between the old oaks, and the emerald sward was ablaze with coltsfoot, daffodils, and daisies. Fungi clustered in the shade beneath the grey-barked beech trees, and the sun that pierced the branches above seemed to lie on the shrubs like powdered gold.

Godwin stared about him in wonder, as hundreds of white petals, the discarded blossoms of many trees, drifted around him like snow. On every side were throngs of harebells and clouds of feathery ferns. They danced beneath the trees in an almost dreamlike shimmer. And the trees grew together in defiance of their natures. He was used to woods where one type of tree dominated over the rest, usually oak or beech, but this was like an ideal forest, a vision of health and beauty. Misterell was a haven for green, growing things, a sanctuary for natural life.

Elgiva turned to her companions. "No wonder this place is enchanted," she said. "It guards itself against intruders. This is a special place."

"It's wonderful," agreed Godwin. He inhaled, savouring the scent of the rich, dark earth, the radiant flowers, and the woody perfume of the trees. It was as life-affirming as the first breath after birth.

Grimalkin's nostrils flared with delight. "It smells delicious."

"Spring always comes early in Misterell," explained Trystin. "One of the Founder's gifts to us. This place is good and beautiful. There's no forest like it in all the land."

"I never expected this," said Elgiva. "My people fear Misterell as a place of evil."

"Perhaps it's evil now," sighed Trystin, "but it wasn't always so. Misterell is enchanted, and other kingdoms have feared its power, but they don't know the truth. The wise man feared to come here too, but when he did, he realised that Misterell is sacred, not evil. He said the enchantment comes from Faine and we should feel honoured to live here. Faine brought all the people together at a place we call the Hill-Shrine, and he did great magic there long ago. We used to go there to worship his memory and share our love for the Earth, but now the penalty for worshipping Faine is death. Grandfather says that Vieldrin is jealous of the Founder."

"Misterell has been fickle before," said Elgiva. "Bellic told me some of the legends, how the people of Misterell turned against the Founder and so he left them and never returned. And when they realised their loss, it was too late. All they had left were guilt and remorse."

"So it's said, lady. Before Faine left, he blessed the forest, and he wouldn't take back such a gift. Not even in anger, Grandfather said. I don't believe we lost his love, either. The elders still argue about it, but I'm sure Faine forgave us. Grandfather told me our forebears repented and the Hill-Shrine was consecrated and dedicated to Faine. But then the guilt of the people began to infect the forest. It withered and shrank back into itself. So, when the spring returns each year, it makes us both happy and sad. As Grandfather says, we remember Faine's love and also how that love was spurned. Now the enchantment Faine gave to Misterell has become a thing of fear. The forest is warped by guilt."

Elgiva grasped the elfling's arm and made him look at her. "This is a sorry tale indeed, but I do think you're forgiven. The Founder wasn't easily spurned, and it seems to me he trusted you above all his other kingdoms because he left the Lorestone in your keeping."

Trystin stared at her with hope in his gaze. "If the Lorestone's really here . . ."

"That's what we have to find out. But first, I'd like to see this shrine."

Trystin's gaunt features brightened, and he took her by the hand. "It's this way, Lady Elgiva."

Trystin led his companions through a coppiced area and then across the ford of a shallow stream. A well-trodden path took them on through the trees, through clumps of sow thistle and betony, and skirted round a group of abandoned huts that had fallen into decay. Trystin moved at a quicker pace and averted his eyes from the crumbling huts, as though some horror were crouching there. A cloud of dark memories crowded around him, and he touched his healed cheek, as though it helped to steady him on his course.

At length, the path snaked out into a clearing, and at its centre was a shallow knoll. Rowans grew around its base, and buttercups swarmed on the grass below it. Trystin stopped and grinned at his friends.

"The Hill-Shrine," he announced.

Elgiva prepared to climb the knoll, but Trystin tugged at her sleeve. "No, Lady Elgiva, it's forbidden. The penalty is death!"

"I will climb this knoll, no matter what," she said, her eyes bright with purpose.

Trystin chewed his finger and watched Elgiva climb the knoll. Then he looked at Godwin, but Godwin merely shrugged and sat upon the grass, as though he had resigned himself to waiting. Trystin had been delighted by his friends' response to his home and excited to be their guide, but now that he was back in Misterell, the old fear began to resurface. He searched for courage, made his choice, and then scampered up the knoll.

The flat crest of the Hill-Shrine bore a crown of flowering plants, a ring of purple self-heal nearly a foot in height. Trystin stepped into the circle and stood at Elgiva's side.

"They always grow like this here, lady." He pointed at the flowers. "Grandfather says Faine ordained it. They represent the counsellors who stood with Faine at his first court."

Elgiva merely nodded at this simple explanation. "Self-heal," she mused. "Is that the Founder's message to Misterell? To Elvendom itself? And what about these rowans, the trees with power over death?"

Trystin was lost. "Such things are beyond me, lady."

She knelt upon the grass and placed her palms on the ground. "There's power here. It's sharing itself with me." She looked up at Trystin and smiled. "But there's something else too. Some memory. A residue of something wonderful. A feeling of oneness."

Though Elgiva continued to smile, her eyes sparkled with tears.

Godwin waited patiently. Out of respect, he stifled the yawn that threatened to crack his jaw, but he longed to stretch himself full-length upon the deep, rich grass. The forest's balmy, fragrant air was making him feel drowsy.

At length, Elgiva and Trystin walked down the slope of the knoll, holding hands. Their faces shone like those of children who were on their best behaviour.

Godwin clambered to his feet and tried to look alert. "Should you make a sacrifice or something?"

He felt pleased to make a contribution to the proceedings, but Elgiva's pert nose wrinkled, as though he had uttered an oath.

"What sacrifice do you have in mind? We don't shed blood in the name of Lord Faine. He taught us to love our fellow creatures, not kill them."

Her expression darkened, and she stood for a moment, toying with her hair; her sudden demand startled him.

"Give me your knife, please, Godwin!"

He tensed with apprehension. "What are you going to do?"

"Don't worry," she reassured him. "But you were right, as usual. I destroyed a forest. I was showing off when I should have shown mercy. I can't shed blood to honour Faine, but a sacrifice of some kind is required."

Perplexed and concerned, he gave the knife to his friend. Elgiva tested its edge with her thumb and then turned and ascended the knoll. Once on the summit, she took the blade in one hand and her long black hair in the other. Without hesitation, she severed the gleaming tresses and scattered them on the grass, as though they were contemptible.

Godwin winced at this, and Trystin gasped in horror.

"Oh, Master Godwin," he cried. "Elven ladies never cut their hair!"

The Exile of Elindel

But Godwin wasn't listening. His attention was drawn to his friend as she stood on top of the knoll.

"I've been guilty of vanity and I've misused the power you gave me, Lord Faine. So I sacrifice this symbol of vanity to make amends with you. Forgive me, if you can, and guide me to a truer path." Elgiva drew a deep breath and straightened herself, as though shrugging off a burden.

Godwin understood the necessity of her action, though it galled him to see it. He placed a hand on Trystin's shoulder and opened his mouth to speak, but his attention was snatched away by a rustling in the shrubs nearby, and he spun to confront the unknown threat.

Trystin's mouth fell open in horror and Grimalkin let loose a snort of alarm as three elves sprang into the glade, each carrying a spear. They halted several yards from the knoll and assessed the situation. Spangles of sunlight flashed on their spears.

"So," cried one. "Intruders, you defy the laws of the king!"

"The penalty is death," yelled another.

Two of the elves, grinning with anticipation, levelled their spears and strode towards Godwin and Trystin.

"Be gone," commanded Elgiva. "Leave us alone, or I will attack you."

"Yah!" jeered the first elf, and he and his companion marched on.

Godwin thrust the elfling behind him and drew his sword. His hand shook badly, but trying to steady it only made it tremble more. While he tried to look menacing, the third elf stalked towards the knoll.

"In Faine's name, stop," Elgiva cried. "I don't want to harm you!"

But her warning was ignored. The two elves got ready to throw their spears.

Hampered by Trystin's clinging presence, Godwin couldn't move. He looked towards Elgiva as she raised the knife and pointed it at the two attackers. The next thing Godwin knew, there was a great flash of light. He and Trystin fell to the ground as a beam of force spiralled past them. When he could bear to open his eyes, he saw two bodies on the grass ahead of him.

The remaining elf was taken aback, but he soon threw off his shock. With vengeance gleaming in his eyes, he started to climb the knoll, and as he reached the summit, he drew back his arm to strike.

Godwin scrambled to his feet and ran to save Elgiva, but the spear had already been released and was sailing towards its target.

The weapon, however, appeared to hit an invisible wall, and Godwin watched in disbelief as it tumbled to the grass.

The attacker gaped and watched the spear roll down the knoll, as though it had betrayed him. For several moments, his eyes flipped back and forth between Elgiva and Godwin. It was then Godwin noticed the ridge of scar that twisted the length of the elf's right cheek. Recovering his wits, the elf scuttled back down the knoll and fled into the forest.

Godwin sheathed his sword and bounded up the slope. He reached Elgiva, seized her by the shoulders, and turned her round to face him. Spent magic glimmered in her eyes, and her face looked strangely puzzled. The knife slipped from her grasp.

"Are you hurt?" demanded Godwin.

She shook her head. "No, I'm fine."

He smiled with relief. "By Frigg, don't look so thunderstruck! Does your power amaze you that much?"

She seemed confused. "But I didn't do anything."

"Didn't you kill those two?" He nodded towards the two dead elves lying on the grass.

Elgiva recoiled in horror. "Yes, oh, Godwin, yes! I keep on killing, don't I? But I had to. You and Trystin . . ."

He tightened his grip on her shoulders. "Stop. It's okay." He stooped to retrieve his knife.

"I don't know what made me do it, but I used the blade to channel the power. Iron must be a good medium. Perhaps too good. I kill too easily."

Godwin pushed the knife into his belt. "You saved our lives," he reminded her.

"Yes, I'm glad of that, but I could do no more."

"I assure you, that was enough," said Godwin with a grin.

"No, no, I mean . . . I used up my strength with that first bolt of power." She looked at him intently. "*All* my strength. I was desperate."

Godwin's composure was shaken. "What?"

The Exile of Elindel

"When the elf attacked me with that spear, I didn't defend myself. I couldn't." She glanced around her, as though searching for words. "Something helped me. Something stood between us and knocked the spear away." She shivered and placed her hand on his arm, as if his solid presence were an antidote to her fear.

Godwin didn't know what to say or how to accept this impossible truth. As they stood in silence on the knoll, he felt they were not alone, and a shiver ran up his spine.

They descended to level ground, where Trystin sat staring at the dead elves. He was chewing his nails as usual and looked terrified. He ran to greet them and threw his arms around Elgiva, babbling thanks for his deliverance, but she too seemed appalled by the sight of the two corpses and was unable to return his embrace.

Godwin pulled the elfling aside and enlisted his help in dragging the bodies into the underwood. Together, they hid all trace of the elves.

Elgiva suddenly gasped in panic. "Godwin, where's Grimalkin?"

Trystin was startled. "Oh, Lady Elgiva, she was scared. She must have run away."

"She can't have gone far," said Godwin. "No doubt she's found something to eat."

"We'd better find her," Elgiva decided. "Trystin and I will search for her. We know the ways of forests. Stay here and rest awhile, Godwin; you look like you could do with it. I'm sure we'll be back before that elf returns with reinforcements." She touched his arm.

Godwin wasn't entirely convinced, but Trystin agreed with Elgiva.

"The elf will have gone to the royal hall, and that's a long way off, Master Godwin. And they won't come back here looking for us. We'd be mad to stay after what we've done."

Mad indeed. He acquiesced and watched his friends depart.

When they had gone, he sat by the knoll and tried to relax, but it wasn't easy. He drew his sword, stroked the blade, and mused to himself that, as usual, his dubious skills as a warrior had been completely superfluous. Magic had saved the day.

Beneath the warmth of the afternoon sun, the forest was very still, but Godwin had disquieting thoughts, despite the pervasive calm. Perhaps his friends would never return. Perhaps they had never existed. Perhaps he was really in the throes of an illness and would wake up back at the settlement, his lumpy straw pallet beneath him and his travels but a dream.

He got to his feet and stretched until his bones cracked. The dream, however, persisted. He looked up at the Hill-Shrine and decided to climb to the top. What prompted this move, he didn't know, but he told himself the top of the knoll was a much better vantage point, where he wouldn't be taken unawares. Yet, this was only a part of the reason. He was too sleepy to be on guard.

He lay down in the circle of self-heal, like a sacrifice to the spring, the gleaming lengths of Elgiva's severed hair strewn around him in the sunshine. Laying his sword upon the grass beside him, he let the warmth soak into his bones.

Birds trilled in the treetops, and insects droned in the tepid air. Warmth, drowsiness, and enchantment flooded like a sleeping draught into Godwin's limbs, and his eyelids closed, cradling him in darkness.

Drifting for a time, as though freed from all his fears and doubts, he became aware of a figure strolling through the blackness towards him. It drew into focus, and he could see it was Rowena. She was talking to an unseen companion, and behind her, the mead hall sprang into being, its walls shivering like a mirage. As the vision sharpened, his wife's words were clear.

"Yes, our lord says he will bargain for the captives' return. In my heart, I know Godwin will come back home to me."

She was smiling, that well-remembered smile. The long, flaxen hair. The blue eyes like sapphires. If only he could reach out and touch her.

He sat up with a start, and the vision burst like a bubble, leaving him bewildered and lost. He gasped at the pain of separation.

Rowena!

He rubbed his eyes and looked around. There was no sign of his friends. No sign of enemies, either. The glade was deserted and quiet, an island of unimpeachable stillness in the tangled, lush-leaved forest.

Before he could wonder at the strangeness of his dream, an inexplicable compulsion made him lie down again. Whatever it was, he couldn't resist it. His eyelids felt like slabs of marble, and he was

The Exile of Elindel

forced to close them. For a time, he floated in a lazy warmth, a silken breeze caressing his skin and filling his lungs with the scents of the forest. Lulled by a bone-deep feeling of security, he was surprised to hear a voice, a voice that seemed to be in his mind, a mild and soothing voice that spoke to him without words, yet he understood the meaning. It hummed around him and within him, like the very air he breathed, a voice of authority, but gentleness, too. An anodyne that flowed into his veins like peace. He fancied that, if the Earth could speak, she would speak in such a voice.

"They who persecute evil shall prosper
"And come to their inheritance.
"The sword now sleeps,
"But awakened, it shall guard the good.
"The iron shall be invincible,
"The metal made mighty,
"The steel strengthened.
"The light-of-battle will protect its lord."

Godwin rolled over onto his stomach. Surely he must be awake? Why couldn't he open his eyes? The ground he lay upon seemed to yield, and his body sank gladly into it, as though it sought oneness with the Earth. He opened his mind once more to the voice.

"'Tis time thy natal gift to claim,
"The warrior's fame that was forsaken;
"So when in peril, say its name,
"Then Taranuil will awaken."

Chapter Twenty-One

"Are you asleep, Master Godwin?"

Godwin struggled to wake himself. Shafts of sunlight sliced through the clouds, dappling his vision with the shadows of leaves. He sat up, fighting his confusion. He couldn't remember where he was, but he felt as though he had slept for many hours.

"We found Grimalkin," Trystin informed him. He turned and scampered back down the knoll to join Elgiva.

"She cast off most of our baggage in her hurry to get away, and we were forced to retrieve it," said Elgiva. "Luckily, she left us a good trail to follow, and as you predicted, the local plants are much too tasty for her to stray very far."

"How long were you gone?" asked Godwin.

"Not long at all," she said. "But we'd better make a move, I think."

Godwin nodded his assent, though he needed more time to gather his wits. His recent dreams had clouded his brain, but he had to acknowledge the need for haste. He followed his friends as they left the glade, but his mind wandered still in visions.

Hardly had they left the clearing when a skirl of shrill cries snatched their attention back to the top of the knoll. A host of birds had descended on the Shrine, and each one picked up a hank of dark hair before taking flight again. Their cries rang with triumph as they bore their spoils aloft. Elgiva seemed briefly taken aback, but then she laughed with delight.

"At least I have some use in this world, even if only for lining nests."

Her companions shared her amusement, and with Trystin leading once again, they set off through the forest.

As they threaded their way through the undergrowth, it grew

increasingly thicker, thwarting their need for both speed and stealth.

"We're making no headway at all," complained Godwin, stabbing at the shrubs with his sword. He suspected that Trystin was leading them astray, but he didn't want to offend the elfling's overly sensitive nature with ill-considered criticism.

To ease his frustration, he took a swipe at a low-hanging branch with his sword. The weapon cut cleanly through the bough, as though it had been a twig.

"This fellow was sired by an axe," he said. "Whoever forged this weapon gave it the temper of stone."

"Must you mutilate the trees to prove it?" asked Elgiva behind him.

He didn't deign to answer this, for his answer would have been hurtful. Perhaps it was an answer she deserved for having deflated his pride. No, what had happened in the Forest of Shades was something best forgotten.

He plied the blade once more to the vegetation that blocked their way, clearing the path of obstructions. Trystin gave up the position of leader and followed in his wake.

At length, they came to a small clearing. Daylight was leaving the forest, but there was enough left to threaten their safety away from the underwood's concealment. They looked at each other, and by some unspoken agreement, they decided to cross the clearing.

As if from nowhere, a tiny figure appeared from the trees, a sackful of firewood strapped to its back. At once, the four companions melted back into the forest.

A flock of rooks cawed across the darkening sky, and the tiny figure jumped in alarm. She watched them speeding home to roost and then, as silence drifted down once more upon the glade, she went on with her chore. The sack she carried seemed cruelly large, but she continued to fill it with twigs, as if inured to the task.

"That's Kinchine," declared Trystin. "She's my friend!"

Without further consideration, he broke from cover and ran to meet her. His companions shared a thoughtful look and then followed his example. When Kinchine saw Trystin running towards her, she dropped the twigs she carried and covered her mouth with her hands.

"Kinchine, what's wrong? It's me. It's Trystin!"

"Go away," she wailed, stepping back. "You ran off. They'll catch you! They'll kill you, and Kinchine, too! I mustn't talk to you. Haldrin said so."

Trystin turned to his friends for support, his large eyes full of hurt.

"Don't be afraid, little elf," said Elgiva, smiling at the child.

"Kinchine not afraid of you! Kinchine afraid of warriors! Kinchine wants to go home now!" The child's gaze darted about in panic.

Godwin sheathed his sword and approached the elf-child. "There's really no reason to be afraid." He gave her a generous smile. "Nobody saw us come to this place, so Kinchine is quite safe."

She pouted at him while she considered his statement. He moved forward, scooped her up, and held her in his arms. A tiny squeal escaped her lips, and she tried to pull away.

"Don't make a fuss," said Godwin. "We won't let them get you, and we won't hurt you, either, but you'd best be quiet, or someone might hear." He squatted on the grass and sat her on his knee, and at length, the tiny elf relaxed. "There we are. That's better."

She looked at him from under her lashes. "Wilthkin," she said in a small, awed voice.

"That's right," said Godwin. "What a clever girl you are. I'll wager this is the first time you've seen one, isn't it? Do you think we could be friends?"

Kinchine nodded, a tentative smile on her lips, while her small fingers plucked at the hem of her robe.

Godwin looked at Elgiva. "The poor mite's afraid to trust anyone."

"She trusted me once," said Trystin.

Elgiva smiled at the elf-child. "Time you went home. It's getting dark."

"Goodbye, Kinchine," Godwin said, setting her on the grass.

"No," she protested. "Let Kinchine come, too, and ride on that great big horse!"

Grimalkin emitted a loud snort.

"Take Kinchine home, please, lady? It's not far."

Elgiva seemed to consider this for a moment, and then she ran her fingers through her shorn locks. "Perhaps it might be a good idea to meet the other elves," she said. "What do you say, Trystin? Will this child's kin embrace our cause?"

"Oh, yes!" he affirmed. "They all hate the king, though they're too scared to say so."

"Very well," decided Elgiva. "Godwin, lift Kinchine onto Grimalkin's back, if you please, and we'll see her safely home."

Godwin hoisted the tiny elf onto the animal's broad back.

"Now, Grimalkin," he said, "I hope you're not going to complain at so small a burden."

"The last thing I want to do is complain," said the pony, and then she swung her head round and glared at him. "But it's still on my list."

Kinchine's home was a sprawl of huts, dwarfed by a ring of elms and oaks. Godwin decided it wasn't a welcoming sight to anyone in need of comfort. The circular huts, two dozen or so, were warped and weather-worn, their thatched roofs thinning with age. Above them, the trees seemed to sag with despair, as though their roots were buried in gloom, and the air was thick with the smell of decay. *What keeps this collection of daub and wattle dog-holes from falling apart?* he wondered.

A paltry fire burned in the centre of the settlement, and before it sat an elderly elf, his shoulders slumped forwards. Upon hearing the arrival of strangers, he raised his hoary head, but seemed too apathetic to show his surprise.

"Look at Kinchine, Haldrin. Look!" squealed the elf-child. "Kinchine's riding a great big horse!"

"Where have you been to, spindle-shanks?" demanded the old elf, not unkindly, his wizened face a sullen mask in the firelight. "'Tis late. Who is that with you?"

"Kinchine met nice friends in the forest. Trystin's come home, too. Trystin's naughty, isn't he?"

"Trystin is a fool," the old elf snapped. "Come here by the fire, all of you. Don't skulk in the shadows like thieves. What is your business here?"

Trystin yanked at Elgiva's sleeve and urged her towards the fire. Lifting the elf-child and her burden of firewood from Grimalkin's back, Godwin strode towards the elder.

"My name's Godwin," he said, setting Kinchine gently down. He held out his hand in greeting, but it was ignored. "This is Elgiva from Elindel, and our pony is Grimalkin."

"From Elindel, you say?" An expression of mild curiosity flitted across the elder's face.

"Yes," replied Godwin. He folded his arms across his chest. How could such a shrivelled old creature make him feel so ill at ease?

"Come here, girl," scolded Haldrin. "Stand where I can see you. I cannot abide skulkers. Now that you are back, Trystin, make yourself useful. Go and find some food for these folk and put that gnat to bed before she falls asleep where she stands." He turned to face Elgiva and Godwin and looked them up and down. "Sit down beside me, the pair of you."

Trystin scuttled to obey. He seized Kinchine's tiny hand and led her away. Elgiva and Godwin sat by the fire and subjected themselves to the old elf's careful scrutiny. He studied them intently, as though they were items on a market stall and he a wary buyer.

Finally, he deigned to speak. "Now, you are from Elindel and he is a wilthkin. What else have you to say for yourselves?"

"We'd rather not say too much," said Elgiva. "This is a dangerous place to be, and I fear your king has many spies."

"What?" croaked the elder, his temper rising. "If all you can give me is insults, you can go on your way at once! If he has any spies or supporters, I am not among their ranks. I may be a menial now, but I have my conscience and my principles, no matter what you think. I was a free elf once, you know, until I defied our so-called king, may Faine tie his entrails in a thousand knots!"

Godwin looked at Elgiva. The elder's outpouring of wrath was startling, but perhaps also rather reassuring.

"You said 'Faine,' " Elgiva ventured.

"Oh, I see," he cried, "the light has suddenly dawned! You are spies of that jumped-up jackanapes yourselves, and you have come to trick me, have you? Well, he might think he is a deity and better than the Founder, but the filthiest heap of dung on the Earth would avoid his foot for fear of being tainted. There, take that back to your master. I have lived too long as it is!"

Godwin had to smile at this. The scrawny-limbed ancient had climbed to his feet and was flailing his arms about. The sight of such infuriation, dancing about in a tattered robe, struck Godwin as both sad and amusing. The elder's behaviour was excessive and his courage pathetic, for it seemed to be no more than the death wish of a foolish old man who could well afford a reckless concern for what life he had left.

Elgiva jumped to her feet and reached out to the elder, but he recoiled from her touch. "Calm yourself, please. We're of the same mind. Vieldrin is our enemy. In fact, I mean to challenge him."

The old elf cocked his fists on his hips. "Hah! I never trust the words of strangers. I know Vieldrin and his tricks. You may have fooled Trystin and Kinchine, but it is not so easy to fool me." He jabbed a finger in her direction. "How can you prove what you say?"

"Elgiva's the Queen of Elindel," broke in Godwin, somewhat vexed. He got to his feet and stood at her side, as if to show his allegiance. He would have said more, but the elder forestalled him.

"What proof is that, then?" the elder said. "I am not too keen on royalty."

"I had hoped for your support, but if you don't trust us, so be it," Elgiva said. "I dare say we can live with it. All we ask for is your silence."

It was at that moment Trystin returned. He carried a loaf and a jug of ale, which he placed before his friends, and he seemed embarrassed to have intruded into this atmosphere of hostility. He smiled and stepped back.

Elgiva frowned at the offered food. "If this is all you can provide, how thoughtless would we be to take what little you have?"

"If our food is not good enough, 'tis your look out," snapped the elder. "Vieldrin keeps us short of food to make us weak and pliable. Eat it or not, I don't much care."

"There's really no reason to be so rude," Godwin said. "We came here in peace and are used like enemies."

"If you don't like it, you are free to leave and find better company elsewhere. I still don't know exactly what you are doing here, so why should I welcome you with open arms?" Haldrin glared at Godwin with blatant contempt and then hitched up his robe and sat.

After a short and uncomfortable silence, Elgiva, Godwin, and Trystin followed his example.

Elgiva sat staring at the fire, and while she nibbled on a chunk of bread, she stirred the soup of her thoughts. She and her companions needed to move forward. They should leave now and proceed on their quest, but for some reason, they had ended up here. Perhaps it was meant to be, and if they could glean some hope or help from the elves of this strange kingdom, it mustn't be discounted. But Haldrin's unfriendly manner disturbed her. She didn't want to go and leave him so angry and bitter. She needed to convince him of her integrity.

She turned towards Godwin. His friendship was the only thing she could rely on, and in his gaze, she saw an echo of her own thoughts: it was time to take some kind of action, to make some kind of statement.

She got to her feet, her sudden movement startling those around her. "Haldrin," she said, "we can't presume upon your hospitality, and it seems to me we should leave you in peace, but before we go, let me make amends for any offence we have given you."

"How?"

She shrugged. "My magic is unpractised, but it is at your service."

"Now just you harken to me, girl . . . " Haldrin pushed himself upright, his face creased with annoyance. "I am leader of the Eldership of Misterell. In youth, I was chief mentor to the late, good King Eldruin. I was Ministrant of the Rites of Faine First-Father." His head snapped back, as though he expected his audience to gasp at the sound of these appellations. "And I tell you this, I will not be mocked by magic trickery." He drew a deep breath and puffed out his chest.

Elgiva admitted defeat. "As you wish."

"No, Grandfather," bleated Trystin. "Lady Elgiva would never mock you. She's good and has great magic. Good magic, look." He tugged at the old elf's sleeve. "She healed my scar. She healed me!"

"I know what the wardain can do!" snapped Haldrin. "They conjure up things to make us afraid. They use us for their sport. She healed you, did she? So? A small demonstration of magic, and you become her willing thrall! You are too gullible, boy. Did Vieldrin not promise us many things when he set the dead king's crown on his head? We trusted him and were betrayed."

The Exile of Elindel

"Elgiva's not like that!" Tears of frustration welled in his eyes as Trystin went on. "You alone of the elders, you knew Eldruin well. You said he was a good king. And Faine, Grandfather, Faine, wasn't he a wardain?"

"Be silent, boy," commanded Haldrin, his eyes livid with outrage. "Don't dare to argue with me! You ran away, and now you presume to tell us what to think. Good Eldruin might have been, but he sired an evil monster, so there was something rotten in him, for all his good intentions. Let go my sleeve, you silly knave, or I will cuff your ears!" He pushed him away. "Magic can kill as well as heal. Have you forgotten so quickly the murder of your parents?"

Trystin covered his face with his hands. Godwin frowned at Haldrin's callous outburst, got to his feet, and drew the sobbing elfling into a warm embrace. Angered by the elfling's distress, Elgiva knotted her fists in her robe and felt the coils of her power unfold, like a serpent preparing to strike.

She had reached a decision. Something had to be done, if only to mollify Trystin's pain. If only to purge herself of anger.

Turning on her heel, she walked several yards and then spun to face the fire. She threw back her mantle, spread her arms out before her, and focused her will on the wielding of magic, her anger the spark that would kindle the flame.

"Haldrin, I wish to show you there's still such a thing as good magic in this world. Allow me to entertain you in payment for your hospitality, and if you remain unconvinced of my integrity, Godwin and I will leave you in peace," she told the elder.

Haldrin cocked his fists on his hips. Elgiva suspected he would have liked to storm off, but curiosity compelled him to remain where he was.

Elgiva's magic was now fully awakened, and it ached to obey her commands, but hesitation held her back. Self-doubt or fear seized her heart. What was she doing, and why was she doing it?

Why was it so hard to let go?

From the shadows that flickered beneath the trees, a snort of amusement reached her.

"Show the old bastard what's what."

Grimalkin's wicked suggestion almost made Elgiva laugh out loud. Confidence flooded into her mind and dissolved the dregs of her doubt. Drawing a deep breath to steady herself, she gathered words for a spell.

"I think this fire does not suffice
"On such a night to melt the ice,
"So I will try to be precise
"And make it brighter in a trice."

Bringing both hands together, palms down, she levelled them at the fire, and magic coursed down her arms. "Stand back!" she warned.

Her friends obeyed at once, and even Haldrin made no protest.

The fire hissed and then flared with an angry roar. It grew in size and soon, the flames were over ten feet tall. The night drew back, as though startled, and the shabby huts were illuminated by a billowing orange glow. Their shadows capered in the underwood, like the dancing souls of dwellings.

Elgiva continued her incantation, pausing between each line.

"Fire dance and flames arise.
"Mirror the colours of the skies.
"Red, orange, yellow, and blue,
"Imitate the rainbow's hue.
"Change to violet, then to green.
"Now all together, they are seen."

As she spoke, the turgid flames obeyed her commands. Their colour began to change, and as it did, it softened. Her companions were no longer dazzled by the brilliance of the fire but could watch the display without shielding their eyes. The darkness around them thickened once more and took on a rosy hue as the fire billowed scarlet.

The flames rippled like tongues of blood, and their crackling pulsed with vigour. Then the flames were streamers of rich orange light, filling the glade with amber warmth. A moment later, the fire became a dazzling cowslip yellow, a citrine coruscation as clean as summer sunshine.

The aureate splendour of the flames deepened, transforming itself into azure. Like a cloudless sky, it spoke of freedom and the vast tracts of the heavens. Trystin clung to Godwin's tunic, and his thin face glowed with wonder, but Haldrin, still unmoved, stood like a pillar of granite.

The azure melted to lavender and then darkened to purple. The

The Exile of Elindel

wall of flame swarmed with magical power and hinted at the opulence of royalty.

With a sudden flare the fire changed again, and now it was green, a bright, luxuriant emerald so redolent of spring that the air actually carried the smell of its leafy, growing life, as if in celebration of the power of the Earth. The trees around the clearing stiffened, and Elgiva felt them strain towards the fire, as if they meant to feast upon the vigour of the flames.

Elgiva continued to stand still, her arms levelled at the fire and power coursing along them. She waited, confident that when the final change came, she would see the flames reflect the colours of a rainbow. But soon, she realised the last line of the incantation had been ineffective. In a sterner voice, she repeated it, but the green sheet of flame remained unaltered.

There was a change in the atmosphere. The air began to hum with the striving of magic that strained itself to the limit without success. Godwin could see Elgiva trembling, her small fists clenched with effort, as she stood in the eerie emerald glow. He glanced at Haldrin, who still stood blank-faced, and was taken aback by the number of elves who now stood in the clearing. Aware that magic was at work, they had crept from their beds to investigate. They now stood cowed and silent, both fear and wonder reflecting in their eyes as they gaped at the grass-green blaze.

Elgiva's voice ruptured the silence.

"Fire, obey and flames be true!

"Reflect entire the rainbow's hue!"

She chewed her lower lip. Mirrored in her feverish gaze, the green flames were unchanged. She lowered her arms. "I'm sorry. Have patience. I'll try a little harder." She closed her eyes and lifted her arms, her forehead glazed with sweat.

"Mighty fire of Mother Earth,

"Be kind to one who knows your worth.

"Forget your roots are in the land.

"A rainbow be, as I command!"

A grimace of pain appeared on her face, and trembling racked her limbs. The fire writhed with violence, but its colour didn't change.

"Stop it," hissed Godwin. "You'll hurt yourself. Enough!"

The green glow flickered and faded, and then, with a tremendous whoosh, the fire shrank back to normal. Darkness swooped back into the glade.

Elgiva staggered, lost her balance, and fell to her knees with a groan. Godwin's muscles tensed as he fought his desire to run to her aid. He didn't want the elves to see how badly she needed support, how inept she was at magic. This display must have cost them the trust of the elves, but acknowledging Elgiva's weakness would only make things worse.

When Elgiva's vision swam into focus, she was startled to see so many elves and all of them apparently dumbstruck. She panted with fatigue. Her lungs felt scorched and her stomach churned, but she struggled to her feet. The forest canted around her for several sickening moments.

So much for trying to impress people. All she had succeeded in doing was to demonstrate unreliable power and her lack of control in its use. The Misterellians would never see her as a serious threat to their king.

She mopped her brow with the sleeve of her robe and stared at the crowd of elves. An embarrassed silence stifled the air. Why didn't somebody speak?

Into the feverish calm, she said, "I have to ask your pardon. I've over-taxed myself."

She looked at Godwin; he responded with a tight smile and folded his arms. Elgiva tried to smile back, but the muscles in her face weren't working, and she feared her grin might be somewhat lopsided.

"A fine thing, by Frigg," said Godwin, sighing as though disappointed. "All these folk assembled here, hoping for entertainment." He shook his head. "And you call that magic?"

Godwin would never know how grateful Elgiva was for those words, for his supportive humour. The tension lifted, and she sagged with relief. The faces of the gathered elves made her think of bewildered sheep, staring wide-eyed at the antics of a brace of large, mad dogs, and despite her empathy for them and her guilt at causing their consternation, her need to giggle was irresistible.

The Exile of Elindel

Careless of the consequences, she sat on the ground and laughed.

The Misterellians muttered in the shadows, but Haldrin snapped at them to be quiet. Then he strode forwards and stood before Elgiva.

"Forgive me," he said with the hint of a bow.

Elgiva peered up at him. He glowered down his nose at her.

"Perhaps I misjudged," he admitted. "If you can find such amusement in failure, then I am inclined to trust your intentions. Perhaps not all the wardain are evil. Vieldrin would have torn us all limb from limb had we been witness to a failure of his power. You ask pardon for your weakness. You greet your companion's disdain with laughter. We have seen all this, and yet, we still live. And above all . . . " He paused and nodded, as though acknowledging some truth. "I have seen magic this evening of a kind I never thought I would see again. It honours Faine, and so do you."

Haldrin smiled and seemed almost embarrassed at having to use a blatant expression of pleasure. He let his gaze wander over the elves in the glade and then nodded to himself, as though he had reached a decision.

"Well, fellow thralls, it seems to me that we are not in the mood for sleep," he said. "So why don't we have some food and wine in honour of our guests? There may be work afoot, and we should be apprised of it. Shall we drink to the death of Vieldrin? He is an abomination in the eyes of the Founder!"

Chapter Twenty-Two

THE FIRE HAD been refuelled, the tables and benches dragged out onto the grass, and under a star-filled sky, the slaves of Misterell were gathered for a feast, a feast that would leave them short for tomorrow, but living in Misterell had taught them that tomorrow might never come.

Elgiva sat at one of the tables with Godwin on her left and Trystin next to him. All around them, the elders sat feasting and chattering, in good spirits. The chance to speak to these elves all together was one Elgiva welcomed, but it would be unwise for her to trust too freely. Their sudden change of heart was odd, and perhaps it didn't ring true; however, Elgiva was responsible for it, and she couldn't just walk away. She got to her feet.

"My fellow Eldrakin," she said, "your hospitality gives us strength for the challenge that lies ahead of us, and for that, we are very grateful. Misterell must be purged of evil, and her people must be free once more. Your king is a tyrant who breaks the laws of the Founder. If we are to be free of him, we all must do our part. Mine is to oppose him. I hope I have the strength for it, but your support will help me."

A few apathetic murmurs greeted her remarks. Only Trystin's worshipful gaze and Godwin's generous smile offered her any encouragement, but they weren't enough. She sank back down.

An elf with steel-grey hair caught Elgiva's eye.

"May I, Lorac, be so bold as to comment on your words?" He linked his hands together, his elbows on the table. "What you say is all very well, but Faine, you know, is spirit now and we are flesh and bone. My dear, what spirit may endure the flesh and bone cannot. You say we all must do our part. You speak of strength, but you are a wardain. To you, such things come easily. We, however, have no power, merely the strength of our sinews and limbs, and most of us are either too young or too old to boast of any prowess there. The fittest among us were chased away or murdered by the king. What kind of support do you expect? What use are we in the fight against evil?"

"And we are forbidden to worship, you know," another elf broke in. His eyes peered warily from under a mop of thick white hair. "If we are seen to be praising him, to be seen praising F-F-Faine, we have earned ourselves a speedy death."

"Can't you worship him in your hearts?" asked Elgiva.

"I think Elgiva has a point," said Haldrin with a frown. "I believe we should listen to her."

"Old fool," snorted a female elf from an adjoining table. "When have you ever believed, or trusted, even in the early times, when we were still free elves? What's made you change your hide so quickly? Has one display of magic robbed you of your wits, or are you going senile?"

Haldrin opened his mouth to speak, but Trystin intervened.

"I wish you wouldn't argue!"

The depth of his feeling drew everyone's gaze, and he seemed overcome by shyness. He leaned closer to Godwin, as if to draw courage from the nearness of his friend.

"I love Lady Elgiva," Trystin went on. "She healed my scar, and I trust her with my life. She wants to help us. Why won't you listen?"

"Help us, hah!" spat the white-haired elf. "Help us stir up Vieldrin's wrath and put us in our graves. I want it known that I, Aldric, want no part of this."

Trystin glanced at Godwin. "It's better to die once than die a little every day," he ventured. "You, you're elders, you're wise, aren't you? Can't you see the wisdom in that? Lady Elgiva is good. I know. She hates the king, and so do we. So we should stand together."

"Look, lad," said Lorac. "You fail to see the danger we are in. Yes, we know she possesses magic. We may even accept that it is good magic. But good or bad, is it strong enough? I think we already know the answer."

Trystin pouted. "You're blind," he muttered. "A chance of freedom tries to take your hand, and you turn your backs on it."

"Chance, aye," said Lorac, "and chance isn't good enough. What we need is certainty."

"Excuse me," Godwin said, "but as to the strength of Elgiva's magic, your king doesn't doubt it as you do. He has tried to persuade her to be his ally." He hesitated for a moment, his confidence clearly wavering as he looked around at the elders. "Look, I know I'm only a wilthkin, so all this is beyond me, but I know what I know. I know what I've seen. We've met your king, not once, but twice. And we're alive to speak of it. That's not Vieldrin's way."

"What would a wilthkin know of his 'way'?" Lorac said with a sneer. "He is a creature of caprice, yet there is method in it."

Godwin pretended to ignore this. He took a large swig of wine and pressed on. "Perhaps great magic isn't required. Perhaps there's other help to be had." He paused and cleared his throat. "Haven't you heard of the Lorestone?"

Elgiva grabbed his sleeve in protest, but he shrugged her hand away. The elders merely stared at him.

"The Lorestone," Godwin persisted. "It's a stone of great power to be used against evil, and legend has it Faine left it hidden . . . here."

"Legends?" said the female elf. "What use have we for legends?"

"Well, we're looking for it."

He made the three of them look ridiculous. The striving after the Lorestone consumed them, but in the eyes of these elders, they looked like lunatics chasing moonbeams.

"Sit down and shut up," Elgiva hissed at him, somewhat exasperated by his lack of discretion. "This isn't helping our cause."

He didn't listen.

"Legend or not," he said, "if Vieldrin gets the Lorestone first, then he'll be invincible."

"He already is," sniggered Lorac.

A murmur of bitter laughter greeted Lorac's words.

"He believes it exists," said Godwin, undaunted. "He's searching for it now."

"Not now, I think," said Lorac, with a yawn. "If he has any sense, he'll be in bed, which is where we all should be."

"He mustn't get his hands on the stone," Godwin said. "You have to help us. You must help us, if you want your freedom. The time for action has come, and what's more . . . " He took another swig of wine. "We all know what it's like to be a slave. It's insupportable. And you,

The Exile of Elindel

Lorac, you speak of danger, yet you haven't the faintest idea what the real danger is."

"What is it, then?" asked Lorac, his head cocked. "Enlighten us, wilthkin, do."

"Well, I, er . . ."

Elgiva tugged once more on Godwin's sleeve, and this time he sat down, and rather heavily, in her opinion. He folded his arms across his chest and glowered at the table. Around them, the elders muttered softly, and their eyes were wells of disdain.

It was then that a tiny elf-child tottered towards them across the grass. In her long white shift of linen, she looked like a wraith that wanders the night, searching in vain for peace. She rubbed her eyes with her knuckles, and her soft voice stunned the darkness.

"I wish Mamma would come home. Aunt Everil, where is Mamma?" She looked at the elf-woman, the phantasm of a nightmare glimmering in her dark eyes.

Elgiva stood up and stepped towards her, and taking the child's tiny hand in her own, she turned to face the eldership. "This is innocence," she said. "A sight to gladden the Founder's heart. Can you stand by and see it corrupted, trampled on, despised? Will you sacrifice her right to be free for the sake of your fears? The old should prepare the way for the young."

She stared at them while the elders shook their heads and muttered.

Trystin sprang to his feet.

"Let's celebrate!" he shouted. "Let's celebrate good magic and look to the future and freedom!"

He raced across the grass to the huts. Curious but wary, the elders watched in silence. When he returned, he held a reed pipe, which he began to play.

"Quiet, lad!" hissed Aldric. "We've made enough din for one night. Someone is bound to hear us."

"A curse on the spies!" cried Everil.

The elders visibly jumped.

"Why should we be quiet?" she went on. "What's wrong with merry-making? Let the forest ring with laughter and song, and these sad, old trees will be proud again!"

Haldrin nodded. "Indeed, we must honour the Founder," he

said. "We have not been true, I least of all. I was always the first to praise his name; now I am the most disloyal. My friends, we have sinned against our lore, our duty, our very natures. Our shame is great indeed."

The old elf straightened himself in his seat, as though restored to his former authority when he led the elves in their devotions. Now, instead of bitterness, he wore a look of zeal.

Chapter Twenty-Three

GODWIN WAS UNNERVED by the elders' sudden change in mood. A surge of energy had brought them all to life. They hastened to their dwellings to awaken their grandchildren, nephews, and nieces, to unearth their hidden pipes and lyres. They built up the fire to a roaring blaze and fetched more flagons of wine.

The night was old by the time Elgiva sought him out. Godwin didn't notice her standing at his side, so lost was he in his gloomy thoughts, and the sound of her voice made him start.

"You look unhappy, my friend," she said.

He searched her features, gauging her mood. Her face was etched by fatigue. Her reserves of energy had all been squandered, performing tricks to amuse the children.

"They're certainly in high feather," said Godwin, inclining his head towards the elves. "But Vieldrin is still their master, and they are still his slaves. Nothing has changed, Elgiva."

"And that has made you unhappy?"

He skirted round the question. "I fear for them in their madness, don't you?"

"Some of the elders welcome discovery."

"Really?"

She ignored his cynical tone. "They believe even Vieldrin's guards secretly hate their master, and with a little encouragement, they'd willingly change sides."

Godwin found this hard to accept. "I think we should be more cautious."

"Perhaps," she said, "but it's too late now. The elders are determined. I talked with them, and they told me things, things I'd rather not know. Remember I told you of Smirill? Vieldrin venerates his name and wants to follow in his footsteps. There are powers hidden in the earth, good and bad, and the bad are better undisturbed. But Vieldrin will disturb them, you can be sure of that. And he will bend them to his will."

Godwin had heard enough, but Elgiva hadn't finished.

"Many ages of knowledge and wisdom lie between us and Faine, but in his day, there was goodness and love. Now there is hatred and greed. Knowledge has corrupted our race, and our path has reached its conclusion in Vieldrin. He's as lorewise as my great-uncle, and his personal power surpasses that of any wardain in the land, but worst of all, he has no conscience. Vieldrin doesn't care. He'll do whatever he wants to do, and he'll do it because he can. If he frees the dark things in the Earth . . . "

"But the Lorestone, Elgiva—"

"If the stone holds the key to Faine's power and Vieldrin finds it, then we're lost indeed," she said. "What is my power against the might of the Lorestone combined with Vieldrin and the powers of darkness?"

"But he doesn't have the Lorestone. He hasn't beaten us yet!" Godwin tried to subdue the note of hysteria in his voice. "We can't give up now, no matter what the odds and what the elders say. Is it just conjecture? They've frightened you with gossip. They don't know what Vieldrin's up to any more than we do. And he's flesh and blood, by Frigg! He can be destroyed, can't he?"

The arrival of Haldrin curtailed this discussion. He approached them with confidence, Trystin at his heels, and his voice calm and steady.

"Now is the time we should make plans," he said. "We have renewed our bond with Faine, and though we risk what little we have, we will help you all we can. Trystin says tomorrow, he will guide you to a place he knows where the stone may be hidden.

"And while you search," continued Haldrin, "the rest of us will stage a rebellion to occupy the guards. Word will be sent to the other slaves who live in Misterell. Let us hope they will join us. The guards won't know which way to turn, but they are not all bad. Most of them serve Vieldrin out of fear that he will harm their kin. They may deal kindly with us."

At that moment, the music ceased and the revellers clapped and called for more, though their mad carousing had passed its peak.

The Exile of Elindel

The night had grown cooler, and Haldrin suggested they all return to the fire, but as they were strolling across the clearing, Godwin's worst fears came to pass.

An ominous rustling among the trees made them all turn to face its source. A silence fell over the glade, and no one dared move. A band of elves strode out of the night, two of their fellows bearing torches. Their swords were drawn, and the firelight gleamed upon their leather armour.

The elders stood and watched, slack-mouthed, as the warriors marched into the glade and sneered at those assembled. Godwin caught sight of the leader's face, and his heart missed a beat. Too well, he remembered that twisted scar.

The guards edged nearer with scowls on their faces and firelight on their swords, and as they did so, the elders retreated.

"What's going on?" demanded the elf who appeared to be in charge. He took a step forward, his fists on his hips and a deep frown on his brow. He had the look of someone kept reluctantly from his bed. Crossing him would be unwise. Clearly, he outranked the others, for they cringed when he spoke. "A rebels' get together, eh? Making an infernal noise. Enough to wake the sun. And a wilthkin! This is serious, lads!"

"Captain," hissed the elf with the scar, "I'll wager they're worshipping Faine!"

"Shut up, Snarkin, I know what's afoot. If you hadn't done such a rotten job, we wouldn't be scouring the forest in the middle of the night. Spare me your bloody opinions."

Snarkin ducked, as though from a physical blow, and drew back.

"Now then, I want the ringleaders. They'll pay for this, and they'll pay in blood. Sound the horn for assistance!" The captain strode forward menacingly. He searched every face for a sign of guilt, and then he turned back to glare at Snarkin. "Damn you, Snarkin, are you asleep? Sound the horn, I said!"

Snarkin made haste to obey the command. The clarion blare made everyone jump, but Elgiva stepped calmly forwards.

"Listen," she said, "we want to help you—"

The captain snorted with laughter. "Gah! Shut your noise, lest I use your guts to lubricate my sword. I'll do the talking here."

Elgiva was undaunted. Clearly uplifted by the support of the elders, she held her ground, defiance sparkling in her eyes. "Threaten and bluster all you like. We will worship Faine no matter what."

"You have signed your own death warrant, my girl." The captain snarled with relish.

"And furthermore," Elgiva went on, "I will rid this kingdom of Vieldrin."

The captain laughed and spun round to face his warriors. Their faces clenched with terror. "You hear that, do you, dogsbodies? Treasonous talk, that is! She wants to rid us of Vieldrin, but he's a generous master. We don't want rid of him, do we?"

One of the warriors was about to reply to this, but his companion nudged him in the ribs.

"Do we?" bawled the captain.

"No, Captain," said the warriors.

The captain's gaze whipped back to the elders, his mouth a smirk of cruelty. "Well, my lads, do you fancy some sport? We'll take that one there for a start." He pointed at Elgiva. "She seems to be their leader. Then the old codgers should give us some fun before reinforcements arrive. Snarkin!"

"Captain?"

"Take her, Snarkin. Alive, if you can."

"But Captain, she killed Rancill and Vendriel. She struck them both dead with a glance!"

The captain spun round and slapped Snarkin. "Don't question an order, milksop! Why can't you do as you're told?" He grabbed Snarkin's collar and thrust him forward. "Now get her, worm. We're wasting time. And mark me, cretin, I said alive. We must learn all the names of her fellow conspirators. But if she gives you any trouble, you have my permission to show no mercy."

Snarkin moved forward slowly and began to stalk Elgiva. "Now you, don't you make no trouble."

Elgiva confronted him, clenching her fists, but then her soft lips parted and she cast her gaze back at her friends and looked at Godwin. In her eyes, he saw a horrified look, a look that said, "I have no strength."

Oh, Frigg, we're done for!

Godwin shook from head to foot, but he fought to gain control of his limbs and ran across the clearing. He halted between Elgiva and Snarkin, and looking into the elf's scarred face, he raised his sword with a hand that trembled and said in a quavering voice, "Another step, and you die!"

"Yah, wilthkin!" Snarkin spat upon the ground like a snake discharging venom. "Hey, Cadrinell, get over here and sort him out for me!"

Another elf crept forward and stood at Snarkin's side. The three antagonists faced each other, reluctant and uncertain. Even the tips of their swords were trembling.

"What are you dithering for?" barked the captain. He folded his thick arms across his breast and grimaced with impatience.

Thoughts raced through Godwin's mind. He saw himself fighting to defend the settlement. He saw his masters practising swordplay. But none of it helped him now. He didn't know what to do. If only he had a longsword to swing at his attackers. Then he could have cut them down before they got too close. But all he had was this blunt-edged blade and a leaden body palsied by fear. And what if they both attacked at once? Would it be slashing or stabbing? What would Elric have done? Where was Cerdic when you needed him? Frigg! He couldn't move a muscle. He was rooted to the spot like an idiot. Rooted to the spot and only half sober. The elders were old and weaponless. Elgiva had used up her strength. So much for their fanciful notions. Craven old fools! How in the name of all the gods had he ended up like this?

Cadrinell made his move and thrust his sword at Godwin's chest. Godwin parried the blow, amazed at his own reaction. The flat edge of his sword clashed with Cadrinell's blade. Though his arm twisted, he managed to knock the weapon aside and deflect it from its target.

Cadrinell struck again, and Godwin parried. Inexpertly handled, his sword glanced off the elf's. Together, they stabbed and sliced, while Snarkin stood grinning, his own sword poised with its tip against Elgiva's throat.

Godwin's heart pounded. Cadrinell's elven agility gave him the edge; he may as well have had winged feet. The warriors jeered with encouragement.

"Cadrinell, he's tiring!"
"You'll soon finish him off!"

They were right. Godwin's strength was failing, he couldn't clear his head, and he was retreating, inch by inch, towards the fire. Feet shuffled behind him as the elders moved out of his way. Trystin's terrified pleas were ignored, and a child sobbed in the shadows. He heard these sounds from a distance, and they didn't seem important; his only concern was to save himself and to keep Elgiva from harm, though an instinct for self-preservation begged him to flee and end his involvement with elven affairs.

There were shouts in the forest, more warriors summoned by the blare of Snarkin's horn. By the gods, he was going to die like this, pierced by the blade of this leering wretch far away from home. Why didn't somebody help him? Why was he on his own?

As Godwin continued to back away, panic flooded his brain and an image, unbidden, sprang into his mind: a hill with a crown of purple flowers and words that made no sense. Yet, one word floated uppermost on a sea of desperation. He couldn't resist the need to speak this word.

Under his breath, he gasped, "Taranuil."

Like a startled animal torn from sleep, the sword tensed in his hand. Its edge took on an eldritch gleam, as though fresh from the forge. Still edging backwards, he drew the blade across the pad of his thumb. He could see its lethal trenchancy, yet the blade was blunt to the touch. How could this be?

Godwin's enemy moved in for the kill, and as he sprang forward, Godwin prepared to meet a painful death. He raised his sword, convinced it would be his last act on the earth. His legs were too leaden for flight. He had no choice but to die, and die well.

To his utter disbelief, he was pulled forwards. His sword denied his cowardice, urged him into battle, and his veins were flooded with confidence. With impossible ease, he parried the blow that should have struck his head. Cadrinell didn't have time to strike back. Godwin slashed at him, from left to right and upwards.

Cries of horror escaped from the elves as Cadrinell's head was severed from his neck. It rolled several yards and came to a halt, wearing a look of surprise. The headless body fell backward on the ground.

Godwin was even more surprised, yet he had no time to wonder. He turned to face Snarkin.

The Exile of Elindel

Perhaps watching the fight had put Snarkin off guard. Whatever the reason, as he now raised his sword to threaten Elgiva, he clearly didn't realise she had edged farther away from him. Seizing the opportunity, Godwin sprang at him, raising his sword, and Snarkin clumsily parried the blow. Deep down, Godwin was glad of this. He didn't want Snarkin to die without the chance of defending himself. With Taranuil in his hand, Godwin was invincible.

Snarkin swung at Godwin again. This time, the edge of Godwin's sword clashed with Snarkin's blade. The latter broke in two, and Snarkin stepped back in ashen-faced horror. The warriors gasped in unison, while their captain swore with rage.

Godwin could show no mercy, for they who persecute evil shall prosper. He lunged at Snarkin with all his strength and impaled him on his sword. Snarkin sagged against him, his face a grimace of pain. Godwin pulled the sword from his guts and watched him sink to the ground, excited and sickened by what he had done.

The warriors gaped at each other, and the captain fought to rally them, but none volunteered to take Snarkin's place. The elders clamoured, inspired by Godwin's triumph, but the blare of a horn and loud voices sounded in the forest.

The captain flashed a cruel grin, as the underwood burst open and a party of armed elves sprang into the glade. Emboldened by the reinforcements, the warriors brandished their weapons.

Panic seized the eldership, and they snatched up the children and scattered. Tables and benches were overturned in the hope of foiling pursuit. The torches were extinguished and dirt kicked onto the fire. In his frenzy to get away, Haldrin collided with Godwin.

"Too many to fight now," he shouted. "Flee!"

Godwin spun around. Darkness occluded his vision. Objects hurled by the fleeing elves were flying through the air, and dim shapes ran past him, left and right. Eager to help the elders, the dogs milled about, snarling at the warriors and snapping at their heels. Godwin couldn't make sense of it all.

Grimalkin charged into the glade and galloped round in a rage. She kicked at everyone, regardless of who they were, and whinnied, "Bastards! Bastards!"

Godwin looked round for Elgiva, his pulse pounding in his throat, and was relieved to find her beside the fire. She was standing like a statue, staring at the embers. He ran to her side, grabbed her hand, and dragged her across the clearing. She neither complied, nor resisted.

They passed Grimalkin as they fled, and he whacked her on the rump, urging her to gallop out of reach of danger. The thought that he could have told her to run didn't register in his mind.

They ran for a while, and then Godwin stopped to clean his sword on the grass. The weapon was smeared with gore, and the sight of it made his stomach clench.

There was madness in the forest, cries of panic and promised violence echoing in the night. Soon, the sun would rise again, and hiding places would be few. The rebels couldn't run forever.

Without warning, Godwin and Elgiva stumbled into a dell. Its sloping sides were covered with ferns, its edge disguised by willows. Sliding and slithering down the bank, they came to a halt at the bottom. Their nostrils were assailed by the stench of rot, but despite the murkiness and filth, they were well-hidden. Motionless and hand in hand, they crouched in the stagnant water, trying not to breathe too loudly.

After a while, the sounds of pursuit passed them by.

"So, that's that," said Elgiva. She dropped his hand, and Godwin could sense her anger mounting. "Our allies have scattered in panic. The whole of Misterell knows we're here and we've lost our companions. Why did you drag me away like that? I ran away like a frightened mouse. They'll think my magic's all show and no substance!"

Godwin couldn't believe what he was hearing. "Well, isn't it?" he countered. He had more than earned the right to give a frank response. "How can you say such a thing, Elgiva? After I saved your life. You used up your strength on magic tricks. Showing off again, by Frigg!"

"How dare you!" she cried. "I could have put the fear of Faine into all of them!"

"Perhaps one of us did just that!" he snapped.

Only a whisper of moonlight penetrated the dell, so he couldn't see her face clearly enough to gauge her mood. They sat a few moments in silence, and then Elgiva drew a deep breath and ran her fingers through her hair. She leaned against Godwin's shoulder.

The Exile of Elindel

"I'm sorry, Godwin. You did well. You were very brave. I didn't know you were such a warrior."

"I'm not," he said, "but what else could I do? The elders were scared, and you couldn't help me."

"You didn't need my help."

Something strange about her tone made Godwin look at her. "No, Elgiva, but..." He searched the dark blur of her face. A feeling of secret amusement seemed to cross the space between them, and his senses reeled with a sudden horror. "You mean you could have?" He gripped her by the shoulders and angrily pushed her away. "By Frigg, you just stood there and watched!"

"Forgive me," she said softly. She pulled herself towards him and knotted her hands in his tunic so he couldn't thrust her away. "There was a reason. At first, it's true, I'd exhausted my powers, but while you fought with Cadrinell, my strength returned. I decided not to intervene, because, my friend, you doubt yourself and it's destroying you. I know how it feels to doubt your own power. Now you know how much courage you have. Do you think I'd have just stood by and watched, had you been in any real danger? Can you really believe that of me?" She paused and withdrew her hands. "And now I know, when magic fails me, I need have no fear with you at my side. You made a vow to protect me, and you have honoured that vow. Better than I have honoured your friendship."

Silence stretched between them. Godwin felt torn by conflicting emotions, not knowing if he should be angry at Elgiva or ashamed to have doubted her. Either way, he promised himself he would understand elves or die in the attempt.

"I suppose I should thank you for giving me faith in myself," he said.

She shrugged. "I'm only returning a favour."

Was that all it meant to her? "But Elgiva, there's one thing you don't understand. You see, it wasn't me. I couldn't have done what I did without the help of..."

"Of what?"

He faltered, expecting only derision for what he had to disclose. "Of..." How could he say it? He didn't understand or believe what had happened in the glade. He looked away and lowered his voice. "Without the help of my sword."

Elgiva laughed at this, but it was laughter devoid of malice. Even so, it made him sigh. To his surprise, she put her arms around his neck and hugged him.

"Poor Godwin, I am cruel, aren't I? Wilthkin say such funny things, but silly elves should learn respect. Please, don't be offended. It wasn't you I was laughing at."

She yawned and snuggled up to him, succumbing to her fatigue.

"What were you laughing at?" he asked.

"I sensed it," she said. "In fact, I've always known. Why are you so shy about it?"

"What do you mean?"

"It's nothing to be ashamed of. You own a magic sword."

Chapter Twenty-four

GODWIN JUDGED IT safe to leave Elgiva where she slept for a while and venture out to find their companions. It had rained during the night, and the morning air was fresh with the smell of flowers and wet earth.

He cast a glance back at the dell and then walked a short way across the grass. A path ahead snaked between the trees. It was little more than a ribbon of earth, but he felt a strange compulsion to set his foot upon it and follow it to its end.

He walked for a while on the beaten track until a nagging doubt made him falter. Perhaps he ought to return to the dell. What if Elgiva awoke in his absence? She wouldn't know where he was.

A noise from beyond the trees to his right made him stop and listen. It was the sound of water, a fresh, tinkling murmur that called to his thirst. He left the path and hurried towards it, wading through the bushes, and as he approached it, the sound deepened, hinted at refreshment.

The shrubs drew back, and he found himself in a tree-ringed glade. Across the glade, a waterfall cascaded down a shallow escarpment. The waterfall, a torrent of silver, plunged into a pool, and the overspill formed a bubbling stream, which seemed to dance across the glade and vanish into the forest. Reeds cooled their feet in the shimmering pool and on either side of the waterfall, the rock face was covered with flowers and shrubs.

Hastening forward, he knelt by the pool and drank the clear water in grateful gulps. The beauty and calm of his surroundings gave him a feeling of optimism, of hope. He tried to pinpoint the source of this feeling, but it slipped away from him.

There was movement behind him. He spun around, his hand on the hilt of his sword. Grimalkin approached the pool and lowered her head to drink.

Godwin relaxed. "Oh, by Frigg . . . it's you! Must you sneak up on people like that? Where've you been, you old nag?"

"If you're interested, Brit, I've found Trystin. Look, here comes the little whingebag now."

The elfling skipped towards them, grinning. He halted at the edge of the pool.

"Master Godwin, you found it, then?"

"Found what?" demanded Godwin.

"The place the wise man spoke of. Faine's Lynn—the heart of Misterell. Come on, Master Godwin. Let's climb up here and start our search!" cried Trystin, and he scurried towards the escarpment.

In hardly any time at all, the elfling had reached the top of the rock face.

Godwin glowered at him. *Damn your agility.* Then he shrugged off his irritation and moved towards the cliff. "Trystin, it's too steep! I don't think I can climb it."

"Plenty of footholds, Master Godwin!"

Godwin shook his head and began his ascent. The cliff was as sheer as the side of a barn, and the rocks were slick with spray; nevertheless, he managed to scramble halfway up before his strength deserted him.

"Trystin!" he cried between ragged breaths, "What is the point of climbing up here?"

"Point or not, I should make less noise," Grimalkin whinnied from below. "The whole of ruddy Misterell will know what you're about."

Godwin twisted around to hurl an insult at the pony, but his foot slipped and he began to slide. He scrambled to find a purchase, his muscles taut with strain, but he slithered downwards through the plants into the path of the waterfall.

Then he lost his footing completely and braced himself for the inevitable.

The impact stunned him for a moment. Trying to regain his feet, he found himself pummelled by gallons of water, and the breath was pounded from his lungs. He lost all knowledge of who he was or what he was trying to do. Blinded by water, he crawled on all fours, knowing only that he needed air.

All at once, the pressure ceased and left him gasping in a cool, moist shade with red specks flashing before his eyes. Beneath him, his fingers clutched soaking wet soil.

Gradually, his dizziness faded. He was astonished to find himself kneeling behind the waterfall in a tiny chamber of solid rock several yards in diameter. Though straight, the walls of the chamber looked as if they had been gouged from the rock by some incredible heat. In places, the surface of the stone ran like solidified wax.

He hauled himself to his feet. The waterfall fell like a silvery curtain, concealing the outside world from his gaze. In his confusion, it seemed impenetrable.

But he wasn't alone for long. Trystin, wearing a look of concern, squeezed his way past the waterfall and hurried to his side.

"Are you all right, Master Godwin?" Runnels of water ran down the elfling's face.

"Yes, yes. No harm done." Godwin drew a deep breath to compose himself. "We'd better continue our search."

"No, wait!" Trystin cried. He studied the walls of the chamber, as though he were searching for veins of gold. Then, with a grin of delight, he turned towards Godwin. "Don't you think this would be a very good hiding place, Master Godwin? Somewhere safe and secret?"

Godwin cocked an eyebrow at this. "Be reasonable, lad. These walls are solid. You couldn't hide anything here."

Trystin gazed round with an expression of wonder. "But the walls, Master Godwin, they don't look right."

Godwin walked to the end of the chamber and explored the cold stone with his fingers. "Well, no, they're odd, but they're still solid rock. If anything lies behind these walls, there's no way we'd ever find it."

Trystin grabbed his arm. "But it must be here," he protested. "It wouldn't be out in the open for anybody to find!"

"How do you know?" asked Godwin. He pulled himself free from the elfling's grasp. "Look, Trystin, lad, we can't walk through stone, and I can't see a door. Can you? We'll have to search elsewhere."

Trystin, however, was adamant. "No, Master Godwin. Where's Lady Elgiva? She'll know what to do. Perhaps we need magic to get through this stone."

"We're wasting our time."

But the young elf refused to leave the chamber. "Faine loved this place."

"No doubt."

Godwin turned to walk away, but Trystin barred his path.

"I can feel his love, Master Godwin," he insisted. "I can feel it here."

The strange and wistful gleam in the elfling's eyes made Godwin hesitate. With a groan of exasperation, he unsheathed his sword. He suspected that, once awakened, his sword could penetrate anything.

"All right, I give in," he said. "If it's magic we need, then there's magic in this."

"Yes, yes, I saw!" said Trystin.

"If this won't do it, will you be satisfied?"

Trystin nodded and grinned.

Godwin brought the blade to his lips and whispered, "Taranuil."

Convinced his blade would be unharmed, Godwin didn't hesitate. He walked towards the back wall of the chamber and stabbed at the rock with all of his strength.

As steel and stone made contact, an explosion of light and a blast of air knocked Godwin and Trystin off their feet. Taranuil sang like a bell and sent shivers up Godwin's arm until he was forced to drop it. Cries of terror thronged in his throat, but the force of the blast had left him mute. Both he and Trystin shielded their eyes as the brilliance raged about them, and the rush of air sucked the breath from their lungs.

When it was over, a cold, damp peace filled the granite chamber. Godwin got to his feet and stood, catching his breath. The waterfall sounded unnaturally loud, but louder still was the pounding of his heart.

In the wall of stone ahead of them, a tall, arched doorway had appeared. Beyond this lay another chamber, bathed in a ghostly light. Trystin stood up and grasped Godwin's arm, and they looked at each other, open-mouthed. Godwin saw his own amazement echoed in the elfling's eyes.

Godwin summoned what courage he could and approached the threshold. Trystin followed close behind, his fingers fastened on Godwin's tunic.

The chamber was perfectly round with a sunken floor, and the walls were of polished stone. After a brief inspection, Godwin managed to extricate himself from Trystin's grasp. Half expecting it to sting him again with its power, Godwin retrieved his sword, but the blade was cold and inert, mere metal. He and the elfling shared a look of caution and then, brandishing Taranuil, Godwin returned to the doorway.

Trystin tiptoed behind him, as though he feared to awaken whatever nameless horror might be lurking in the cavern. Three stone steps beyond the doorway led them down to the sunken floor. There they stood and looked about, waiting for their eyes to grow accustomed to the dimness. The smell of cold stone and damp earth made them shiver in their sodden clothes.

Though the chamber walls were sheer and round, the ceiling was made of dark, wet earth, enmeshed with writhing tree roots and, here and there, a few fine cracks that let in strings of sunlight. The only feature in the cavern was a pedestal made of polished stone. Godwin and Trystin stepped softly towards it.

On the pedestal was an oaken casket, bound with bands of iron. They looked at the casket, and then at each other, and then at the casket again. Finally, Godwin straightened himself, transferred his sword to his other hand, and slowly lifted the casket's lid. He and Trystin sucked in their breath.

A smooth, round opal, as large as an apple, lay nestled on a bed of white silk, and beneath its milky surface were suggestions of blue, green, yellow, and red. A ray of sunlight pierced the globe, lit up the casket, and bounced off again, spangling the walls with muted reflections. The light flashed and winked on Godwin's sword, as though they shared some arcane communion.

Stunned by the opal's beauty, Godwin felt like a trespasser, a defiler of ancient relics, while Trystin nervously chewed his fingers and stared at the opal's perfection, as though it were an elixir that could heal his anguished past.

Eventually, Godwin found his voice. "By Grim," he whispered. "The Lorestone."

Trystin clutched at Godwin's arm, his face alight with joy. "I knew it, Master Godwin! I knew it wasn't a myth!"

Godwin glanced at Trystin, and his own sense of accomplishment was mirrored in the elfling's expression. A thrill of excitement raced up his spine, and he fumbled as he sheathed his sword. Steadying himself with a deep breath, he reached out to touch the globe. Its cold, smooth surface glimmered under his admiring gaze.

"By Frigg, it's beautiful!" he gasped.

"How shall we carry it, Master Godwin?"

"Carry it?" Godwin scowled at him. Move it from its quiet abode? Seize it with rough, mortal hands? The idea was appalling, but of course, it was why they had come. "Carry it, yes. Well, I don't know. We must keep it somewhere safe."

He lifted the opal with care, surprised at its weight. Beneath it was a piece of parchment. Balancing the stone in one hand, he picked up the parchment. The words it contained meant nothing to him. He had been raised by a race unfamiliar with writing, but even if he had been able to read his own language, this must be Elvish. Despite Elgiva's gift of languages, this was beyond him. He handed the parchment to Trystin and set the opal back on its bed of silk.

"Can you read?" he asked. "Does this make sense to you?"

Trystin studied the parchment for a moment, nodded, and then began to read aloud.

"The stone's discoverer,
"Orphan and slave,
"Shall unlock the door
"With a magic glaive.
"Let him be honest,
"Sure and leal,
"And take it for
"The elven weal.
"Whoever should wish
"To light its flame,
"Must seek and find
"The Lorestone's name.
"The sacred grove,
"The sarsen ring,
"Where Nine Wise Men
"Are heard to sing.
"There stands the tallest,
"Like a tower;

The Exile of Elindel

"Beneath his feet
"A word of power.
"This word invoke
"To weave the spell.
"But have a care
"And use it well."

They gawked at each other for a moment. A sudden need for haste made Godwin snatch up the opal and turn to leave the cavern. Trystin padded behind him, the parchment thrust into his tunic. As they left the second chamber, the doorway vanished and became once more a wall of solid stone.

Grimalkin was still devouring the plants as Godwin and Trystin edged round the tumble of the waterfall, her copious tail lashing at the flies that swarmed about her rump. She lifted her ungainly head as Trystin capered up to her and hugged her scrawny neck.

"Grimalkin, we've found the Lorestone!" he cried, and he danced about with joy.

"Well, that may be," she snickered. She glared first at Trystin and then the ground beneath his feet. "But that's no reason to tread on my dinner."

Chapter Twenty-Five

SLEEP WAS A fathomless pit of oblivion, and Elgiva was sorry to leave it. Her senses were sluggish, her mind was fogged, and discomfort registered slowly. She stretched herself and scanned her surroundings.

Her nose was assailed by the stench of the water that had seeped into her clothes. Her hair and skin were stiff with dried mud, her kirtle torn and soiled, and her cloak was wrapped about her body like a filthy cerement. Broken fern stems pricked her limbs, and she itched all over.

Pushing against the bank of the dell, she heaved herself to her feet, wincing at the effort. She searched round for Godwin. She needed her level-headed friend, and his absence alarmed and puzzled her. She was alone. She swallowed down a sudden surge of panic.

She peered up through the branches. The sun was high in the sky. She had slept too long.

Her pulse quickened with hope when the leaves on the edge of the dell rustled. She squinted through the foliage. A dark shape sat on the top of the bank.

"Godwin?" she whispered. "Is that you?"

There was no response. Scrambling through the trees and ferns with the sun drawing water from her eyes, she wondered at the sudden dread that writhed in the pit of her stomach.

When she reached the top of the dell, Elgiva reeled at the sight of her foe. The forest seemed to spin like madness, and terror churned her stomach. Vieldrin sat on the grass in a long black robe. He was disturbingly handsome and wearing a grin of cold, malicious triumph.

"I could have assumed his appearance, dear heart," Vieldrin said

The Exile of Elindel

with a smirk. "An amusing subterfuge, I think, but rather underhanded." The arch of his eyebrows sharpened, clearly enjoying the fear in her eyes. "In any case, such shape-shifting tends to be demeaning. Those wilthkin are so ugly. And how could I be so cruel? I know how much he means to you. I see it in your heart. Why, I could almost be jealous."

"What . . . how did you find me? What are you doing here?"

"Faine-worship has reared its ugly head. The guards who reported back to me had news of an insurrection. Who else would be behind it but you?" He smiled widely, exposing his perfect white teeth. "As for seeking you out, dear heart, I merely followed my nose. But I would have found you, filthy or not. Magic has an odour all its own, but I would not expect you to know that."

"What do you want? I believe our contest is not yet over." She tried to maintain an icy calm.

Vieldrin smiled and smoothed back his hair with a strong, elegant hand. "How quickly you reach such serious matters," he said. "I had hoped for some lighter conversation on so fine a day."

Elgiva frowned at his smugness. She looked away and searched for the easiest route of escape, but Vieldrin snaked out one arm and closed his fingers round her wrist.

"I shall speak of our contest soon enough. There are other vexations I wish to discuss, the most recent being that little rebellion. Your attempt to incite my subjects was, fortunately, a failure, and soon, they will all be rounded up. I have assured them of my leniency, providing they abandon their foolishness and return to their duties. However, it would appear four of my warriors managed to get themselves killed. I do not feel inclined to show mercy to murderers."

Releasing her wrist, he leaned back on his elbow and glared down his nose at her. His contempt and the bitter sting of failure stirred Elgiva's anger. With a primitive hatred, she raised her clenched fist to attack him, but he grasped her arm, twisted it, and then pulled her towards him.

"I dislike your hostility, dear heart," he said in a calm, soft tone. "That is no way to treat a friend."

For a moment, his eyes were aflame with power, and then magical force lanced up Elgiva's arm and pierced her heart like a dagger. The pain, though brief, left her gasping with shock and far too stunned to retaliate.

"If you . . . if you harm my friends, I promise you, I'll kill you!"

He laughed and released her. "Well, dear heart, what are four warriors? I can be generous, Elgiva. I can forget such trifles. I will think about it." He looked at her with unsettling softness in the depths of his large, dark eyes. "If only they had your mettle, my dear. I have five hundred warriors in Misterell, and not one of them has courage like yours."

"Five hundred?"

"Someone has told you differently?" He feigned a look of astonishment. "Well, no one can be trusted."

"You least of all," she said.

He grinned. "Your presence is so refreshing. You never agree with me, while everyone else—"

"Everyone else has neither the courage nor the power. You're nothing but a tyrant with a kingdom of terrified slaves."

"I know," he said. "It has been a labour of love, my dear, to get the old place how I want it."

"And Elindel?"

"Is coming along. My plan to take Queen Gilda's lands is also well in hand. Tandrin's, too, eventually. Peranduil will be next, I think. But enough of all that. It is tiresome. Let us return to the list of your crimes, and let us start with the Forest of Ethephon—the Forest of Shades, as some have called it. I wish you had spared it, Elgiva. That was my favourite haunt. For ages untold, the wardain of Misterell have ruled the land about the Forest of Ethephon. Its destruction hurt me deeply, you know. Very deeply, in fact." His gaze sharpened like a whetted blade.

"The forest was evil," she exclaimed, but even as she said it, she realised the truth. "It wasn't the forest. It was you."

"In my younger days, I practised there. Ah, the spells I wove, the enchantments I learned. How easily I could invoke the bitter wrath of the trees."

Elgiva's whole body was cold with revulsion. A gyring emptiness sucked at her mind, and she swallowed the gorge that rose in her throat. When she was finally able to speak, her words felt like gouts of abomination.

"You had no right—"

"No right?" he growled. "I had every right! The world belongs to those with power, to those with the strength to take what they want. The forest was mine by inheritance and mine by conquest, too. How can you talk of rights, Elgiva, when you destroyed the forest? You set flame to the living trees. What are you but a murderer?"

"The trees were in torment . . ."

"Some misguided notion of mercy killing?"

"You have no respect for Nature . . ." Her voice trailed away in sobs.

"Nonsense," he said. "I respect its power, and I intend to use it."

"Like Smirill used it?"

"Smirill was a fool." His eyebrows arched. "Smirill made too many mistakes. I intend to make none."

Elgiva strove for self-control, to find the focus she needed. "You have royal elf power. Nothing more. What can you do with that?"

"You pretend to hate me," Vieldrin went on, his tone now soft and indulgent, "because you think you should. Even the elven vow to Faine cannot change your mind. I fail to understand, my dear, no matter how I try. Why do you refuse to acknowledge the fact that you find me so appealing? I do not mistake the look in your eyes. I am well-acquainted with desire, little elf." He held up his hand to silence her protests. "But that aside, Elgiva, if desire and vows have no effect upon your stubborn heart, there is one thing that will." He grinned at her for a moment and then lay back on the grass, his hands behind his head. "I have risen above mere royal elf power. Forgive me for ending the fun so quickly, but our contest is concluded. Elgiva, I have found the Lorestone."

"I don't believe you . . . I . . ." She could barely find the strength to keep breathing.

His sensuous lips stretched into a smile. Then he sprang erect, seized Elgiva's upper arms, and dragged her to her feet. For someone so slender and elegant, he was also frighteningly strong. He studied her face with the manner of a father vexed by a stubborn child.

"Yes, it exists," he said, "and I have always known it. I have spent much time in the search for the stone, and now I am rewarded. I win, Elgiva, and you must surrender."

"You can only use it once," she gasped as she dangled in his grip.

"Once will more than suffice," he returned, his tone hinting at future horrors. "Then Faine's power will be unleashed, and it will enter me, increase my might a hundred-fold!"

He tightened his grasp, and Elgiva's arms throbbed with the pressure of constricted blood. She was weak. She had failed. Fresh tears bled from her eyes, and runnels of sweat ran down her spine, but the need to escape from his evil grip burned in her brain like panic. She drew her being into focus.

"But meanwhile," she said, "you have mere royal elf magic."

Angry, scarlet fire blossomed along her arms. Vieldrin gasped with pain and was forced to release her. Scowling dangerously, he stepped back and prepared a bolt of his own. Power blazed from his fingertips with concentrated violence, and it sent Elgiva reeling backwards, rolling her like a wind-tossed leaf upon the forest floor. For several long moments, it clung to her skin and burned her with white-hot agony before the power was spent.

Vieldrin laughed, his fists on his hips. "Before you presume to do battle," he jeered, "consider with whom you do it. I am your senior. In my prime. And I have had years of practice." He stepped forwards, seized her arm, and hauled her to her feet. "Yours is the magic of an infant."

Her vision was smeared with tears of pain and she tried to focus on his face, but all she saw was a blur of evil. "You think you're clever with your tricks and threats. You might have the Lorestone, but you won't be allowed to use it!"

He pushed her away, laughing with scorn. "And who is going to stop me? Queen Gilda? Tandrin? How would they do it? They must confront me face to face, but they could never enter my realm without alerting me. I would have the advantage and be the first to attack. And anyway, Elgiva, who will protect their people and lands if they come after me?"

"This war . . . It's a diversion—"

"Allow me to finish, dear heart," he snapped. "Your uncle—I hesitate to call him great—that old fool, Bellic. He will prevent me, will he? I have him in chains in Elindel, chains that cannot be broken save by magic stronger than his. He is defeated. There's that wilthkin friend of yours with his puny little sword. I would not waste my power. And of course, there's you. Who would win in a duel of magic? I think we know the answer, do we not? I have your measure now." Folding his arms across his breast, he gazed at the forest, as though he were bored.

She combed her fingers through her hair, and her mind ran through a host of escapes, alternatives, and choices, but time and again, the spectre of death blocked her every move.

"Why don't you use the stone?" she asked. His gaze swooped towards her, but he said nothing. "If you are to be the master of all, why do you delay? Why don't you stop the war, Vieldrin? There's no need for any more bloodshed."

"What care I for bloodshed?"

He glanced away, but she thought she saw a flicker of something; doubt or vexation, she couldn't tell, but she drew courage from it.

"The truth is, you can't use the stone. You don't know how to use it. Nobody does, do they?"

"Be silent!" he snapped. "These matters are beyond you. I do not have to explain myself to you or to anyone else. All that need concern you is I now have the Lorestone, and I have the power to kill your uncle and your friends. Know also that they will be spared if you become my queen."

Elgiva needed time to think, but her mind was numb. She swallowed hard. It seemed there was only one way forward; it was purely a matter of survival. Pride, anger, revulsion . . . such things must be pushed aside. If she and her friends could stay alive, at least some hope would flicker on in all this darkness. Owning the Lorestone was one thing; using it was another. Until its mysteries were unlocked, she must play along with Vieldrin.

But it wasn't going to be easy.

"Well?" he rasped. "Do you agree to become my queen, or will your uncle be flayed alive?"

Faine, Siriol, somebody, help me.

"I am waiting, little elf."

Elgiva drew a deep breath. Cunning and compliance were now her surest weapons. "I have no choice, do I? I can't argue with what you've said. I'm no match for you, and I admit it. I'd be a fool to oppose you now." She averted her face and sniffed back her tears. "Do with me as you will."

Chapter Twenty-Six

"I CAN'T UNDERSTAND where she's gone," moaned Godwin.

He was sitting near the dell, Trystin, solemn-faced, beside him. A small fire spat and crackled before them, its ration of branches nearly consumed. They had waited several hours, perplexed and worried by Elgiva's absence, but neither knew what to do about it. Concern tightened the skin of his brow into a frown as he turned to the elfling.

"Are you sure there are no messages? No marks? No elven signs?" he asked.

Trystin sighed and then stood and stretched his legs.

"Master Godwin," he said, "forgive me, but you have asked me this question several times already. My answer must be the same. We both know. Something has happened to Lady Elgiva."

"How much longer must we hang about here?" demanded Grimalkin. She tore up a bunch of greenery and lumbered towards her companions. "Cabbage hearts, I'll get cracked heels, standing in all this mud. Why don't you do something? Why don't you search?"

"Because it's far too dangerous," said Godwin. "Vieldrin's patrols are everywhere, and where would we search? It's a bloody big forest. Or hadn't you noticed, you stupid beast?"

"Call me stupid, would you?" she retorted. "Me, who can jump higher than a tree."

"Don't be ridiculous," he said.

"You ever seen a tree jump?"

The sound of someone running towards them brought their banter to an end. Godwin leapt up, sword in hand, ready to confront the intruder. An elf hurried along the path that ran parallel to the dell, and Godwin immediately recognised him: Aldric of the eldership.

THE EXILE OF ELINDEL

"Aldric, stop!" called Godwin.

The old elf started, spun to face the sound, and his furtive look changed to one of anger. He strode towards the companions and wagged a reproachful finger at them. "It's all your doing!" he hissed. "Betrayers!"

"What in Frigg's name are you on about?" demanded Godwin.

"Have you not heard? You led us all a merry dance, and now your plan has borne fruit. I thought we were wrong to trust you."

Folding his arms over Taranuil, Godwin sighed with frustration. "Explain yourself."

Aldric's brow was creased with vexation, and he fidgeted where he stood. "Your friend has betrayed us. She's going to be Vieldrin's queen. It's just been announced. What treachery!"

This information was so absurd that Godwin could have burst out laughing. "What?"

"Didn't you know? Deceived you, too, then, has she? The two of them are going to be wed, and all of Misterell—what's left of it—must go and pay them homage or be slain for disrespect. Tomorrow at noon, if you want to know, they're announcing their betrothal. Pah! No more chatter, or I'll be late. I'm a weaver by trade, and Vieldrin has ordered me to make a special cloth for his wedding. When Vieldrin commands attendance, only a fool would disobey. If I'm not there before dusk falls, then my head's off, for sure."

"Wait!" cried Godwin, raising his sword.

The elder began to back away, but Grimalkin butted him between the shoulders and thrust him forward with her nose, until he stood within an inch of the tip of Godwin's sword.

"Are you mad, or lying, or what?" Godwin asked.

"I tell you it's true," bleated Aldric, flinching from the sword, "and my advice, for what use it is, is that you go and pay homage, too, or be found by the guards and slaughtered."

"I don't believe it," Godwin said.

"Please yourself," snapped Aldric, "but there's something else you ought to know, though you won't believe that either. That Lorestone you spoke of. He's found it."

"Found it?" Godwin looked at Trystin, not knowing how to react, and Trystin stared back in bewilderment.

"A murrain upon him!" cursed Aldric. "I suppose that's why your friend gave in so soon. I always suspected she was a coward, but it strikes me she's changed sides a bit too quickly even so. Not altogether unwilling, I think. I've heard about these Elindelians. Power-mad . . . and that's not all—"

"By Frigg, will you shut up! For a man who's anxious to take to his heels, you've a ruddy good lot to say for yourself. Now, tell me this. Where are we to pay homage?"

"The royal hall, of course. Where else?"

"All right," said Godwin. "Be off with you, then, or be well-acquainted with the edge of my sword."

Aldric glared at him with contempt and then turned and fled into the forest. Godwin sheathed his sword, musing on the nature of the Misterellians. They were cowards. But it was easy to think such thoughts with anger in his heart and a magic sword, easier to chide and bluster than to try to understand. He sighed at his own hypocrisy and turned to his young companion. The gods be thanked, Trystin, at least, was always on the side of right. Or was he just besotted with Elgiva? He was, perhaps, too easily swayed.

"Well, lad, what do you make of all this?" he asked.

"Stuff and nonsense!" proposed Grimalkin.

"I wasn't asking you."

"Why not? Never heard of horse-sense?"

"Master Godwin," ventured Trystin, "I agree with Grimalkin. Lady Elgiva must have been tricked. She wouldn't do this willingly. She's playing along with the king."

"Yes, it must be so," agreed Godwin. "In which case, Trystin, we must make sure she knows we have the Lorestone. We have to do this ourselves. No one else can be trusted."

"Hate to get on my high-horse," snorted Grimalkin, "but exactly how, may I ask?"

"Well," decided Godwin, "we'll have to go and pay homage, and perhaps we can speak to her privately."

"Some hope of that. More likely, they'll grab us, Brit."

"Shut your noise, you ugly brute. You're always so pessimistic."

"You wanted to talk to animals," she reminded him, "so now you're stuck with it."

Godwin ignored her. "Trystin, it's going to be a long, cold night. Do you know where we can get some food?"

The Exile of Elindel

The elfling stiffened like a frightened hare. "Everil will help us. But it means going back . . . " He paused and drew a deep breath, and then his eyes lit up with purpose. "But I'll go, Master Godwin."

"Good lad, but wait till dusk. Bravery won't conceal you from the king's patrols quite as well as darkness."

Trystin appeared surprised, delighted, and embarrassed all at the same time and surely wouldn't have been more taken aback had he found the crown of Misterell discarded in a ditch.

Vieldrin stepped from the royal hall into the lambent morning. Elgiva was ahead of him. She stopped, stood ankle-deep in the rich, green sward, and gazed down at her new clothes. Her blue silk gown rustled in the breeze, its train a swathe of sky upon the grass.

He had wondered at her cropped hair and told his female servants to wash and brush it. They did what they could and then covered her head with a square of white silk held in place by a gold circlet shaped like a two-headed serpent. The circlet sparkled in the sunlight and the white silk fluttered beneath it, seeming too light and ethereal a thing to be a part of the Earth. A brooch set with garnets gleamed at her breast and when she moved, frail chains of gold, adorned with tiny trinkets, tinkled like bells on her ankles and wrists.

As Vieldrin watched, she resumed her walk across the grass, and he sauntered after her in his equally regal attire, his jet-black outfit studded with pearls. He raised his hand and reached out with his dark power to hold her back, the fleshless fingers of his coercion gripping her with their unseen talons. He held her still while he strolled to her side.

She turned to face him with a half-smile on her face and took the arm he offered.

Floating somewhere in the mire of his heart was a tiny vestige of pride untouched by evil. Gazing at his future queen, he was dazzled by her radiance, though it troubled him to find such pleasure in beauty. As she looked up at him with her large, dark eyes, he wondered if the affection he pretended to feel had some small shred of truth in it.

He laughed to himself. *No. Idle thoughts. Remember who you are, Vieldrin, what you have to do. This pleasure comes solely from gloating. When those slaves see their avowed ally, the good and lovely Elgiva, sitting beside her enemy, helpless and submissive—and soon to share his bed—how they will despise her!*

He congratulated himself on the way things had turned out. Elgiva had abandoned her quest to find the stone and that left him more time to search for it himself. Of course, there were those prophecies, but if destiny really did intend Elgiva to be the stone's discoverer, then what did it matter? He would be there to take it from her.

"When are you going to show me the Lorestone?"

Unnerved, he flashed her an evasive smile. Taking her small hand in his own, he raised it to his lips, but it was deliciously perfumed and only increased his unease. He dropped her hand with a frown of displeasure, and she stepped back in alarm.

"Later, my dear," he promised, forcing himself to sound gentle and calm. "After the oath of fealty. Be not so impatient." He grasped her hand again.

She offered him a mysterious smile. Was this artful creature playing games with him? Did she really believe he had won? Well, it would be a small thing to kill her if she gave him any trouble.

"Will you be going to Elindel?" asked Elgiva.

Vieldrin gave her a questioning look.

"You'll take me with you, won't you?" she said.

He shook his head and feigned regret. "You will stay here and rule in my stead. These scoundrels need to be constantly watched."

And so do you, my dear. And I would not allow you anywhere near Bellic or Gilda.

"How fares my cousin, Thallinore?" she asked.

"Ah, none too well, I fear."

"What poison do your agents glut him on?" she asked, her tone still light and casual.

"Poison? What need of poison? Mix royal blood with narwardain, and you have an unstable compound. Poor Thallinore is mad and weak and not long for this Earth."

Elgiva appeared to consider this, and then she nodded. Stepping away from him, she strolled towards the nearest tree, the train of her luxurious gown dancing in her wake. Placing her hand on the trunk, she stood for a moment, clearly lost in thought.

The Exile of Elindel

"How is my great-uncle Bellic?" She traced the patterns on the bark with her fingers, but her eyes seemed to be focused elsewhere.

"Old," Vieldrin said with a smirk, "but otherwise quite well. He is not ill-treated, but he is helpless. His powers are blocked by the chains he wears. A clever spell of mine. I have allowed him to live, dear heart, but if you decide to turn against me . . . " His voice deepened, hinting at horrors.

She shrugged and leaned back against the tree. She wriggled her toes in her sandals, watching their movements with interest and then, without looking up, she spoke. "What's the use? I knew this was all a waste of time. Anyway, why should I care?" She turned her dark eyes full upon him, and they were livid with anger.

He summoned up his powers, preparing to defend himself.

"Why should I be the only one to take responsibility? This burden was dumped at my door by those who once despised me. I can't be held responsible because, you see, I can't. I haven't the power! You can see it, why can't Bellic? All those years I spent as a slave. They had no right to do that. But I have the right to enjoy my life, just like anyone else."

"My dear?"

She strode towards him, and he tensed, uncertain of her mood.

"Bellic let me find things out the hard way, and while I suffered, a fool sat on my throne. Was that just? Wasn't I entitled to any respect? Should a queen be treated like a slave? And fool that I was, I tried to save the life of my so-called master, and what did they do? They banished me. Sent me out to fend for myself. Did anyone help me? Did Bellic? Oh, no. But then I'm told I have a mission, and I'm sent on a dangerous journey, and I try to help a bunch of stupid old men who run away at the drop of a hat. I go from one form of slavery to another, and nobody ever asks my opinion. How dare they do this to me!"

With a shaking hand, she massaged her brow, as if to erase the deepening frown there, and then she sighed and lowered her gaze. "Bellic doesn't realise how hard it is using magic when you've never been taught. He doesn't realise how much it hurts, how terrifying it is."

Vieldrin watched her aslant, but said nothing.

"Strange, but I was never treated like a queen when I lived in my own kingdom." She paused and stroked the fabric of her gown, and her fingers trembled, as though aroused by the decadent touch of the silk. "I've never worn fine clothes like this, and I never had homage paid to me, until now. And I tried to be good, but being good got me nothing but abuse. All the things I ever wanted, they denied me, and I loved them for it."

"And it pleases you, of course, that I can so easily provide you with all the trappings of power," he said. "Whatever you want shall be yours."

She averted her face, but he caught her chin and forced her to look at him. Silvery tears ran down her cheeks, and Vieldrin experienced something unfamiliar. He stumbled mentally for a moment, but he was able to name the unsettling sensation: compassion. It threw him off balance. For a second, he thought of striking her, but her doleful gaze seemed to plead for restraint. He wanted to hold her in his arms.

Confound the bitch. He would show no weakness. He would not jeopardise his plans for the sake of a fleeting and misplaced sensation, nor would he stoop to her level. He would be a figure of purpose and power, and she would always fear him.

And she could never be trusted, no matter how genuine her change of heart might seem.

Of course, if it were genuine, it was further proof of the axiom by which he lived his life; everyone could be corrupted by flattery, power, or wealth.

Vieldrin was pleased. Of course the little fool's tears were sincere. Either they were tears of frustration or tears of self-disgust. Whatever the cause, he was glad. It boded well for his plans. Perhaps it was odd how quickly she had changed to his way of thinking, but she was young and impressionable, and years as a servant had left her with a weak will and a damaged heart. A good thing for him, but sad, too. He had bargained on a worthier foe, a more experienced bride. In any event, it seemed she would be willing to help him, would even enjoy using her power against the ones who had spurned and abused her.

But be on your guard, Vieldrin. She may get ideas of her own advancement when she has had her fill of revenge.

He saw the path ahead of him, all obstacles swept aside. With

Elgiva's power to aid his own, he would rule Elvendom. He would be the Elwardain. Then all he needed was an heir, and he could dispose of his queen.

"You no longer wish to be Queen of Elindel in your own right?" he asked.

"When you are Elwardain, I shall be queen," she said with her usual power to unnerve him. "And Queen of Misterell, too. And queen of wherever I choose. Why cling to the hope of one throne, when you can give me so many others and make them a reality? You said I'd see sense, and you were right. I should have heeded your wisdom. I've been a fool to uphold my ideals, because they weren't mine at all. They belonged to other fools who wanted to keep me in my place. They made me a slave and then expected me to be noble and unselfish. Such attributes belong to a monarch." She smiled.

Damn the little bitch. Was she being sarcastic?

"Would it be so very wrong to take the easy way out? I see no point in struggling, when all the odds are against me. And anyway, Vieldrin, we might make excellent rulers. Elvendom could be strong again." She looked at him strangely, frowned, and edged a little nearer. "I hope, I hope you haven't put a spell on me to make me think like this, to make me talk like this. No, no, I hope you have, because if not, then how can I cope with the truth? Oh, Faine, I wish—"

"No spell," he said, unnerved by her change of mood. "We all must accept what we are."

"I don't know what I am," she exclaimed. "I've never known! It's so confusing, and I'm so tired of it all. I can't go on like this. If I just had time to sort out my thoughts . . ." She turned away, and her body trembled.

He regarded her for a moment, and a strange hunger almost overcame him. She was beautiful and vulnerable, and it would be easy for him to crush her with his bare hands, to snap her bones like twigs.

On an impulse, he grabbed her shoulders, pulling her towards him. He lowered his head and kissed her. She tensed in his embrace. Was this revulsion or merely shyness? He would not tolerate either. She had agreed to be his queen and she must fulfil her duties.

Summoning his power, he spun a web of coercion about them,

an aura of sensual fire, and felt her revel in the heat of his passion. She seemed to melt in his embrace, but he saw in her mind a hint of reluctance.

For a moment, she seemed about to yield, but then she stiffened in his grasp and reasserted her autonomy.

"No!"

The word seemed to hang in the air before his eyes. Her power flared in self-protection, and his web of coercion melted away.

"No, please," she gasped and pulled away. Her eyes were dark with abomination.

"Coy, dear heart?" he murmured.

She gave him a tight and nervous smile. For a time, they looked at each other, and then Vieldrin shrugged, deciding to dismiss her resistance. Perhaps some beakers of wine would make her less intractable.

"Come, my dear," he said. "Let us take our seats. The horns are sounding in the forest. The slaves will soon be here."

Godwin was one of the last to arrive, Grimalkin nagging in his ear and Trystin trudging behind him. The scabbard at his belt was empty, and Godwin hoped it would betoken peaceful intentions, but in reality, he didn't want his sword to be confiscated by Vieldrin's guards and had hidden Taranuil in a nearby grove of oaks.

Ahead of them, the slaves of Misterell were trudging into the glade before the great hall, impelled along by the king's warriors. Vieldrin watched from his throne, Elgiva seated to his left. Godwin managed to catch her eye, but she looked away. Her face didn't betray her thoughts, and he feared he might never get a chance to speak to her.

Godwin and his two companions mingled with the crowd of elves.

Warriors stood around the throng, facing inwards, their swords at the ready. Their captain stood on Vieldrin's right and folded his arms across his chest. He looked out over the gathering of elves with a scowl that promised torment should anyone dare to step out of line. An elf at the front of the crowd turned to face them and bellowed an order. The slaves humbled themselves and knelt upon the grass.

THE EXILE OF ELINDEL

Vieldrin thrust himself to his feet, his dark eyes flashing with menace, and he made a brief oration, praising his future consort for the excellent choice she had made. Having completed his monologue, he commanded his subjects to pledge their fealty and renew their oath to serve him.

When their half-hearted mutterings trailed to an end, Vieldrin nodded with satisfaction, a perfect smile on his perfect lips, and reseated himself on his throne. He scanned the assembly for several minutes, clearly relishing their wretchedness, and then he reminded them of the Lorestone and the absolute power he now possessed.

While the elders muttered in consternation, Godwin smiled to himself. While Trystin still guarded the parchment, the Lorestone was wrapped in a piece of sacking and stowed in Grimalkin's pack. Perhaps he had been foolish bringing it here, but he doubted that anyone would suspect, and as far as Vieldrin knew, the Lorestone had yet to be found. Godwin was excited by its secret presence: if only Vieldrin knew just how close he was to the stone.

Elgiva glanced at Vieldrin. He was clearly enjoying the crowd's dismay. He turned towards her and placed a hand upon her arm in a gesture of ownership.

"Your companions are here," he said.

"They worship me," she said, allowing a hint of a smile to dance upon her lips. "I dare say they're waiting for me to trick you."

His eyebrows lifted. "But you cannot, my dear."

She looked at him with outraged innocence. "Will not, my lord," she said. She flashed him a charming smile. "They will have to accept that things have changed."

He nodded. "Will you address the slaves, dear heart?"

"If it pleases you."

She got to her feet, surveyed the assembly, and then shook her head. "So, you surrendered like cowards, and now you are cringing before me. Is there an ounce of courage among the lot of you?"

Several sneering faces glared back at her from the crowd, but no one dared speak. She glanced at Godwin; he was frowning and seemed perplexed. His honest blue eyes were pleading with her. She snatched back her gaze and found herself looking straight at

Haldrin. The glint of triumph in his eyes made her hesitate, but she didn't have time to wonder at it.

"Why I wanted to help you, I really can't imagine." She tilted her head back. "Now, everything has changed. Thanks to my future husband, I will have what is rightfully mine. I was born a queen, but I lived like the bastard child of a beggar. They made me feel unworthy, fitted only to serve . . ."

Fitted only to serve. And so she was. Bellic had been right.

There were mutterings in the crowd, and Vieldrin drummed his fingers on the arm of his throne. Elgiva drew herself back into focus.

"Well, Elindel will be rewarded for what it did to me." She took a deep breath, swept her gaze over the gathering. "I despise it. I despise you—"

"Do you despise Lord Faine?"

There were gasps of horror among the crowd, and Elgiva's heart clenched with dismay at the sound of Godwin's voice.

"Who dared to interrupt me?" she demanded.

"I did," said Godwin. "You know it was me."

Vieldrin sat bolt upright, a cruel smirk on his face.

"Come forward, wilthkin!" ordered Elgiva.

Ignoring the sudden weakness in his legs, Godwin obeyed Elgiva's command. He knew the risk he was taking, but he had to speak to Elgiva and tell her about the stone. Despite her angry demeanour and the speech she had given, he felt he could trust her, whatever happened.

He wove his way through the crowd of elves and walked towards his friend. A space of about four yards lay between them when she held up her hand to stop him. He wanted to be nearer, to look into her eyes and see the covert messages she was bound to send.

"I've heard your little speech," he said. "I don't believe a word. You wouldn't change sides like this."

"Why not?" Her voice had an icy edge. "This is the way—the only way—for me to get what I want."

"Are we no longer friends?"

Elgiva frowned at him. "We can be, if you swear you are loyal to me, whatever path I choose."

"I don't think I can follow this particular path," he said.

The Exile of Elindel

"That is most unfortunate."

Her mouth was set in a hard, cruel line, but surely her eyes were laughing at him, sharing some secret joke. He hoped he didn't mistake her meaning. He laid his mind wide open to her, begging her, somehow, to reach him.

"Do you think this is a game?" she asked. "Do you doubt my intentions?"

Godwin wasn't certain how he should react, but she spared him no time for deliberation.

"Well?" she snapped. "Do you doubt me?"

"It seems I can't, but I don't believe it. You can't be so false-hearted." He confronted her with a look of outrage, believing that was what was required. "Is this what I've been striving towards? So you could be with him?" He nodded towards Vieldrin.

"Striving, wilthkin?" she said. "What is your striving compared with destiny? Destiny can't be overruled. I have always believed that."

His lips drew apart, but he couldn't speak. Only his eyebrows questioned her. She laughed and gave him an arch look, and then her expression changed to one of anger.

"You should never have interfered with the lives of the Eldrakin. Your meddling has been your downfall. Were the trivial affairs of your own kind not enough for you?"

For a moment, Godwin faltered. The ground at his feet was suddenly unsafe, and his heartbeat quickened with panic. Had he done the right thing in coming here?

"There's no need for this," he said, his voice cold. "You have no further use for me. I had better return to my trivial affairs."

"You can't do that," she told him. "Oh, no. I won't allow it. I may not have a use for you, but I can, at least, have my revenge."

He gaped at her. "Revenge? For what?"

You told me not to doubt you, but you're not making it easy!

"I haven't forgotten the Forest of Shades. Remember when you attacked me? You wanted to cut my throat."

Vieldrin leaned forward in his seat, a look of glee on his face.

"Evil magic made me do it!" protested Godwin, hurt and embarrassed by her words.

"You would have me think so," retorted Elgiva.

225

The ground sagged beneath Godwin's feet once more, and this time, nothing could save him. "How can you be so petty, so unreasonable?"

"How dare you!" she cried. "I ought to kill you where you stand."

Hardly had she said these words, when Trystin fought his way through the crowd and stood at Godwin's side.

"No, Lady Elgiva, please don't!"

With a frown of genuine annoyance, Elgiva raised her hand. Her power leapt through the air, and Trystin grew suddenly wide-eyed and rigid. Then with a groan, he sagged and slowly fell to the ground, where he lay as still as a stone.

Godwin was speechless with horror. He fell to his knees at Trystin's side. How could this happen? This was impossible. Elgiva wouldn't do this. But his friend's limp body said it was so.

He stared up at Elgiva, unable to comprehend what she had done. "Elgiva, you . . . you've killed him."

He couldn't decipher the look on her face. She was about to speak, but Godwin didn't want her words. He jumped to his feet and staggered towards her, uncertain of his intentions. Vieldrin leapt up to forestall an attack and raised his hand to lash out with magic, but before he could do so, Elgiva's power stopped Godwin in his tracks. He crumpled to the grass and plummeted into darkness.

Vieldrin studied his future queen. Her face was flushed, her eyes were bright, and her lips were stretched by a strange, grim smile. *The addiction of magic will teach you the truth about yourself, my dear.*

And how well she used this power. How swift and dramatic it was. He felt it growing, unfolding, and its after-glow made him shiver.

Of course, he must not let her know how adept she was becoming.

Elgiva sank down onto the throne, gripping the arms tight, while Vieldrin gazed across the crowd, pleased to see them mute with horror.

"Well done, dear heart," he whispered. He seated himself on his throne. "The fools are frightened out of their wits."

The Exile of Elindel

"As they should be," she panted. A distracted expression slackened her features, and a gleam of wetness shone on her cheeks.

"Tears, my love?"

She smiled at him. "Ah, no. It's nothing. Power hurts." She scrubbed away the evidence, as though her tears had betrayed her.

He raised his eyebrows. "I think you have tired yourself."

"Oh no, my lord. The use of power has left me a little dizzy. It's a new experience... one I like." She caught sight of her fallen friends and looked away.

"I will have the bodies removed, my dear," he offered.

Elgiva spun to face him. "They're not dead," she blurted out, and then she seemed to compose herself and gave him an arch look. "Do you think I would let them off so lightly? I will have my revenge, and I will savour it. They'll suffer before they die." Her face lit up at the prospect. "We can do anything now, my lord. With power, we can do anything. I never knew it could be so easy to make others do one's bidding."

Indeed, little fool. How right you are.

He patted her hand. "The easiest thing in the world, dear heart."

Chapter Twenty-Seven

Godwin was floating back to the world from a distant time and place, where colours were brighter, scents were sweeter, where pain and sorrow had no meaning. He had soared over fields and farmsteads, twisting streams of polished steel. He had wandered through sun-swept meadows, and rising before him, a stately hall had opened its massive doors. He drifted through them like a ghost, into an atmosphere vibrant with laughter.

And there . . . was it Woden, the High-God, rewarding the warriors for their valour? And was he welcome in their midst?

And he was one with all of it; all things were one with him. And in the air around him purred a soft, familiar voice.

Be at peace, Godwin. All is well.

Clouds of petals fluttered down upon him. Each petal reflected the sun like a chip of coloured glass, and he found himself on the boundary between what is and what should be.

He opened his eyes. A narcotic languor clung to his mind, and he stretched himself and murmured, "How soft are the clouds . . . How soft . . ."

"Master Godwin!" hissed an urgent voice.

He turned his head to find the source of this irritating noise and discovered it was Trystin, but he was fuzzy round the edges and clearly not important. "Go away. You're dead." He tried to return to the land of his dreams, but the vision was lost forever. His mind abruptly cleared and he sat up, startled, and looked around. "Dead? But you're . . . What's going on?"

"Don't be afraid, Master Godwin. I'm alive, and so are you, thanks to Lady Elgiva."

Godwin struggled to focus. He was in a small wooden building, but he couldn't gauge its height or width. The flickering stump of a

The Exile of Elindel

candle stuck to the floor was the only illumination. But one thing he knew for certain: the creature kneeling at his side was definitely Trystin.

"Trystin, what's going on?" he gasped. "I saw her strike you down."

The elfling shook his head. "No, she only pretended to. I heard her voice in my mind. 'Fall down. Feign death. All is well.' A good trick, Master Godwin. But you knew that all along."

"I did?"

"Yes, you made to attack her. A good idea. It made it look more believable. Vieldrin would have killed you, but she was too quick for him. She made you fall asleep. Now Vieldrin thinks he can trust her, because she turned against us. But we knew we were safe, didn't we?"

Godwin smiled to hide his shame. "Where are we, lad?"

"In a hut near the hall. It's dark outside. There are guards everywhere, too. Would you like a drink of water?" He handed Godwin a beaker. "Lady Elgiva said we'd make good slaves. That's why we haven't been killed. They even let us have some light." He pointed at the solitary glim, as though it were a beacon, and his face wore a grin of triumph.

As Godwin gulped the water, he thought of something and almost choked. "Trystin, by Frigg, Grimalkin!"

"She's tethered outside, Master Godwin. Don't worry, she still has the stone. No one suspects we've got it. No reason why they should."

Somewhat reassured, Godwin tried to relax, but a noise outside the hut made him tense with alarm. As he and Trystin watched with dread, the heavy drape that covered the doorway fluttered and moved aside, and bearing an oil-lamp before it, a cloaked and hooded figure stepped in, chased by a giant shadow.

For a moment, the captives and their visitor confronted each other in silence, and then Elgiva set the lamp on the floor. "Hello, you two," she greeted them. "Are you both all right?"

"Yes, lady," Trystin said.

"Elgiva!"

She knelt beside them and pushed back her hood.

"Vieldrin's a little the worse for wine," she told them with a knowing smile, and she paused, as if to savour some secret victory. "He's sleeping so soundly nothing will wake him, but he won't be left in peace for long. There's been some trouble near the hall. Some fighting, I think, but I don't know the reason. I told the guards to investigate and said I would keep an eye on you. They weren't exactly willing to go, until I threatened to complain to their lord and master. But I must be brief. I daren't stay away from the hall too long."

"I suppose I should thank you for saving my life," put in Godwin, feeling sheepish for having doubted her. "I wasn't thinking sensibly when I came forward like that, was I?"

Elgiva looked downcast for a moment, as though she shared his guilt. There was a tension in her movements, as if she no longer trusted her limbs. The strain of their quest was beginning to show. The light from the lamp underscored her features, making them look heavy and tired, and her eyes had developed a fitful gleam, as though too much energy had been tapped.

"You both put me to a great deal of trouble," she said. "In a way, it was a good thing. It put you both in my control, so to speak. Now at least I know where you are, and hopefully, I can protect you. But you didn't make it easy for me. I was lucky, Godwin, to make a move before Vieldrin did."

"You don't have to worry about him now," Trystin said, his face aglow. "Lady Elgiva, you won't believe it, but we've found the Lorestone."

"Hush, Trystin, not so loud!" said Godwin.

Elgiva drew nearer and grasped Trystin's arm. "What? It exists? You've found it? Are you sure?"

"It must be. It's so beautiful. And we found this with it, lady."

Trystin slipped his hand inside his tunic and drew out the piece of parchment. With a grin of triumph on his face, he offered it to Elgiva. They all lapsed into silence while she scrutinised the contents.

"We have to find this place," said Elgiva, handing the parchment back. "But where it might be, I've no idea. If I could contact Uncle Bellic, perhaps he'd know where these Nine Wise Men are."

"And then you could use the stone," said Trystin, "and free the people of Misterell."

"And kill Vieldrin," added Godwin.

Godwin heard a protracted scraping, the sound of a sword being

The Exile of Elindel

drawn from its sheath. He winced at the sound. There was someone outside.

"Come out, conspirators!" shouted a voice.

Grimalkin's frantic neighing filled the air.

"Be still, you beast," cried a second voice. "Let go of my sleeve, or I'll slice you!"

The neighing persisted. At first it was muffled by the sleeve, but then it rose in volume and became a string of invectives against all two-legged creatures.

There was a dull thud, followed by an outraged squeal of pain. Someone had hit Grimalkin, and Godwin bristled with anger. Careless of the consequences, he dashed out of the hut. An elf stood near the pony, his staff raised to strike her again. Godwin seized him, swung him round with a snarl of contempt, and punched him on the jaw. Then Godwin looked about him and saw, to his utter dismay, that he was greatly outnumbered. Two more guards stood by the hut, their torches searing the night, and two more sprang from the shadows, each one holding a spear. One of them pelted towards him and let loose a chilling scream. Horrified and helpless, Godwin staggered backwards, but a kick from Grimalkin's hind legs lifted the warrior into the air and sprawled him on the grass.

This wasn't enough for Grimalkin. Her blood was up, and she trampled on the fallen elf, her hooves crushing out his life. Godwin tugged at her thick mane.

"Stop it, Grimalkin!" The sounds of purposeful movement echoed through the forest. "Listen! You must save the Lorestone. Run!"

"I'll wait!" she snorted. "At that place where Elgiva cut her hair." She turned and sped away.

Godwin glanced down at the mangled elf and almost retched, and then he turned towards the hut. Should he attack the other guards? Perhaps he should run away? But none of these choices seemed feasible, and in the end, it didn't matter. A band of warriors broke through the trees and quickly took him prisoner.

Elgiva was already out of the hut, and she felled three guards with a blast of power, but others soon took their place. She raised her arm in preparation for another elf-bolt, but one of the warriors swung at her with his heavy wooden staff.

Godwin cried out as his friend collapsed on the grass. Any resistance was pointless. Trystin was dragged from the hut and beaten and kicked to the ground, where he lay in a sobbing heap.

"Stop it," moaned Godwin. "He's only a child!"

As they bound his hands behind his back, Godwin cursed the day of his birth. He should have put up a fight, rather than let them drag him away, unresisting, to meet his doom.

Grimalkin would have a very long wait.

All too soon, the guards and their captives had reached the royal hall. Elves filled the space inside and spoke in nervous whispers, while the air grew thick with the smoke from the torches, and the great dogs stood in the corners, trembling.

At the end of the hall stood a dais, and on it, a table and an empty throne. The guards hauled Godwin and Trystin towards it and threw them to their knees. Elgiva's limp body was dumped beside them, her head wound seeping blood. Godwin, unable to help her, could only watch as the thin red rill dripped onto the wooden floor.

Only the worst could happen now.

There was a sudden stillness, the bowing of heads, as the king strode into the hall.

Godwin dragged his gaze away from Elgiva. Vieldrin was robed in midnight blue, his face a mask of fury as he glared down at the captives. But all Godwin could think of was the precious blood draining away, of the hopes smashed like footling trinkets; he would never see his family or his home again.

Lightning flashed in the elf-king's eyes. "So, you plot to kill me, do you? It seems I should have known better than to trust the words of that false-hearted bitch." He clicked his fingers. "Rouse her, someone."

A female servant bowed and ran from the hall. She returned moments later with a jug of water, which she poured over Elgiva's head. Elgiva gasped and opened her eyes, squinting at the light. Once she had gained a sitting position, she looked around the hall.

Godwin tried to meet Elgiva's gaze, but she shied away from him, as though she expected an accusation. Raising her head, she wiped the water from her eyes and peered at the king. A deep frown creased her brow.

"So, little rat, you thought to fool me, did you?" raged Vieldrin, anger reddening his cheeks. "Wilthkin!"

Godwin's heart raced as the king's cold gaze swivelled towards him.

"Tell me about the Lorestone."

Vieldrin snapped his fingers and a servant ran forwards, bearing a jug of wine and a silver goblet. While the goblet was filled, emptied, and replenished, Vieldrin watched his prisoners closely. Then he kicked the servant aside with his foot. Godwin's relief at not being made to answer the elf-king's question was overshadowed by his fear of how his death and that of his friends would be meted out.

Vieldrin sat on the throne, smirking at his prisoners. "It may interest you to know that this is not the first time I have been dragged from my rest tonight. You three were not the only ones hatching a plot against me, so do not think yourselves privileged, though it may have been your example that set other fools on their suicidal course."

He gulped down the wine and motioned for more. The servant scuttled towards him and filled his goblet.

"Apparently, they had some notion of killing me while I slept, but they were captured outside the hall. A small band of elders, easily dealt with. The ringleaders were brought to me so I could question them. You remember Haldrin, I suppose? I dealt him a lethal bolt, and the other rebel—I forgot to ask her name—she made such a fearful caterwauling that it was necessary for one of my lads to run her through with his sword. Well, we cannot have such a deplorable din in the middle of the night."

Trystin sobbed. "Grandfather, Everil, no!"

Trystin's anguish seemed to reach Godwin from a distance. He glanced at Elgiva. Her legs were folded beneath her and her head was bowed, as if in prayer. Her hands lay open on her lap, as though despair had taken their strength, and a drop of blood splashed onto her robe. She seemed beyond the touch of grief.

For Frigg's sake, Elgiva, do something!

"The Lorestone, Elgiva. Where is it?"

Silence settled like a heavy fug, while everyone looked at Elgiva, but it was clear she had no intention of answering Vieldrin's question.

"Do not play games with me! I know you have the stone." Vieldrin reached inside his robe and drew out a piece of parchment, which he waved at his prisoners accusingly. "If you have this parchment, you also have the Lorestone. So tell me, where is it hidden?"

Godwin ventured to reply, but his throat felt like dust and his voice was a mere croak. "We thought you had it."

"Damn you, worm. My lads heard you. What have you done with it? It is hidden somewhere, curse you!"

"Then you'd better look for it, hadn't you?" Elgiva suggested.

"Death and destruction!" roared the king. He hurled his goblet across the hall, and everybody ducked. The vessel struck the wall with a clang, and the terrified servants scattered. "You will tell me where it is. Voluntarily or under torture. I will get the truth out of you. Guards! Take that wilthkin and the brat and tear them limb from limb if you have to. Just get me the Lorestone!"

Four guards stumbled forwards, clumsy in their haste to obey, and seized the hapless prisoners. Vieldrin strode up to Elgiva, grasped her by the elbows, and hauled her to her feet.

"As for you, little rat, we cannot allow you to stay alive, or our plans will be imperilled. But let it never be said that I did not give my foe a sporting chance." Releasing her, he stepped back, his fists cocked on his hips and his mouth a curve of anticipation. "Come on, then, noble adversary. Work a spell against me!"

The assembled elves sucked in their breath, and the guards holding Godwin and Trystin froze in their tracks, as though unwilling to miss a contest of magic.

Swaying with fatigue and despair, Elgiva looked too weak to work a spell. Vieldrin smirked triumphantly, but conflicting emotions churned in his breast. He would have to kill her, wanted to kill her, but what about his plans? What about the progeny that would carry on his work? With dissention at home and the war going badly whenever he was absent, he was stretched too thin; he was alone against the world. He must have the Lorestone to guarantee his right to rule all Elvendom.

Confound you, Elgiva. I almost believed we could work together. But there are others with whom I can work. Oh, yes. I have only to set them free. These friends of mine, they would turn the blood to ice in your veins.

"Come now, dear heart," he said. "Just one little spell, that is all I ask." It was sad she would have to die, but she would not see reason. What made her persist in opposing him, when she knew she was beaten? Such foolishness surpassed him.

He wished he could explain his desire to reach out and touch her injured forehead, reach out and heal it with magic.

A twinge of alarm stung him when Elgiva's eyes opened fully, revealing the ire brooding in their depths. Her finely arched brows drew together in a frown of contempt.

Anger churned in his breast, but he was as angry with himself as he was with her. She was his enemy. Was he losing his mind, allowing her to prise tender feelings from his heart so easily when no one else ever had? He would make her suffer for it. He cast his cloak aside with a deliberate flourish and planted himself before her importantly.

"Do not hope for a quick death," he growled.

Elgiva's attack took him by surprise. Magical fire blazed in his face, and he staggered backwards. Humiliation seethed in his breast, and he threw magic back at his adversary, a dense cloud of sparks whirling in her direction. Their light was dazzling, forcing the onlookers to shield their eyes. The sparks enveloped Elgiva like a swarm of maddened wasps. She tried to protect her face with her hands as the sparks spat out their magical venom. As the sparks gyred around her, the air thrummed and crackled with force.

The vortex of sparks was stretched apart by a barrier of force. It thrust them outwards as it expanded. The sparks glowed white-hot as they tried to burn a path through the shell of power, but Elgiva's might enveloped them, and they burst like harmless bubbles.

Unable to accept that Elgiva's magic had bested his, Vieldrin clenched his fists. At least now she looked exhausted and he could land a killing blow, but before he could make his move, she threw a volley of force at him. It spun around him, like a boiling thunderhead, and lashed at him with bolts of lightning.

Confused, maddened, Vieldrin fended off the shafts of power and fell back against the table. Rage, pure and feral, rose up from the depths of his being. A power surge of terrible strength exploded from his hand. He slashed at Elgiva's storm cloud, sending chunks of it wheeling about the hall. Tables and benches were caught in the blast and hurled in all directions, and jugs of wine were smashed upon the floor. His anger receded somewhat, and laughter bubbled up in his throat at the sight of the assembled elves. They drew back with howls of fear, trying to dodge the flying plates and beakers. The tapestries flapped against the walls, the torches scattered sparks, and the great dogs scrabbled at the doors, desperate to escape.

Elgiva's magic battled with Vieldrin's. The tumult grew until it could grow no more, and then the hurricane of force exploded with an ear-splitting bang. In an instant, the magic exhausted itself, and everything caught up in it fell to the floor with a crash.

Vieldrin fought to appear unaffected by the contest, although he swayed a little where he stood. But his opponent suffered far more than he did. Elgiva had collapsed and lay gasping for air, her features slack and grey with effort.

"So that is the best you can do," he said calmly. "The magic of a child. A great display, admittedly, but there was little substance to it. Now I shall complete my work."

He turned, sat on the great oak throne, and glared down at his prey. Elgiva raised herself on her elbows.

"Rats should be poisoned," said Vieldrin, "but they should suffer, too. Slow poison is my weapon of choice. An incurable sickness that finds no relief. A fatal fever that lingers on, making each minute an age of misery, wasting the body and tormenting the mind. To go mad with thirst, yet fear to drink. To be tortured by slow incineration, and then to die in pain and despair. That is the way we deal with rats who invade our homes with their insolent cunning."

He made a series of gestures before him, his hands slicing through the air like knives. A thread of darkness curled through the air and hovered around Elgiva before settling upon her.

"The spell is done and cannot be undone, except by magic greater than mine, which means that you will die, little rat, for no one in Elvendom can surpass me. Two days I give you to wait for death."

Elgiva's lips parted, but she said nothing. A look of resignation dimmed the light in her eyes. As she sank to the floor, the sigh she made sounded like relief.

The Exile of Elindel

Godwin's legs had lost the ability to hold him upright. There seemed no reason for his heart to go on beating, and a darkness moved across his vision, but he grappled mentally with himself, refusing to let his senses forsake him. At his side, Trystin was sobbing, but there was nothing Godwin could say or do to bring him comfort.

"Hurl this trash out of the door. It has no further use," cried Vieldrin, waving a hand at the destruction around them. "And get this accursed mess cleaned up!"

The elf-king turned on his heel and strode out of the hall. Some of the elves followed his example, while others began to clear away the debris.

The great oak doors were thrown open, and a cool night breeze flowed into the hall. Two servants lifted Elgiva and carried her from the hall, while a third elf lit their way with a torch. Godwin and Trystin were marched outside in their wake, and as the hall doors closed behind them, a cold darkness swooped down on them all.

Godwin blinked, trying to accustom his eyes to the dimness. Ahead of him, the servants carried his friend like a broken doll. Desperate to reach her, Godwin remembered what Haldrin had said about Vieldrin's guards serving him only out of fear. He had to hope this was true, that these guards might take pity on him. He struggled to twist round so he could plead with them.

"Please," he begged. "Let me say goodbye. A final farewell. I beseech you!"

The four guards looked at him in silence.

"I can hardly help her escape, can I? What would be the point?" He almost choked on the words.

"All right," said one, "but just for a moment. No tricks, you understand? Hey, you two!" The elves ahead of them stopped and looked around. "Put her down for a minute. Let this one say his farewells." He jabbed his finger at Godwin.

The guard loosed his hold on Godwin's arm and pushed him forwards. The servants lowered Elgiva, stepped back, and folded their arms. As Godwin knelt beside her, he noticed the deep flush on her face and the sheen of sweat. Already, the fever was taking hold.

Was this the end of all their strivings?

"Elgiva," he gasped. "My dear . . ." He fought to hold back his tears.

She whispered something in a thin, hoarse voice, and he drew a little nearer.

"What is it? I can't hear you."

She stared at him, but her eyes were unfocused. "No sentimental nonsense. Not dead yet. Keep talking. They mustn't hear. Listen . . ."

Godwin fought to master himself, although it wrenched his heart. "Elgiva, you can't. You mustn't die!"

She licked her lips and struggled to speak. "Something I can do for you. My fault, all this. Make amends. Keep talking."

He swallowed down a knot of anguish. "We must say farewell. But my hands are tied. I can't even hold you."

The guards began to shuffle their feet, and one of them cleared his throat in a manner that hinted at impatience. Godwin's heart was thudding with panic, and somewhere behind him, he heard Trystin sob.

"I've found your sword," Elgiva whispered. "I can summon it. Keep talking!"

Tears blurred Godwin's vision. Yes, he ought to keep talking. All he wanted to do was weep, but she needed more time.

"Get on with it!" growled one of the guards.

"The sword comes to your aid," she sighed. "Now, a goodbye kiss, Godwin. Take the magic, while I have some left . . ."

Take the magic? He obeyed without hesitation, lowered his head, and kissed her mouth. Her lips were hot and dry. Almost at once, a wave of force surged into his body. It flared in his limbs like vitriol and was almost too much to bear. Tears of pain sprang from his eyes as magic, raw and powerful, shuddered through his flesh.

The ropes fell from his wrists.

Elgiva turned her head away, releasing him from the kiss. "Use it. Can't last," she said faintly.

Silver flashed in the air overhead, and something heavy fell into his hand. He closed his fingers around cold, hard metal.

Taranuil!

He wanted to laugh at the sudden conviction that he was ten feet tall.

The Exile of Elindel

"What's going on?" shouted one of the guards.

Godwin spun around to face the elves. Nothing could stand in his way now, and he had never been so wide awake, never seen so clearly. There was nothing he couldn't do.

The warriors gaped at the sight of the sword and then drew their own weapons with practised speed.

"Taranuil," whispered Godwin.

The metal rang with power, and the might it contained merged with the magic in his veins, an ecstasy of avenging force.

The servants, unused to fighting, backed away in horror, but the guards strode forwards, their swords upraised.

Godwin's strength was that of ten as he fought with his attackers. Two lay dying at his feet, and a third keeled over, spurting blood. The fourth guard ran at Trystin, but Godwin reached him first and struck the guard's sword with a jarring crash that broke the other blade and left its owner helpless. The guard stepped back and fumbled for the dagger in his belt, but he was far too slow. Emboldened by magic, Godwin lashed out, slicing through flesh and bone, and the guard was dead before his body hit the ground.

Taranuil hummed with pleasure; its edge shone with a gleam of relish.

The servants had edged their way towards the margin of the clearing. When Godwin looked in their direction, they turned and ran for their lives. Godwin caught one by the arm and quickly slit his throat, but the other two made good their escape, and it would be folly to chase them.

He sprinted over to Trystin, who was kneeling on the grass. The elfling's face was a mask of bewilderment, but when he saw his friend approach, his large eyes glowed with wonder. Godwin dragged him to his feet. With one swipe of his sword, he severed the ropes that bound Trystin's hands. Trystin continued to stare at him.

"Now, let's get out of here." Godwin wiped his sword on the grass and slid it into his scabbard.

"Master Godwin, you—"

"Don't be afraid. It's only magic." Godwin smiled at the admiration in his young friend's eyes, and then he frowned at his own pomposity. "And it isn't mine."

Trystin shook with shock and exhaustion, but there was no time for sympathy. Surely someone in the hall had heard the clash of swords. They might be too scared to investigate, but they would soon find someone who wasn't.

And the magic was fading. Godwin felt sick, as though he'd been spinning round and come to a sudden halt. His limbs were cold and heavy, and the sweat seemed to turn to ice on his brow. But he had to make one last effort and get his friends to safety. He grabbed Trystin's shoulder and thrust him forwards.

"Damn you, get moving!" he rasped.

Trystin stumbled forwards on legs that seemed to be devoid of bone.

The flaming brand the servants had dropped still guttered in the grass. Stamping out the last of its fire, Godwin stooped to lift Elgiva, and his head reeled at the exertion.

"Leave me, fool. I'm dying," she croaked.

"I still can't hear you," he said.

Chapter Twenty-Eight

DAWN HAD BROKEN on the eastern horizon, but in the depths of the forest, the trees were wrapped in a pearly mist and they guarded the dregs of darkness. The companions had stopped to rest, concealing themselves in a hawthorn thicket, and for a while they sat in silence, listening for sounds of pursuit.

Godwin was past exhaustion; his muscles ached after carrying Elgiva through the forest. She now lay motionless in his lap, dark shadows beneath her eyes and her face as pale as the mist. Trystin, sniffing back tears of despair, leaned his head on Godwin's shoulder.

"What shall we do, Master Godwin?"

Godwin looked up and sighed. The sky was lightening; the tree-tops were limned with orange and pink, and the brightness hurt his eyes. "We'll meet Grimalkin at the shrine. We'll take the Lorestone to Elindel." His eyes felt full of grit, and he scrubbed at them with the back of his hand. All he wanted to do was sleep. "But first, let's lie low and rest awhile."

"But what about Lady Elgiva?"

Godwin looked at the inert body stretched across his lap and struggled with a surge of panic. "If she dies, we must make sure the stone is in safe hands. Her uncle—"

Trystin sat up. "I don't care about the stone! Curse the wretched thing!"

Putting his arm around Trystin's shoulder, Godwin tried to be strong. "Calm yourself, lad. Elgiva would want us to finish the work she started, because if we don't, it's all been for nothing. Be reasonable, Trystin. No use getting angry. That won't get us anywhere."

Trystin pulled away and glowered at the ground. Godwin closed his eyes and forced himself to relax, but it wasn't an easy matter with the nausea of expiring magic pulsing in his veins. Even though his body ached for sleep, he ought to stay alert. He wondered how long it would be before Vieldrin's warriors found them. Misterell was vast and thickly wooded, but for those who knew it well, it would be no more difficult to search than an orchard.

Elgiva opened her eyes and stared at the trees above her, and her pale, cracked lips began to form words. Godwin inclined his head to listen.

"A spell once spoken cannot be broken. Cannot be broken. The web is woven."

Godwin sighed. This was the end of their quest, and it had all come to nothing. He swallowed down a constriction in his throat before he spoke. "Elgiva, can you hear me? You used up all your strength on me, foolish little elf."

"Take me farther from the fire," she pleaded. "I'm too close. I'll burn." She struggled in his arms, but he held her fast.

"Master Godwin, can't we do something?" Trystin rose to his knees. "Is this the end of everything?"

"Trystin, we must have faith."

"Faith," moaned Elgiva. "You and your faith. Faith in me, and look where it's brought us. You and your faith."

"Be still," said Godwin. "Rest. We're leaving soon. We're going to Elindel."

"Through the flames? The red ones, the yellow ones, the blue ones like flowers? I commit my body to the flowers." She closed her eyes and fell silent, but her breathing was rasping and shallow, as though her lungs were scorched.

Trystin was sobbing, and Godwin didn't dare meet the reproach in those tear-filled eyes. He clasped the hilt of Taranuil, seeking some kind of solace, and tried to clear the shambles that filled his aching head. His mind was all chaos and darkness, save for one tiny spark . . .

"They who persecute evil shall prosper

"And come to their inheritance . . ."

Frowning at the unnamed hope that flickered in his brain, he drew his sword and gazed at it, as though it held the answer. And he saw the Hill-Shrine in his mind. It was a place of power, and its secrets had been forgotten.

But that didn't mean they were lost.

He well remembered the blissful sleep that had overtaken him there. The peace. The circle of nodding flowers. But was he right to believe, to have faith in . . .

His hand was clumsy with excitement, and he struggled to sheath his sword. Optimism flooded his limbs, thrusting him to his feet. He lifted Elgiva into his arms; she was as light as his heart. "Trystin!"

"Master Godwin?" The elfling sat up straight with alarm.

"Get up, lad. I've got an idea. We're going to the Hill-Shrine. Now! If we want help, we must ask for it. Remember what Vieldrin said?"

Trystin shook his head.

"Never mind. He was wrong anyway. There *is* magic stronger than his. Faine's magic. It's our only hope. Don't sit there with your mouth open. We've no time to lose. Come on!"

Dusk was falling upon the forest. Godwin knelt on the Hill-Shrine, Elgiva cradled in his arms, and many yards below stood Trystin, Grimalkin beside him, munching the grass. It had taken them some time to reach the shrine. They had avoided the paths and glades and hidden when they heard noises that might have been the sounds of pursuit. The going had been tediously slow. At intervals, Trystin found edible plants, which he shared with his wilthkin friend, but they were barely enough to still the nagging hunger. Elgiva grew heavier in Godwin's arms, though she was a burden he willingly carried, and his strength was almost gone.

Now he lifted tired, dry eyes to the stars that winked in the sky. It felt as though he had been here forever, waiting for something to happen. He had believed some healing power would manifest unbidden. Now, he feared he would be disappointed.

Elgiva stirred and her eyelids fluttered open, but she didn't seem to know who he was.

"Darkness, it calls," she murmured.

Godwin hugged her feverish body to his breast; he wouldn't let death snatch her away. "Don't talk like that," he said. "I won't let you go."

"Tomorrow, a broken promise. Night calls me to the grave."

He tightened his grip on her slender form and shook her slightly in his frustration. "Faine will hear us, Elgiva." He looked up at the sombre sky, not knowing what he sought. "Faine, release her from this spell!"

"Fetters," she sighed. "Death, the key. Unlock them."

"Faine, First-Father," Godwin prayed.

"Why cling?" she said. "Let go."

"Faine, I believe in you," said Godwin through gritted teeth.

"Water," said Elgiva, struggling in his grasp. He lifted a water-skin to her lips; she drank a little and then pushed it away. "Poison, poison!"

"I have faith. I have faith in good magic." But Godwin's heart felt as though it were breaking.

Night deepened all around them. Elgiva writhed in Godwin's arms, and her body burned with fever. She was like kindling, apt for immolation. Tears ran freely down his face, but he had made a vow, and he would uphold it to the last.

"Elgiva," he cried, and he shook her again. "Elgiva, believe in Faine!"

"Faine . . . good . . . peace . . . death . . ."

By Frigg, I'm not going to lose you, girl!

He shook her yet again, and his anger tightened his grip. "Focus, damn you! Concentrate! One last effort of will! Think of Faine. Believe in Faine!"

"I do believe. I do," she gasped, "but you, you're hurting . . ."

"Ask Lord Faine to help you!"

"It's hot. It's far too hot!"

"Forget the fever. It'll pass. Lord Faine will release you."

"Yes, release my spirit."

"No, Elgiva, release you from Vieldrin's spell!"

Elgiva went limp, and her eyelids closed. Godwin slackened his grip. His hands were shaking, as though he had lost control of his muscles. He brushed the sweat-slick hair from her face, allowing her some moments of peace. He hated himself for his ferocity. It would be kinder to let her drift, let her succumb to the spell and die. He well knew the heartache of forcing sick children to take potions that tasted foul, but made them better. He had the strength for such things, and he had an inner conviction that what he was doing was right. To be deserving of help, one must first ask for it.

"Elgiva!" he said.

She didn't respond. He turned her head towards him and said her name again. The merest breath soughed through her lips. Gritting his teeth, he drew back his hand and slapped her lightly on the cheek. This time, her eyes flew open and she looked at him with such fear and surprise that he almost abandoned his purpose. Gently, he cupped her face in his hands.

"Elgiva, please, you must ask Faine to release you from the spell. Say it!"

"Faine, release me from this spell."

"Faine, heal me."

"Faine, heal me," echoed Elgiva.

"Good magic is stronger than bad. Believe it." *It has to be. It has to.*

Her eyes closed again and she drifted away, and this time, he left her in peace. Nothing more could be done. He lowered her to the grass; her limbs were heavy and still, her skin so pale that it seemed translucent.

Overcome by his own exhaustion, he let his gaze wander. At the foot of the shrine, Trystin lay sleeping. Grimalkin, her head bowed, stood beside him, the Lorestone safely in her pack.

If only Elgiva could use it.

Of course, she would never use the Lorestone merely to save herself. A breeze stirred the branches of the trees and at first, he inhaled the cool air gratefully, but as the darkness thickened around him, its chill breath made him shiver. The thought of summer crossed his mind, but it seemed so far away, and what would summer be without Elgiva? And what would become of this beautiful land, if Vieldrin weren't destroyed?

Two images vied for his attention. One was of his daughters dancing in a meadow full of cornflowers; the other was Elgiva, cold and lifeless in the grave. He couldn't reconcile the two.

He thought then of the prophecies that had brought her to this sorry end. The prophecies, orphan and slave. But *he* had found the Lorestone. A slave indeed, but an orphan, too? Sadly, he dwelt on the parents he couldn't remember, now dead, unattainable. Doubly lost.

Had Bellic misinterpreted the prophecies? But Godwin couldn't use the Lorestone. He had no magic, save for his sword. He drew the weapon from its sheath and peered at it in the darkness.

Taranuil had been the key that opened the door of the secret cavern where the Lorestone lay concealed. The sword had been the trigger. The sword and the cavern were worlds apart, but they had one thing in common: magic. The magic of the Earth . . . of elves . . . of Faine. The sword had no ability to act itself unless it was awakened, and then perhaps as a spark for other forces . . .

There were energies in the Earth and here, at this sacred spot, perhaps they came together. This was the heartland, the hub, of Faine's power.

It was worth a try.

He whispered to the night, "I believe. Faine's spirit will answer me." He lifted the weapon in both hands and cried out, "Taranuil!"

The sword gleamed in response, and he plunged it into the earth. Then he lay down with a prayer on his lips and stared at the star-flecked sky.

He was overwhelmed by drowsiness, yet he fought off sleep, anxious for proof that magic was at work. But all that stirred were the leaves on the trees; they rustled like slivers of darkness.

Oh, for a flash of lightning, an otherworldly voice, the sight of something supernatural!

But the knoll lay quiet beneath the sky, and the now cold and clammy hand Godwin clasped in his own was limp and dying.

"I have faith," he whispered.

And Taranuil, embedded in power, communed with the hallowed earth.

CHAPTER TWENTY-NINE

GODWIN HAD BARELY surfaced from sleep when something large blocked out the light. There was an inexplicable snuffling noise. He pried his eyes open in alarm to see Grimalkin's yellow teeth grinning inches from his face.

"By Frigg!" he gasped.

"You getting up, your lordship?"

"Must you always creep up on people?"

"His lordship's a little grumpy today," nickered Grimalkin. "Anyway, thought you'd want to know, the boy and me heard noises."

Godwin sat up and rubbed his eyes. "What are you talking about, you old jade?"

"Noises in the distance, Brit. Could be warriors. We'd better hoof it. No need to worry, though; I've had breakfast." She turned away. "I expect they're armed to the teeth, so you'd better make your peace with Frigg Or Woden. Or whatever." She picked her way back down the slope.

Godwin had slept too well. For a moment, the concern that nudged at his mind went unnamed, but then he reached for Elgiva, hardly daring to look.

To his surprise, her skin was cool. The dark stains of illness still circled her eyes, and her skin seemed even paler, but she had an air of recuperation, and under the dried blood in her hair, her wound had almost closed. Her breathing was now deep and regular, and for a while, he smiled with relief and gazed at Taranuil.

Trystin came bounding up the slope, and in his eyes there was only one question.

"The crisis has passed," said Godwin.

Relief and wonder lit up the elfling's face.

Godwin got to his feet, straightened his tunic, and then drew his sword from the earth. For a moment, he gazed at the slumbering blade. "We'd better leave. We've stayed too long. And yet," he added, "not long enough."

"Yes, Master Godwin," Trystin agreed. In his voice was a new, deeper respect.

Sliding the sword back into its scabbard, Godwin drew a cleansing breath, filling his lungs with the morning air. "How does one give thanks?"

Trystin clearly had no answer to give him. Godwin suspected they shared the same sense of awe. They had witnessed something neither could understand, something great and terrible.

Godwin pulled himself together and smiled at his young friend. "Go and tell Grimalkin that she must carry Elgiva until she can walk unaided. Take the water-skin with you, lad."

Soon, they were wading through lush grass and spring flowers. Finding a bubbling rill of water, Godwin called a halt so they could replenish their water-skins. The thin stream tinkled away into the forest's green embrace, followed by a retinue of slender reeds. Despite the beauties of Misterell, Godwin felt ill at ease and sensed his companions felt the same. They had no idea if they were being pursued and, if so, by how many. This feeling sharpened as they neared the forest's edge. Ahead of them lay a vast tract of land that would leave them prey to hostile eyes.

Godwin remembered the village Trystin had spoken of and was overtaken by curiosity. In that village were people of his own race. He asked the young elf if they would pass near the village.

"It's on our way, Master Godwin. It's in a valley, before the hills, and the village lies on the west bank of a fast-flowing river."

Godwin nodded. "I see."

"You wish to go there?" asked Elgiva in a voice still drained of energy.

"If there's time," he said with a shrug.

Elgiva smiled. "I understand. You want to meet your own kind."

"No time for social visits," snorted Grimalkin.

"Time enough, I dare say," Elgiva returned. "We hold the stone."

"We need food, too," Trystin said. "Perhaps they'll let us have some."

The Exile of Elindel

"That's settled, then," whinnied Grimalkin. "Food, it is. Let's go."

As the companions pushed on, the trees thinned out, and on either side of their path were tracts of grass that swarmed with nodding bluebells. Silence drifted through the mist like the spirit of the forest. Misterell was hard to leave.

At length, the trees were behind them, and they stood before the prospect of the open plain ahead. Godwin looked at Elgiva, but her thoughts were elsewhere, her gaze unfocused, her hand clenched around Siriol.

They had travelled less than half a league when Grimalkin drew up with a snort and swung her large head towards the forest. Elgiva and Trystin followed her gaze, and Godwin winced at the fear in their eyes.

"What is it?" he asked.

"Shut up!" hissed Grimalkin, her long ears swivelling back and forth.

Godwin listened, his muscles tensed, but his effort was unrewarded; he lacked the sensory range of his friends.

"Vieldrin!" gasped Elgiva.

"What do we do, lady?" Trystin asked.

"Sprout wings and fly seems a good idea," said Grimalkin.

Godwin searched about him for some way of escape. Ahead of them stood a clump of oak trees, their branches lifting new leaves to the sun. "Elgiva?"

She nodded and urged Grimalkin into a canter. Snatching hold of Trystin's hand, Godwin stumbled after them. As they approached the nearest oak tree, Grimalkin stopped at Elgiva's command.

"It's no use," said Elgiva. "We can't hide here. They'll see us."

The steady thud of approaching hoofbeats drew nearer until even Godwin could hear them.

"Elgiva, by Frigg," Godwin said. "You must do something . . . quick!"

"I don't think I have the strength," she said. Anxiety sharpened her features. "Perhaps, perhaps if you help me. Yes, you must help me. All of you!"

Her sudden authority calmed their panic.

"Lady Elgiva, we'll do anything," said Trystin, his eyes bright with trust.

"Grimalkin?" asked Elgiva. "Are you able to concentrate on anything other than food?"

The pony snorted.

Elgiva drew a deep breath. "Very well. Godwin, stand on my right side. Trystin, on my left. We will make a circle of power. We must be in physical contact." She held out her hands. "Put your free hands on Grimalkin. No matter what happens, don't let go until I give the word. Do not break the circle."

Godwin reached up and grasped Elgiva's hand then he glanced at the forest. A score of horses dashed from the trees. The desire to unsheathe Taranuil almost overcame him, but he obeyed Elgiva. Trystin had seen the horses, too, and he trembled in his rags.

Elgiva's voice rose over their fear, and it steadied them with a promise of power.

"Believe that we're invisible. Close your eyes and concentrate. Think until it hurts, but you must believe it. I tell you, we are invisible. We are nothing but air. Not even a shadow on the grass. Our enemies will pass, but will not see us there. Believe it, my friends. Don't fail me."

Godwin wanted to feel secure, to trust in Elgiva's magic, but it was hard, so hard. It was as though closing his eyes had left him alone in the darkness, while peril thundered towards him, like a huge beast of prey.

How on Earth could he be invisible?

He thought as hard as he could, bullied himself into the notion that flesh and bone could be transmuted into something unseeable. It was hard to imagine what help he could give with a mere exertion of will, and once again, he had to trust in the reality of magic.

I am air. Not even a shadow. I am air.

He heard the rumble of hooves, the exhalations of galloping horses, and in his mind, they were slavering beasts with barbed tails and flaring nostrils. More like dragons than horses. His legs buckled, but the earth assured him of its permanence, its readiness to uphold him, and a strange throbbing in the air closed about him like a shield.

Air. Not even a shadow.

Elgiva's magic tightened around them, and its desperation churned his guts. The hooves came nearer, pounding the earth, and his heart beat in time with them. How long could he uphold his concentration? His head ached. He was air. When would it stop?

He was air. Not even a shadow.

Shuddering, febrile bursts of magic buzzed about his ears, making the skin crawl over his flesh. This caul of force was stifling him, yet it held no malice. He wondered how Trystin was faring.

Elgiva strengthened her grip on his hand. She trembled, and her palm was slick. He shared her pain as she forced her power to the limit and beyond. He feared that the cords of her being would snap. She was untutored. How much longer could she maintain this spell? And surely Vieldrin could see them. Perhaps he could sense their presence. No. They were invisible. They weren't even a shadow on the grass.

The ground vibrated beneath his feet, and a whip cracked. Godwin winced, but there was no complaint from the horse receiving the blow. All he could hear were explosive snorts and the thunder of hooves as the riders raced by in a frenzy of speed. And then they were gone.

The thunder receded. What felt like an age of terror had lasted less than a minute.

They stood awhile, cloaked in silence, and then Elgiva loosened her grip on his hand.

"Relax."

The small voice above him wasn't Elgiva's. It was weary and hollow, drained of every emotion. But it was also the voice of someone who had survived an ordeal and gained from the experience. It had passed through fire to purity, and there was a strange duality in it: enervated, yet charged with power.

He opened his eyes to see the after-gleam of magic that still writhed in hers. It glittered for several moments more, and then it shrank back into an angry darkness.

Grimalkin snorted. "Will you take your hot little hand off my back!"

Grimalkin's remonstrance startled him. He withdrew his hand, sighed, and scrubbed the sweat from his eyes. Somehow, their wills had strengthened the magic, impossible though that seemed. He looked across at Trystin, who was ashen-faced, but managed a smile before sitting down heavily on the grass.

But Godwin had no time for him. Elgiva was all that mattered. Her face was blanker than a linen sheet, her eyes surrounded by circles of sickness. He offered her his hand, and after a moment's hesitation, she returned to herself and allowed him to help her dismount.

They looked into each other's eyes, and there was no need for words. He had shared her magic in Misterell; he understood how it felt.

Her legs gave way, and she fell into his arms. He carried her to the nearest oak tree and lowered her to the grass. Taking off his cloak, he covered her with it to keep off the morning chill. Then he made to rise from his knees, but she grabbed him by the sleeve.

"There's something I must tell you, Godwin. When the slaves paid homage, I . . . I realised it then. Kendra was right, and Bellic, too. They tolerated my treatment when I was a servant. It fitted me for service to Elvendom. It taught me humility. What might I have been without it?" Her hand slipped from his arm, and her eyelids began to droop. "So much power and wealth to be had . . . there for the taking. So many temptations. Yet it held no appeal for me. Does suffering give one strength after all?" She smiled, but then her eyes flashed open. "But Godwin, my powers are stunted. I can't develop them to the full. I don't even know what that is. Perhaps I'll never know."

Elgiva fell back with a sigh of exhaustion. Godwin didn't know what to say. She needed a wardain's guidance.

"Don't worry," he said. "We'll go to your uncle. He'll know what to do."

"But Vieldrin will get there first. He might—"

"Rest now," said Godwin. "We'll worry about that later. The danger's passed, and we have the Lorestone."

Elgiva didn't sleep for long. Some nagging sense of urgency dragged her back to the world. In her mind, she pictured Vieldrin racing towards his destiny, and she was a part of whatever that involved. She was wasting time, had to be moving.

And Siriol had been warm.

Supporting herself against the tree, Elgiva struggled to her feet. Her head reeled and her legs were weak, as though her bones had melted. Her body felt scorched by magic. Her powers were growing stronger, but she lacked the strength and skill required to protect herself from their intensity. She felt like a shallow river, broken-banked and choked with stones, unable to cope with a fierce spring flood. She cursed her weakness and also the fever that had cost her so much energy, yet she smiled at the irony of it all. The more she exercised her powers, the stronger they became; the stronger they became, the more they weakened her. She was on a downward spiral that could only end in death, and perversely, there was pleasure in it, for it was true what Vieldrin had said: power was like a drug.

But it was pointless bemoaning her weakness, and she had no time to convalesce. Only magic mattered; she was born to serve it and if it destroyed her, so be it.

She turned her attention outwards once more. The threat of rain had darkened the sky, but that was the only menace, so she allowed herself to relax. Her friends were among the trees. Godwin clung to a swaying branch while his legs kicked out at the air, Grimalkin was neighing derisively, and a group of birds wheeled overhead, filling the air with their cries.

There was movement some yards to her right. Trystin stirred and sat up.

"I heard birds," he said, rubbing his eyes. "They were calling for help."

Relinquishing the tree's support, Elgiva walked towards him. She knelt at his side and tried to smile. "I think our friends are robbing nests."

"Stealing eggs?" cried Trystin.

She drew a deep breath that hurt her lungs. "Needs must, I dare say."

Trystin appeared to accept her words, but she suspected he lacked the strength to argue.

"Trystin, you look sad," she said, reaching out to stroke his cheek. A trite remark to make, perhaps. In truth, her friend looked dreadful. He seemed thinner, and his bare, bruised limbs were like sticks. His hair was a wild and dirty tangle around his pale, gaunt face. It wrenched her heart to look at him.

"I'm tired, and I think of former friends," he said.

He hadn't intended any reproach, but she felt it nonetheless. If only she hadn't intervened, Haldrin and Everil and countless others wouldn't have lost their lives.

They sat in a thoughtful silence, and Trystin chewed his nails.

"Well," said Elgiva, at length. "I think you need cheering up."

She smiled, hoping he would do the same, but his sadness ran too deep. Placing her arm around his shoulders, she gave him a gentle hug. She longed to lift his spirits; he was too young to be so sad. But how to go about it?

Of course, there was only one way. But would she be doing it more to punish herself than to gratify him?

"I need some serious practice. What magic shall I perform, Trystin?"

His eyes grew large with reviving interest. "Oh, Lady Elgiva, I don't know!" Then he saw the birds circling the trees, and he turned to her with a grin. "I've always wondered what it's like to fly."

Elgiva arched her eyebrows. "Fly?"

"Yes. I've always wanted to know what it feels like to be really free."

She thought for a moment and then swayed to her feet. "Stand up. I'll see what I can do." She straightened herself and held out her arms, while Trystin grinned with excitement.

"Rise, little Trystin, take to the skies.

"Size is no object when Trystin flies.

"Light as a winter moth in the night,

"Wingless, arise, ascend, take flight!"

They waited for something to happen, and Trystin chewed his nails. All of a sudden, he was lifted a few inches off the ground, and he hovered above it for several moments.

"That's not good enough," said Elgiva.

Without some strong emotion to fuel it, the magic was sluggish and weak, but it would be no use to her if it waxed and waned like the moon. It had to be controlled.

"Be spry and fly; be light, take flight!

"Soar in the ether, though lacking feather.

"A blur, a streak, though lacking beak.

"In air, be fleeter than any worm-eater!"

Her mind sharpened with clarity, and a rush of force surged in her limbs, a gleeful burgeoning of power. It was savage, alive, and wonderful. Confining it within the bounds of her will, she directed it slowly outwards. The magic was a sparkling river, and she the valley through which it flowed, no longer blocked by the dregs of disuse.

Now you will do my bidding.

But still she was holding something back. The magic frightened her.

Trystin began to rise from the ground. He squealed with delight. The magic lifted him higher and higher, and he began to dance in the air, spinning around like a wind-tossed leaf. His laughter made Elgiva laugh, too.

"Oh, lady, this is fun!" he shrieked.

For a while, she giggled at his antics, at the grimy tunic that flapped round his legs, like the feathers of a windswept crow, but then the power ebbed.

"I'm sorry. You must come down now, Trystin."

Once the elfling's feet were on the earth, he ran to Elgiva and hugged her. "Oh, Lady Elgiva, you're so clever!"

Elgiva wanted to return the embrace, but a wave of giddiness made her gasp. Her vision swam with scarlet motes, and the blood throbbed in her skull. Tears sprang to her eyes at the knowledge that power was killing her, yet she was compelled to use it. It was almost as though she enjoyed the pain.

She looked at Trystin's beaming face, and it seemed a small price to pay.

Chapter Thirty

THE SUN WAS hidden behind the clouds that toiled towards the valley, and the river seemed grey and sluggish, as though it were clogged with detritus. Between the river and the hills lay the British village, a sprawl of shabby dwellings, like the refuse of a bygone age.

Godwin and his companions looked down at the village from the east bank of the river. They were weakened by hunger and exhausted by travel, and the village's gloomy aspect did nothing to lift their spirits.

"It looks like it's been abandoned," he said. "A place without hope."

"No, Master Godwin, there are people here," Trystin said.

"More of Vieldrin's work," said Elgiva. "There is some enchantment here."

"Shall we go and say hello?" asked Trystin.

"You and I had better stay here . . . at least for the moment. They might mistake us for friends of Vieldrin." She paused. "Godwin?"

He nodded. "Yes, I'll go."

He made his way down the slope towards the rickety bridge that spanned the river. Unbidden, Grimalkin trotted behind him.

"Wait for me," she snorted. "Don't want to miss anything."

A number of villagers looked up in alarm when they heard the sound of neighing, but the sight of the two intruders seemed to reassure them, and by the time Godwin had crossed the wooden bridge, a gathering of people had turned out to meet him.

He stood before the silent, sullen crowd and tried to recall the only words he knew of his people's language. Then he checked himself. Of course it wasn't necessary, because of Elgiva's gift.

"My name is Godwin," he said, his mouth suddenly dry. He

moistened his lips. "I'm of your race, but as a child, I was taken by the Saxons and taught their customs. I mean you no ill."

They looked him up and down, curious yet wary. An old woman in a grubby brown robe stepped out from their midst. She stopped a few yards in front of him and thrust her staff in the earth, as though to indicate the point beyond which he mustn't go. Her wispy white hair spoke of age and frailty, but her sharp eyes were keen as a blade.

"Brought up by Saxons, you say? Yet you speak our language as well as we do," she said, a frown deepening on her brow. She shared a look with the villagers, and their silence invited her to continue. "Ceara is my name, and I speak on behalf of the tribe. What is your business, stranger?"

The villagers stared at him, their faces blank. Godwin shuffled his feet. He didn't know what to say, where to begin.

"Courage, son," hissed Grimalkin.

"I've come to help you," he said.

"Cabbage hearts! It's food we're after!"

"Have you, in sooth?" Ceara said. "My friends, it appears that we are saved!"

Humourless laughter greeted her words.

"I'm not alone," said Godwin, crossing his arms. "The powers of good are with me."

"You are an angel?"

"I don't know what you mean," said Godwin, annoyed by the old woman's rudeness. "I heard you were in trouble, and I've brought good magic to aid you."

"A half-wit," Ceara said.

"I know about the enchantment. Vieldrin of Misterell is the source."

The villagers fell silent and glanced at each other through narrowed eyes.

"But there are good elves, too and one such travels with me. She's determined to kill Vieldrin."

A young man stepped forward and sneered. "And who is this saviour? Is she too afraid to meet us?"

"She is an elf," said Ceara, "and they are all agents of Satan."

"I don't know what you mean. My elven friend is the Queen of Elindel," Godwin told her angrily.

"We know of no such place."

"Never mind," said Godwin. "We've stopped on our way to Elindel to offer you some assurance that your plight can't last forever."

"In sooth, it cannot," she said, "for we cannot live forever."

"Why don't you ask about food?" nagged Grimalkin.

Godwin ignored this remark. "We heard that your chief is dying—"

"He died a week ago," Ceara said.

"I . . . I'm sorry for that. I had thought to bring him hope."

"Hope? He is past hope. He is well out of it." She hobbled towards him and raised her staff.

Godwin stepped back.

"From whence do you come with this hope?"

"From Misterell. We escaped from Misterell," said Godwin.

The villagers muttered in consternation.

The young man turned to address the crowd. "They have sent him to spy on us!"

"No, Aled!"

A young woman with dark red plaits moved through the throng. "You are too quick to judge, brother," she said. She stopped at the young man's side. "What has become of our hospitality?"

Aled turned away, and the young woman smiled at Godwin. "My name is Angwen, stranger, and I am niece to Morvyth, sister of our late chief. Morvyth is our leader, but she is old and sick, so I will speak in her stead. I know she would aid a traveller before she questioned his purpose." She glanced at her people reproachfully, and they shrank beneath her gaze. "Godwin, I bid you welcome, both you and your elvish friend, and I hope our hospitality will make amends for the slights you have suffered. My friends, he is a stranger, true, yet he is of our race. Is it his fault the Saxons took him? And have you forgotten that once, we lived with the faery folk in peace?"

Godwin was touched by her gracious manner. "Thank you, lady. We're hungry and tired, but we aren't welcome in this place, so to spare you any conflict, I think we'd better move on."

"Call your friend," said Angwen. "No harm will befall her."

Godwin looked at Grimalkin, and her eyes seemed to echo his

decision; Elgiva could take care of herself in a rabble such as this. He walked over to the bridge and beckoned with his arm.

"There are two elves," he said to Angwen. "My friend is called Elgiva, and the boy with her is Trystin. He was born in Misterell and has lived life as a slave since Vieldrin murdered his parents."

Angwen frowned and watched as the figures crossed the bridge. "Welcome," she said as they drew near. "Godwin has explained your purpose. Please eat with us and rest awhile. My name is Angwen, and it would please me to hear your story, if you would care to tell it." She stepped towards Trystin and took his hand. "Poor child. So young to be an orphan and a slave."

She moved away, and the villagers drew apart before her. Unsettled by her final remark, Godwin shared a look with Elgiva, and then they followed in her wake.

Night was falling like a cloud of dust, and a mist-ring hugged the moon, but inside Angwen's dwelling, the fire threw warmth against the walls and tallow candles glimmered. Elgiva told Angwen a little about their adventures, and a meal of goat's cheese, bread, and ale chased away their hunger. Now, they sat before the fire, at ease in Angwen's presence.

Angwen moved around the hut, lighting candles and refilling beakers, yet always attentive to the words of her guests. Unlike the other villagers, Angwen seemed hardly affected by the gloom in the valley, yet now and then, Godwin saw a trace of sadness in her blue eyes. For a while, she expressed wonder at the tales her guests brought to her door, but the sadness reasserted itself, and she sat beside them, staring at the flames that danced cheerily on the clay hearth.

"It behoves me to explain the sorry state we are in," she said. "As you know, Gwion, our chief, died seven days ago. He was much loved by all. So long had he been our leader and guide, I think we forgot he was mortal. His death was a terrible shock to us—more so to Aled and myself, for Gwion was our father."

Godwin made to convey his condolences, but she waved his compassion away with her hand. "Death comes to us all. It must be so. There is a saying: death is not the end of a short life, but the centre of a long one. And do not grieve for Gwion. He acquitted himself with honour while he lived, and he died a very old man. Now he dwells with God. It is we who suffer by losing him, for we are bereft of his wisdom and love. In his youth, he was famed for his courage and skill, as a leader of men and a warrior. Even the Saxons respected him, for Gwion knew no fear." She turned her face towards Godwin, her hair gleaming like copper in the firelight. "Perhaps you have heard of him, Godwin?"

Godwin shook his head.

"Well, you are young," she went on, as though she herself were older than she appeared. "Now, Morvyth is our chief. When Morvyth dies, I shall take her place, but I cannot rejoice at that. I would rather she lived forever. Not only do I love her dearly, but I fear the burden that is my inheritance." She paused and a soft sigh escaped her lips. "Well, we have suffered much, but perhaps our sufferings are for a purpose. We may be a conquered race, but please God, we will rise again."

"And your village, lady," said Elgiva, "it's cursed by an enchantment. I've felt it, and I'm sorry to say, my magic can't undo it."

Angwen didn't seem surprised. "It is as you say."

"Yet you are undaunted."

"I pray to God for endurance."

"My great-uncle once told me that some of your people are blessed with a special gift. You know the Earth's magic, and it protects you."

Angwen raised her eyebrows. "It is said that the Druids believed such things, and I would not deny their wisdom, but God protects us now."

Elgiva acknowledged this with a smile. "God has many names."

Angwen regarded her thoughtfully and then nodded.

"You doubt your fitness to lead this tribe—you who are the most worthy to do so. There's power in you and strength," said Elgiva. "Surely you've always known it?"

Angwen was taken aback, and Godwin changed the subject to save her from further embarrassment. "There's a lot I don't know about my people. Perhaps I ought to meet your chief. Pay my respects. If there's no objection."

"You may indeed, if you so wish. I am sure she would be

The Exile of Elindel

honoured. But I doubt you will learn much from her, for she is old and wanders in her mind, more so since Gwion died. I think her heart is broken." Sighing, she got to her feet. "Now I will leave you to get some rest. I will sleep at Morvyth's."

With a weary smile, she walked to the door, but she stopped and turned to Elgiva. "Tell me, my friend. Are elvish folk mortal?"

Elgiva didn't seem surprised by the strangeness of this question. "Indeed we are," she said, "but we are a long-lived race, Lady Angwen. An elf who has seen a hundred summers can expect to see many more. Yet in the end, all things must die."

"One hundred summers? That is cruel. One hundred winters, too," said Angwen. "Surely there are times when elves must weary of life, like the rest of us. A shame they must wait much longer for their heavenly rewards."

For a moment, she stood in the doorway, a pensive expression on her pretty face, and Godwin's heart went out to her. She was too young to be so sad. He noticed also, with a pang of shame, the grace of her movements, the sheen of her skin, and the soft, round curves of her body beneath the plain homespun of her gown. He thought of Rowena and the joy to be found in the arms of a woman, and he drew a deep breath and turned away. A wave of loneliness made him sigh.

He shouldn't let her leave like this without a word of comfort. But it was too late; Angwen had gone.

Elgiva was watching him, and he felt himself flush with embarrassment, believing she had read his thoughts.

"Angwen is special," Elgiva said. "Someone should try to convince her of her suitability for leadership when Morvyth dies."

Godwin stared at her questioningly.

"She will be good for these people. She has inner strength, Godwin. Didn't you notice?"

"Notice what?"

She smiled. "I didn't enchant her."

The security and drowsy warmth of Angwen's dwelling granted the three travellers their first untroubled sleep in many nights, and they slumbered longer than they had intended. By the time Godwin ventured outside, the morning was already old. Elgiva emerged shortly afterwards, Trystin at her heels.

A promise of rain weighted the clouds, and they hung in the pale sky like clumps of grey wool. The air was warm and clammy. Godwin looked round, hoping to speak to someone who would know where Angwen was, but Grimalkin was the only other living thing in his line of vision. She snorted at him.

"All nice and cosy, tucked up indoors, eh?" she said. "Don't worry about me, left outside all night, will you?"

"Good morning to you, too," said Godwin. "And you weren't left outside, as you well know. I put you in an animal shelter, and you were fenced in. What are you doing here?"

"No one fences me in," whickered Grimalkin, "not while my back legs still work."

"We're not welcome here as it is," said Elgiva. "Destroying their property isn't helpful, Grimalkin."

A woman in a homespun gown walked towards them with a basket in her hand. She kept her eyes on the ground, stopped, and placed her basket beside Elgiva.

"Angwen sent this," she said and then scurried away before Godwin could speak to her.

Elgiva peered into the basket. "Food."

Grimalkin's ears pricked up.

"For us," said Godwin.

They ate their stale bread in silence, and even Grimalkin had nothing to say. Was it the gloom of the overcast sky, or perhaps the draining effects of the enchantment that stifled cheerful conversation? Whatever the cause, Godwin had an odd conviction that something unpleasant was going to happen. The atmosphere was charged with tension. It turned the food into hard chunks in his belly and made him restless and fidgety. He even fancied that he and his companions were drawing together mentally against an unknown menace. To his sensible, practical brain, this idea seemed very strange indeed.

"I bet that's shit, isn't it," said Grimalkin.

"The food, you mean? Yes, it's pretty bad."

"Don't I know it," snorted the pony. "Their hay is older than I am. Celery stalks! I wish you'd seen what I saw earlier on. They even eat rats, you know. Filthy mixen-dwellers. Don't know what they're cooking for later. Smells just like stewed puke."

Godwin threw his bread at her. "Sometimes you go too far."

The Exile of Elindel

"I'd go a lot farther, given the choice. Far away from here."

"Grimalkin, that's enough," said Elgiva. "These people have to eat something. If all they can find to eat are rats, that's Vieldrin's fault, not theirs."

"I never thought it would be like this," said Godwin, shaking his head. "I had some idea that my people . . ." Disillusionment filled his mind. The Saxons had sneered at his people, laughed at their weak and desultory ways, but in the privacy of his heart, he had cherished a different picture; one of nobility, courage, and strength. But perhaps the Saxons had been right.

He glanced at Elgiva and she smiled with understanding, but this didn't hide the grip of fatigue, the pallor of her skin. "You're ill yet, my dear. Too little food and too much travel. You haven't recovered your strength."

She twisted a curl of hair round her finger. "My mind fares worse than my body," she sighed. "These Nine Wise Men . . . I wish I knew just who or what they are. Our quest has become an aimless trudge." Her hand slipped down to the amulet. "And there's something else that puzzles me."

Trystin bolted upright and pointed towards the hills. "The wise man is at home!"

They followed the direction of his arm and saw on the top of the highest hill, a ribbon of dark-grey smoke.

"So that's where he lives?" said Elgiva.

"So he told me, lady."

Elgiva toyed with the amulet. "I think I should meet him."

"Do you think he'd know where the Nine Wise Men are?" Godwin asked.

Elgiva looked at Godwin, but she seemed to be focused elsewhere. "What? Oh, yes, the Nine Wise Men."

"He's bound to know," Trystin said. "He knows everything, Lady Elgiva!"

Elgiva grinned. "You may be right," she said and got to her feet, her pale skin suddenly flushed with excitement.

"We're going now?" asked Godwin.

"I go alone," she said.

Godwin was unprepared for this. "Alone? But why? Be reasonable. Those hills are practically mountains."

"Yes, lady," said Trystin. "They're very steep and covered with scree. You'll have a difficult climb."

"Don't worry," she said. "I'll get there." She touched them both on the shoulder and then her gaze returned to the hills. "It looks so quiet and cool up there, and the solitude will do me good. Stay here and rest and wait for me. I must be alone. I need to think."

Godwin took her hands in his. "You will be careful, won't you?"

She smiled. "Guard the Lorestone while I'm gone, and please don't worry about me." She squeezed his fingers.

Reluctantly, he let her go.

Godwin looked at Trystin. He saw no reason to put into words the feelings they shared. "I'm going for a walk," he said.

Trystin merely nodded and withdrew inside the hut.

"And you," Godwin said to the pony. "Stay here and don't wander off."

Grimalkin snorted. "Everyone's going their separate ways. What kind of a quest is that?"

Chapter Thirty-One

Godwin walked parallel with the river. The air was growing warmer, more humid, and the water beckoned.

Without warning, the image of his wife and daughters emerged from the recesses of his mind, like a guilty secret. A sensation like panic churned in his guts and forced him to walk more quickly, as though he meant to outrun his thoughts.

But they scuttled behind him and caught up.

What kind of man would abandon his family and go off seeking adventure?

His throat constricted, and he feared he would choke on his shame. If Godwin had learnt anything from the Saxons, it was the importance of kin and the duty one had to one's family. His daughters were his responsibility. They depended upon him. And they were so far away.

What on Earth was he doing here?

If he persisted with these thoughts, his heart would surely break, so he trudged on through the tall, coarse grass, leaving the huts behind, and lost himself in motion.

Head down, he almost blundered into the willows that formed a clump at the river's edge. Their delicate limbs, adorned with new leaves, drooped over the shimmering water. He slid in among them, cast off his cloak, and stood a moment on the sloping bank.

He laid his sword, sheath, and knife beside him and then rose to his feet and unclasped his belt, dropping it on the grass. He threw off his stained and ragged clothes, ran to the river, and plunged in.

Swimming was a popular pastime with the Saxons during the summer months, and Godwin had learned to swim at an early age. The shock of the cold water was soon replaced by the pleasure of weightlessness and the warming effects of exercise; for some time, he lost himself completely in the experience.

When he returned to the world of air, he was gasping, his skin glowing from his exertions. He shook the water from his hair and eyes, and cleansed of all his emotions, he clambered up the riverbank and flopped onto his cloak.

He had to await Elgiva's return. Better to wait in this sanctum of trees than to spend the day listening to Trystin's bleating or Grimalkin's continual grousing.

As always when he felt at a loss, the sword seemed to call to him; once dressed, he drew it out and examined the edge. As usual, the sword appeared sharp and ready for use, yet when he touched the blade, it felt dull. To test it, he took a strand of his hair, pulled it taut, and ran the edge of the sword across it. The blade made no impression on the lock of hair. It was completely blunt, and he had nothing with which to sharpen it. He would need to find a whetstone when he returned to the village.

Then a thought occurred to him. This was a magic sword, and perhaps it needed to be awakened first.

"Taranuil," he said.

The sword hummed at the sound of its name, and its edge took on a trenchant gleam. He nodded to himself, seized another hank of wet hair, and sliced the blade across it, being careful to avoid his fingers.

The sword still refused to cut his hair. He frowned, made another attempt, and another, but still, the blade made no impression.

He stared at the weapon in puzzlement. Surely he wasn't mistaken? The edge of the sword was keen, thin as a sliver of seashell. Gingerly, he ran his finger down the length of the blade. His finger told him it was dull, as blunt as a rusted ploughshare. Was there something wrong with his vision?

"I don't understand," he said. "Damn it, I've awakened you. Why are you so dull?"

He stood and walked to the nearest tree, drew back his arm, and brought the weapon down upon a slanting branch. Taranuil cut through the bough and those beneath it, as though wood and air were the same, lacking any substance. So easily was this act performed, Godwin had to grab the trunk to stop his own momentum.

The Exile of Elindel

The severed branches fell away, and half of the willow flopped with a splash into the river below. Godwin watched the amputated limbs drift downstream. His mind refused to grasp the sight, and he scowled at the shining blade.

"By Frigg, don't toy with me!"

He gripped the blade and squeezed, but felt no sharpness. He clenched his fingers tighter, until the pressure hurt him, but when he uncurled his hand again, his skin was unmarked.

He sat on his cloak and stared at the silent river. He needed an explanation, but there was none to be had. He looked at the sword, at its razor-sharp edge, and confusion gave way to fear. He flung the weapon aside, as though it were something loathsome.

The sword hummed in the grass, but he refused to listen.

There was rustling among the trees behind him. He got to his knees, snatched up his knife, and twisted around to confront the unknown threat. Angwen emerged from the willows, her long hair braided with pale-blue ribbons. She glowed like a flower in early spring, despite her shapeless linen robe with its belt of plaited rope.

She was clearly embarrassed by his startled reaction and clasped her hands together at her throat. "Forgive me," she said. "One should know better than to creep up on a warrior."

Godwin dropped his knife on the grass and pulled himself together. "Good morning, Lady Angwen."

She smiled and sat down beside him. "The sky is full of rain."

"Yes, indeed," he said.

She gazed across the river. "I spoke with Morvyth earlier. She would like to meet you today."

Godwin tried to sound casual, and the effort it took surprised him. "How is she, Lady Angwen?"

Lowering her gaze, Angwen stared at her hands, folded in her lap. "Her time diminishes swiftly. She wanders in strange realms. Yet, sometimes she speaks and sees so clearly . . . but it is often thus with the dying. For now, thank God, she sleeps."

Godwin wanted to sympathise, but could think of nothing to say. Whatever he did say was sure to sound trite. Angwen was clearly a person well acquainted with death and the loss of her kin. Embarrassed by his own awkwardness, he waited for her to continue.

Angwen raised her hands and pulled the ribbons from her hair, and the gleaming, dark red tresses flowed like a river of polished bronze. She sighed, as though she had been freed from some unbearable constraint.

Godwin swallowed hard.

"My aunt is so good, so full of wisdom," Angwen said. "How shall I cope when she dies? We have lost too many elders and have no one to guide us. How shall I lead these unhappy people? I have no husband to help me." She raised her beautiful, lucid eyes and turned their gaze upon him.

Unsettled by her scrutiny, he looked away, drew up his knees, and hugged them to his chest.

"There is no one eligible for my hand, and even if the elf-king permitted us to leave, I do not know where I would search for others of our race. Aled is not fit to lead. It pains me to admit it, but he is too impetuous and has no common sense. And I am the tanist. As eldest child of Gwion, this burden must be mine." A worried frown disturbed her brow. "Our village cannot last much longer. We are diminishing, dying . . . like our chief." She looked up with regret and placed her hand on his arm. "But I am thoughtless, Godwin. At least I have a tribe. I know where I belong, but you . . ."

"My people must still live somewhere, lady, but where they are, I'll never know. And perhaps it's better I don't. I've been taught the Saxon ways, and I think I'm too old to learn new ones."

"Was life hard for you with the Saxons?" she asked. "Being apart from your own people must have made you sad at times."

"Only when I thought about it," he said.

"I should like to hear about it."

Angwen waited for his answer, but Godwin shrugged. "Another time, perhaps."

"Of course. Forgive my curiosity, but we are isolated here. News from the outside world is all the more valued for its rarity. I did not intend to pry." She paused and lowered her eyes. "Sometimes, I find myself wondering if there really is an outside world."

"There is," he said, "but that doesn't mean it's something worth talking about."

"What will you do, my friend?" she asked.

"Do?"

The Exile of Elindel

"When you have helped your elvish friend. If you succeed . . . what then? Elves and men cannot live together, and surely you would not return to the Saxons?"

But he had to. Rowena . . . the children . . .

He opened his mouth, determined to tell her the reason why he must go back, but somehow, the words wouldn't come. Gazing into her eyes, eyes so like his own, he knew he needed his own kind, knew he needed her . . .

But the image of Rowena refused to be suppressed, and he got to his feet. All he wanted to do was escape. To escape from Angwen, from everyone, from all of their demands and needs.

Angwen was also on her feet. "Dear God, I have offended you."

"No." No. He had offended himself. He had been false to himself.

There were too many vows to be kept. He had a duty to his family. He had pledged to protect Elgiva. He had promised himself freedom. Why were there so many choices now, when once, he had none at all?

He drew a deep breath to steady himself. No, he mustn't be false to Angwen. Perhaps he had used Rowena to mitigate his loneliness, to make himself feel secure and accepted. Perhaps he had used Elgiva to escape from the very security Rowena had provided and to satisfy his need for excitement. Yet, he loved them both . . . didn't he?

No, he mustn't use Angwen. He mustn't betray his own people. And she alone had defended him against the tribe. He decided to tell her about Rowena, but Angwen grasped his arm and looked into his eyes.

"In you, I see loss and loneliness," she said.

Please don't. You sound just like Elgiva.

"I, too, am lost and lonely," she went on. "Forgive me if I seem over-bold, but it is the custom of our race to speak what is in our hearts."

I have no heart.

"I feel there is a bond between us," she said.

The touch of her hand on his skin and the glow of affection in her soft eyes were altogether too much. He grabbed her waist and pulled her towards him, kissing her on the mouth. She threw her arms about his neck and returned the kiss with hungry lips.

He held her away from him, appalled by her need, and looked into her eyes.

"I knew," said Angwen. "One day, I knew, if I had faith, there would be someone . . . someone special . . . for me."

Angwen smiled, clasped his hand, and pulled him down to the grass. They sat and watched the sun-dappled water lapping against the riverbank, and she leaned her body against him.

"Could you find it in your heart to love someone like me?" she asked, a tremor in her voice.

Who couldn't? "Angwen, you're very beautiful, and well, if things were different, I'd stay by your side forever, but—"

"You are my warrior—"

"I'm nothing of the sort," he said.

"But I can see," she said. "You are a true son of our race."

He wanted to deny this, but her trusting gaze stifled his protest. In her eyes, he could do no wrong.

Angwen could know nothing of his past, his self-doubt, and his cowardice. He travelled with elves and braved hardship and danger, apparently because he wanted to. He carried a sword and was born of a race of warriors. So she clearly took his valour for granted. No doubt in her mind, he represented someone she could lean on after years of supporting others.

How could he shatter her illusions, when she had little else?

With her encouragement, could he become the kind of man she already believed him to be? Might he finally realise whatever potential the Saxons had denied him? But such thoughts were fantasy. He couldn't stay here.

Could he?

Someone called him from the distance. Godwin heard his name, but it took some time for him to give the summons his full attention. It was Trystin, and the urgency of his plea demanded an answer. As he pulled away from Angwen, a great abyss yawned between them, and it sent a shiver down his spine.

"By Frigg!" he cried. "What now?"

"Your friend sounds very distressed," she said.

"That's nothing new." He grimaced and stood. "Trystin, over here!" He held out his hand to help Angwen to her feet. Gathering up his knife and cloak, he led her out of the trees.

The Exile of Elindel

Trystin stood on the riverbank, nervously chewing his nails. "Come back to the village, Master Godwin! You must . . . Grimalkin . . . she's . . . there's trouble!" So saying, the elfling took to his heels.

Godwin sighed and made to follow him, still holding Angwen's hand.

Master, don't leave me!

Oh, Frigg, he'd forgotten the sword!

"Angwen, please go on ahead. I must go back and fetch my sword." He smiled to dispel her anxiety. "Don't worry, I won't be long."

As Godwin neared the village, Grimalkin was calling his name, and her neighs were both urgent and angry. Soon, she came into view, kicking and bucking, surrounded by a ring of people. A length of rope dangled from her neck.

"Piss off, you turds," she screamed at them, "or my hooves will churn your guts!"

Godwin thrust his way through the noisy crowd. Angwen stood with the villagers, and she looked relieved when she saw him. He stopped next to Grimalkin and glanced round at them.

"What in Frigg's name is going on?" he demanded.

"Your beast tried to run off, so we brought her back," said a middle-aged woman. "Then she started playing up. Kicking and jumping about like a mad thing."

"It's that time of year," remarked an old man. "She must have got wind of the wild nags that live beyond the hills."

The villagers nodded.

Godwin cocked his fists on his hips and gave the pony a menacing glare. "Curse you," he muttered under his breath. "You were left in charge of the stone!"

"We all need to sow a few wild oats," retorted Grimalkin, tossing her head. "I saw Angwen sneak off after you."

Grimalkin's candid and thoughtless remark left Godwin speechless with rage.

The old man scratched his scanty beard and shook his head at Godwin. "She's a stubborn brute. A killer. Never seen a more mettlesome beast."

The villagers muttered agreement.

"You'll have to give her the stick," said the woman, offering her staff for the purpose. "Show her who's the master."

Heads nodded in the crowd.

"The first dog that takes a stick to me gets his nose bitten off," cried Grimalkin.

"Shut up," said Godwin. "You've caused enough trouble."

"Listen, Brit," she whinnied. "You only know their side of it. The bastards wanted to eat me!"

"Don't give me that. You're full of tricks."

"Seeing as she's unmanageable, stranger, would you care to sell her?" The old man looked at him hopefully.

Godwin turned to confront him. "Sell her?"

"I have nothing much to barter with, just a couple of trinkets, but my family is starving, you see."

"She would feed a great many of us," cried another man in the crowd.

"Told you," snickered Grimalkin.

Godwin looked round at the hungry eyes and lean faces taut with desire; some were even licking their lips. A shudder ran down his spine. "No, I'm sorry, I can't. She's too useful."

Then Ceara hobbled towards him, waving her staff in the air. "You would see us starve, then, stranger? The Saxons taught you well!"

"Ceara, please!" cried Angwen. "The pony is his, and this man is our guest."

Ceara's lip curled. "Did we send him an invitation?"

"You can't make me sell her." Godwin placed his hand on Grimalkin's neck in a gesture of ownership and whispered to her, "Don't panic. I'll protect you."

"And who'll protect you?" she whinnied. "Look at 'em. They're getting nasty!"

"You have no charity, stranger," Ceara said with a sneer of contempt. "You have eaten our food, which we cannot spare, and what need have you for a pack-horse? Your covetousness is a sin."

"You shall not have my pony."

Angwen touched Ceara on the arm. "It is not fitting that we should fight," she reminded her. "And if we abandon our courtesy, then we become barbarians." The two women looked at each other. Angwen inclined her head, and after a moment's consideration, Ceara gave her a tight-lipped smile. "Whoever harms this animal will answer to me. Now, back to your work, all of you."

With much muttering, the villagers dispersed, and Angwen turned to Godwin, her hands spread in apology. "Forgive them, Godwin, but they are broken and dispirited. They were not always so callous."

"I understand," he said.

"I think you had better tie up your beast. I wonder that this was not done before."

"I trusted her too well."

He glared at Grimalkin, but she regarded him with indifference. He moved to her side and tugged at the pack, pretending to check that it was still in place, but really to reassure himself that the Lorestone was safe and undamaged.

The woman who had served him breakfast approached. She stopped before Angwen, made a slight curtsy, and then muttered something Godwin couldn't hear.

"Thank you, Angharad," said Angwen, and she turned to Godwin. "Morvyth has asked to see you now," Angwen announced, and she held out her hand. "Let us first secure your animal, and then I will take you to my aunt's dwelling."

Taking her hand, Godwin followed her, and when they reached the meagre hut, they found Trystin hiding behind the door. Frightened by the angry crowd, he had run indoors. Seeing Godwin, he sighed with relief and threw his arms about him.

"Go and fetch a bale of hay to keep Grimalkin out of mischief," said Godwin as he pried himself from the elf's embrace.

He tethered Grimalkin and gave her a scolding, though he knew he was wasting his breath.

Then he followed Angwen across the village to the home of the dying chief.

Chapter Thirty-Two

Inside the dwelling was a sunken room, a low fire hissing on the hearth. There were shelves laden with heirlooms and ornaments, and from the rafters hung bunches of herbs, adding their fragrance to the air. The vague shapes of benches and chests squatted in the shadows.

Godwin stood beside the door while Angwen crossed the room and stopped beside the raised bed.

"Aunt Morvyth," she said, "the stranger, Godwin, is here to see you."

A frail hand fluttered on the coverlet, beckoning Godwin to approach. Angwen drew up a three-legged stool and stood it beside the bed.

"Greetings to you, lady," said Godwin.

"And to you, traveller," said the old woman. "Will you sit awhile?"

Her voice, though feeble with sickness, had a warm, maternal quality, and Godwin felt at ease in her presence. Smiling, he lowered himself onto the stool.

"Some light, Angwen," the old woman said, "and then you may leave us, my dear."

"Yes, Aunt."

Angwen lit two torches on the wall beside the bed, kissed her aunt on the brow, and tiptoed from the room.

Now that Godwin could see the old woman more clearly, it was obvious how sick she was. Her skin was wrinkled, sallow with illness, and her lips were drooping and slack. Upon the pillow was a cloud of soft white hair.

"I forget your name, stranger," she murmured.

"My name is Godwin, lady."

The Exile of Elindel

"Godwin, I am pleased to meet you. Angwen has told me some of your tale, but forgive me, my memory cannot be trusted, and I go soon to meet my maker." The candour of her statement caught Godwin off guard, and she smiled at his discomfiture. "Be of good cheer, young man. I do not worry, nor should you. Now, it would please me to hear you talk. I do not lack for visitors, but they tell me nothing new."

Godwin thought for a moment, wondering where to begin. "Angwen told you I was brought up by Saxons?" When Morvyth nodded fractionally, he went on, "I was very young when I was taken in a raid, and my sister . . . they killed my sister. I don't know what became of my parents, nor do I know what tribe I'm from." He paused as the old pain came to the surface. Odd that it still had the power to hurt him after so many years. "I dream of it still, though I don't remember all of it. I've always hoped . . . I've longed to meet others of my race."

"Ah, be not sad, my son. Curiosity is natural, and such ordeals as yours were all too frequent once, but life must go on for the sake of the tribe. We may be a persecuted race, but we are not defeated yet. I believe we will rise again."

"But Morvyth, somehow I feel . . . cheated. I'm ignorant of my people, their customs, their beliefs, and there's an empty place inside me . . . " He stopped himself. He hadn't intended to talk this way, but there was something about this woman that made him want to unburden himself.

"I can tell you nothing of other tribes, only the history of ours."

"I'd like to hear it, lady."

"And I should like to tell it." Morvyth chuckled. "My memories of the past are sharp, and elders love to tell tales, do they not? But do not worry. I hope to be brief." Her thin lips curled with humour, and Godwin smiled back at her.

For a moment, she paused and gathered her thoughts.

"We are of the Gododdin tribe—of whom we are surely the most unworthy, the lost ones who strayed too far from home. Cunedda, our chief, brought us down from the northlands many long years ago. My father was among their number, a mere boy who aspired to live as a warrior among warriors, and in his thirtieth year, he fathered Gwion, my brother, who became heir to the settlement our father founded. Eftsoons, I followed.

"At that time, we lived farther east. The Romans had abandoned this land, but they left us their houses, their towns, and roads. But soon, the invaders came. The Angles and the Saxons. They were warlike and hungry for our land. Many of our kind fled west, and we were forced to follow, but the Saxons could not be stopped. The High-King himself made a treaty with the invaders. We knew they were treacherous and were not surprised when they broke the pact and laid waste the land, destroying the towns and villas. The future promised us nothing but conflict. My father was slain in battle, and Gwion became our chief. Ah, such a man, my brother. No finer warrior ever lived."

A glow of pride glimmered in Morvyth's eyes. "He married late in life, you know. Ethne. Young, she was, and beautiful. She gave him a son and then a daughter. Ah, those two! I loved them. As dear to me as if they were my own. They were tiny chits when their father became our chief. And they were always together. Alas, poor Verica never knew the joys of fatherhood, for I have always been barren."

Godwin laid his hand upon the old woman's arm, but she didn't seem to notice his attempt at consolation.

"I believe it was in the year 479, a party of Saxons fell upon us. A terrible day. Gwion lost not only his children, but also his wife, Ethne. And I . . . I lost my Verica. The raiders stole what they could and burned our homes, and then they went. Gwion and I sought solace together . . . Many long, long nights of grief.

"But still, the tribe remained. We could not forsake our people. So, we decided to retreat farther north, and Gwion threw off his sorrow. He knew that without his leadership, his people would be lost. He took a second wife. Her name was Caronwen—half his age and the temper of a wild cat! But he loved her. She bore him Angwen and, later, Aled.

"For some years, all went well. Our tribe moved on, and we made our settlement here. We did not lose touch with the ways of the world, and we were safe from the Saxon menace. But then there came a great famine and a pestilence that covered the land and took so many from us. Caronwen . . . she was one who succumbed, and Gwion was left a lonely old man, trying to hold his tribe together—the remnants of it, at least.

"Not long after we came to this place, we discovered there were elves nearby, but our race and theirs have ever been friends and we had no cause to fear them. They left us undisturbed . . . but alas, a new king ascended the throne."

"Vieldrin," muttered Godwin.

"I believe that is his name. He took our gold and horses because we refused to acknowledge him sole master of these lands, and rather than destroy us, he placed an enchantment upon our village. Should any try to leave this place, it compels us to turn back. Indeed, I fear that if we could defy this spell, the result would be certain death. So, Godwin, we are trapped here and time has stopped for us. The price of our freedom is to worship Vieldrin as our lord and master, but that we can never do, for God is our only master. But this elf-king will not kill us. He enjoys our torment and knows our race scorns death anyway. And Vieldrin is insane."

"Morvyth, did Angwen tell you that my companions are elves?" Godwin asked.

Morvyth nodded. "They are good elves, she said."

"And one is very powerful. Our intention is to destroy Vieldrin. If he can be slain, we will do it."

"My son, such a hazardous task. We cannot help you, for we are helpless ourselves. Whatever we had of value was taken from us by force, by the Saxons, the pestilence, and the elvish king." She shook her head in dismay. "All I can give you are my prayers and my blessing, such as it is. God guard you in your quest."

"This god you worship," said Godwin. "I have little knowledge of him. As a child, I was taught some things by a man called Aethelwulf, a wise man among the Saxons, but your beliefs are a mystery to me. Aled said I was a . . . a heathen?"

Morvyth frowned. "Aled has no manners. No blame attaches to you, my son. Each man must follow his heart."

"The Saxons have many gods, Lady Morvyth, and I have believed in them, but . . . " Godwin thought of the Hill-Shrine. Since Faine touched his heart, he had become aware that there might be more supernatural entities at work in the world than he had ever imagined.

"Godwin," said Morvyth, "I know God helps me. He gives me comfort and strength. We all seek different things in life. We must all tread different paths. Faith and belief are private things, which you must discover for yourself."

Her hand sought his upon the coverlet and squeezed it, and for a while, they sat in a thoughtful silence. At length, Godwin needed to talk.

"It's strange, the things I remember. When the Saxons took me from my tribe, my sister and I were outside the village. I think we were sitting under a tree and we'd been picking blackberries. We had a basketful."

Morvyth lifted her eyebrows; he assumed she did so out of polite interest.

"I was carried away by a tall blond man, and the basket was scattered on the grass. And there were some wooden toys, I think. I see it more clearly in dreams, but also I see my sister . . . He killed her." He swallowed and turned his head away as the old pain tore his heart.

Morvyth clutched at his sleeve. "Blackberries, you say?"

"Yes. Apart from those cruel memories, this is all I have of my past."

He drew his sword from its sheath and held it up. The smooth steel gleamed in the torchlight. Morvyth propped herself on one elbow, and there was a wildness in her eyes which filled him with alarm.

"Please, Morvyth, I'm sorry. Don't be afraid!"

"No, let me see it! Let me see!"

He lay the sword on the coverlet, and she touched the hilt with quivering fingers.

"Is it you?" she gasped. "After all these years? Brave blade, you have been true to your master!" She turned her gaze upon him, her eyes awash with tears. Her frail body shook with emotion. "Oh, God be praised. Indeed, we are saved."

Godwin jumped to his feet. "Morvyth, what is it? What's wrong?"

"Nothing. Nothing is wrong, my son! No, Godwin, it is wonderful!" Morvyth fell back on the bed, torn between weeping and laughing.

"Be calm, Lady Morvyth. I'll fetch your niece."

Morvyth grabbed him by the sleeve. "No, stay, my son!" she begged between sobs. "Sit down, please. You must not leave me, not a second time!"

Frowning, Godwin hesitated, and then he complied with her

The Exile of Elindel

plea. She held out her hands, and he took them in his own, and her agitation slowly waned, her breathing returned to normal. She stared at him all the while, and tears ran down her cheeks.

"Bear with me, Godwin. Do not be alarmed, for I have another tale to tell, and when I have told it, I am sure to die happy."

She released his hands and took a long breath while Godwin watched her, confused and uncertain, impatience gnawing at his guts. He tried to keep still and hugged his chest, seeking to hold down the sense of panic that told him he was going to hear something astounding. Something unbearable.

"Many years ago," said Morvyth, "while our father was still alive, Gwion went out one day alone, searching the land for allies. He travelled west and found a great forest beyond the hills. Hearing the cries of a child in distress, he urged his pony in her direction. He found a little elf-child who had fallen into a ditch and broken her tiny foot. She was fearful of the warlord, but he soothed her and bound her injury. The elf was afraid to go home in case she was scolded for wandering off on her own, so Gwion lifted her onto his pony and offered to take her there and ask her elders to be lenient.

"He entered the dark forest, and the elves soon spotted him. A party came out to meet him with the elf-queen at their head. Gwion asked pardon for trespassing and that the child be spared from punishment, for she was so tiny and had been hurt. Admiring his courage and compassion, the elf-queen thanked him for what he had done and promised she would send him a gift to repay him for all his trouble. For indeed, you see, the child he had rescued was the elf-queen's very own daughter.

"So, Gwion returned to his Ethne, and two days after his homecoming, their son, Aidan, was born.

"Some days later, a stranger arrived. A handsome elf in gold and white came riding into our village. He would not dismount and said he would only speak to Gwion. When Gwion appeared, the elf held out to him an object wrapped in gold-coloured cloth. 'We know of your joy, my lord,' said the elf, 'and my lady, the queen, has sent you this gift to reward you for your kindness. It is for your son. It will protect him always, and it is his alone, for by the magic employed in its making, it can never leave him, save by his express command.

Likewise, it was forged in such a way that it will never injure him, regardless of who wields it.'

"Gwion thanked the elf, but the messenger's errand was not yet complete," Morvyth went on, "and he said to Gwion, 'In accordance with custom, it has a name peculiar to itself by which its magic is awakened. Awakened for as long as is necessary to serve and protect its master.'

"The messenger beckoned Gwion closer and whispered so that no one else should hear. Then he sat up straight and said, 'My lady the queen also undertakes to welcome your son as her own, should he ever lack for home, help, or kin. He need only ask for her protection, and it shall be his.' Gwion asked the elf to thank his queen, and the elf rode away.

"Gwion unwrapped the elf-queen's gift, and we gathered round to see it. It was a fine sword, with strange runes on the hilt. An elf-sword, Godwin . . . yours!"

The very foundations of Godwin's being seemed to crumble inside him. A weird, aching numbness filled his body, and the room began to sway around him. He leaned against the bed, digging his fingers into the coverlet.

"Aidan, you have returned. Gwion knew you would," cried Morvyth. "Ah, had you but reached us sooner, you would have heard these things from your sire. A cruel, cruel destiny to keep flesh and blood apart so long and then cheat them at the last.

"Gwion knew. He knew you would return to us. Oh, Aidan, dear nephew, he never forgot his firstborn son! He called to you on his deathbed. There were many things your father wanted to tell you—the most important of all, how much he loved you."

Godwin tried to get to his feet, but she gripped his arm and held him fast with a strength that belied her frailty.

"He intended to tell you about the sword when you were man enough to use it. Ah, Gwion. A champion of our race. And you, his son, a warrior, will lead us out of darkness!"

"No, I can't!" he protested.

"Yes, yes! This sword has power," she said. "Can you not feel it, Aidan? It is a power for good. For good! This is the sword you carried when they took you away from us. I remember. I remember only too well. They could not take it from you . . . it would not let them take it. Forged never to leave you, it exerted its power over them. To take the sword away from you, they would have had to take your life."

"No! I was never so brave, and they were never so cruel! And they did take my life, don't you see?" The tears rolled freely down his face, and he struggled in her grasp. "Morvyth, by Frigg! Please let me go."

"You defend them," she said, "but perhaps you are right. Your father, despite his grief at your loss, told me all things have a purpose, so there might be a purpose in your abduction. It was an old custom among our race to foster our children with others. In this way, we thought to enlarge their minds, teach them things we could not, and widen their skills and experience. Perhaps you have learned many things with the Saxons?"

He shook his head in despair.

"Now you will lead us, Aidan," she said.

"No, Lady Morvyth, I can't."

She didn't, wouldn't hear him. "Here, take this." She fumbled to unclasp a thin chain at her neck. It carried a silver ring on which was a tiny red dragon, fashioned from chips of garnet. Unable to undo the fastening, she broke the chain, drawing blood from her flesh. She thrust it into his hand. "This is the symbol of our race. It was your father's ring. Wear it, Aidan. Put it on!"

He took the ring, and Morvyth lay back upon the pillow with a sigh of spent emotion, but then she frowned.

"But Aidan, the sword. Without its name, it cannot be awakened, and I do not know it. I do not know it!" Her eyes flashed panic at him. "Only Gwion knew its name, and he took it to the grave!"

Godwin returned the sword to its scabbard. "Morvyth, listen, I know the name."

She gaped at him.

"I know it, Morvyth. Be at peace."

Tormented by her infirmity, Morvyth sobbed and moaned, and her body was seized by spasms. Godwin placed his hands on her shoulders, trying to calm her.

"Gwion!" she cried out. "Brother! Your son has returned! Do you see?"

"Morvyth, you should rest."

"No, I must have my fill of you, my Aidan. Home at last!" She sobbed, as though her heart would break. "And now, at least I can die happy. Angwen! Angwen!"

Her eyes became glazed. Godwin stepped back, shaking with the shock of what had been revealed, and then a sudden realisation hit him.

Angwen!

He made for the door and flung it open. A rush of daylight dazzled him, and some moments passed before he saw that someone was at his side.

"Godwin, what's wrong?"

His sister reached out and touched his arm.

"She needs you," he said.

He blundered past her and ran through the village to the hut where Grimalkin stood tethered. She lifted her ungainly head, tufts of hay jutting from her mouth. He had no intention of giving her any opportunity to vent her spleen, so he hid himself behind the hut and sank to his knees.

So, these were his people, the once proud Gododdin. And Gwion had been his father. If only he had come sooner. Just one short week in a lifetime of loss before he found the Lorestone. His father had called to him on his deathbed. He alone had occupied his father's last thoughts on Earth. But Godwin would never hear from his lips how much his father loved him.

He hugged his chest, his heart aching. This couldn't be happening, could it? Could destiny really be so cruel? Had all of his dreams been leading to this? His sister, his uncle and, worse, his own mother, murdered by Othere's men. Perhaps by Othere himself. Taranuil, an elf-sword. And Angwen . . .

His father had been a warrior, had led men into battle. He had called to his son, and his son was a slave and a coward. His son was a man who deserted his children, a man who felt lust for his own sister.

He took a deep breath to quell a rush of nausea, and then he clambered to his feet and staggered away, supporting himself on the wall of the hut. He needed some dark and secret place in which to hide his anguish, but as he rounded the corner of the hut, a large shape blocked his path.

"Gall and wormwood, Brit!" it said. "What did that old hag do to you?"

The Exile of Elindel

He gave the pony an outraged look. "By Frigg, leave me alone! I don't need you, not now!" He put his hands on her flank and pushed. "Damn you, get out of the way!"

"Not till you tell me what's wrong," she said.

"Grim take you!" He leaned against her body and drew a shuddering breath.

"It seems these scum have offended you."

He glared at her in amazement. "You dare to insult my race!"

"How often have you insulted mine and thought nothing of it?" she asked.

"You don't understand," he said.

"Then make me."

"Grimalkin, these people . . . They're my people! The tribe I was taken from by the Saxons!"

"Ah."

"It's taken me over a score of years to find out who I am."

"Cabbage hearts! Are you really that old?"

He intended to rail at her, but in her eyes was a gentle humour he had never seen there before. Was she actually trying to cheer him up? He relaxed a little and steadied himself. "To be fair, I should thank you," he said, "for that rumpus you caused earlier."

"Really, Brit? Why's that?"

"You stopped me from making a dreadful mistake. I was about to . . . I was falling in love with my sister." The confession stung his throat.

"That's bad, is it?" she asked.

"Grimalkin, in the name of Frigg!"

"Sorry, Brit. Different standards, you know."

He tried to relinquish Grimalkin's support, but he was trembling all over. The pressure of his anger and grief was threatening to tear him into pieces.

The pony's large head shook from side to side. "You're having a rotten time, aren't you? Wonder how our elf-queen's doing?"

Elgiva! His shame deepened at the realisation that he had forgotten her so easily. "Oh, Frigg, I forgot all about her!"

"Hardly surprising," said Grimalkin. "She'll be all right, though. She's got magic."

Godwin grimaced. "Oddly, so have I," he said. "My sword was made by elves."

"All things return full circle, Brit."

He curled his fingers into her mane and tried to explain his heartache. "My father, Gwion, he died a week ago, and I was too late."

"Poor orphan and slave."

"Grimalkin . . . I can't bear it!" He threw his arms about her neck and surrendered to his tears.

"That's right, old son, have a good weep and let it all out. Do you good. Too much on your plate." She stood unmoving, supporting his weight until he regained his composure.

At length, he mastered himself. "Where's Trystin?" he asked.

"Little whingebag buggered off. Think he was bored," she said. "With all the excitement going on, no wonder he feels left out."

Godwin sighed and scrubbed the tears from his eyes. "I thought I tied you up, you old nag?"

"There isn't a rope made that these old teeth of mine can't handle," she told him.

"Next time, I'll use a chain. Anyway, I think I'll go inside and rest."

"Good idea. It's starting to rain."

Godwin glanced at the blackening clouds. "Perhaps I should go and find Elgiva," he said with a frown. "She was far too weak to go on her own."

"Have a nap first," Grimalkin said. "Then everything will be in its proper perspective."

Whatever that is. He patted her neck and then made to leave.

"I say!" she called, and he glanced back at her. "What is it that is given to you, belongs to you alone, yet is used by your friends more than by you?"

He shrugged.

"Your name!" she said.

"You and your riddles!"

"So," she snickered, "what *is* your name, Brit?"

"My name's Godwin. I don't know how to be anyone else."

Chapter Thirty-Three

There was a hammering at the door, and someone was calling an unfamiliar name. Godwin turned over on the bed and huddled against the wall, but the annoying noise persisted. He dragged himself from his rest, stamped towards the door of the hut, and quickly heaved it open. An old man stood on the threshold. Rain pattered on the hood of his cloak, and thunder cracked in the late afternoon sky behind him. Godwin stared, fuzzy with sleep.

"Aidan," said the old man, "there are things we need to discuss."

"Oh, for Frigg's sake, leave me alone," said Godwin.

"Aidan, this cannot wait."

"My name is Godwin, old man."

The elder tutted with exasperation. "Godwin, then . . . Please, will you come? The elders are waiting to speak to you."

"What if I don't want to speak to them?"

The elder sighed, but said nothing, and Godwin shrugged. "Oh, very well."

The man set off across the village, and Godwin trudged in his wake. Soon, they reached a large wooden structure, open on all sides, like a barn no one had cared to complete. It sheltered a roaring fire, and around the blaze, the elders sat, cross-legged and solemn-faced, waiting in silence for them to arrive. A gathering breeze lifted sparks from the fire, and they floated like motes of gold-dust above the elders' heads.

The old man took his place with his peers and beckoned Godwin to join them, but Godwin stood outside their circle, his arms folded. Evidently embarrassed by his aloofness, the elders regarded each other, as if none was prepared to speak first. Another roll of thunder drummed across the sky.

While Godwin waited with growing impatience, the sound of hoofbeats plodded towards him, and Grimalkin sidled up. Moving into the shelter, she took her place beside him, rain steaming off her hide.

"That nag seems to follow you everywhere, brother," said a soft, sly voice from the circle of elders. "Indeed, you seem to prefer a dumb beast to the company of your own people."

Aled sat smirking in his direction with provocation flashing in his eyes, but Godwin merely frowned at the youth, refusing to be baited. Beside the youth sat Ceara, scowling and stiff with contempt.

"Aidan," said one of the elders, "I am Llewellyn, the oldest here. I welcome you to your long-lost tribe on behalf of us all. We have heard the news from Angwen. As eldest and strongest surviving child of our late chief, Gwion, you will be chief when Morvyth dies. We acknowledge this as your right."

The elders waited for Godwin's response, but he had no words. He felt confused and giddy and placed his hand on Grimalkin's withers, trying to hold himself steady. At least he would show them no weakness.

"You've all been against me from the start," he said, "and I don't see why I should talk to you."

"Circumstances have changed," said Llewellyn. "Morvyth believes that you are truly Aidan, and you bear the elf-sword."

"That is no proof!" cried Aled. "He could have stolen it!"

"Peace, Aled!" said Llewellyn. "That accusation is unjust."

"I am the son of Gwion, and I will say what I choose," said Aled. "And I say this man is a heathen, raised by the barbarians who took our land. How is he acceptable? He is a stranger who travels with elves. He knows nothing of how we have suffered—"

"Fit or no, his claim is just," said Llewellyn.

"I will have proof!" cried Aled.

Godwin didn't want to participate, yet he knew he must before his future was decided for him. "You are my tribe, and I acknowledge the right of the elders to choose who will be chief. However—" he pointed a finger at Aled, "—I do not acknowledge him. He has no place among the wise and should be with the children of the tribe."

Aled jumped up, his face dark with rage. "I am Chief Gwion's son! I have a right to be here!"

The Exile of Elindel

"Calm yourself," admonished Llewellyn. "Aidan, you too are unjust. It is not fitting that brothers should quarrel. Let us sit down and talk peaceably."

With a grimace, Aled reseated himself, and Godwin joined the elders sitting round the fire. He forced himself to concentrate, but he wanted to be alone, to untangle the skein of his thoughts. And one thought dominated over the rest: what had become of Elgiva? Her absence gnawed at him like panic. He glanced across the village at the gathering dusk. Even if he searched for her now, he would never find her in the darkness.

"So, Aidan, you are the tanist," said Llewellyn, "and you will lead us when Morvyth dies."

"But is he warrior enough to lead us?" said Ceara. "Aled requires proof of who he is, but I would like proof of his mettle."

"And how can we be sure his allegiance is not with the Saxons?" said Aled. "They might have sent him to search out his race and help his masters to destroy it!"

"Aled speaks wisely," Ceara said. "We cannot trust a man such as he." She jerked her chin in Godwin's direction. "Not only is he a heathen, he consorts with a demon in animal form!"

Godwin almost laughed out loud. In the capering shadows beyond the fire, equine expletives singed the air.

"This is ridiculous," said Godwin. "I won't waste breath arguing with you, but I will give you proof of my identity, and then, by Frigg, you can take it or leave it." He got to his feet, unsheathed Taranuil, and brandished it like a reproof. "I suppose you all know the history of this blade?"

"Indeed," said Llewellyn. "Its origins are well known to all the elders. It was the birth-gift of an elvish queen."

"It was more than that," said an old man beside him. "It was a token of friendship between our people and theirs."

"Yes," said Godwin, "and you know this sword has a name that awakens its power, and only Gwion knew that name. But I, as the sword's rightful owner, have learnt the name . . ." He hesitated and then cast all caution aside. "I learnt by the grace of good magic, which spoke to me through this very blade. This sword was forged for Aidan, son of Gwion, alone, and it is forbidden to do him harm. If you need proof that I am he, I am happy to provide it."

He took half a dozen steps backwards so nobody would hear him as he whispered to the blade. Then he offered the weapon, hilt first, to the highest-ranking elder. "Llewellyn?"

The old man regarded him with a puzzled frown. Godwin's unflinching gaze, however, drew him to his feet. He approached and grasped the hilt of the sword. Godwin bared his left arm.

"Cut me. As hard as you like."

Llewellyn's eyebrows lifted in horror. "I cannot! Aidan, there is no need for this!"

"Do it!" snapped Godwin.

The elders stiffened round the fire and became as silent as stones. Then Llewellyn moistened his lips.

"I cannot do it," he said.

"Then let me do it!" said Aled. He ran up and snatched the sword from Llewellyn. "I will try this heathen's mettle, and I am stronger than you!" A smug smile stretched his lips. "Shouldn't you brace yourself, brother?"

"Get on with it," said Godwin. "I haven't got all day."

Aled's grin faltered, and then a cruel frown scored his brow. He lay the cutting edge of the blade on his brother's naked flesh, and with obvious relish, he sliced the sword along Godwin's arm.

Godwin felt the drag of the blade, and its dull scrape set his teeth on edge.

The elders gasped in sick horror, and a flash of lightning ripped through the sky and lit up the night.

Aled and Llewellyn both looked in disbelief at Godwin's arm, and he held it out for them all to see. There was no cut, no injury of any kind.

Godwin repossessed the sword and stepped to the edge of the shelter. He struck at one of the sturdy stanchions that held up the wooden roof. It offered no resistance, and the sword cut through it. The elders recoiled as the roof collapsed on one side, lacking the broken spar's support.

"So there!" snickered Grimalkin.

Perhaps he should chide himself for showing off in front of these people, but Godwin was unaccustomed to such a feeling of power, and he wanted to savour it.

Llewellyn stepped forwards.

The Exile of Elindel

"No one can doubt your identity now, Aidan," he said, "so if you refuse to lead us, we must decide what we are to do."

Something shifted the old man's gaze. Godwin turned to see Angwen and Trystin walking towards the shelter. Both of them were soaked to the skin.

Angwen stepped into the shelter, a distraught look in her eyes. "Morvyth is dead."

Her gaze was directed at the elders, but she was looking straight through them. Godwin heard gasps of shock behind him as the elders digested the news. Angwen turned towards him, but embarrassment prevented him from holding her gaze for long.

Aled strode up to his sister. "Here is our new leader."

Angwen shook her head. "No, it was Morvyth's wish, her dying wish, that Aidan be our chief."

Godwin avoided the elders' eyes. On top of everything else, would he now be forced to disregard a dying woman's last, desperate wish?

"How can he lead us?" protested Aled. "He is a stranger, a Saxon spy, a heathen!"

Angwen glared at her brother. "Aidan is a warrior. Morvyth believed that when our people fight back against the Saxon hordes, only men like Aidan can lead us."

Godwin gaped in horror. Battling against the Saxon hordes? As well might an ant try to hold back the ocean!

"When Aidan's friend has disposed of Vieldrin," Angwen continued, "we must begin our search for our people, for they are strong and many in number. Aidan will lead us west to their strongholds, and we will flourish as before. Then we will prepare for the war that will rid us of these Saxons forever."

Everyone but Godwin welcomed these words. It was so remote from what really concerned him. He wanted to know where Elgiva was, what was happening to her. Unable to endure another moment, he left the shelter. Lurching into motion, Grimalkin lumbered after him.

The rain was now transforming the earth to a sticky slime that foiled all desire for haste. He had barely measured out three yards when Aled intercepted him.

"Where are you off to, Saxon-lover?"

Rage erupted in Godwin's breast. Lashing out with the back of his hand, he sprawled the youth in the mud, and before Aled could get to his feet, the lethal tip of Taranuil was resting against his throat. Aled's eyes were round with fear.

"Carve his tripes out," suggested Grimalkin.

Godwin couldn't help smiling at this. Aled clearly mistook his amusement for a sneer of cruelty, and his lower lip began to tremble.

"I have only to say one word," Godwin said, "and I'd have the power to cut you into a hundred pieces, and with no more effort on my part than it takes to cut up a rotten apple, but because you're my brother, I'll spare you. It's your youth that makes you so insolent. But Aled, mark me well. That won't excuse you forever. You'll have to learn some tact and humility if you wish to live as long as these elders. Now get up, you arrogant little worm, and be assured, the next insult you hurl at me will be your last, I promise you."

Aled gasped with frustrated anger, but he was powerless to protest. Dragging himself from the mud's wet clench, he shambled back to the fire.

Godwin turned to the elders with a weary sigh. "You have to play along with Vieldrin while those entrusted with the task do what they can to cause his downfall. You've done your part by sheltering us. As for the question of choosing a leader, I refuse to accept the title and grant that honour to Angwen, if she will take it."

They were hanging on his every word, and for the first time in his life, he felt fully the master of a situation. His confidence took him by surprise.

"You can't remain as you are," he said, "insular and suspicious. There are changes happening in this land, and they won't pass you by forever. My knowledge of the Saxon ways might have helped you fight them, but that self-same knowledge tells me such a fight would be useless. The Saxons are here to stay, and they are unstoppable. But there are other ways of defeating an enemy apart from slaying him in battle." He hoped they understood, but the elders merely stared at him.

With that, he walked away, squelching through the mud, and made for Angwen's hut. Trystin and Grimalkin followed, like his personal retinue, and Angwen hurried to join him. She caught him by the sleeve. With a frown of vexation, he turned to face her and rivulets of rainwater ran into his eyes, forcing him to squint so that his sister appeared as little more than a benighted blur. But he was relieved not to see her eyes; they were bound to be raw with entreaties.

"Aidan, do not leave us," she said. "Not after so many years apart. God has sent you to us."

"Perhaps he has," said Godwin, "but you misread his purpose, sister."

"Aidan, brother..."

He seized her by the shoulders, determined to make her understand, but a flare of lightning showed him her face, livid with pain and loss. He grasped her hand and made for the hut.

Together, they stumbled into her dwelling, and Angwen rekindled the fire. Before Godwin could close the door, Grimalkin squeezed her way over the threshold and stood against a far wall. Godwin caught Angwen looking at him askance, clearly puzzled by his lack of reaction to the pony's intrusion, but he didn't have the energy to explain. He merely closed the door behind Grimalkin and moved to the fire to warm himself. For a time, he and Angwen stood in an uncomfortable silence while steam plumed from their wet clothes.

"Angwen—"

"Aidan, I—"

"No, Angwen, listen, please. I'm leaving as soon as Elgiva returns." Godwin met her gaze, and she blushed. "I think it's best."

"Forgive me, brother." She looked away.

"No, Angwen." He relaxed and put his arm around her. "It's you who must forgive."

Tears welled in her eyes. "How were we to know?"

Godwin sighed. "I've wronged you, sister."

She frowned at him, searching his face.

"Yes," he said. "Before I knew we were brother and sister, I was false in my dealings with you. My heart and my duty lie elsewhere. I'm already married. I have a Saxon wife."

"A Saxon wife?"

"Angwen, you are still very young, and when this evil is removed, your people will be able to travel and trade again. You'll find someone to help you lead them."

She nodded, but the gesture lacked conviction.

"I've too many duties elsewhere," he said. "Not only a wife, but children, too. And leadership ill becomes me, Angwen. This is your destiny, not mine."

Clearly uncertain, she chewed her lower lip. He hugged her to him and stroked her hair.

"You told me once that your village was dying and you'd lost too many elders," he said, "but that's no reason for despair. It means you can start afresh. Some of the old ways may have been lost, but they aren't always the best ways. You need to find new ones, and I know you have the strength to do it. I ask you to take this burden from me, in the name of the blood we both share."

She studied his face and then smiled and hugged him. "I gladly accept, then, brother, because it is your wish, but I shall always think of you as leader of this tribe, no matter where you are. I will lead the tribe on your behalf, and your humility will be my guide."

He kissed her brow, and it struck him how like Elgiva she was. Both were too young to be weighed down by frightening responsibilities, yet both had unquenchable inner strength, and neither of them knew it. Both of them needed his love and support. How cruel that he must choose between them. Crueller still that he had to abandon his long-lost family yet again.

Deserting people had become a way of life for him.

For a while they stood, wrapped in each other's arms, as if they knew this embrace would be their last.

She lifted her eyes to his. "Will you return to us?"

"Who knows what the future holds?"

"God be with you, brother," she said, in a small, but courageous voice.

"And with you, sister," said Godwin.

She stepped towards the door, and then she looked back, smiling. "You are wrong, Aidan."

He raised his eyebrows.

"Leadership becomes you well."

With a sigh, Godwin turned back to the fire just as Trystin entered the hut carrying a basket, which he set upon the floor beside Godwin. It was a few moments before he realised the elfling was offering him some bread. He put his arm round Trystin's shoulders.

The Exile of Elindel

"I've been ignoring you, haven't I? I'm sorry, Trystin."

"I did say he was bored," snorted Grimalkin. "Not that anyone gives a mare's cuss."

Godwin refused to be baited. "The storm's here for the night, Trystin, and unfortunately for us, we're far too kind-hearted to leave a poor creature out to fend for itself, so we're holed up here with some rather dubious company until it stops."

"I was thinking the same myself," said Grimalkin.

Chapter Thirty-four

Elgiva had to be near the top of the hill by now, but blinded by rain, it was hard to tell. The hill was steeper and taller than it had appeared from the ground, and before she had even reached it, she had braved Vieldrin's enchantment and broken through, and this had cost her dearly. During her ascent, the loose shale shifted constantly underfoot, while sharp rocks scraped the skin from her hands. Only blind determination kept her toiling upwards in defiance of her exhaustion.

A loud concussion in the sky made her heart leap into her mouth, and she had to rest again while blood pounded in her ears. Too many rest stops. She must keep going.

She closed her hand around Siriol, and it answered her need with a glow of heat. It had to be Bellic. It had to be. Because if not...

She strained to see through the helm-cloud that covered the top of the hill, but it hid the summit like a cloak, concealing whatever promises her fevered mind had imagined. All she could do was clamber on. She ignored the smart of her bruises and cuts, the pain in her lungs, and the flashes of lightning. She was almost there; she had to keep moving.

A hint of light at the top of the hill flooded her mind with relief and hope. She heaved herself higher, and spasms of pain tormented her arms and shoulders, while the guttural boom of thunder roared at her toiling form. She stopped and squinted through the darkness.

Some yards ahead, a tall, dark shape stood on a narrow ledge. A cave behind the figure gave off a warm and inviting glow. The figure bent towards her, and its long robe fluttered in the wind, the trailing sleeves and voluminous hood hiding its face and limbs.

"You have come this far, my child," said the figure. The voice was familiar, yet it had a strangely hollow quality. "A few feet more, that is all."

She struggled on in desperation, scrabbling for holds on the slippery rocks, and her breath sobbed in her throat. "Please," she begged. "Your hand!"

"Alas, I cannot!"

"But I can't make it. I can't!"

"Do not surrender now, my child. A little more effort, and then you can rest."

The figure turned and was gone. She tried to call him back, but her voice was a feeble croak. With one last pained exertion, she managed to reach the ledge. Crawling on all fours, she entered the cave, collapsed on the floor, and let out a groan of relief.

Then, like a stone, she dropped into darkness. It covered her like peace, and she lay for some time in welcome oblivion. At length, she heard a caring voice, and it lifted her into the light.

"Forgive me, child. I can do nothing to remedy your distress."

Elgiva lifted her head, and her senses drew into focus. In front of her, the heat of a cheery fire bled warmth into her bones. When the tightness in her chest had eased, she sat up and scanned her surroundings.

The cave was bleak, its only sign of habitation a trestle bed, but the bare frame showed it hadn't been used. The rear of the cave tapered away into blackness, and only an overhang of rock protected the cave from the weather. To her surprise, Elgiva saw a raven sitting on a ledge, and to her right, chewing its cud, was a goat with curling horns.

"Greetings," croaked the raven.

"Greetings," bleated the goat.

Hidden within the folds of his robe, the figure watched her across the fire. "You like my little refuge, Elgiva?"

Still puzzling over the figure's companions, Elgiva nodded.

"Ah, these are my friends. Rork the raven brings fire in his beak." He indicated a pile of spills lying on the floor. "Eswen the goat carries wood up the hill. But lately, I have not needed fire, except to signal my presence. No need for fire to warm my bones, when I have none to warm. You chose a bad night to visit me, child."

"Lord Bellic, or should I call you Uncle?"

The dark hood nodded in answer.

"By Faine, I'm so happy to see you!"

"You do not see me," he said. "Come nearer the fire and dry yourself."

"Uncle, remove your hood."

"I cannot," he said. "I am not in the flesh. I appear to you in spirit, while my body lies sleeping elsewhere. You know I am in fetters, chained by a spell I cannot break."

"Oh, Uncle Bellic!" Her voice cracked with emotion, and hot tears burned her eyes. How she longed to embrace this kindly old elf who had taught her, protected her, loved her.

"I used to come here in body, too. In sooth, I had thought to bring you here and teach you the uses of magic. Things did not turn out as planned, did they?" he said. "My dear, you have been gravely ill. Alas, poor child, I lacked foresight. Is this what I have brought you to?"

"No, Uncle Bellic. Don't blame yourself."

"You have been touched by evil magic. Tell me about it, Elgiva."

"Vieldrin." She paused and drew a deep breath. "But I'm free from his spell now, Uncle. That's not what I need to discuss. There isn't time. I need your help. So many things I need to ask."

"You have the Lorestone?" asked the elf-lord.

"Yes, I have the Lorestone, Uncle."

His hood bobbed in satisfaction. "Then all is not lost."

"But nothing is gained!" she protested. "A parchment with the stone bore a clue to the whereabouts of its name. Without its name, the Lorestone is useless."

"Faine would not wish it to be used without effort. Where is this parchment, Elgiva?"

Elgiva looked away. "Vieldrin has it."

"I see." He considered this fact for a moment. "Do you remember the words of this clue?"

"I'm not sure."

"Try, Elgiva."

Elgiva did her best to recall the verse written on the parchment. She felt like a child again, repeating the morning's lesson.

"The important part is about a sacred grove, a sarsen ring, where Nine Wise Men are heard to sing," she said. "There stands the tallest, like a tower, beneath his feet, a word of power. That's all I can remember."

"It is sufficient," said Bellic. "Well done."

"But, Uncle, there's something that worries me," she said. "You believe I am the one ordained to wield the stone, but perhaps you are mistaken."

"Why so?"

Elgiva thought hard for a moment, trying to remember more of the verse that had been written on the parchment.

"The beginning of the verse was something like, 'The stone's discoverer, orphan and slave,'" she said, and then she remembered where she had heard that before. Kendra had recited it from her leather-bound book. "For one thing, I didn't find the Lorestone. It was found by my friend, Godwin, a Briton who bears a magic sword."

The elf-lord flinched under his robe, as though her words were blows. "Then I have erred. Alas, I misread the Ninth Book!"

"Perhaps the discoverer and the wielder are one and the same, or perhaps not." Trystin was also present when the stone was found. Another orphan and slave. She decided to keep this to herself.

"If my conclusions have been false, I hope you can forgive me, child, but if it is any consolation, I still believe you are the one destined to use the Lorestone."

"In which case," she said, "I have to find the Nine Wise Men."

"In this, I can be of service. These Nine Wise Men are menhirs, my child. They stand upon a broad glade, a circle of stones surrounded by oaks. The tallest is the kingstone, and the others are his eight sons. A wilthkin legend would have it that Arawn, King of the Otherworld, punished them for their arrogance by turning them into stone, for they were wise as wizards are wise and thought themselves greater than they were. On the night of the summer solstice, they sing their remorse to the sky, or so it is believed."

Elgiva decided to intervene before this turned into a lesson on wilthkin myths and legends. "Yes, but where are they?"

"Once you have left these hills behind, you must head southwest. The grove in which you will find the menhirs lies in a hollow in the land. It is like an enormous bowl, ringed by mounds of earth. It should take you two days on foot."

"Two days!"

"Have patience, Elgiva. Vieldrin does not have the stone, and were he to find the sarsen ring, the name is useless without the stone, as the stone is without its name. Now, while you are here, what other matters assail you?"

She thought for a moment, trying to be calm, but she felt ridiculous sitting there when she should have been racing back to her friends to tell them what she had discovered. "Tell me, then, about Siriol."

His hood moved slowly up and down. "It had but one spell and one spell only. Magic for use when there was need, but only for good, of course. The power it held would endure for as long as you wished it to, and no longer. Thereafter as an amulet, it was effectively useless. Whatever appeared to happen subsequent to that was entirely down to you. You could say I lied to you, my child, but I had hoped, by providing a focus, it would help to awaken your powers, give you confidence, and perhaps show you your courage. The most important requirement for using magic is belief. You had to believe in Siriol and believe that something would happen. And hopefully, it did."

"I suppose you were right," she said. *But sometimes it made me too confident and gave me more courage than wisdom allowed.*

"Perhaps I took a grave risk," he said, "but what else could I do at the time? Then Vieldrin arrived in Elindel, and I was unable to leave. I suspect he made himself known to Thallinore some time before you were banished. To Tarkinell also, perhaps. Indeed, he may have suggested your exile to isolate you and test your powers. You may wonder now why I did not come to you in spirit sooner, but I only have strength enough for short trips, and I feared Vieldrin would sense what I was up to. I knew where you were. Animal friends told me about the Saxon settlement, and I was counting on Kendra being able to tell you whatever you needed to know. I did not intend to leave you at the mercy of someone as dangerous as Vieldrin, yet I do not believe he planned to kill you, or you would not be alive still."

"He wants me as an ally." She hesitated. "And as his queen."

The elf-lord didn't seem surprised. "Yes, he must have heirs, no doubt. I am sure he regards you as the one most suited to his requirements. Alone. Untrained. Having power without knowledge. The ideal prey. Easy to corrupt."

The Exile of Elindel

Elgiva lowered her eyes, recalling the elf-king's seductive embrace, his charm and lavish promises. True, she had resisted him, and resisted, too, the addiction of magic that yearned for satisfaction. But it hadn't been easy.

Elgiva's self-doubt didn't escape the attention of her great-uncle. "Do not chide yourself, Elgiva, for being a little in love with him. No matter how good we think we are, some darkness lives inside us all."

She glared at him in outrage, but it was futile to protest. It was too near to the truth. And if Vieldrin weren't the evil monster she knew he was . . .

"And if it did not," Bellic said, "we would go against the balance that resides in all of Nature's works. We would not exist."

"Vieldrin must know we have the stone, but perhaps he thinks I'm dead by now, or that my friends have been captured and forced to reveal where the Lorestone is, so I dare say this gives us some space to breathe—"

"I fear he must know," Lord Bellic said with a sigh. "We must not underestimate him, and he is sure to have spies."

"At least he has no more power yet than any other wardain."

"My dear, that may not be the case. He has been trying to summon up the dark things that dwell beneath the earth. These things are called fetchen, and they are ancient shades of evil. Indeed, in Elindel—"

"But how?" she asked.

"Best we do not dwell upon it, for there is much in this world and beyond that even the Eldrakin do not know. Our magic is of the Earth, and the wardain use it for good, but again, there must be a balance, so evil exists there, too. And these Nine Wise Men are sources of power. They stand in a place where the magic is focused, as do all circles of stone. In such a place, many spells may be woven and powerful magic released."

"Such things are beyond me." Elgiva shuddered. "I don't feel equal to any of it. I can't use my magic properly, and powerful magic frightens me, and I feel . . . I feel like I'm dying. The power is destroying me. Vieldrin overmastered you, yet you are a powerful wardain. You have years of practice behind you. You can be in two places at once! What hope do I have of succeeding, when my own power turns against me?"

"Elgiva, your magic is very strong, but you yourself are weak," he said. "Your aura is faint, and you have not been strengthened in preparation. In childhood, all wardain must struggle this way, but for them, of course, it is easier. They have instruction and practice. But remember, this power is inherent in the Earth, and it is right and natural. It is your ally, not your foe."

It doesn't feel like an ally. She shook her head. She felt like a scrap of parchment that someone had screwed up and cast aside. She had counted on her great-uncle being able to unfold her and smooth out the creases.

"We are directly in touch with this natural power. It is ours for as long as we are the medium through which it expresses itself," he said. "At the final test, it will not fail you."

"No! I still don't know how to summon this power to my aid."

"You do not need to know," he said. "You merely need to feel. And inasmuch as you use the power, the power is using you, for the energy must find some release."

"But I can't sustain it!"

"Because you are weak. Prolonging the magic will come with practice."

"But there's no time for that!" She groaned.

"You fear, and that is why you fail."

She got to her knees, angry and hurt. "It's true, I'm afraid, and by Faine, I have cause to be! All this has been thrust upon me, and it's a burden I can't bear!"

"Nevertheless, it is your inheritance."

"Uncle, I've always feared magic because I believed I had none . . . and now it's too late to learn otherwise." She glared at him.

Bellic seemed unperturbed. "Niece, you do right to rail against me, but it is too late for recriminations. All I can do is give you advice, though you would not be blamed for resenting it."

He paused. She sank back onto the floor and folded her hands in her lap.

"Magic is passion," he continued. "Does not your power stir most when you are beset by anger or fear?"

She nodded.

"Such feelings concentrate the mind, if not the very being, too. Use them to focus yourself on the magic, to become as one with the energy. Your entire being, Elgiva, body, mind, and spirit. They must be one with the power. This power is good and will not destroy you, though it leaves you not entirely scatheless. I perceive you are dissatisfied with this, but I tell you, you must master this power. Do not let it master you. And if you fear it may surpass you, then channel your magic through some other medium, something strong and of the Earth. Direct its force away from you. But one day, you will have the strength and will wonder why you were so afraid." He paused to let his words sink in. "You see, we are like the standing stones. We must let the power flow through us, as they do, pure and unhindered by fear and self-doubt."

She shook her head and sighed. *You're asking me to let go, to give myself to this terrible force. As always, you ask too much.*

"Hesitancy will undo you. Vieldrin is devious, clever, and quick. He will strike an opponent without any warning." The elf-lord paused, and then his voice grew stern. "Elgiva, you must listen well, for I need your help also."

"My help?"

"Yes," he said. "Though you will refuse to accept it, you are stronger than I. You must release me from my fetters."

"No," she said. "It's impossible!"

"You have revered me, this I know, but I am a wardain, not a god, and I am no longer in my prime."

Elgiva covered her face with her hands.

"Do not falter. Vieldrin must be stopped. The war must be ended, peace restored, and the balance re-established. And Elgiva, your cousin is dying."

"Dying?"

His hood bobbed briefly in affirmation. "Your throne awaits, Elgiva. Prove yourself worthy to claim it. Nothing that is valuable in life is ever attained without effort."

"But Uncle, to fight Vieldrin, I must break my oath to Faine First-Father. Thallinore..."

"Yes, child, I know. I am sure Faine will understand."

She gazed at her great-uncle, hollow-eyed. She hadn't found the comfort she craved. Her mind had reached out to him in anguish, but he seemed unequal to her need.

"Tell me, Elgiva, how is Trystin?"

The change of subject left her floundering. "I dare say he's fine."

"Care for him. He is a good elf. And Godwin, your friend, is a Briton, you say? They are attuned to the power of the Earth. It is well you travel with one."

"That's exactly what your daughter said." She wondered what his reaction would be, but Bellic merely nodded.

Bellic stood. "I must depart. Someone comes, and they may try to awaken my body. Do not tarry here. The firewood is all gone. There is a quicker way down the hill than that by which you ascended. Eswen will be your guide."

"But Uncle, must I go? There's more. There is so much—"

"Have courage, my dear, and trust in Faine. He has chosen you for a purpose, and his choices were always well made. Be of a good heart, Elgiva."

Chapter Thirty-Five

A CALM LIKE sea-brume hugged the village, and beyond the fields, a shimmering heat-haze blurred the seam that joined earth and sky.

In a grove of trees beyond the stronghold sat Aidan and his sister Eluned. He was very young, she a little younger, and they giggled over their spoils, plunging their hands into the wicker basket to draw out the dark, sweet blackberries.

"Save some for Mother," said Eluned.

Licking the juice from his fingers, Aidan peered up through the oak leaves and saw the swollen cloud-mass, a black grume that devoured the sun. The rain would force them to go home. He didn't want that. Being indoors was dull. But now his sister was busy about some task, and it claimed his attention.

"What you doing?"

"A daisy chain. For you, 'cause you'll be chief one day."

"I won't have a crown, Ellie."

She ignored this and placed the daisy chain on his head. He struggled to draw his sword, which was far too large for his childish grasp, and then he marched up and down on his chubby legs.

"Mother will be angry when she knows you've got the sword," said Eluned. Aidan pulled a face at her, and she burst out laughing. "Will you forget Ellie when you're chief?"

"Never!"

"We'll always be together, won't we?"

A drizzle of rain began to fall. Aidan sheathed the sword and glanced at the curdled clouds. The raindrops tickled his face. A hint of lightning scoured the sky, and the grass was ruffled by a freshening breeze.

"Better go home now," said Eluned.

A clamour in the village went unheeded at first as they gathered up their wooden toys, but then the noise grew louder. There were shouts and clanging, metallic sounds. Black smoke curled beyond the trees.

"Ellie, what is it?"

People were running towards them, pursued by strangers. There was fighting, yelling, and panic everywhere. Huddled together, terrified, Aidan and Eluned watched as their neighbours were slaughtered. The breeze carried smoke that stung their eyes. Their village was burning.

The children were spotted. "Take them!" came a cry. Tall and blond with a curling beard, a raider marched into the grove, in his hand a death-dealing broadsword, already stained with gore.

"Aidan, run!" screamed Ellie.

She turned to flee, but transfixed by terror, Aidan couldn't move. The raider seized him, crushing him under his brawny arm. The basket of fruit was overturned, and the daisy chain fell to the grass.

Ellie ran back to help her brother and kicked at the raider's shins.

"Leave him alone!"

The man roared at her in his rage, but she only kicked him harder. In the distance, a horn sounded urgently. The raider, anxious to obey the summons, shoved Ellie aside with his foot, but she leapt up again, tried to grab his sword arm.

Aidan watched in horror as the man lashed out at her.

He struggled in the Saxon's grip, but there was nothing he could do. His sister lay dead on the grass. Around her lay the trampled blackberries, the abandoned wooden toys. In her soft, young neck, a deep red gash leaked her life's blood into the earth.

The raider ran to join the others. Aidan struggled under his arm, his eyes blinded by hot tears, and his screams became part of a roar of darkness that carried him away . . .

. . . And he floated with it willingly until he found himself stretched like a sacrifice, lying on top of a knoll. A ring of flowers encircled him, enclosed him in a peaceful void, as though he were a precious thing they wanted to protect.

The Exile of Elindel

And outside the circle of upright blooms, every pain he had ever felt was crouching in the darkness.

Godwin sat up with a start.

His chest was heaving with ragged gasps. It was dark, and he didn't know where he was, nor even *who* he was. Thunder cracked above him, increasing his alarm.

He swung his legs off the low bed and sat, hunched forwards, hugging his chest. Sweat cooled on his skin and made him shiver.

Eluned.

Was that her name? And was she lost to him forever? He knew now that she wasn't. 'We'll always be together,' she had said. Nothing was ever lost, only changed.

This time, the nightmare had been clearer. Now he knew why his sister had died. She could have run away, but instead, she had tried to rescue him, while as usual, he had behaved like a coward. He refused to let himself make allowances for the young child he had been then, for Eluned had been even younger.

He made a pact with himself. From now on, his life would be worthy of his sister's sacrifice.

He straightened and took a deep breath, and then he looked around the room; in its centre, the embers of the fire glowed red and gave off a meagre light. Trystin lay sleeping on his bed, his outline dimmed by darkness, and in the shadows beyond the fire, Grimalkin snuffled softly.

The door scraped open.

A figure swayed on the threshold, a silhouette of lightning. Godwin's heart pounded with shock. He sprang to his feet and searched for his sword. A whinny escaped Grimalkin's lips as she was startled from her sleep.

Then the door creaked shut and the figure walked in and knelt before the fire. Shivers racked her frame. "Sorry I took so long."

Godwin sagged with relief. Elgiva pushed back the hood of her cloak, and muttering a few words under her breath, she raised her hands to the fire. It threw out tongues of yellow flame and hurled her shadow against the far wall.

"Bring more wood," she said.

Godwin didn't hesitate. As he fed the fire, he looked at his friend, shocked by her condition. Her arms and legs were cut and bruised, her clothes were torn and soiled, and her eyes had a hollow, vacant look. He yearned to offer some comfort, but he felt himself unequal to it.

A distant growl of thunder proclaimed the passing of the storm.

Godwin placed his hand on her shoulder. "I was worried," he confessed.

She lifted her head.

"What happened?"

Elgiva shrugged. "It rained."

"The wise man?"

"Uncle Bellic," she said. "In spirit only, of course." With a wry smile, she shifted her gaze and stared into the fire. Steam began to coil from her gown, as though her will had turned to vapour.

For a while, they sat without speaking. The silence had an abstract quality that made Godwin feel he might still be dreaming.

"What's wrong, Elgiva?"

She sighed. "I expected too much."

"I know," he said. *I know.* He slipped his arm around her, and she leaned her body against him. "Tell me about it, my dear."

"He told me where to find the Nine Wise Men. They're standing stones," she explained. "He said Thallinore is dying. He said he's been wrong about the Ninth Book. He said that I was weak. He said I must learn to master my powers, but I still don't really know how."

Godwin knew only too well the smart of shattered hopes. "We'll prevail," he said.

She shook her head. "Vieldrin seeks to control the dark forces that slumber in the earth."

Godwin didn't want to hear about that. "We've got some food here, Elgiva. You should eat."

Grimalkin took several steps forwards, pricking up her ears.

"Hello, Grimalkin," said Elgiva. "Have you guarded the Lorestone in my absence?"

Grimalkin looked at Godwin and flashed the whites of her eyes.

"Her behaviour can always be relied upon," Godwin said with a wry smile.

The pony emitted a satisfied snort.

"The storm's passing," Elgiva observed. "We should leave."

The Exile of Elindel

"Indeed," said Grimalkin. "We've dallied too long with these clodhoppers."

"I'm sick of your insulting remarks about my people," Godwin said.

"I only insult, Brit, but you renounce."

Godwin opened his mouth, but found himself strung between anger and shame and unable to answer this accusation. Elgiva relinquished his support and turned to face him with a look of concern.

"Godwin, what does she mean?" she asked.

"Why don't you tell her, Aidan, lad?" suggested Grimalkin.

He didn't know where to begin, so he showed Elgiva the dragon ring. "Morvyth gave me this. The symbol of my race. It belonged to Chief Gwion . . . " He stopped, swallowing down a lump of emotion. "By Frigg, Elgiva, you've no idea. It's unbelievable!"

"My friend, what is it?" she asked, placing her hand upon his arm. "In Faine's name, tell me what's happened."

In Faine's name, it had all happened. Taranuil. Faine's Lynn. The Hill-Shrine. Orphan and Slave.

Oh, Grim. Oh, God.

"These are my people! And I'm Aidan, Gwion's son, his long-lost son, his heir!"

Elgiva gasped with astonishment, and he proceeded to tell her the rest. His talk with Morvyth. The elf-blade. The elders. Eluned. Angwen.

But when he spoke of Angwen, there were things he hadn't the courage to say, and he looked at Grimalkin with a silent plea: *As I spared you, spare me likewise.*

"Godwin, you refused to be chief?" asked Elgiva.

"I don't want that," he said. "I'm not trusted here, and there are things, more important things, I have to do."

"More important than your inheritance?"

"It's not what I want."

"Am I the cause of this?"

He shook his head. "Elgiva," he said, "it's not as simple as that. I wish it were."

Her eyes searched his, but she said nothing, and he was grateful for her silence.

She got to her feet, crossed to the door, and opened it.
"The storm has passed," she said. "The night has been washed clean. It's time for us to quit this place."

Chapter Thirty-Six

For the next two days, the companions travelled on, the hills and the elf-bane behind them. Elgiva knew a quick route through the former, thanks to Eswen the goat, while the latter had been breached by the agency of magic and the united willpower of the quest. Elgiva set a brisk pace, and their rest stops were marred by a nagging feeling that they had no time to waste.

On the second day, as the four of them walked along together, Elgiva became increasingly aware of the low spirits of her companions, Godwin in particular. He was staring at the ground, deep in thought, and she felt bound to ask him what was amiss.

"I wonder what Angwen and her people thought of me when they found out I'd run off like a fugitive," he said. "Without a word of thanks. Without saying farewell. I didn't even ask to see my father's grave."

"Well, there wasn't much time, was there?" said Elgiva. "If we succeed, Godwin, we can go back, you know. Make amends. You can visit your father's grave and pay your respects."

"I can't do that until I feel worthy enough," he said.

"But you are worthy."

He shook his head. "I keep abandoning people."

"You haven't abandoned me," she said.

"Give him time," snorted Grimalkin.

"Shut up, Grimalkin. That was unkind," said Elgiva. "Godwin, listen. Being at your village was a strange episode in our lives. We both learned things that are hard to accept. You're bound to feel unsettled by it all."

"Staying at that place wasn't exactly fun and games for me, either," snickered Grimalkin, "but you don't see me being all sorry for myself."

"And here's me thinking you always have a long face," said Godwin, giving the pony an arch look.

Grimalkin snorted, while Elgiva and Trystin laughed.

They carried on walking and soon, they were clambering up a ridge of land. Once at the top, it was clear they had reached their destination. Below them was a large grove of oaks. The plain on which these old trees grew was surrounded by ancient earthworks, so they seemed to be standing in a dish moulded out of the land.

Hidden within this ancient oak grove, the Nine Wise Men guarded their secret of power.

Elgiva led them on, and they scrambled down the man-made bank and hastened towards the oaks. At the edge of the grove, Elgiva halted and turned to face her friends.

"We must be careful," she said. "I dare say Vieldrin has many spies."

She surveyed their surroundings, but nothing could be seen or heard, only the innocent presence of birds.

"Lady Elgiva," Trystin said, "you don't think he's still here, waiting for us?"

"Don't smell him," snorted Grimalkin.

Elgiva squinted through the trees. "I'm sure Vieldrin's been here. He has the parchment and he's lorewise, so he'll know, or will have discovered, what the Nine Wise Men are."

"And if he believes we have the stone, he knows we must come to this place," said Godwin.

"This dithering is getting me down," said Grimalkin. She lowered her ungainly head and snatched at a tuft of grass.

Godwin unsheathed his sword. "We're getting nowhere standing here."

He made his way slowly into the oaks, and after a nod from Elgiva, his companions followed his lead. Soon, they were within the centre, a glade where daisies grew in abundance, and towering above the tiny blooms, nine monoliths of sandstone were planted in the earth. But the largest stone had been ripped from its roots. It lay on its side, splintered and charred, the victim of wanton violence. The four friends grouped themselves around it, like mourners paying their last respects.

Elgiva looked down at the riven stone, as though it were a symbol of her broken hopes, and in the hole where the menhir had stood, she could see an oblong box made of marble. It gaped open to the air, blank and empty, its lid discarded on the grass. Whatever it had contained was gone.

For a time, they brooded over the shattered kingstone.

"Think we're too late," said Grimalkin at length.

Elgiva raked her hair with her fingers. "I don't know what to do," she said. She looked at Godwin, pleading for guidance.

"Well," he said, "whatever happens, we can't let Vieldrin get the stone. Not now. Now he can use it."

A sigh escaped Elgiva's lips, and she nodded. "We're compelled to follow him, and he knows it. We have no choice. He must be stopped, and the Lorestone is the only way. If he releases the fetchen, then only Faine's magic can stop him. We must find a way to use it."

Godwin sheathed his sword. "But how do we sneak into Elindel without letting the stone fall into his hands?"

Elgiva shrugged. "I don't know, Godwin. I must think. Let's camp here tonight. I can't . . . I need some kind of plan."

He nodded and then turned on his heel and went to get wood for a fire.

When Elgiva woke Godwin later to take his turn on watch, he greeted it with a sense of relief. Strange dreams had beset him while he slept, dreams of barrows where dead men lay rotting among their treasures and spirits roamed in an earthbound stupor, envious of the living.

It was still several hours before the dawn, and a clammy brume rose about the circle and curled round the feet of the lofty stones. The spring night was sharp and cold, and Godwin added more wood to the fire and sat close to it, rubbing his hands. An owl hooted urgently from the trees, but Godwin paid it no heed.

But he became aware that something wasn't right. An inexplicable feeling of apprehension rode the chill night breeze. He noticed the strange, coiling mist that rose from the ground like steam and watched as it crept towards him. It clung to his clothes with pulpy fingers, stroked at his skin. Scanning the darkness on either side, he couldn't see anything to account for the dread that writhed in his guts. Elgiva and Trystin were fast asleep, and Grimalkin stood with her head lowered on the edge of the circle of stones. Above them all, the moon and stars winked between gaps in the clouds.

And yes, it was far too quiet.

He almost let out a yell of fear when a ghostly shape swooped past his eyes, scant inches from his face. It was only the owl, but it had been startled, and as it soared noiselessly over the circle, it hooted, "Beware!"

Just then, a twig snapped in the blackness somewhere behind him, and he stumbled to his feet in panic. There was stealthy movement, sly rustlings in the grove of oaks, and his body tensed with foreboding. The merest hint of a whisper reached his fear-sharpened hearing. Perhaps it was nothing more than the breeze in the leaves, yet the breeze had dropped and the stillness was stifling, like the build up of pressure before a storm.

His hand shook as he drew out his sword, and the noise it made was loud in the thick and clammy silence. The rustling in the bushes ceased. Whoever he had been listening to was also listening to him. Godwin hardly dared to move as he glanced towards Grimalkin. Her ears were twitching in all directions, and the firelight showed him the whites of her eyes.

The mist thickened and swelled and moved of its own volition, needing no wind to propel it. It gleamed with an inner glow. Godwin looked down, but couldn't see his feet, for they were enveloped in fog. Likewise, the stones rose out of the clouds. He tried to move, but he couldn't. The turgid vapour that hugged his legs gripped him as though it had muscle and bone. He wanted to call out a warning, a protest, but some coercion stopped his throat. Horror squeezed his heart as the fog seeped over the grass and rolled towards Grimalkin. It coalesced around her form, like a cloud of pulverised nacre.

And then the rustlings started again.

Grimalkin whinnied in terror, but then the compulsion of the mist forced her into silence.

Whispers hissed in the shadows, and vague shapes scuttled towards the circle. Godwin fought his helplessness and tried to master himself. He tightened his grip on the hilt of his sword, and with every ounce of will he possessed, he struggled to gasp out a single word.

"Taranuil..."

The name broke from him like a yelp of pain, and the sword responded at once. A shiver of clean power coursed down the blade, flashing retribution at the mist. It helped Godwin to fight his inertia. He slashed at the cloying fog and carved it into gaseous chunks. The fog recoiled like a living thing, and he was released from its narcotic power.

He hastened to where his friends lay sleeping, cocooned in a cloud of vapour; it drew aside before him. He shook them both, and they struggled to open their eyes.

"We're being attacked!" he cried. "You must wake up. There are creatures beyond the circle!"

Elgiva scrambled to her feet, and her gaze flew straight to Grimalkin. By now, the fog was up to the animal's withers.

"This fog is unnatural!" Godwin cried. "Elgiva, you must do something!"

"They're after the stone," she said.

Grimalkin let out a whinny of fear as the enveloping mist slid away from her, allowing dark shapes to take her captive.

The companions dashed towards Grimalkin, but long before they reached her, three elves sprang into the sarsen ring, moonlight glinting on their swords. Godwin ran to confront them, his sword pulling him behind it. He plied Taranuil to the purpose for which it had been forged and soon two of the elves lay dead at his feet, their blood pumping in runnels over the grass. The third elf drew back, a featureless shape against the background of glowing mist. Godwin prepared to attack him.

But the surrounding vegetation, and even the night itself, rose in a palpable mass and become a wall of darkness. It enclosed the circle of standing stones and boiled with malevolent power.

Weird cacklings and whisperings filled the night air. Trystin screamed with fear, and his distress made Godwin hesitate, allowing the third elf to make his escape. The dark wall opened to let him out before sealing itself again.

An elf with a staff mounted Grimalkin. She reared and bucked madly but she couldn't dislodge her attacker. The elf hit her with his staff, and Grimalkin whinnied in pain. Godwin ran to her rescue, but he slipped and fell on the blood-soaked grass. The wall of darkness thickened, and Grimalkin was lost from view.

"Grimalkin!" he cried. "Grimalkin!"

All that answered him was the pounding of hooves as Grimalkin galloped away, and Godwin almost wept at the thought that everything was lost.

Darkness closed in around the companions. It became a flapping, shapeless mass that looked like a flock of large, deformed birds caught up in a whirlwind. Godwin was pulled towards them, and a visceral fear warned him that their touch would be lethal.

"Elgiva! Where are you?" he shouted. "Help me!"

A sudden burst of blue-white light scorched across the circle. The darkness flinched and drew back. Freed from its influence, Godwin spun round and raced to Elgiva's side. She was standing before the campfire, which the poisonous air had almost put out, and Trystin was hunched at her feet, his body racked by whimpering cries.

Elgiva's bolt of magic had banished the whirling shapes, and they flew to the edge of the sarsen ring, hissing with displeasure. But they drew inwards again, like a tide of black, polluted water.

Elgiva grabbed Godwin by the sleeve. "Vieldrin left a trap for us! He left some elves to steal the stone, but he also left this darkness! Godwin, these are the fetchen! They can recognise other powers. They isolated the Lorestone so the elves could take it from us."

"And Grimalkin!"

"And their reward will be to kill us before they return to their lairs," she said. "But I don't intend to die just yet!"

Elgiva threw another bolt of magic at the hissing, fleshless creatures, and they recoiled, but those behind her seethed nearer than before. She spun to hurl her power at them, and the wall of darkness grew in size, rising higher round the circle. The air above the sarsen ring began to boil with whirling shapes, and their whisperings and moanings became like the roar of the sea.

The shapes danced above them; though black, they were transparent, like veils suspended in the air. And they flitted ever nearer. Godwin didn't know how to protect himself, but he stabbed his sword at the cackling wisps, and the fetchen capered away from the blade, leaving it to ache with frustration.

The Exile of Elindel

The fetchen revolved within the circle of stones. Their extremities took on the shape of claws, and within the blackness of the horde, skeletal faces gibbered with glee. Their voices became an eerie howling that filled the sky with abomination.

A desperate beam of scarlet force shot from Elgiva's hand towards the murky mass. It sizzled as it went past Godwin. Though it sounded full of power and fury, it splashed against the writhing shapes of the fetchen and dripped to the grass like wasted blood. The fetchen roared their hate at Elgiva, and she blasted them again. Again and again, she threw out power, but the fetchen stood their ground.

It was hopeless. Elgiva couldn't hold back the loathsome ranks of the fetchen. She stopped to catch her breath, her head swimming with effort, and was forced to confront a grim fact. It was fear that restrained her, fear of the light as much as the dark.

Let go, she pleaded with herself. *Let go.*

But she couldn't. She didn't want to die. Her flesh was too frail to wield magic. The thought of unreined power appalled her. She was unskilled, untutored, weak.

Faine First-Father . . . help me!

She unleashed her magic once more at the fetchen, but it was the product of desperation, ill-timed and ill-directed, a widely diffused discharge of power that rebounded off the fetchens' might. They hurled it back at Elgiva, and she and her friends were knocked flat by the blast. It burnt her skin like acid, and surely they must feel it, too. She cursed herself for allowing them to suffer this pain.

Regaining their feet, they clung to each other while the fetchen advanced.

Godwin raised his sword, and Elgiva's heart might have ached at this pointless attempt at self-defence had not her eyes been drawn to the blade. It was still awake and eager, angered by its master's plight, and ready to strike at the enemy. She didn't know the weapon's name, but it was an elf-blade and had been forged in such a way that magic couldn't warp its metal. And it had magic of its own.

She had used Godwin's knife when they were attacked at the Hill-Shrine. And Bellic had given her advice. *Channel your magic,* he had said.

A rush of excitement quickened her pulse. "Godwin! Give me your sword!"

"What?" he asked, but she tore the weapon from his hand and closed both hands around the hilt. Power hummed down the blade. *Forgive me for the Forest of Shades. You shamed me with your metallic integrity. I will not give you cause to do so again. Let us now work together as friends.* "Godwin, Trystin, get down!"

They obeyed at once and knelt at her feet while the black shapes howled around them.

She held the sword out straight before her and summoned her powers. A beam of light pulsed from the elf-blade's tip and cut through the fetchen, scattering them like old, dry leaves. Their shrieks of anger pierced the night. Elgiva turned, slicing through the whirling mass, but when the beam had passed them by, the fetchen regrouped and shared their strength.

Her limbs shook with effort and sweat ran down her face, but this time, she wasn't prepared to give up. *I have to focus. Body, mind, and spirit.*

The magic shaft intensified, becoming a blade of azure. Godwin and Trystin shielded their eyes. The sword hummed and jerked at the force that scorched along it, but the elf-blade wasn't surpassed. Adding its own might to Elgiva's, it began to throb with mounting glee.

Let go, it told her. *Let go. Let go.*

Elgiva abandoned all her fears and gave herself to the magic. It filled her limbs like ecstasy, and nothing else existed. Her entire being revolved around it, and power monopolised all of her senses. She became a part of all the magic that ever was or ever would be.

Her power flooded into the night, and the sword accepted it, channelled it away from her, and threw it at the fetchen. A searing white beam of destruction, it lit up the whole of the sarsen ring, like an exploding star.

While the blade keened with power, Elgiva spun round and round, cutting through the ranks of the foe. She stood at the hub of a wheel of might. The fetchen gyred around her, like pieces of black and helpless anger, trying to swoop towards their prey, but Elgiva's magic pushed them back.

Then a new sound filled the air, a chiming rife with energy. The monoliths were singing.

The Exile of Elindel

Laughter welled up in Elgiva's throat. Now she knew what magic was. Magic was ecstasy, abandonment, freedom. Magic was total awareness. Magic was oneness with everything that was natural, pure, and good.

The ringing of the sarsens' song rose to the sky, like the voice of the Earth. They called to Elgiva's magic, and it hummed through their sandstone hearts.

In a rush, the fetchen flew from the circle, swirling in all directions with a noise like beating wings. The speed of their departure left a gust of air in its wake. It snatched at Elgiva's clothes and hair and howled off into the distance. The black shapes melted into the night.

But as they went, their fading cries sounded more like triumph than defeat.

For some time, nobody moved or spoke. In the stillness, Elgiva's ragged breathing was abnormally loud. Dawn was breaking beyond the trees, and birds were starting their morning songs, as if nothing had happened in the power-scourged glade.

Elgiva's hands were clenched at her sides, and her eyes had a faraway look. Taranuil lay at her feet, and Godwin stooped to retrieve it. Trystin clung to his side. As Godwin hefted the blade, he thought of the differences between them. Elf and wilthkin; female and male; magic and mundanity. He and Elgiva had lived their lives in disparate worlds, spanned by a yawning gulf. Taranuil was the bridge.

"So," said Elgiva. "He's done it."

"He has the Lorestone," said Godwin.

She flashed a look of hatred at him, and an after-glow of magic glinted in her eyes. "I'm a fool!" she cried, gasping with anger, and he winced at the violence that crackled in her gaze, though it wasn't meant for him. "I should have kept the Lorestone beside me!"

"If we'd been attacked by elves alone, we'd have been able to stop them," he said, "but those other things . . ."

"By Faine!" she cried.

Blue flames slithered down her arms and dripped to the grass with a sizzling sound. Godwin stepped back in alarm.

"I'll crush him," Elgiva said. "I'll break him. I'll burn him. I'll snap every bone in his worthless body!"

With a cry of frustration, she hurled her magic into the pallid sky. The bolt soared upwards and burst high above like a monstrous flower, illuminating the sarsen ring down to its roots.

"I've failed." Elgiva sank to her knees and began to sob.

Godwin placed his hand on her shoulder. "Don't give up yet. We have to follow Grimalkin. Perhaps she's managed to hold them up. We might be able to catch them."

Chapter Thirty-Seven

Halfway through the following day, Elgiva and her friends came to a steeply rising ridge. Rocks gleamed like splinters of bone in the grass. Following the pony's trail, she led them up the slope to a level crest. The land before them dropped sharply down to a vast, flat plain.

Elgiva emitted a gasp of delight and closed her hand on Godwin's arm. "I'd no idea we were so close. Look over there. Elindel!"

Godwin followed the line of her gaze. "I see a hint of darkness on the horizon," he said. "Is that it? It might be as much as two leagues away."

They followed the trail along the ridge. The ground fell away, and before them was a narrow rift. The tracks of elves ran along the rift and out across the plain, but the hoof marks ended at the edge. They peered into the fissure. A soft moan rose from the darkness below, and they gazed at each other in horror. The plaintive murmur was unmistakable.

"Grimalkin!" cried Elgiva.

"Lady Elgiva, what shall we do?" said Trystin.

"We'll get her out at once!" she said.

"In Frigg's name, how?" Godwin asked.

"The quickest way. Levitation." Elgiva smiled at Trystin. "I've already had some practice."

Godwin knelt upon the grass and peered into the rift. "I've no idea what that is, but I don't care, as long as it works. Grimalkin! Can you hear me? Don't worry. We'll soon have you out of there."

Ragged breathing answered him from the darkness of the rift. Godwin looked at Elgiva with hope in his eyes. She drew a deep breath and raised her hands. Then she spoke.

"From out of this abyss, dark and drear,

"Grimalkin, arise, and have no fear.
"The power of Good suspend you high
"Above the sharp rocks where now you lie.
"Float towards me, friend so fair,
"Like a mote that rides the warm spring air."

A dim shape rose from the fissure. Elgiva continued her incantation.

"I order you stop, but do not drop.
"And float towards me, slow and sure.
"Lie at my feet; the spell is effete.
"Gently down and heavy once more."

Grimalkin's unconscious body obeyed Elgiva's commands and drifted over the grass, coming to a halt at Elgiva's feet.

They knelt beside the pony, and Elgiva ran her sensitive hands over the animal's body.

Elgiva smiled with relief. "There's nothing broken. This creature is made of iron. But she's badly bruised, and she's had a bad knock on the head." She nodded towards Grimalkin's pack and then sat back on her heels. "They've taken the Lorestone, of course."

"They pushed her down there on purpose," said Godwin.

"They were far enough away from us and near enough to Vieldrin. Grimalkin was no longer needed." She began to unstrap the pony's pack.

Godwin snarled. "The bastards could have just turned her loose."

"Poor Grimalkin," said Trystin, his large eyes full of tears. "Lady Elgiva, will she be all right?"

Elgiva hugged him. "Yes, she'll be fine. Don't worry. But she won't be able to travel for a while, and we haven't time to wait for her." She scanned the darkening sky and got to her feet. "The day grows old. We must go."

"But we can't just leave her here all alone!" Trystin's gaze flitted back and forth and finally settled on Godwin.

Godwin smiled. "I'll stay with her."

Elgiva spun round. "Godwin, I can't leave you behind!"

"We'll catch up with you. Anyway, you don't need me. Go to your uncle. He'll know what to do." He paused a moment and then added, "Take my sword, if you wish."

"Godwin, I can't do that," Elgiva said. "It's yours!"

THE EXILE OF ELINDEL

His generosity touched her, but her attention was snatched away by a shout from Trystin. The elfling had jumped to his feet and was pointing across the plain, his eyes wide with wonder.

"Lady Elgiva, what is that?"

She followed the line of his gaze. A cloud of dust issued from Elindel, and as it drew nearer, the sound it made resembled thunder. As the nebulous shape approached them, Elgiva saw within it a herd of horses. Their coats were white, but their manes and tails were black as ebony. They galloped nearer, their necks thrust forward, dirt and grass flying from their hooves.

"The Royal Herd of Elindel!" cried Elgiva.

"They're beautiful!" squealed Trystin.

The great animals skidded to a halt at the bottom of the ridge. They stood there, snorting, their large hooves raking the earth.

"By Frigg," breathed Godwin. "I don't know anything about horses, but I'll wager that's the finest herd I'm ever likely to see."

The horses raised their noble heads to the figures atop the ridge. They thrashed the air with their raven-black tails, which fell to the ground in silken splendour, and their black eyes glittered, as if they knew themselves to be without equal.

Then one of the horses pranced forwards. It was Alsiann. "I have come for the one who once cleaned my stable, whom now I honour as my queen."

Time rolled backwards for Elgiva to the days when she and Alsiann had travelled together from Elindel, Elgiva refusing to ride the great horse because, as a nar-wardain, she knew her place. Needing to be back among her own kind, the animal had eventually left Elgiva on a shallow hilltop, looking out at the bleak landscape of her future. It was there that Elgiva had finally confronted the reality of exile. She clung then to the one piece of advice Alsiann had given her. *Find an oak tree. One that is rich in years. Oaks are lords of the forest. Their wisdom is well known.*

Briefly, a threat of tears choked off Elgiva's voice, but when she found it again, excitement at this reunion with her old friend was hard to suppress. "Greetings, Alsiann Fiorin. Greetings to you and the royal herd."

"The king is dead," Alsiann said. "We have awaited you. Lord Bellic told us you would come."

"Alsiann, these are my friends. This is Godwin, who found the thing we sought, and Trystin, who knew where it was hidden. And this poor beast is Grimalkin, who kept it safe as long as she could until she was taken by wicked elves."

Alsiann nodded. "You must return at once. Elindel has a new king."

"Vieldrin, of course," said Elgiva.

Alsiann snorted. "I am leader of the royal herd. I alone have the right to carry you."

Elgiva didn't hesitate. She slithered down the grassy slope and ran towards her friend. Her joy at seeing Alsiann could no longer be contained, and she threw her arms around the horse's neck.

"Dusk falls soon," nickered Alsiann. "Vieldrin has creatures about him at night. And he has the Lorestone. We cannot tarry, my long-awaited friend." The elf-horse nuzzled Elgiva's cheek and then drew back her head.

Elgiva wrapped her fingers in the mare's flowing mane and leapt onto her back. "You'll stay, then, Godwin?" she asked.

He nodded.

"Trystin, what about you?"

The elfling chewed his finger, and his eyes flicked back and forth between Godwin and Elgiva.

"What should I do?" he asked.

"You'd be safer here," said Elgiva.

"I'm not afraid," Trystin said. "And when you kill Vieldrin, I want to be there to see it." He pulled back his shoulders, as though he were trying to look brave, but his thin legs trembled beneath his tunic.

"Girasol will carry you," Alsiann announced. "He is gentle and surefooted. The best of mounts for a young elf."

A handsome young stallion trotted forwards and intercepted Trystin as he scampered down the slope.

Alsiann swung her head round. "And what of your human friend, Elgiva?" Elgiva whispered in her ear, and the great horse turned and stared at Godwin. "So, Godwin, is it your intention to follow as soon as that pony revives?"

"It is," said Godwin.

"Then I shall leave you my eldest son. Tanarus Aquila will carry you when you are ready to travel. That pony will not be up to the task."

The Exile of Elindel

Trystin swung onto Girasol's back, and the herd prepared to leave. Elgiva looked back at Godwin, but she couldn't say goodbye. They might never see each other again, but saying goodbye wouldn't help; it would only make the fear more real. With a twinge of loss, she turned to look ahead, grabbed hold of Alsiann's mane, and the herd thundered off towards the forest.

Godwin made a small fire and sat beside it, watching the evening fall upon the land. In his lap, he cradled Grimalkin's head. The few provisions he had found in her pack had done little to fill his emptiness, but the loss of Elgiva bothered him far more than the gnawing of his stomach.

The herd had galloped away with his friends, their milky hides sucked out of sight like a cloud of vapour, and it had filled him with secret shame. He feared the forest of Elindel. It was a place of magic and peril, a place where he surely would founder and fail. The final test had come, and it had found him wanting.

He looked down at the pony. He was glad she had been unable to speak to the royal horses, for her form and manner would have been greeted with nothing but disdain—as he would suffer the scorn of elves were he to go to Elindel. Better both of them stay where they were.

For a while, he fell asleep, but Grimalkin stirred and woke him. She staggered to her feet, and Godwin shifted to avoid her hooves. She shook her head, then her body, and finally, her matted tail. She cast off sleep like a chrysalis and emerged with a vigorous snort.

"Cabbage hearts, I'm reborn!" she exclaimed. "Dreamed of warm hay and spring greens."

"I'm glad you're up. My legs had gone to sleep." He rubbed his thighs to alleviate the stab of returning life. "Your head weighs a lot for something so empty." He clambered to his feet.

"You make a fine pillow, if nothing else. So where has everyone gone?"

Godwin explained the situation.

"So, you stayed behind to look after me, eh?" She thrust her long muzzle into his face and tried to lick his cheek.

Godwin recoiled in disgust.

"I gave them trouble, you know. Kicked one in the gizzard. The other thought he was dead." She bared her yellow teeth in triumph.

"Quite brave of you, I suppose," said Godwin, "but they made you suffer for it. They pushed you down that chasm."

"Celery stalks! I've been in worse plights. Suffering's my lot."

"Well, at least you're feeling better."

"I'm in agony! But who am I to complain?"

Godwin's attention was drawn to something in the distance; two parallel lines of light were moving slowly towards the ridge. He squinted to try to make sense of them. Just then, Alsiann's son joined them, striding up the bank, his body dim grey in the darkness. The animals weighed each other up while Godwin pointed across the plain.

"What's that?"

"Don't ask me," said Grimalkin.

"It comes from Urith-Endil," Tanarus said.

"Should I put out the fire?" asked Godwin.

"We have already been observed."

And so they waited.

The strings of light-beads threaded their way closer to the ridge, and as they drew nearer, they formed a torchlight procession. Eight male elves in gold and white livery walked between these two rows, and they carried a golden litter.

The procession halted fifty yards from the bottom of the ridge and from its midst, four riders came, three bearing golden lances. When they reached the bank, they stopped and looked up, and one of them hailed the three companions. "Who are you and what is your purpose?"

Grimalkin snorted. "None of your business, nosy!"

The elf who had hailed them scowled. "I am Tercel, Captain of the Guard. My lady, Queen Gilda, will know your business, if you have any sense."

Grimalkin hissed in Godwin's ear. "Think the old slicer is due for an airing. Better safe than sorry."

Godwin unsheathed his sword.

In a cave deep in the forest sat Bellic, Elgiva, and Trystin. Between them, a small fire kept the darkness at bay. Merrill, the Captain of the Guard of Elindel, stood in the maw of the cave, a gloved hand poised on the hilt of his sword, ready to fend off intruders.

The Exile of Elindel

"Well, Trystin," Bellic said, "it makes my heart glad to see you alive, though I wish we had met at a happier time. But I see you have left behind more than your former slavery." He reached out and touched the elfling's cheek.

Trystin nodded and then turned to Elgiva and smiled. Bellic gave her a look of approval.

Elgiva was anxious to avoid all talk about her success with magic. "I'm glad to see you alive, too, Uncle. Vieldrin hasn't harmed you."

"I have Merrill to thank for that," he said. "He has been my jailer for many months and pretended to be my tormentor, too, to spare me the malice of others."

Elgiva stared at the iron bands on Bellic's wrists and ankles and the chains that restricted his movements. "Forgive me, Uncle. I can't break the spell that binds you."

The creases round Lord Bellic's eyes tightened. "Even if you could, perhaps it is better you do not, for now," he said. "If I were to be seen without my shackles, it would arouse suspicion."

Bellic was skirting round the truth, but Elgiva had to face the fact that she could never equal Vieldrin in power, let alone surpass him.

"I'll never confront Vieldrin on any terms but his own," she said, "and that's something I can't risk. He can use the Lorestone whenever he likes, and he has the fetchen to boost his power, and compared to that, I'm nothing."

"My dear," said Bellic, "you must not give in. There must be a way. I sent a message to Gilda, and she is on her way. Behind her marches an army. Perhaps some diversion can be contrived."

Elgiva frowned. "What good will that do?"

He winced, but then he recovered his composure. He stroked his grey beard.

"When Vieldrin uses the Lorestone, I think he will use it against you only," he said.

"You think, but you don't know."

Bellic disregarded this. "Against his other enemies, he will use his personal power and that of his creatures and guards. You must stay here and hide until Queen Gilda arrives. Possibly the three of us can defeat him in magical combat."

"If we can take him unawares."

"If Gilda's army attacks," he said, "it may distract him long enough for us to use our powers."

Elgiva shook her head. "But why should he use the stone against me? He could destroy me without it. In fact, he could kill us all at once. Postponing the moment makes no sense."

"No one knows the Lorestone's might or what it is capable of, my dear, and you have forgotten something: Vieldrin's caprice and arrogance. You defied him, Elgiva. You made him look foolish, and then you escaped. He must make you pay for that, and publicly. He will want to gloat on your defeat. We must be thankful our opponent is bereft of reason. It gives us more time to make our plans."

"Forgive me, my lord," Merrill said. "It is time we should go."

"A few minutes more," said Bellic.

"The fetchen will be out soon," said Merrill. "My lord, the curfew has passed."

"Curfew, Uncle?" asked Elgiva.

Bellic nodded. "We must keep to our homes after sunset. Those who do not may fall prey to the fetchen. At night, they terrorise the forest, but they must return to their lairs before dawn, until their master finds a way to free them forever by wielding the stone." Bellic's hands fretted in their chains. "I am unable to defend myself. These chains block my powers, and I must fear the fetchen no less than the lowliest of the nar-wardain."

"If I can't remove your chains," said Elgiva, "perhaps Queen Gilda can."

"She is a powerful wardain, my dear, but do not worry on my account."

"It's difficult not to," said Elgiva. "We need your powers, Uncle."

Bellic was disconcerted. Clearly he had hoped for more personal a concern.

"We need all the help we can get. I know what evil the fetchen possess. I dare say their touch could freeze the soul. They attacked us at the circle of stones."

"How did you purchase your escape?"

His question called up thoughts of Godwin and twinges of self-reproach. It had caused her pain to leave him behind. "I told you of my friend who bears a magic sword? I used that sword to channel my power. I unleashed great force without harming myself."

"You did not bring it with you?"

Elgiva glared at him. "It belongs to Godwin. It was a gift, his birth-right, Uncle Bellic, and I couldn't take it from him. Even though he offered me the use of it, I refused."

"Refused?" He lifted his eyebrows.

"He wished to stay with our injured pony," Elgiva said. "How could I take his sole means of protection?"

"I admire your concern for your friend, Elgiva, but the future of Elvendom is more pressing. You should have compelled him to come with you."

"Compelled," she said. "I'm not Vieldrin!"

Bellic nodded and then smiled. "Indeed you are not."

"Please, my lord," Merrill said.

With a weary sigh, Bellic hauled himself erect. "I must go," he said. "I fear you must put out the fire, lest its light draws prying eyes."

Trystin jumped to his feet. "Why can't we steal the stone?"

"It is always at Vieldrin's side, and he is surrounded by guards," said Bellic. "Could you steal it without his knowledge?"

"Turn me into a mouse," said Trystin. "I'll get into his hall—"

"And how will you carry the Lorestone, Trystin?" Bellic smiled.

"Then I'll make him use it on me!"

"He would not," said Bellic. "You would throw your life away needlessly."

"But we must do something!"

"For now, we must be patient, Trystin. Impetuous acts will only undo us. When Gilda arrives, we will think of a way to foil Vieldrin's plans."

Trystin pouted and sat down.

"Good night, my dear," said Bellic, kissing Elgiva on the brow. "Good night, Trystin. Try to rest. Stay in this cave, and you will be safe. I sent the royal herd to look for you because they come and go as they please, so their movements do not arouse suspicion. Nobody knows you are here." He turned towards the captain. "Merrill, I am ready."

Elgiva threw dirt on the fire, and the cave was plunged into darkness. She and Trystin sat in silence, wrestling with their thoughts.

"Why don't you try to rest awhile?" suggested Elgiva.

"Lord Bellic is wrong," said Trystin. "We should do something now. I could do something."

"What could you do?"

"Vieldrin will be in the great hall," he said. "I'll go there. He'll have the stone with him."

"You don't know where the hall is, and anyway, you'd just get yourself killed," she protested. He slumped further into himself, and she sighed. "I'm sorry, Trystin, but it's no use."

He didn't respond, and she left him to sulk, too tired for further discussion on the matter. She rested the back of her head on the stone behind her. Soon, she began to drowse.

"I don't care what you say . . . I'm going!" cried Trystin, springing to his feet.

He bolted out of the cave. His sudden departure took Elgiva by complete surprise, and he had gone before she could stop him.

She tore after the elfling, fearing to shout in case the fetchen or the guards heard her. She hurled a thin ribbon of harmless fire in his general direction, hoping to bring him to his senses. She could easily have killed him to prevent whatever reckless act he intended to perform, but she loved the elfling far too much. She resolved to make no further attempts to hinder his progress by magic. She feared what her anger might unleash, and she couldn't afford to alert whatever patrolled the benighted forest.

She was forced to rely on her native speed, but Trystin was younger and faster and fuelled by determination. He flitted through the underwood, the distance between them increasing all the time. She would never catch him. Soon, he was swallowed up by the trees and the all-embracing darkness.

Chapter Thirty-Eight

GODWIN EXPLAINED THE situation as briefly as he could to Captain Tercel. The dour-faced young captain was every inch a warrior as he sat on his handsome horse, one hand resting on the pommel of his sword. He gave Godwin a cursory nod, said something to his horse, and the animal wheeled about and trotted back to the litter.

Sword in hand, Godwin waited while the captain spoke to whoever was concealed behind the sumptuous golden drapes. At length, the captain hailed him.

"The queen requests you to descend," he said. "She would have speech with you, wilthkin." His tone made it clear that this was an order, not an invitation.

Godwin clambered down the bank, Grimalkin and the elf-horse following close behind. He made for the golden litter, escorted by the lance-bearing guards. When he had approached within a few yards, the captain cried, "Hold!" and Godwin stopped in his tracks. The golden drapes were swished aside.

An apparition of loveliness moved from the litter and set her golden sandals upon the torch-lit sward.

Queen Gilda appeared to be middle-aged, old enough to be his mother, but it didn't matter; Godwin was stunned by the vision before him. The black hair falling to her waist had the merest suggestion of silver in it, while her body, though slightly plump, moved with the elegance of a swan. Her face had a comfortable aspect, the fine lines at the corners of her mouth showing a predisposition to laughter, while her dark eyes glittered like gems. A circlet of gold stars crowned her head, and each star had a pearl at its centre. In the long white robe that skimmed the grass, she possessed all the trappings of royalty. And she radiated power.

She scrutinised Godwin, and her eyes seemed to see right through him. She smiled with such warmth that he felt his heart melt.

"Invaginate your sword, young man," Queen Gilda commanded, her eyebrows arched with mischievous humour.

He lifted the sword and gaped at it. He had no idea what he was supposed to do. At the sight of the blade, the elf-queen's face lit up with pleasure.

"Come closer," she said.

Godwin stepped towards her. The nearer he was, the greater became Queen Gilda's emanations. She shimmered with benevolent power. Magic had touched him so many times that he could now easily sense its presence, and before him stood a being whose powers were fully matured; they took his breath away. But with this knowledge came a sudden, unwelcome realisation: Elgiva totally lacked this aura.

"Your sword, if you please," said Queen Gilda.

Godwin extended the weapon, and she took it from him with a smile. To his surprise, it began to hum, as though overjoyed by her touch.

"Many moons have travelled the sky since last I held you, Taranuil," said the elf-queen. She flashed her glittering eyes at Godwin, and he almost dissolved into the grass. "Do I enchant you, Aidan?"

Godwin stood, mesmerised, a yearning for the elf-queen throbbing in his veins. "You . . . you're so beautiful."

She grinned, revealing her perfect white teeth. "It would seem that I do. Please forgive me."

The queen touched him on the cheek. For a moment, his brain reeled with desire, and then the night congealed about him and drew into focus.

"Aidan, dear, I am glad to see that you have treasured my gift," she said. "Has it shown you your courage?"

Godwin was taken aback. "Your gift?"

"Use the proper form of address," muttered the captain beside the litter.

"Quell your indignation, Tercel," chided Queen Gilda. "He is unfamiliar with our ways. We will dispense with formalities."

The captain bowed stiffly. "Yes, Your Majesty."

THE EXILE OF ELINDEL

"How fares your father, Aidan?" asked the queen.

Godwin fought for self-control. "My father is dead, my lady."

"Ah, me!" Her expression darkened with sorrow. "He was a good wilthkin. And what of your mother?"

"She, too."

"I am sorry for that," she said.

"My lady, this is all a bit too much for me to take in. Did you say you gave me this sword?"

"It was my birth gift to you," she replied. "The magic it contains is mine."

"Then I must thank you," said Godwin.

"There is no need." She smiled. Her warm, melodic voice took the edge off his confusion, and he started to feel at ease.

"You travel with little Elgiva. She has gone to see Bellic, I am told, and we also are planning to meet him. It is my intention to treat for peace in the hope this will buy us some time—though how we shall use the time so gained is a matter quite beyond me. I have heard of this Lorestone, of course, but lacking lore wisdom as I do, I know little about such things. I must hope Lord Bellic contrives some means of foiling Vieldrin's plans. My army follows close behind. I intend to make camp here and wait for them." She turned towards the captain. "Tercel, my dear, we will rest here."

"Yes, Your Majesty." The captain marched down the procession, barking orders at the elves.

Queen Gilda glanced at Taranuil. "Sleep now," she said as she handed the sword back to its master.

Godwin slid the sword back into its scabbard.

"Will you eat with us, Aidan?" asked the queen. "You have a lean and hungry look. A little food would be welcome, I think."

She offered Godwin her pale-skinned hand, and they strolled towards a heap of wood the servants had stacked upon the grass. With a glance, she set it alight.

"When I made you the gift of Taranuil, I also made a promise, my dear," the queen said. "I offered you my protection, should you ever lose your family. Perhaps you are a little too old to be in need of adoption, yet I will have you as a son, in memory of your dear, kind father. He was so good to my own child. And now, I may deal kindly with his. Hold out your right hand, Aidan."

When he complied, she grasped his hand and pressed their palms together. There was a brief sensation of heat, and when she withdrew, there was a mark upon his skin—a brand in the shape of a star, and within it, a rune that meant nothing to him, but it was identical to the marks on Taranuil.

"That is my mark," explained Queen Gilda. "No matter where you travel, this brand guarantees safe passage through all the elven lands. Likewise, no elf who sees this mark will refuse you food or shelter. From now on, you are elfryth—elf-friend."

Godwin was lost for words. All of his thoughts revolved around the magic of the elf-queen's touch. A servant scurried forwards and offered him fruit on a golden tray. He helped himself without looking.

"Henceforth, you may call yourself my son, and if my counsellors disapprove, still they must accept it. They will throw up their hands in horror, of course, and fret about the unthinkable—a wilthkin inheriting Urith-Endil!"

Godwin almost choked on the fruit. Looking up, he saw Captain Tercel standing some yards away. His face was humourless and dark with disapproval and, Godwin suspected, a touch of envy.

The queen's mellifluous laughter rang in Godwin's ears. "Aidan, do not worry. I have two sons and a daughter. They and their issue will rule after me."

The future was nothing if not uncertain, and there were no guarantees. Godwin forced a smile to conceal his disquiet.

"I am honoured to be your adopted son," he said, bowing.

"And I am glad you accept the title."

Godwin searched the grass at his feet, looking for some composure, and then he remembered his obligations. "Lady, I think I should leave now," he said.

Queen Gilda's eyebrows lifted in query.

"I intended to follow Elgiva as soon as our pony was able to travel." He looked out over the landscape. The dawn was breaking in the east.

"Indeed. Your friend is dear to you, and you wish to be at her side. Forgive me for detaining you. I am loath to let you go, my dear, but perhaps if you rode on ahead of us, you could forewarn Lord Bellic of our arrival. That lovely elf-horse will get you there swiftly."

The Exile of Elindel

Godwin eyed the great stallion warily. He had never ridden a horse and his experience of equines was limited to Lord Othere's docile pack ponies.

"I can't ride him," Godwin said.

"The old pony, then?" Queen Gilda lowered her voice. "But she is ewe-necked, poor dear, and has too little heart-room. A perilous mount, to be sure. You do not intend to ride her, my son?"

Godwin blinked at Queen Gilda. He didn't intend to ride either of them, but he understood the need for haste. How could he give in to cowardice when he was the son of an elven queen?

As if to mirror his thoughts, she said, "You must ride a beast that accords with your rank."

Godwin had no choice. Bowing to the queen, he went to meet his fate.

"Hold, my son!" she commanded.

For a second, Godwin ignored her, already forgetting his newfound status. The ensuing silence reminded him, and he turned to face the queen.

"No son of mine, by birth or adoption, shall walk the land like a beggar," she said. "Those filthy rags must be transformed."

Filthy rags? He looked down at himself and saw, as if for the first time, the dried blood that stiffened the material of his leggings. It puzzled him for a moment until he remembered the sarsen ring and how he had slipped on the gore-caked grass. His clothes were stained and ragged. They were filthy, and so was he.

She made a brief gesture in the air, and he was engulfed by a golden light. It spiralled about him and then gradually receded. To his astonishment, Godwin was now attired in Queen Gilda's colours. His clothes were new and impeccably white, and on his tunic, above his heart, a gold star was embroidered. Magic had combed out the knots in his hair and scraped away his itchy beard. He felt as fresh as the dawn.

He gaped at his new garments. "By Frigg!"

Queen Gilda laughed, and her beautiful hands were clasped at her breast with delight. "What a fine elf you would make, my son!"

Godwin smiled and bowed his thanks and then turned towards Tanarus. The muscled bulk of the mighty horse loomed over him. Godwin touched the animal's mane and felt him flinch.

"Look," said Godwin, "you don't want me on your back any more than I want to be there, but we have no choice in the matter."

He tried to mount the great horse, while behind him, the queen's attendants muffled their laughter. A sharp word from their mistress prompted several of them to come to his assistance. They heaved the reluctant warrior onto the animal's back. The ground reeled far below him, but between the hard earth and Godwin's fear was the bulk of the haughty stallion, a creature of frightening power and speed.

"Tanarus," asked Godwin, "can I hang onto your mane?"

"If you must," said Tanarus, stamping his foot.

"Go with all haste," Queen Gilda urged. "We will follow anon. Goodbye, my son."

"Goodbye . . . er . . . mother," said Godwin.

With a horrible jolt, Tanarus set off, and Godwin clung to his mane. Every muscle was tensed to stop him from sliding off the smooth back while the world flew past him. This was a new experience for Godwin and one he wouldn't care to repeat. He risked a glance behind him. Grimalkin was tearing after them, and he feared she would overtax herself, but he was grateful for her presence.

Here was the chance for Trystin to prove himself by redeeming Faine's gift from the clutches of evil. Now was the time to show his friends that he was an asset to them, not merely an item of baggage they had brought from Misterell, a silly elfling ruled by his fears. But he must be swift. He ran through the leafy bowers, avoiding the pathways and glades where dwellings lay still cloaked in sleep.

At last he found the great hall. Crouching low in the underwood, he took stock of his surroundings. A handful of guards stood outside the main doors, talking in lowered voices. Torches were set in the ground before them.

Life in Misterell had taught him stealth, and he knew how to move without making a sound. He noticed a door at the side of the hall and crept towards it, like a shadow. A lone guard patrolled the flank of the building, and Trystin sat and watched him, wondering how to divert the sentry's attention so he could slip in through the door.

The Exile of Elindel

Then the guards at the main doors started to quarrel, and their voices rose in contention. Scowling, the sentry left his post and joined them. Trystin seized his chance and within moments, he was at the side door. The latch was unbolted, and his heart leapt with joy at his good fortune.

He slipped inside, into semi-darkness with only the light of a solitary torch that smoked above the hearth. Closing the door behind him, he tiptoed over the wooden floor.

Beside the hearth lay a massive hound. It lifted its head and snarled. The dying embers of the fire cast a reddish light on the animal's back, and its large eyes glowed like rubies.

"Hush, friend dog," whispered Trystin, a finger against his lips.

"You're after the king," growled the hound.

Trystin's heartbeat quickened its pace, but the hound laid its head between its paws and let out a weary sigh.

"You're welcome to him. Over there. He's sleeping behind those drapes."

Trystin padded the length of the hall towards the curtained chamber; then, after a moment's hesitation, he summoned his courage and twitched the hangings aside. Vieldrin lay on a raised bed, a woollen blanket pulled up to his chest. On the bench beside him, a chunk of candle glimmered in a sconce. In his arms he cradled the Lorestone, as though it were a baby.

Trystin's heart was in his throat as he looked at the slumbering king, and his mouth was parched with terror. Yet, he wished he had brought a weapon. How easy it would be for him to kill Vieldrin where he lay.

He heard a cry from outside and flinched as though he had been hit. Blades clanged together outside the hall.

Vieldrin stirred and frowned in his sleep. Horrified, Trystin stepped away and hid in an alcove. The elf-king cursed with rage; his feet thumped on the floor. The swish of the drapes made Trystin snatch in his breath.

"What's going on?" demanded the king. "Who dares to wake me with this noise?"

Vieldrin marched across the hall, and the hound stood up and barked at the sight of its angry master.

"Silence, you worm-riddled cur!" yelled the king. Picking up a flagon of wine, he flung it at the dog. With a yelp of fear, it scuttled away, its tail between its legs.

The king hurled force at the hall's main doors, and they threw themselves open so violently that all of their hinges buckled. Trystin's heart pounded as Vieldrin strode out into the night.

"I will have you all throttled with wire," roared the king. "I will feed your guts to the hounds! I will teach you to quarrel when you are on watch! Get back to your posts this instant!"

Confused and angry as he was, Vieldrin had left the stone behind. Trystin sneaked back through the drapes. The Lorestone lay on the blanket. He darted forwards and snatched it up. Then, quitting the chamber, he made for the side door, overjoyed at his success. Checking to see that his way was clear, he crept towards the undergrowth.

But there he was caught.

A hand clamped across his mouth, and he was dragged to the grass. Shock and terror threatened to burst his heart. But then he recognized his captor, and he was dizzy with relief. Slowly, she released him.

"Oh, Lady Elgiva!"

"In Faine's name, what have you done?" she hissed.

"I have it. I have it. Look!" He held out the stone, and she sucked in her breath. "Lady Elgiva, take it!"

"What's that noise there?" demanded Vieldrin. He marched from the entrance of the hall, his fists upon his hips. "Ware, you dogs, we have prowlers!"

"Run," said Elgiva. "Back to the cave!"

They fled into the forest, but they didn't make it back to the cave. They had barely left the great hall behind when a wall of darkness blocked their path; a darkness with features and claws.

"By Faine, the fetchen! I can't fight them again. We mustn't let them touch us, Trystin." She pushed the elfling behind her.

Shrieking with glee, the fetchen formed a ring around the elves and herded them back towards the royal hall. Then, suddenly, a gap appeared in the writhing wall of shapes, and the king strode forward into the ring, a clutch of guards at his back.

"Elgiva, my dear, what a pleasant surprise."

The Exile of Elindel

Tanarus left Godwin and Grimalkin at the edge of the forest and trotted off to rejoin the royal herd. While they were deciding what to do next, the sudden appearance of an armour-clad elf took them both by surprise. Godwin quickly drew his sword, but the elf held up his empty hands to show that he meant no harm. His gaze had a distracted look that sent shivers up Godwin's spine.

"Are you Godwin?" he asked. "Elgiva's friend?"

"What if I am?"

"I'm Merrill, Captain of the Guard. Lord Bellic spoke of you. I await Queen Gilda's arrival. Did you see any sign of her on your way here?"

Godwin nodded. Merrill looked him up and down in a puzzled manner. Then Godwin remembered he was dressed in Queen Gilda's colours, but he saw no reason to explain himself to a stranger.

"Don't doubt me, Godwin," Merrill said. "I'm Elgiva's friend, too, and that's the truth."

"Easily said, but not so easily proven."

The captain spread his hands apart in a gesture of helplessness and then let them fall to his sides. "Everything goes amiss. Lord Bellic is under close arrest, and warriors are marching against Queen Gilda. She can't kill them all, nor would she, for she knows they serve Vieldrin out of fear. I have no power to stop them. I'm helpless, and that's the truth. And . . . and, worst of all, my friend, little Elgiva and Trystin are taken."

"Taken?"

"Just before daybreak," said Merrill. "The elfling tried some hare-brained scheme to get the Lorestone and failed."

Godwin cursed under his breath. "Are they all right?"

"As far as I know," replied Merrill, "but Elgiva seemed to have given up. I offered to take care of their confinement, but Vieldrin said I should go to blazes. He put them under some sort of spell—though by the look of those two wretched creatures, he didn't need magic to subdue them. The guards took them somewhere, and others went to get Lord Bellic. I came straight here to wait for Queen Gilda. Didn't know what else to do."

Godwin leaned against Grimalkin and sighed.

"Please," said Merrill, stepping forward. "Come with me to a place of safety—if there's one to be found. The forest's alive with Vieldrin's guards. And we're all to assemble at sunset. I'll try to hide you till then. Vieldrin says there's to be some sport. Faine knows what he's got in mind." He tugged at Godwin's sleeve. "Come."

"I must help Elgiva!" cried Godwin, snatching back his arm.

"Indeed," said Merrill, "but how? Vieldrin has the Lorestone and the means to use it. There's nothing we can do. I don't even know where they've taken Elgiva. And she'll be well-guarded, count on that."

"But you're the Captain of the Guard! Can't you do something? Anything?"

"No one's going to listen to me with Vieldrin breathing down their necks. The truth is, only Queen Gilda has any chance of beating Vieldrin, but even she can't fight the Lorestone. See sense, man. You must hide."

The captain turned and hurried away, and Godwin followed. The world was about to end.

Chapter Thirty-Nine

DUSK WAS FALLING over the forest, and thick clouds curdled the blood-shot sky. In a clearing specially made for the purpose, Elindel's inhabitants were assembled. A handful of armed guards patrolled the scene, while the rest of Vieldrin's warriors were guarding the forest's perimeter.

Godwin, Grimalkin, and Captain Merrill stood at the rear of the crowd, and despite his fear of what was to come, Godwin had to marvel at the sight of so many elves. The forest was huge, but still he wondered how so many beings could live within it.

He looked out over the sea of heads, and in front of the crowd, he saw two platforms. They stood about twenty feet apart and were raised several feet off the grass. With a knot of dread in his stomach, Godwin surmised their grim purpose.

"There's Bellic," said Merrill.

Godwin started and then turned to the left and followed Merrill's gaze. Flanked by two armed warriors, the elf-lord shuffled into the glade, and his age-lined face was slack with defeat. Iron bands circled his ankles and wrists and were bound together by chains. Behind him trudged a younger elf in parti-coloured clothes, and under his arm, he carried a lyre.

"Caspell, the minstrel," Merrill said.

Caspell stood between the platforms and turned to face the crowd. In a quavering voice, he began to sing a refrain in honour of Vieldrin. The strings of the lyre twanged like sorrow.

Soon, Caspell's song came to a mournful end, and a blare of horns resounded across the clearing.

Vieldrin ascended the nearest platform. He wore the crown of Elindel, and his scarlet robe was studded with gems. In the crook of his left arm, he cradled the Lorestone. With his elegant frame and handsome face, he looked every inch a monarch. For a while, he stood, his eyebrows arched, and contemplated the crowd.

"Well?" he said. "No cries of joy to welcome your lord and master?"

There was a distinct lack of enthusiasm in the elves' response. Vieldrin looked upon them all with a cold and steely glare, and Godwin found himself clenching his fists as the dark eyes swept across him.

Vieldrin turned and signalled to his guards beyond the trees, and Elgiva and Trystin were dragged into the glade. The elfling was made to stand at the front, while two guards pushed Elgiva onto the wooden platform opposite Vieldrin. She stood there blank-faced in her tattered shift, her hands hanging limp at her sides.

She had suffered some ill-treatment, and Godwin winced at the sight of her. Raw-eyed and bruised, she looked like a wraith. He wrapped his arms about his chest to still his pounding heart. His mind laboured.

If only he could get to her, offer her his sword.

Vieldrin's voice boomed across the crowd. "People of Elindel, Elgiva and I are here to provide a little entertainment. Perhaps you don't remember her, but she has aspired to be your queen. I am now about to demonstrate that she is unworthy to rule. Her paltry powers would be useless if you needed her protection. A ruler must be strong and bold, and lorewise, too, I think. Three virtues that I own in equal measure, and I shall provide you with ample proof." His cruel gaze scanned the crowd, and he offered them a perfect smile. "I challenge the upstart Elgiva to a contest of magic. To the death."

Anxious murmurs ran through the crowd, and Bellic's weary, desperate voice rose above them all.

"The contest is unfair," he cried. "You possess the Lorestone!"

Vieldrin frowned. "Be still, old fool. Your senile mumblings grate on my ear. What I have, I have by virtue of my courage and cleverness. Two more attributes I possess that mark me fit to rule."

"If you are such a perfect ruler, have you no compassion? Mercy is also a kingly virtue."

Vieldrin glared at Bellic, his eyebrows arched. "Showing mercy is not always prudent, especially towards one's enemies. Mercy is for fools and weaklings. Should I show her mercy and have her turn upon me later, like an ungrateful cur? I offered her joint rule, but she made her position clear. There is no other option."

"Then take away her powers," cried Bellic. "It can be done. You have the stone!"

Elgiva turned to face Lord Bellic, her face a mask of outrage. "How dare you! My powers are my inheritance, to do with as I please. It took me long enough to find them. I don't intend to give them up now! By Faine, I won't surrender, and I'll accept no mercy from a cold-blooded killer like him! I will put my faith in the First-Father, and I will endure what I must!" Her tortured gaze fanned out over the crowd, and then the merest whisk of a smile touched her bloodless lips. "I believe it's better to die once than die a little every day."

Godwin's throat constricted as she spoke these words. He hugged his chest and prayed that her courage would see her through the ordeal ahead.

Vieldrin laughed, though something in his eyes suggested Elgiva's unwavering defiance unnerved him. "You see, Bellic, how no one listens to you anymore? You can teach us nothing. A new era dawns and cowards like you have no place in it. Watch and despair, old fool. Your turn will quickly come." He spun to face his warriors. "Night falls. Light your torches. The audience must be able to see everything that happens here. We do not want them disappointed. But stand well back. I will be inviting some of my friends to this gathering, and they are a little wary of light." Vieldrin grinned with cruel pleasure as the guards carried out his commands. "So, let us have a little prelude to the entertainment, shall we?"

A restless hush fell on the crowd as the elf-king raised an elegant hand and began to chant an incantation.

"I call to those so cruelly banished,
"Come, sweet allies, sage and sear,
"Arise from the clinging darkness here.
"From your deep lairs arise and dance;
"Amuse us with your dalliance.
"The foul sun has been vanquished!"

For a moment all was still, and then, like black fumes seeping from a fissure in the ground, the fetchen floated from their subterranean lairs and circled their summoner. Vieldrin laughed as they swooped round his head.

"Soon, you will be free forever," he promised them. "I shall harness the Lorestone's power and make you immune to the sun. Then what fun we shall have together. But our audience needs warming up before the contest begins. I trust you came prepared to entertain us?"

The formless creatures swarmed between the platforms and spun together in a circle, hissing like serpents.

"Let the sun lie dead and the black mould spread.

"Let the horse be lame that pulls the plough.

"Let the ripe fruit rot; bare be the bough.

"Let the farmer rail and the tall corn fail.

"Let the fungus creep and the children weep.

"Let slime of snail and mildew's scent

"Smother all the innocent."

The elves surrounding Godwin recoiled in revulsion, yet the horrid fascination of the whirling fetchen held everyone where they stood. Vieldrin grinned and clapped his hands, urging his creatures on. Their wild cacophony stunned the trees, profaned the peaceful twilight. Godwin fancied even unseen nocturnal animals must be scurrying for their dens.

The evil song droned on, eating into the air like gangrene.

"See the gelid dead below;

"To clinging clay the bodies go.

"Cankered buds and mildewed leaves,

"Crippled roots and stunted trees.

"Beauty falls, as we arise

"To poison the water and stain the skies."

There was weeping in the crowd, and elflings clung to their parents. Godwin's heart was suffused with outrage. Cursing his helplessness, he rested a hand on Grimalkin's neck, knotted his fingers in her mane, and felt her body trembling.

A guard with a torch stood a few feet away, so Godwin was bathed in a pool of light, but no one remarked upon his presence; all eyes were enthralled by the dance of the fetchen.

Godwin's gaze found its way to Elgiva, lost and alone on the platform, and he couldn't imagine what thoughts racked her mind,

The Exile of Elindel

what hopes she might still be nursing. She seemed subdued and broken, though a flush of anger tinged her pale cheeks, darkening her bruises. If only she could strike Vieldrin before he used the Lorestone, strike him with a lethal blast!

Elgiva turned her head and caught Godwin's eye. She could give him no comfort. She had failed him. Vieldrin had the Lorestone. She would die, and so would her friends.

But accepting failure wasn't easy. Had Faine intended evil to win when he left the stone for posterity? There must be a chance. There must be.

She looked at Trystin, who was spellbound by the capering fetchen. His eyes reflected a hopeless terror that wrenched her heart.

Her friends would die. They would die without hope, the image of her surrender pursuing them to oblivion. For their sakes, if not for hers, she must fight on. Fate had chosen Vieldrin to be the wielder of the stone, but love was still worth fighting for, no matter how futile the attempt. Love, innocence, and friendship were surely stronger than hatred, cruelty, and greed.

She studied Vieldrin closely as he gazed dewy-eyed at his minions, the Lorestone cradled in his hands. His head was tilted to one side, and he seemed unaware of her existence. It was as if the purpose of their meeting was forgotten. His eyes widened with pleasure as he admired the fetchen, and Elgiva couldn't be certain, but he looked a little older. There were shadows of depravity upon his handsome face. Was evil leaching his youth away? Or was it the torchlight playing tricks on her eyes? Whatever the cause, she drew strength from the sight.

Elgiva averted her gaze and followed the dance of the fetchen. As they spewed forth their hatred of all the things she knew to be good and natural, anguish and wrath welled up in her heart, and she screwed up her eyes to hold back her tears. Magic began to shape itself around the hub of her anger, and it lifted itself bold and clean, like a new-forged blade preparing to strike.

Faine, I will not believe it. I will not believe we're defeated.

The pressure of magic inside her demanded to be released, and regardless of the consequences, she had to let it out.

Godwin gasped as a blast of blue light burst from Elgiva and spiralled about the clearing. The entire assembly was jerked to attention, while the fetchen shrieked and capered madly, caught in a gale of magical force. Howls of confusion tore out of them as Elgiva's power scythed through their ranks.

Scowling, Vieldrin threw up a shield of force to protect himself. It shimmered in the air before him like a wall of water.

Abruptly, Elgiva's power went out. She was breathing hard, but her eyes gleamed with defiance as she turned to face Vieldrin. "Enough," she said. "I won't endure this any longer."

"You will endure what you must. You wish me to retaliate?" He held up the Lorestone for all to see, and torchlight sparkled on its perfect surface. "Shall I use this now? Or shall I toy with you awhile? The crowd are expecting some entertainment."

"Crown, come down!" commanded Elgiva.

The crown of Elindel tumbled from Vieldrin's head, clattered across the platform, and rolled into the grass. It wheeled and glittered until it came to a halt midway between the two platforms. Someone in the crowd behind Godwin ventured a nervous giggle.

Vieldrin scowled at the fallen circlet, and then his face grew dark with vengeance. He thrust out his arm. The tree behind Elgiva began to topple towards her. It made a great cracking and splintering sound as its roots snapped free from the earth. There were gasps and cries from the crowd.

Quickly, Elgiva raised her hand, her palm towards the tottering giant. "Stop! Don't drop! Stay in the soil. To land be loyal. Don't lean at all. Stand straight and tall."

The tree paused and swayed, creaking with stress. Then, with agonising slowness, it righted itself, and the crowd gave one long sigh of relief.

Elgiva turned to face Vieldrin; her brows were arched, and her dark eyes glittered. "Are you trying to amuse yourself, or me?" she asked him with the air of one who knew she had nothing to lose.

Vieldrin snarled and tore a gem from the sleeve of his scarlet robe. He hurled it at Elgiva. It rolled through the air, becoming a large boulder as it did so.

THE EXILE OF ELINDEL

"Go home, errant stone!" commanded Elgiva, her hands held up before her.

The boulder halted, hanging in the air, and then it cast itself back at Vieldrin. He didn't have time to deflect it with magic, so was forced to duck to avoid it. The boulder impacted behind him and splintered the planks at the edge of the platform before it rolled away.

Springing erect, Vieldrin hurled a thread of fire at his enemy. It burst against her shield of force, scattering sparks in all directions. The crowd cried in terror and covered their faces, but shackled by their fear of the king, they didn't dare leave the arena of combat.

Elgiva lowered her magical shield and unleashed a ball of lightning that screamed towards her opponent. With an arc of flame, he deflected it and sent it spinning into the sky. It detonated above the forest and illuminated the tree tops.

And so they continued, fire against fire, until the air was blistered and their bodies drooped with exhaustion. The atmosphere buzzed and crackled with power, and the crowd crouched on the grass, whimpering with fright.

Finally, Vieldrin threw up a wall of force between himself and Elgiva. It writhed with angry red flames. Elgiva couldn't breach it with her darts of power, and Godwin could tell she was weakening. Her magic bolts grew thin and faint. Clearly, her power was all but exhausted.

Godwin could bear it no longer.

I made a vow to protect her. I can't let her die like this! Not alone!

He fought his way through the crowd and ran to save his friend. As he neared the front, Trystin looked at him, and the elfling's thoughts seemed to mirror his own. Trystin broke away from the guards, and together, they made for the platform.

"No!" cried Elgiva, extending her hand.

Godwin felt himself halted by some invisible force. Somehow, Elgiva had wrenched a bolt of power from deep inside herself, in spite of her exhaustion, and it was holding him and Trystin where they stood. He struggled to take a step towards Elgiva, but he couldn't. His fear for her left him breathless, his heart pattering in its cage of bone.

"You will not sacrifice yourselves!" cried Elgiva.

"Elgiva, in the name of Faine!" Godwin fell to his knees and wept.

"Godwin, I have faith," she said.

Elgiva turned to face Vieldrin. His mouth was twisted into a smirk.

"Distract her, my dark friends!" he shouted.

The fetchen converged upon Elgiva, hissing and churning, uniting their power against her. She threw weak bolts at their fleshless shapes, but her strength was ebbing. Her well of magic had run dry, and her body could stand no more. A cold paralysis crept along her limbs. Her magic guttered and went out.

Vieldrin nodded with satisfaction. "Now the stone shall work my will!"

Bellic buried his face in his hands while Godwin pulled Trystin to his side and turned the elfling's face away. The fetchen bobbed around Elgiva, their skeletal faces taut with relish, but she tried to stand calm and resolute, squaring her shoulders. There was nothing else she could do.

She needed to look at Godwin; for the last time, she had to smile at him in honour of their friendship, in memory of all he had done for her. His gaze was honest, open, and it reflected the smile back at her. It made her heart ache. Perhaps they could get away. *Faine, please let my friends be saved!*

Vieldrin was glowing with triumph, and yet even in this moment of victory, there was a pang of regret. His sport would soon be over.

And there stood his opponent. She was defeated, but still she regarded him with anger and defiance, her beautiful face flushed with emotion. Her stubborn determination to oppose him had sparked both his hatred and his yearning. Never again would he have such a foe on whom to unleash his might. He desired her. He should have ravished her before this final battle. Now it was too late. Soon, she would be a pile of ash. A memory.

Well, no matter. He would be supreme in Elvendom and finally free of these disturbing emotions. Elgiva's death would purge him of such perversities.

He held up the Lorestone with both hands and showed it to the

The Exile of Elindel

crowd. "Behold, this is the Lorestone," he cried, "and its name is Peronel!"

A gleam lit up inside the stone, and all eyes were drawn towards it.

Vieldrin bent his whole being towards the use of magic, his body trembling with both exertion and excitement. And then he began to chant.

"Destroy Elgiva; shrivel her.
"In fire and torment swivel her.
"Wither her; deliver her
"From life and body. Break her.
"Let breath and soul forsake her,
"And all her friends, and any who
"Opposed my will, or thought to do.
"Grant me power ten times more
"Than any wardain gone before.
"Sole master make me of this land;
"Put awesome power in my hand,
"And make me with one single spell,
"Heir to Faine's magic, Peronel!"

A sound like distant thunder rumbled over the clearing. The ground shook. The trees quivered. Every leaf vibrated.

"Behold!" declared Vieldrin. "The might of the Lorestone is upon you all!"

The opal began to glow in his hands.

It became a pulsing sphere of scarlet, like a bead of blood in the wound of the night.

Then the stone was a globe of amber . . .

A tiny and perfect sun . . .

A ball as blue as a summer sky . . .

An orb of deepest indigo . . .

A jewel of lavender.

One by one, the colours changed, and then the stone was a vivid green. It filled the glade with a rich, warm light and the smell of green, growing things, and it throbbed like the anger of Nature.

Vieldrin felt sated with power, intoxicated with it. He locked his gaze upon Elgiva. He wanted to savour every moment.

But why was she smiling?

And then the colours appeared together, and a rainbow shot from the heart of the Lorestone and arced across the glade.

Lightning exploded in the air and screamed across the cloud-locked sky, and a deafening boom of thunder cracked above the forest, knocking its inhabitants off their feet with one huge detonation.

The might of the Lorestone flooded the glade, hurling the darkness aside. All eyes were sightless before it, all ears were deaf, all mouths were mute, and raw, untrammelled magic rode the night, like the spirit of vengeance.

And as he lay sprawled on the grass, numb to the core of his being, Godwin was aware of nothing—nothing but Taranuil, as it keened in its sheath in fellowship with the Lorestone's awakened power.

Its wordless song was like the laughter of metal.

CHAPTER FORTY

"BE AT PEACE, Elgiva. All is well."

Elgiva opened her eyes and searched for the source of the voice. "Where am I? Who are you? *Where* are you?"

"You are out of your body. You know who I am, and where we are is of no importance."

Elgiva stood wrapped in a pearly mist, and she couldn't see beyond it—perhaps there might be nothing to see. A figure slowly approached her, a young male elf in a long white robe, his black hair falling down to his waist. His large eyes glittered like stars.

"Did you like my trick? The rainbow? I thought it would give you hope." The elfling laughed.

"First-Father?" wondered Elgiva.

He nodded with delight.

"But you're so young," she exclaimed.

"Not really, my child. I appear to you as I did in life, when I was at my happiest. It is the custom in spirit. You see me before I discovered magic, before all my burdens came to me. But perhaps you need me older and wiser." In an instant, he changed, becoming middle-aged and grey-haired.

"Why am I here?" she asked. "Am I dead?"

"You are very much alive, but I brought you here so we could talk."

"What's happened to my friends?"

"Fear not. They are all quite safe."

"And Vieldrin?"

"He is friendless now, for the fetchen are once more entombed in the earth. As for Vieldrin himself, he is somewhat changed."

"What do you mean?"

"You will see, my child." A smile spread across his face. "The

Lorestone contained good magic and could only be used for good. Would I leave such terrible power to chance? Once awakened, it searched for evil and, having found it, acted upon it and righted what was wrong."

Elgiva frowned in puzzlement. "I don't understand this at all," she said. "This means that Vieldrin couldn't win?"

"It is evil that could not win," said Faine. "Had Vieldrin used the Lorestone to benefit Elvendom, he would have prospered by it. He would have been Elwardain, and his name would long be remembered with love in the annals of our people. He would have been my heir, and he would be standing here, not you."

"So I wasn't the chosen one?"

"You were because you chose yourself. You were true to yourself, my child. You resented the burden placed upon you, but even so, you accepted it and you never abandoned it. In your heart, you knew what was right."

"So the prophecies were wrong," she said.

"The prophecies were not wrong, as you shall understand."

"But they told me I was ordained."

"No one was ordained, my child, only the time of evil. I knew how and when my gift would be found, so balance could be restored, but everything else was left to the choices of those involved."

"But they brought me up as a servant. A slave!"

"And had they not done so, you, my child, would not be who you are. And you have proved yourself worthy, because of your integrity, your struggles, and your faith—and most of all, your love. When you faced what you thought was certain death, you made sure your friends could not intervene. You put their well-being before your own, and your last thoughts were of them. And even to the very end, you still had faith in good magic. In me. It was always a question of faith." A broad smile lit up his kind, wise face. "And tell me, had you been the one to unleash the might of the Lorestone, would you have killed Vieldrin?"

"No," she admitted.

"Another reason why you prevailed. You would have found another way. Your heart is good, little elf." He reached out and touched her on the brow. "They who persecute evil shall prosper and come to their inheritance, and you, who are most worthy, inherit my power, child. For a twelvemonth only, I give you this gift, so the balance is preserved."

Warmth flooded Elgiva's soul, and it filled her with strength and vigour.

"You are supreme in Elvendom, and I know you will use this power wisely and act for the welfare of all. There are things you need to do. Go now, Elwardain. It is done."

"Will I see you again, First-Father?"

"You see me now because of the Lorestone. It was a link with my spirit. When it was awakened, it called to me. Now the Lorestone is no more, but yes, you will see me again one day. And then we will have time to talk. All the time in the world." The grin returned once more to his face, and he was again an elfling, his large eyes twinkling with laughter. "Believe it, and it shall be so—and that, my child, is the first rule of magic."

Godwin lifted his head, the cool night air restoring his senses. Something warm was lying beside him. He forced his gaze into focus. It was Trystin. Both of them were uninjured, but to Godwin's amazement, Trystin's bruises had gone and he himself felt whole and well. In fact, he had never felt better.

Then his heart lurched into his throat: what had become of Elgiva? He scrambled to his knees and stared at the platform, fearing what he would see.

There stood Elgiva, robed in white, and her eyes were like embers that smouldered with power. Her pale complexion was flawless and her body gave off a pearly glow, as though she were a creature of moonlight. Her hair fell shimmering down to her waist, and when she moved, it crackled with force.

Godwin stumbled to his feet. What had become of his frail young friend with her bruises and her tattered shift? Now she was a being of fire, Elwardain of all Elvendom. Should he approach her as a friend or as a humble subject, a mere creeping thing in her shadow?

He grasped the hilt of Taranuil and begged it to give him the strength to fight the awesome enchantment that flooded his senses. Then he staggered forwards to where the fallen crown lay glittering in the fitful light of the many abandoned torches. He plucked it from the grass. Elgiva's gaze followed him as he carried the circlet towards her.

She frowned, and he stopped in his tracks, compelled by her gaze as if she had uttered a verbal command. Her eyes were terrible wells of power, and he felt his legs would melt beneath him, but her soft mouth curved into a smile, and the warmth of it filled him with joy.

"Don't be afraid, my friend," she said, "but I don't think you should touch me yet. I think I might burn you if you did. The power has not quite been absorbed."

"What happened, Elgiva?"

"I'm different now, Godwin," she said. "My old self is no more, but it's right and necessary. I feel great magic flowing through me, and it doesn't hurt now. It will never hurt again. Look." She pointed towards the other platform, now a heap of blackened planks.

There before it on the grass, Godwin could see the Lorestone, no longer opalescent, but black and neatly cracked in half. A thin wisp of smoke issued from the core.

"Its power is now mine," said Elgiva.

A sudden movement caught Godwin's eye. Beside the stone, its forepaws raised, a tiny creature sat, twitching its nose. "By Frigg, a mouse!" he said.

The creature squeaked and ran away.

Elgiva laughed. "That must be Vieldrin."

Godwin stared at her.

"The First-Father doesn't approve of killing, when there's another way," she said. "Vieldrin will find it very hard to rule all Elvendom now! And he'll soon know how his victims felt, when he's living in fear of hawks and owls."

She smiled at him again, a smile of knowledge and consummation. He knew she was still his friend, still Elgiva, and she smiled for him alone. As he watched, her fire faded, and it seemed as if she absorbed the power. Soon, she stood before him, complete and in control, the magic as much a part of her as her flesh and blood.

She dropped to her knees and sat back on her legs, folding her hands in her lap. As she bowed her head, he placed the crown upon it, marvelling at her beautiful hair.

He reached out and stroked the gleaming tresses. "Faine returned your sacrifice."

She nodded, taking both his hands in hers, and it pleased him to

The Exile of Elindel

be the sole object of her attention. He glanced to his left, and the affrighted faces of many elves stared back at him, not daring to intervene.

"You're wearing Queen Gilda's colours," she said.

"I'm her adopted son."

This bald explanation seemed to suffice. The questions could wait for another time, but for now, they just wanted to look at each other and share the success of their quest.

Chapter Forty-One

THE DAY OF celebration neared. The royal hall was festooned with garlands, new gowns received their final stitches, ovens sweated in the steam-filled kitchens, and the boughs of trees were heavy with lanterns.

In his hut some distance from the hall, Godwin grimaced at his new attire. The tailors had made him a gold-braided tunic, slim-legged trousers, and a billowing cloak. They were kingly garments indeed, but they were elvish, and he wasn't. He felt he should represent his race, but instead, the elves had absorbed him, as if to make him respectable.

Outside the hut, Grimalkin was surrounded by giggling elves who capered away as Godwin approached. The craze for decoration had gone a bit too far. The pony's mane and tail were plaited with ribbons, and on her head was a green felt hat, with two holes cut out for her ears and roses round the brim. Godwin laughed and thought he might never stop.

Grimalkin snorted and tossed her head, and the hat slid over her eyes. "Now we both look ridiculous, Brit," she said.

Godwin gave her a pained look and pushed the hat back into position.

"We don't belong here."

This observation unnerved him, but he decided to ignore it. "Have you met the other guests yet?"

"Who could see anything stuck out here?"

Godwin agreed with her. It had hurt him to be given quarters so far from the royal hall, but of course, he was a wilthkin and would never be truly accepted here, no matter how many elven queens adopted him as their son. At least the pony had kept him company.

"I did hear dogs yapping," said Grimalkin. "Yap, yap, bloody yap, while I was trying to sleep. What use are dogs, eh? Stupid things. Howling and scrapping and pissing up trees."

"They're wolves, not dogs," snapped Godwin.

"Same stable, different horse."

Godwin strolled up and down on the grass for a while, his scabbard slapping against his thigh. He wanted to ask her a question, but was concerned not to seem too needy. "Have you seen Elgiva?"

Grimalkin peered from under her hat. "She's too busy to bother with us. Lots to do, I'll warrant. Don't fret. It only seems like she's forgotten us."

"Right. I'm going to look for her. Try not to get into mischief while I'm gone."

When at last Godwin found the Elwardain, she was sitting beneath an ancient yew tree, deep in the forest. She didn't stir at the sound of his movement through the underwood, and he suspected there was no longer room for fear in her heart.

His joy at being once more in her presence narrowed his vision to the point where his surroundings were of no interest, until he noticed all of the headstones that filled the clearing, and he felt like an intruder. Elgiva glanced up at him.

"Godwin," she said, "come and sit beside me. It's peaceful here." Her voice was deeper than he remembered.

He sat and leaned against the tree. He was gladdened by the nearness of his friend, and the day's frustrations were forgotten.

"You're paying your respects?" he asked.

She pointed at the nearest headstones; two had fresh flowers at their base. "Those two are my parents, King Ner and Queen Erlina." Beside these stones was a smaller one. "That's me. Do you remember? I died when I was a baby. They called me Princess Elfreyan. The grave is empty, of course."

For a moment, Godwin went back in time to Kendra's lonely little house. "Yes, I remember," he said. He tried not to fidget and waited for her to speak again.

"Not a name I'd have chosen myself." She looked at him and smiled.

Godwin relaxed. "It's so long since I've seen you."

Elgiva looked away. When she spoke, there was tension in her voice. "Less than a week, my friend. I'm sorry it's seemed so long to you. I've been extremely busy. Godwin, you must understand, I'm not merely a wardain, but the Elwardain, as well. I'm ruler of all Elvendom, its guide and its protector."

Godwin nodded, as if he understood, or even cared, but all that really concerned him was Elgiva's translucent beauty.

"This is the oldest tree in the forest," she said.

Godwin wasn't listening. Deep in his heart, he nurtured a hope: that she could remove all of the obstacles with just one wave of her hand; that she could somehow make everything right, and he wouldn't have to leave her.

She was watching him, and in her eyes he saw his thoughts, captured and naked.

"Wh-what?" He blushed and cursed his weakness.

"This tree is perhaps a thousand years old. It grew here long before we were born, and it will still be here when we're dead. Some things never change. I used to sit here as a child, when life was too grim to bear. It taught me how to endure." She touched the flaky bark with her fingers, as though the tree were a sacred relic. "He sleeps. The last time I sat beneath these boughs, I was clad in servant's rags."

"It's a fine old tree indeed," said Godwin, but to him, it was still just a tree.

With a sharp pang of sadness, he realised that Elgiva was no longer childlike and frail and in need of his protection, but independent and powerful. She had come to her inheritance.

They sat awhile in silence. The sun had started to sink in the west, staining the clouds with crimson.

Elgiva toyed with a strand of her hair. "I still find it all so hard to believe," she said at length. "Do you?"

He looked at her. She seemed more relaxed, and there was something in her tone that made him think of the old Elgiva. "Yes," he said. "When we first met, I was the slave of a warlord, a nothing. Now look at me: a Gododdin chief, the son of an elf-queen, and elfryth."

"I, too, began as nothing," she said. "Now I rule the Eldrakin. Their welfare is in my keeping. I'm waited upon by servants. Elders ask my advice. So many decisions and duties. It's strange—ironic, even. By gaining my freedom, I seem to have lost it."

Her wistful tone wrenched Godwin's heart. "A pity we can't go back," he said. "Return to our first meeting. To the days when life was simple."

"Was it?" She ran her fingers through her hair. "Godwin, we can never go back. What's happened to us has been for the best. It was all part of destiny's plan. You always believed in destiny, and you were right; destiny is mapped out for us, but we have the means to alter it by being true, or not, to ourselves. Destiny is like a great wheel, and we stand at the hub, and it's up to us which way we turn. It's the choices we make that cause events to happen as they do. Each spoke is a different lesson, but the destination's the same."

"And what is the destination?" he asked.

"We find out who we are." She paused. "The yew hasn't changed, but everything else has, and for that change, the Eldrakin owe you a debt of gratitude that can never be repaid. Had you not found the Lorestone—"

"But not without Trystin's help."

"If you hadn't found a way to cure me of Vieldrin's spell—"

"Faine cured you, not me," he said, suffused with panic at the thought that their conversation was heading away from what he had intended.

"As you wish." She shrugged and stared at the evening sky.

Godwin waited as long as he could before subjecting Elgiva to the severity of his need. "If your people are so indebted to me, then why am I kept at arm's length? It doesn't matter how grateful they are; they still don't trust me, do they?"

Elgiva lowered her eyes. The sky darkened, the clouds were edged with gold, and in the branches above them, an owl hooted at the coming night.

"Faine spoke to me through the Lorestone," she said. "He put things into my mind. He has a kind voice, but his words are cruel. The wilthkin are spreading over this land. They encroach upon our domains and will continue to do so. Conflict is unavoidable, but Faine opposes war, so the Eldrakin will retreat. We must draw deeper into ourselves, like Misterell, but more so. Do you understand? I alone have the power to do this. Elvendom must be removed to another place entirely. To another dimension."

"Another what?"

"You couldn't understand," she said, "nor do you need to, Godwin. This power I have is given to me for a short time only, and I have things to do. I see what I could never see before, and I know the magic of the Eldrakin will fade at some future time, but perhaps I can forestall it by taking my people away."

"But surely that's a long way off."

"Perhaps, but what is time? A circle. An illusion."

Godwin hugged his chest. "I feel this is the end of everything."

She gave him a sympathetic look. "No, this is the beginning, Godwin, as each new day is another beginning. The old day is dead, but its lessons will never be forgotten. For the Eldrakin, another era begins, and I'm to build a new shrine to Lord Faine to reaffirm our faith. When that has been done, then each of us must face the dawn of another age, and my friends must all go back to their homes. That's where their—your— destinies lie."

"Must I?"

She lowered her gaze and nodded. "I've kept you away from your people for far too long."

"But how can I leave," he said, "knowing I may never see you again?"

"You will forget."

"Forget you?"

"We've talked enough," she said, "and I have many things to do."

"Talked? We haven't talked at all. There are things I need to say to you!"

She looked at him, sighed, and then anger glimmered in her eyes. "Godwin, can't you accept the fact that we can't always have what we want?"

She rose abruptly to her feet, and Godwin's heart was in his throat at the thought he was going to lose her. He jumped up and clasped her cool white hands.

"Elgiva, I just can't imagine my life without you!"

She thrust him away, as though he had offended her, and for a moment, she glared at him. Her face was grey in the twilight, and she was trembling.

The Exile of Elindel

"Godwin, we have responsibilities, people who depend upon us. We must take different paths." She smiled at him and took his hands in her own. "You must go back to your family. For my part, I must marry a wardain to secure my line and protect the magic that must be passed to my heirs. I must lead the Eldrakin out of this world to begin another life. You see, Godwin, I am condemned to the loneliness of absolute power."

"By Frigg, it's too cruel!"

"Do you think I'll find it easy to send you away from me?" she pleaded. "That's why I kept you at a distance. I'd hoped it would make our parting easier, that I . . . " She swallowed, and tears sprang to her eyes. "Godwin, you're under a kind of enchantment still, but it's one you created yourself."

With a shuddering sigh, she released his hands. The weight of her words left Godwin speechless.

"You have a good heart and a good brain, Godwin, and now you also have the chance to put them both to good use. At last you can be your own master. Don't be false to yourself. The future is yours to make of it, whatever you want it to be. How many of us can say that?"

She was right. It had been a selfish hope that they could stay together. He had helped her gain this victory, but that didn't mean she belonged to him, like some prized possession. She belonged to the Eldrakin. She was their gift, not his.

Elgiva stepped forwards and hugged him, and Godwin was too taken aback to return her warm embrace.

"In the end, all things are one, and you and I are one," she said. "The physical world is an illusion." Her voice was as mellow as the dusk, and her smile filled his heart with peace. "Can you and I ever really be parted? We will always be together. Always."

She turned and walked away.

Godwin sat down and stared at the sky, trying to make sense of it all.

And perhaps he understood.

While he and Elgiva breathed the same air, trod the same earth, saw the same moon and stars, they could never be apart. But what of this other dimension? His pulse raced with a sudden panic, and then he remembered what she had said. *In the end, all things are one.* A feeling of peace washed over him.

Yes, he and Elgiva must go their separate ways, and he was being unreasonable if he thought his problems could all be solved by the intervention of magic. *This is the real world, Godwin. You've been a dreamer too long.*

So what was he going to do?

He looked at the mark on the palm of his hand. He could go to Queen Gilda, but he wouldn't be wanted there and what of his family? The dragon ring glinted on his finger. Could he see himself as the leader of his tribe, freeing his family from Othere and bringing them back to live with him? How could he expect Rowena to leave the only life she knew and live with the enemies of her people? And what would become of the Britons when the Saxons tired of peace?

No. He was going to return to Rowena, to the wife with whom he had shared so much, the wife he had loved and forsaken. Running away was all part of the dream. But it left too many loose ends in his life. He must go back to Othere's. But he wouldn't be, couldn't be a slave. He would rather die. Yet, his place was with the wilthkin, and his marriage seemed to be a symbol of the future. Perhaps one day, opposing sides would see that their strength lay in being one.

So, better to see it all as a dream, an adventure, a lesson learned. Better for him to start afresh with everything behind him, with all of his experiences on his back, neatly bound like baggage.

At least he now knew who he was, his life had a solid foundation, and there was one freedom he had gained: the freedom to be himself.

Chapter Forty-Two

A HUNDRED TORCHES illuminated the night and outside the forest's perimeter, beyond the trees that dripped with streamers, tables stood ranked upon the grass, laden with food and wine. Music wafted through the air, laced with the perfume of flowers, and the elves and their guests danced in celebration.

Among the crowd stood Godwin, resolved to be cheerful in spite of his heartache. At least he was in the company of friends, and it was good to see them again.

"Bless me!" Joskin was saying. "Never thought to see Elgiva dressed in all that finery. Looks a bit drowned in it all, eh, Shredwing?"

From Joskin's shoulder, Shredwing agreed.

"She looks wonderful," said Kendra. "By the stars, every inch a queen!"

Greyflanks and Blacktail appeared and renewed their acquaintance with Godwin, and lost in the face of their conversation, Joskin strode off to the nearest table to sample a tray of cakes.

On a flat-topped hummock sat Elgiva, looking down on the celebration, her great-uncle at her side. Garlands of flowers were strewn at her feet. She was dressed in green and gold, and the crown of Elindel sat upon her head. In the folds of her sumptuous robe, Briar, an elderly wild cat reclined, lazily washing its paws.

From the tail of her eye, Elgiva could see her great-uncle smiling at the revelry below, and she would have smiled too, but for the ache in her heart. Thoughts of Godwin were pushed aside, however, as her uncle leaned towards her.

"You have yet to decide about Tarkinell."

"Tarkinell? Did you expect me to kill him? Under elven law, he must have a fair trial, the outcome of which will determine his punishment."

"You will be a merciful ruler, I think."

She cocked an eyebrow at him. "I was well taught."

She got to her feet, raised her right hand, and addressed the crowd below her. "My friends and fellow Eldrakin!"

The crowd turned towards her and fell silent. For a while, nothing stirred under the moon's cold gaze, and even that pallid sphere seemed to be listening.

"Now for a spell long awaited!" she declared. She paused for a moment, drew a deep breath, and then spoke in a loud, clear voice.

"From every spinney, tract and height,

"Evanish, stalkers of the night.

"From wood and forest, tor and dell,

"Arise and harken to my spell.

"Expire, demented shendkin foul;

"Dissolve and die, no longer prowl.

"You things of magic, flesh and bone,

"The Earth no longer is your home.

"You must attend my potent spell

"No matter whereabouts you dwell.

"I charge thee, perish, be no more.

"I bring what you have waited for:

"For your fell bodies death is best,

"But for your souls eternal rest."

A flash of lightning ripped through the sky. From the distance, a dreadful wail carried on the air.

Lord Bellic was on his feet, clutching her arm. "A shendkin!" he exclaimed. "And so close to our home!"

The horror of this information rippled through the crowd below.

"It's dead," said Elgiva, and she called out so everyone could hear. "The shendkin are all dead!"

There was a moment while this declaration sank in, and then a great cheer went up.

"Congratulations, Elwardain," said Bellic. "That was indeed well done, but the last line you spoke . . . you have a kind heart, my dear."

Elgiva looked at him. "I met a shendkin once. It had the most beautiful eyes. I saw a plea there. I think at last I've answered that plea." She turned back to the crowd. "My next duty is to choose a new ruler for Misterell, as it would appear its present monarch is permanently indisposed." The crowd chuckled. "I think there's only one possible candidate. I intend to establish a precedent by offering the crown of that kingdom to one who is not of royal blood, but whose love for Misterell and for Faine gives him every right to claim kingship. Trystin of Misterell, stand forth!"

Upon hearing his name and seeing all eyes turn towards him, the elfling hurried to Godwin's side and clutched at his sleeve. His surprised expression made Elgiva smile.

"Will you accept the crown?" she asked.

Trystin chewed his finger and looked up at his friend. "Oh, Master Godwin, what shall I do?"

"It's your decision, lad," said Godwin. "What is in your heart?"

Trystin's brow creased. "My heart says that Misterell is poor and sick, and it needs help to be beautiful again, but I . . . "

"You know how Misterell used to be, what it ought to be," said Godwin, putting his arm around the young elf's shoulders. "And no one loves Misterell more than you. You know how to put things right. Misterell deserves such a king."

Trystin appeared to struggle with his indecision for a few tense moments, and then he stepped forwards, his head held high. "I accept, Elwardain, with all my heart!"

The assembly voiced their approval.

"This pleases me greatly. You're very young to be king, but I'll send all the help I can, and when you're ready to rule unaided, I'm sure you'll be an admirable king and Misterell will once again be the jewel of all Elvendom. Don't regret your lack of magic, Trystin. Misterell has more than enough of its own." Elgiva gave him a mischievous smile. "Some of it may rub off on you."

More cheering greeted her words.

"I have other rewards to bestow," she went on. "Kendra, you will move to Elindel, and you're assured of a safe haven here until the end of your days. You, I call elfryth, and no one may offer you insult or injury in this land. Furthermore, as a keeper of knowledge, I entrust you with the archives. The preservation of our lore will be solely in your charge. Greyflanks, you and your family may dwell in my fields and woodland. You will always be under my protection, and you may hunt wherever you please. Never again will you need to wander in search of food or shelter. Now, Joskin, what would you ask of me?"

The giant looked up with astonishment. "Bless me! Could do with some thread and some tools, I suppose, and a bigger perch for Shredwing."

"And that's all you require?"

"I have all I want," replied Joskin.

"What you've asked for is nothing and yet, it shall be done. However, there's more that I can do, though it's much less than you deserve." She pointed at the crippled bird still perched on the giant's shoulder. "Fly to me, skyfarer!"

The hawk flapped his damaged wings, took off from Joskin's shoulder, and in an instant, his wings became whole—strong, full-feathered, and sleek. In ecstasy, he soared above the crowd's astonished faces, swooping and climbing joyfully, and then he returned to the towering Saxon.

Shredwing's squawks of gratitude were drowned by a tumult of cheers, and Joskin gazed at Elgiva, clearly too overcome to speak.

"To Captain Merrill is granted the title of Justice General to the Crown," continued Elgiva, "for he's a fair-minded, honest elf. Merrill, I trust you to be the final arbiter in any dispute, if you will accept the position."

In the crowd, Captain Merrill made a low bow. "I will be honoured, Elwardain."

"Now, Grimalkin, what would you ask of me?"

Grimalkin stood at the rear of the crowd, sniffing a plate of honey cakes. She pricked up her ears and looked at Elgiva. "Cabbage hearts!" she snorted. "Haven't had time to think about that, but you can make this hat disappear and get someone to fetch me some more of these buns. I'll have oats for breakfast, too. Apart from that, I'll let you know."

Elgiva smiled and then turned to face Godwin. "My friend, you far surpass any gifts I could give you."

Godwin squirmed as all eyes turned towards him.

"You have many choices ahead," said Elgiva, "but I think you may want to begin afresh, so I will provide you with gold and gems to purchase your freedom from Othere, and the freedom of your

The Exile of Elindel

family, if that is what he demands. Build a settlement of your own. You have the courage to do so. But wherever you decide to live, you and your descendants will be under the elf-ward of Elindel. You made a vow to protect me once. Now it's my turn, I think. I trust that Faine will help me keep my vow as well as you kept yours. Take your pick of my armoury, Godwin, my horses, too, and anything else you may require for your journey. I wish you to ride home in splendour, so the Saxons will see, as I do, a most fearless and constant warrior—Godwin Gildason."

Godwin raised his eyebrows, and then he smiled. "Thank you, Elwardain," he said in a formal tone.

"And," continued Elgiva, "a certain gift I gave you in the past is yours to keep forever, though it's not in accordance with elven law, but to take back a gift that was given in love would violate the teachings of Faine."

Godwin frowned up at her. "A certain gift?"

Elgiva pressed on, ignoring his puzzled expression. "Also, you'll be pleased to know I've removed the enchantment that lies over Angwen's village. Her people have started rebuilding their lives. Messengers have been sent to assure them of our help and protection. And I'll be sending food and other provisions and whatever else I can." She turned to the crowd. "I dare say you've heard enough talk for one night. Minstrels, your merriest tunes! Enough of the past and the future. The now is all that matters. I think we should enjoy it!"

Shortly before sunrise, Godwin found himself part of a procession as it wound its way through the mist-wrapped forest. Trystin was at his side, while around them, the other guests and the inhabitants of Elindel walked along, chattering to each other in an atmosphere of barely suppressed excitement.

Elgiva led them all to a clearing near the edge of the forest. She stood in the centre, where a tumble of stones of various sizes and colours lay scattered. These had been gathered together by servants the previous day. Everyone formed a circle around her and stood in respectful silence.

Elgiva lifted her arms, and a mist rose up from the ground at her feet, and as it rose, it carried the stones and piled them on top of each other. Where the stones met, they welded together. When the mist evaporated, the new shrine was complete. Three solid walls and an arched doorway now stood beneath a roof of polished rock, and along the walls were granite benches, plain and unadorned. Elgiva stepped onto the threshold, a smile of accomplishment on her face.

As the rising sun skimmed the treetops and touched the clean stone of the shrine, a gasp of approval broke from the crowd. The sunlight made every facet as vivid as a chunk of glass, and all of the ores and crystals trapped in the stones glinted with many colours. It was an inspiring sight, as the simple, granite building became a thing of beauty.

"I dedicate this shrine to Faine, First-Father of Elvendom," said Elgiva, turning to face the crowd. "Like him, it's strong and beautiful. It's humble, yet proud with hidden splendour. It's plain and ornate, a thing of both light and shade, created out of the tangible bones of the Earth by the Earth's intangible magic. Let it stand as a reminder of the power of good magic and the balance that sustains the universe. Its separate parts combine into a single, harmonious unity. Thus, it stands as a symbol of all Elvendom. It's a place to be apart and a place to be a part of everything. May it and the Eldrakin endure forever."

The elves applauded Elgiva's words with great enthusiasm. Godwin, however, was only half listening. There was something he had to do.

Ignoring the scrutiny of hundreds of eyes, he walked towards the shrine and entered. Halting on the smooth stone floor, he turned to face Elgiva. "There's no altar," he remarked.

She shook her head, a puzzled expression on her face.

"It needs something. A focal point."

Slowly, he unsheathed his sword and walked to the rear of the shrine. "Tomorrow, Faine," he said, "I won't be a part of your world anymore, but tomorrow is another day. This elf-blade has taught me many things. My heart and mind have been opened. In thanks for that, I offer it to you. Let it stay here as a reminder that, when good is threatened by evil, we need to fight on its behalf."

He selected a central point on the stone floor, and then he lifted the sword in both hands and whispered its name so that no one should hear. He plunged the weapon into the floor. It pierced the thick stone easily and buried two-thirds of its length in the granite.

"Farewell, old friend," said Godwin. "Remain here in my stead where my heart is. But remember, though we're parted, we'll always be together." He paused, and in the silent glade, it seemed even the birds were listening. "And by my express command, you will stay here always and never be removed, save by my hand alone."

He finished the last sentence hurriedly, not knowing what motives had prompted it. Perhaps he needed to leave behind a permanent reminder of his existence, something that would live on long after he lay forgotten in some lonely grave. Or perhaps he hoped that leaving the sword would ensure he would one day return.

Elgiva stepped forwards and put both hands around the hilt of the sword. She pulled, but the weapon refused to move. She smiled and looked up at her friend. "To wield such a sword requires courage," she said, "but far greater courage to give it up."

They gazed at each other and then, linking arms, they walked out into the sunlight.

Chapter Forty-Three

GODWIN CAUGHT SIGHT of the village, and a broad smile stretched his lips. Smoke curled cheerily from the huts, and he could see people busy in the fields. He slewed himself round on the back of his horse. Elgiva and her retinue were making their way towards him, and while he waited for them to catch up, he wandered back in his memory to his sad departure from Elindel.

Leaving Trystin had been the worst moment; Godwin had almost come to regard the elfling as a son. Trystin had clung to Godwin's tunic, his large eyes brimming with tears, and Godwin had done his best to sound stern as he pushed the elfling away from him and held him by the shoulders.

"Is this any way for a king to behave?"

"Kings don't cry," said Grimalkin. "They make cruel laws to make others weep."

"Not me," sniffed Trystin. He started to chew his fingernails, but then he thought better of it. "I'll be a good king, and brave, just like Master Godwin, and I'll never hate wilthkin or be scared of magic or anything!"

"Care for Misterell, Trystin," said Godwin. "A place of such beauty must be preserved."

"Yes, I will," promised Trystin. "I'll care for it, Master Godwin, and if I falter, I'll think of you and follow your example. That way, I'll never go wrong."

"Be yourself, lad, and be it well. That's all that's ever required of us," said Godwin, and then his pretence at fortitude crumbled, and clasping Trystin to his breast, he hugged him so hard, he almost feared the elfling's bones would snap.

"Do you wish to visit Angwen?"

Elgiva was now beside him, her black hair braided with golden ribbons and her green gown draped across Alsiann's back. Her question caught him off guard.

"What . . . ? Er . . . no. Let's move on," he said.

"Are you sure, Godwin? I thought you wanted to make amends."

He shrugged. One day, he would. "Can we skirt round the village? Surely there's some ford or bridge downstream where we can cross?"

"If not, I'll make you one," she said, smiling.

"Yes. Let's move on."

"Move on?" snickered a voice from the rear. "Move on, he says, and here's me thinking I might be in for a rest. I've had enough. Ages since anyone fed me, you know. As for these stones, my poor old hooves are split and buckled and scuffed so badly, I'll wager I'm crippled for life—what little there's left in my ill-used body."

Godwin sighed with exasperation at the sight of Grimalkin plodding towards them, but Elgiva grinned. "I'm sorry, Godwin," she said, "but it was her wish to return with you. I couldn't really stop her."

Godwin nodded. At least some things would never change.

He turned his horse's head southwards.

"From here, you must travel due east," said Elgiva.

They were standing on a small hill, one Elgiva remembered well as the place where everything had started for her. The darkening landscape spread out below, and on the other side of the hillock, her retinue waited to turn back for home.

"You have plenty of food for your journey. It shouldn't take you long to get home," she said.

Sighing, Elgiva urged Alsiann down the grassy slope. Godwin followed. The horses were left at the foot of the hillock, and Godwin stacked wood for a fire.

"Do you like the horse?" asked Elgiva, forcing herself to sound casual. "You didn't really say, but I chose him because he's gentle and not of the royal herd. He should give the Saxons no reason to comment."

Godwin stepped back from the firewood and looked at the placid, grey horse. "Saxons don't need a reason," he said. "By Frigg, what'll they think of me? Bags of gold and dressed like a lord!"

He smiled at her, and she knew he was trying to sound light-hearted for her benefit.

"What can they think, but that you surpass them?" she said. She snapped her fingers, releasing her pent-up emotion with a dart of magic, and the firewood blossomed into flame. Folding her arms, she looked at her friend, and she hoped her gaze held a hint of reproach. "You didn't select a sword," she said. "You left your scabbard behind."

He lowered his eyes.

"A warrior can't go abroad unarmed." She cocked an eyebrow at him and then walked to Alsiann's saddlebag and drew out an object wrapped in gold cloth. Returning to the campfire, she handed the bundle to Godwin. "My parting gift to you."

Inside the cloth was Godwin's elven scabbard, but it had a new occupant: an elf-sword with a leaf pattern on the blade and elvish runes on the hilt.

"That's my mark," she said.

Godwin looked up, clearly both surprised and delighted. "You made this for me?" he asked. "Is it . . . is it magic?"

"That rather depends on how you use it," Elgiva replied, giving him an arch grin.

He fitted the scabbard to his belt, and when he looked up again, their gazes locked. As if sharing the same compulsion, each made a movement towards the other, as though they meant to embrace.

But then the spell was broken as something heavy slid down the bank towards them.

Elgiva cleared her throat. "Why, here's Grimalkin, laden with treasure!"

Godwin looked torn between anger and relief. He drew a shuddering breath.

"And what a weight it is, to be sure, by all that's green and edible!" Grimalkin snorted.

Godwin turned towards her and folded his arms across his chest in an attitude of stern amusement. "So, you old nag," he said. "Looks like I'm stuck with you forever."

"Gall and wormwood, Brit! I'm not immortal, you know!"

Laughing, Elgiva sat by the fire. Godwin sat beside her and for a while, they watched the flames dance as dusk fell all around them.

The Exile of Elindel

It was time to say farewell, but Elgiva didn't want to bring to an end their last precious moments together. And she knew Godwin felt the same.

"You need a story to tell the Saxons," Elgiva said. "They'll want to know what happened to you and why you have all this gold."

"Don't worry," he said. "I've plenty of time to think of a tale on the way home. I won't mention elves, of course. And I'm not going back as Godwin the slave, but as Aidan, son of Gwion, a chief of the Gododdin. My status will dictate my treatment."

"It will?" she asked.

"No matter what you think of Othere, he's still an honourable man."

"I dare say you're right."

"But I'll tell Rowena the truth. My children, too, when they're older. I want them to know who they are." He paused and looked at Elgiva with his honest, artless eyes. "Knowing you has taught me many things about myself. About everything."

"And in you, I met my greatest tutor," she said.

From Elgiva's waiting retinue somewhere behind the hillock, there rose a burst of laughter that seemed to profane their intimacy, and they both fell silent again. From the darkness of a distant wood, a fox screamed for its mate, and its cry was an ache of loneliness.

Elgiva sighed. *Now I begin a new life, although I'm still an exile. But this time, I'm exiled by power, not weakness. This time, being an exile doesn't mean I can run away, and where in all this great, wide world will I find a friend such as you?*

On an impulse, she leaned towards him, threw her arms around his neck, and hugged him tenderly. It was time for them to say goodbye, but her lips refused to frame the word. She pulled away from him, tormented by longing.

"Oh, Godwin," she said, and tears began to flow freely down her cheeks, "we should have been—we ought to be—together!"

He gripped her upper arms, and his eyes were moist with affection. "We are. We always were. We always will be."

They looked at each other in silent anguish, and then they embraced again, and in some other dimension where they were and yet were not, their souls touched briefly in an act of love.

Then Elgiva broke away, rose to her feet. "Well, Godwin

Gildason, this is where we must part," she said. "May Faine always guard you, my friend."

No, I won't say goodbye. My heart is too full for such finality.

Though Godwin sat close to the campfire, a cold and empty feeling was seeping into his heart. He watched as Elgiva turned and stepped lightly towards her horse; watched as she seized the golden bridle; watched her lead the animal to the crest of the hillock; watched as though Elgiva embodied his happiness and it was leaving him forever.

But then, suddenly, Elgiva stopped and looked back at him. Firelight caught the dampness of her eyes, but a slight smile chased the sadness from her face. It was a smile of defiance, full of mischief and affection—a conspiratorial smile. Her voice carried clearly when she spoke.

"I love you, wilthkin."

Then she was gone, Alsiann beside her, and the drapes of darkness closed behind them, leaving Godwin all alone.

Alone and bereft in a world devoid of magic.

Godwin stirred beneath the blankets. It had rained during the night, and his coverings were wet. He cast them aside and crawled to his feet. The sun lay on the horizon like a polished ball of gold, and the dawn was filled with the singing of birds.

After breakfast, he gathered up his blankets and tied them to Grimalkin's back. "We've some way to go," he said. "I don't want to lose any time. I've been away from home too long."

Home. Was Othere's settlement really home, or was home an unknown quantity, somewhere in the future? Whatever it was, the thought of it filled him with excitement.

He had lost Elgiva and his right to lead his tribe, but he could accept that now. He was going back to the Saxons, but he could accept that, too. No matter what life held in store for him, he would accept it all. The road from the past had been long and hard, the road to the future was uncertain, but he faced it all now with his mind uncluttered. At least he knew who he was. And more importantly, what he was. And he knew where his duty lay; he was going back to his family.

The Exile of Elindel

"Have you gone into a trance, Brit? Thought we were in a hurry?" snickered Grimalkin.

Godwin stared at the pony. "I was just thinking."

"Wondering if it was worth it, eh?"

"Worth it?" asked Godwin.

For some reason, the image of Shredwing being healed appeared in his mind. All of their struggles seemed to centre on this single act of good magic. Shredwing had gained his inheritance, the precious gift of flight, and Godwin was proud to have played his part in it. He pictured the once earthbound creature now soaring among the clouds, and he felt a lump in his throat.

"Of course it was worth it," he said, hating the hitch in his voice. He shook his head at Grimalkin and walked towards his horse.

"Well," persisted Grimalkin, "you got lots of gold for your trouble. What reward could be better than that?"

"Myself," he stated.

"Don't go all philosophical. Too early in the morning," she snorted.

He stood with his hand on his horse's withers and thought of Taranuil, the bridge between his world and that of his elven friends. That bridge would always be there.

And we will always be together.

He turned towards Grimalkin. Impatience glittered in her bloodshot eyes, and a grin spread over his face. They had all been changed by what they had been through, but like Grimalkin, like the old yew, like love and faith and hope, some things never changed. They could always be relied upon.

He patted the horse and prepared to mount. "Stand still, Farran. There's a good lad."

As he clambered onto the horse's back, he realised that horses weren't frightening at all when you knew how to talk to them.

Talk to them? By Frigg!

That was Elgiva's "certain gift!" He had forgotten all about it. It seemed as natural now as breathing. He would have to learn how to hide it. The wilthkin wouldn't understand.

He turned to Grimalkin. "Let's go."

He set off in the direction of home. His heart was lighter than he had expected, and spring was blossoming all around him with hope and hidden potential. And the hope was possible, the future was possible, because he had mastered the past. By Frigg, it had all been a great adventure.

Or perhaps the adventure was just beginning.

About the Author

Born in Stafford in the UK, Carol was raised in Crewe, Cheshire, which she thinks of as her home town. Interested in reading and writing at an early age, Carol pursued her passions at Nottingham University and was awarded an honours degree in English Language and Literature. However, fated to lose everything and start again several times, it is only in later life that she has realised her dream of becoming a published author. Now she lives deep in the Cambridgeshire countryside with her cockatiel Sparky and uses words to weave tales like tapestries that she hopes will adorn the walls of your imagination. Her watchword is perseverance.

Other work:
Being Krystyna - A story of Survival in WWII
Amazon US - https://tinyurl.com/jesnssb
Amazon UK - https://tinyurl.com/js4d2ab

An Elf's Lament upon Leaving & Other Tales
Amazon US - https://tinyurl.com/y77wvpjm
Amazon UK - https://tinyurl.com/yc6kmsvo

Author links:
Author page Amazon .com - https://tinyurl.com/ybpbsgh3
Author page Amazon.uk - https://tinyurl.com/y9ytzj5u
Facebook author page: https://www.facebook.com/AuthorCarolBrowne
Twitter : https://twitter.com/@ CarolABrowne
Blog: http://authorcarolbrowne. wordpress.com/
Goodreads: https://tinyurl.com/y9bgne33

About the Publisher

#ExperienceBWP
#BWP
#burningwillowpress

www.burningwillowpressllc.com
http://smarturl.it/BWPLLC

If you enjoyed this book and would like to know when we release more like it please sign up for our newsletter on our website at www.burningwillowpressllc.com

Additionally, if you enjoyed the story or even if you did not, we—the author and the publisher—wish for you to leave a review on Amazon/Goodreads. The number of reviews that an author receives helps them continue to write every day to produce more works like this one and more. It does not matter how long or short. We certainly appreciate this and hope to read it with others like it.

Made in the USA
Columbia, SC
22 December 2017